DIVINE

As Joanna Traynor's ballsy heroine Viv says to her lawyer when a guilty plea is proposed: ' "I'm nineteen years old with a face like the back of a bus. My chances in the job market are nil and in the marriage market even less. Now do me a favour and listen . . . I'm not guilty. My liberty may not mean a great deal to you but it's all I have. If that's the best advice you can offer, sod off." '

You don't quietly tuck someone like Viv away for six months. She wants her day in court – the 'due process' so often overridden by our criminal justice system by a politely negotiated guilty plea between a chummy judge and barristers.

Viv has an Afro-Caribbean father, a white mother, and a brainy sister living in Paris who feels perpetually guilty about a childhood accident that left half Viv's face permanently scarred. Viv also has a group of friends and enough drugs at university to keep self-pity at bay – as long as she isn't trapped in a corner, as now.

Few writers have confronted the subjects of disfigurement and sex so boldly – or race, for that matter, or drugs, or the law. Joanna Trayner is simply a one-off, with an ear for youth culture as keen as that for the legal establishment. There is a driving energy and brilliance to her prose that has developed in this second novel into something arresting and remarkable.

DIVINE

JOANNA TRAYNOR

BLOOMSBURY

My thanks to Sarah Edwards and Nina Tuller

First published 1998

This paperback edition published 1999

Copyright © 1998 by Joanna Traynor

The moral right of the author has been asserted

Bloomsbury Publishing Plc, 38 Soho Square, London WIV 5DF

A CIP catalogue record for this book is available from the British Library

ISBN 0 7475 4379 8

10 9 8 7 6 5 4 3 2 1

Typeset by Hewer Text Composition Services, Edinburgh
Printed by Clays Ltd, St Ives Plc

To Robbie

GOING TO JAIL

Chapter 1

'All Rise!'

The whole room stood.

The judge slipped in silently. Just like that. No fanfare. No huge brass-handled doors opened wide. Not even for him. The grand master. No. He slid in. He sneaked in through a panelled door and then set off on his dodder to the throne. He wasn't unsteady on his feet, more a tired old man, slowly thudding and squeaking his shoes against the wood. One last creaking step up and then silence. The court ushers followed his every move. Like cult victims. Getting themselves ready. No one clapped, although clearly he wouldn't have minded. I couldn't clap because I was handcuffed to a screw. The judge, at last in position, looked down on us all. Waiting. Then, everyone in the know gave it to him. The nod. Like Japanese peasants. Just a feather breath short of a prayer, I'd say. It was me in need of the prayers, not him.

Why didn't he have his red clobber on? Only his nose was red. His moustache was white, tobacco-stained. A red cloak would have made him look like Father Christmas. He sat down, ignoring us, looking at his papers, pulling at the back of his wig like a kid with nits. Put on in a hurry, no doubt. He might have been a priest out of the vestry, on his altar, fiddling with cassock and crucifix. Now he was settled, the rest of us could sit down but to be honest, with all that bowing and scraping going on, I nearly knelt down. He leant forward to speak to a woman in front. Her glasses were falling off the end of her face. She poked her pencil towards the cafeteria upstairs and then laughed. The way a secretary laughs at her boss, with the legs of her mind wide open.

Because the judge was having a chat, we were allowed to

3

talk. Shackled to a screw, I didn't feel that chatty and the screw didn't look like he was up for it anyway. The barristers gabbed to their assistants. They rustled away at their papers, fanned them and then sent them flying across the benches. They reminded me of crows, in their flappy black gowns, almost throwing a shadow across the room. A room dullbright with neon. And I shuddered as I shudder when reading in a sunlit garden and the crows fly overhead, shadowing my book, propelling themselves through the air with pumping muscle. I was coming down off speed.

With so much wood about, the walls, the floor, the seat that I was sat on, I might have been on a boat, getting ready to walk the plank. But then I'd be seeing seagulls, not crows. For seagulls, the barristers needed white flappy gowns and what would that have been like?

The judge found himself a pair of glasses. He was old enough to remember the Empire in full swing. And what was I to him? Black woman in a spotty dress. A shit? Empire excrement on his very own doorstep? He thought he'd left us all behind. But here we are, keeping in touch, in trouble, in court, in your face, Your Honour. He would like to hose me down. But he must get on. Must sort this mess out. Sort me out and throw me overboard. Even I could see he wasn't up to it – into it. He busied himself with pen and paper, to get himself motivated. But after a few seconds, his enthusiasm waned. He rested his head on his hand in disappointment. Another dull day for Judge Benkinson. Another story off the same shelf. Another pulped fiction cardboard cutout of crime, me, standing before him, avoiding contact with his furrowed eyes. Obviously guilty then.

The benches in the court were like pews and there were church-hush tones too. One man and one woman in the public gallery. The woman, God knows who? The man, a journalist with a pad out, as bored as the judge, doodling, chewing the end of his pencil. *I* wasn't bored. I felt the boat about to set sail and got ready for its sway, this way and that. Just as my stomach swerved, this way and that. My eyes tracked movement. Flickering. Flashing smiles. A nod here. A smile there. As the court hushed itself to a silence, flapping sheets of paper clapped the air like mini-peals of thunder. Then there was calm.

The judge turned towards me, with his shoulders this time, heaving himself. A real job on his hands. I defended myself with a mask of contrition and make-up, but not too much. Light on the rouge, mascara and lipstick but heavy on the camouflage. So that I might blend in more easily with expectation. From out of his dull cloud the judge leant forward towards me. In Dick and Dora language, with an air of charity, generosity even, he explained that what was about to take place was not a trial. Not for you maybe, arsehole, said my eyes, for the very first time, resting rather than flitting across his fleshy cheeks. *This is the captain of the ship* . . . No, what was about to take place was a farce – to see, in short, if indeed there was, on one of the counts I was to be tried for, a case to answer, said the judge, from somewhere up there. To see if my own confession to a serious crime could be ruled *inadmissible* as evidence to the court.

'And, said the judge, 'as you can see there is no jury present.'

Using his elbows as stabilisers, he swivelled round on his wooden throne and addressed the empty jury benches. Pointing. See? He turned back towards me . . . I could almost hear the ropes whining in the wind as the ship was shaped up. See? he was saying. This is my court and I call the shots. Get it, Viv?

'Yes, Your Honour. I understand.'

My head was throbbing off. The night before I'd gone to see Irish for a chat and some draw – something to calm me down. Whoa! But there was a drought on, see! A drought of draw, hashish, pot, dope, marry joanna as the judge called it. Utterly exhausted already, I let my head fall, chin to chest. My black disc of a head dangled before him.

It was all Irish's fault. The not feeling well. If Simmi had turned up, I would have been all right. But Simmi had not turned up. Nor Vinnie. So that put a lid on it. The final strike, the knell, the dong, the belly full but am hungry. So I went on the whizz coz there wasn't any draw. I felt myself go wrong the moment the powder touched the delicate membranes of my nostrils, burning my fragile pink nasal lining, the dart of the drug hitting like the spike of a hunter's medicine arrow. Sniffffffffffffff, up to my brain, down to my heart, thump, thump, tearing down my stamina, my highfalutin ideals, my innocence. Innocent women don't take speed the night before. The judge had nailed me down already, had spotted my weakness, had boxed me off. I stood in the dock with my head bent down, oozing guilt.

'Come on, Irish, you must have a stash somewhere. You're holdin' back. I just know you wouldn't go this long without a smoke.'

'Listen, you know I'd sort you out if I could but I'm all out. Like everyone else. Bev's out, right? Well then. If Bev's out, half of Brimmington's out. It's the worst drought since Christmas.'

All I wanted, the night before this persecution, was a spliff, a feeling of deliverance, a calm. But because the spliff was not to be had, I'd rushed myself. I'd busied myself with the bother of it all, the panic, the injustice, the falling down. The falling away. Immersed in my strife, I wanted to get out of my head, on anything, on anything, with friends with attitude, with a strong belief that I'd been stuffed, been dealt with, the key thrown away and floating down some sewer under Pucklechurch or Holloway. That's how cracked up I was. So I did some whizz. Whizz, whizz, Billy the Whizz. Irish and me holed up in his flat chopping lines.

Bev said a parcel of hash was due any sec, any minute now. The whole of the town was waiting for the man. In rooms across Brimmington, there were people waiting by telephones, waiting for deliveries from London, Manchester, Nottingham, anywhere and everywhere. People across Brimmington drank tea, cleaned out hash pipes . . . waited. Waited for a smoke. The lucky ones broke into stashes, stashes carefully preserved for Christmas, the baby's birth, the emergency. For when it all ends in tears. From secret stashes they dug out Durban Poison, Manali, Sinse and Temple Balls.

The brave ones went down on the street, getting off on going no-go, where the police will go and pick your pockets for a laugh and a chat and soon rush you off up the cells if they score. If they don't, you carry on fine, looking for a man to sell you a bag of twig or wax. Irish and me did all-around-the-mirror-fuck-off lines of whizz. Which was dead stupid because I was up all night gabbing, chewing my lip off, and now, sat in front of Judge Benkinson, was as wired as hell, jumpy, paranoid and scared. I swallowed some blood from my chewed-up lip.

There was a stir in the court. Not so much a stir. More someone sticking their oar in. Mrs Bodene, my brief, my barrister, was up on her feet. My foot tapped. Nerves twanged. My mouth furred up with inedible air. Bodene swayed across the bows. She looked too small compared to Ratface, the prosecutor, persecutor. And a bit too nice. And her woolly wig suited her. That wasn't good. The wig shouldn't suit the brief, because then . . . then the face sticking out from underneath didn't look menacing enough – mad enough. She should have passed on the lipstick too. Stupid cow. That would have helped. Without their rosy dip, them lips of hers would look pretty mean and thin – make more of a din.

I'd only met the woman twice. Was she that clever she could defend me with a bundle of notes, two meetings and a promise?

'I'll see what I can do.'

A pretty flimsy start, to be honest. But Alan Cunningham, my solicitor, said it was all sorted. I had to believe in him. Just trust him, he said. Even that morning they'd begged me to plea. The pair of them.

Before all this trouble, there was no reason to go down to Regent Crescent, to walk on those pavements, strumming my fingers across the taut strings of shiny black-painted railings, each spike a pointed reminder that each gate was a gate to jail or freedom. I'd ridden past many a time, delighting in the view, the white Georgian façade rising as a slither of a silver

moon, above and away from the grey containers of Brimmington that were across the green. Along the Crescent shone
golden plates engraved with names like Cunningham and
Braddock, Marshall and Duke. No Puddleton and Giggleswick, or Shalloprop or Metherwick. Braddocks and Dukes
from the grammar school. Through the long elegant windows
I fancied I could see county balls being danced and ladies in
corsets fanning their window-framed faces with a flicker. Or
men in suits with fountain pens, slugged over desks of green
blotters and wooden work, choked by dickie bows on hot
summer days.

The men wore hats and watch-chains that dangled from
their bellies. All the time in the world. They parked their cars
in a crescent of cars. The women walked fast in fussy collars
and black tight-arsed suits with every right to be there. And
then there was me, in jeans, in the Crescent, with an appoint-
ment. Every set of eyes averted its gaze, looked past me,
around me, anywhere but at me. They knew. My fate was
sealed. I'm not exactly the Elephant Man, but still, you
wouldn't want me on the meat counter at Tesco's. From
two hundred yards, you probably wouldn't notice much
wrong with me. On Regent Crescent, with my black skin,
you would.

'Take a seat. He'll be with you in a minute.'

The smell of leather yet no leather seats. *Country Life* to
read. *Country Life* for the fraudsters and the divorcers.
Tycoons and tax-evaders. Sure, they'd read *Country Life*.
Look! There was Mr Giggleswick, page 5. Gone up in the
world, I'd say. Up to Scotland with the rest of them. There
they all are. On page 11. A right team.

The ceiling rose was at the end of the room, rather than in
the middle, and painted thick into a chalked clog. They'd
made two rooms out of one, or maybe three or four. Packed in
tight. I eyed the clock, ticking ten minutes past my time. Just
sit and wait till I was called, she said, and then spat me out of
her mind, the minute she ticked me off her list. She must have
seen my file. A lady wincing with sadness was now upon her.

The receptionist was able to give her a big wide puppy-dog smile that almost certainly agreed with the woman's case for the woman had fur on her collar and perfume to kill flies. Her situation was of course unpalatable.

'We're all behind you, Mrs Hegarty,' smiled the receptionist.

Sure! The receptionist had read my file. She could barely murmur when she directed me up to the office. She kept her head down, ashamed I was allowed to walk on her blotter-green carpets, afraid of a bumper car crash into *cliente importante*. I lost my grip on the steep staircase and slipped a few steps, just saving myself from making a great noise. That put me on edge.

That was the first time I met Bodene. She sat beside Cunningham like a caged exotic bird, agitated, waiting for her seed tray – me. As soon as I was seated she attended to her business. Unusual, she said, almost an honour, she made out, that I should get to meet my barrister before a court date. There were issues she needed to discuss with Mr Cunningham and I should consider our meeting felicitous, since one of those issues she wished to discuss was the brief for my case. She gave me the impression that the brief had done the rounds and landed on her desk last. Just as the music had stopped. The brief stops here. Our meeting would have to be quick, she said. The questions necessarily pointed and direct. No time for niceties, she said. Well, bloody well get on with it, I thought, and stop yer waffling.

In future, she said (as if advising on my career ambitions), I should not bargain with the police in a police station, without a legal representative on hand. However, I had done. Possibly . . . no, probably, I'd bargained my way into a prison cell. The question was, almost certainly, how long the spell in the cell should be. Mr Cunningham, either wisely or unwisely, had gone along with my decision to be tried in Crown and not opt for a guilty plea in the magistrates'. (The clerk in the magistrates' had been peeved about this. All wired up for his frizzy busy court. My opting for Crown seemed to short-circuit him. He looked quite ill when he wandered away from

Cunningham without a result.) Why had I not pleaded guilty to the charge of supplying cannabis and let the prosecution drop the more serious charge? Most people would. Why hadn't I? Oh, I see, she said. You're innnocent. Mr Cunningham had had faith in me. Now Bodene wanted to see where he got it from.

I wondered which the most criminal. Dealing out drugs or justice. Justice, that very expensive dessert served up after the main course of the crime. There would be no big helping for me, not without a fight. Bodene's bored expression told me that. So was she up to it? Into it? There'd be no big profits to make out of me. She wanted a career carving feast to tuck into but Cunningham presented her with me.

She didn't recognise my physical misfortune. Just business. Just work. She never showed a glint of pity, and I'm telling you, I look for this stuff. Cunningham leant sideways across his desk, in her favour, like a manager at a fairground stall, holding open the fronds of curtain. She leant forward with her shoulders, then with her nose she pecked away at me. She pecked as if blind, guessing at where the birdseed might be. Peck. Peck. Peck. Any answer I gave, she gobbled, then swallowed and pecked again. Hurriedly. Impatiently. A blind bird scrabbling about on the sandpaper, scraping up a living. Me.

'I'll give it a bash,' she said, not looking up from her page or out from her cage.

Then Cunningham closed the curtains. He stood up and walked in front of her. Time's up, show's over, pushing me out of the room with the flick of a wrist to see his watch and, 'My! Isn't time getting on?'

'I am innocent, you know,' I said.

'Indeed,' she said. 'I believe you. Though whether we can convince a jury is another matter. Without witnesses, the case is thin, to say the least. You may still like to consider a gui . . . Let's see what happens at court, shall we?'

Thank you and goodbye.

I trod lightly, politely, down the creaking stairs of carpet. As I approached the reception kiosk, I noticed jewellery and pinstripe, a middle-aged couple closely knit, asking for Mr

Cunningham, *my* Mr Cunningham. I had to squeeze past them. When the couple felt me they turned and then, with some urgency, they squashed themselves inwards, closing in on the receptionist. It was on my mind that pinstripe and jewellery wouldn't get a woman barrister. They'd get a man with broad shoulders and bushy eyebrows who sat back and took it all in his stride. And won, probably.

Fellow criminals told me that Cunningham was good. They told really good prison stories too. Bodene worried me. Being so thoroughly short with me, she'd almost convinced me that she was actually in control of my case. That all my worry was for nothing. That she would ensure, with a few well-chosen words written to the right people, to have done with the case and done with me and here I was, in court, she not having done bugger all, it would seem. Perhaps, at this stage of her career, she had to take on hopeless cases for practice.

'Your Honour, my learned friend . . . Miss Vivian Jackson is here before the court . . .'

Bodene leant over her bench, her arched hands as tripods, weak and wavery. She was shaking. For Christ's sake! She was leaning on the bench trying to hide it but I could see she was shaking. Her elbows were giving way. She was looking up to the judge, pleading and squeaking out my case. Ratface wasn't even listening to her. He was turning around, looking for someone, something. Not in a desperate way. Looking for his lunchbox, probably. All I could hear was shuffling feet and people squeaking their shoes together. Bodene's voice sounded like one of those squeaks, only more persistent and more irritating.

Ratface up.

Bodene down.

'Your Honour, given the significance of *all* the evidence concerned with this case, which my learned friend here (turning to her and smiling – thinking he's on telly) considers of little note, we feel it imperative that *all* the circumstances of this crime be brought to your attention. I take it my learned friend will be calling the accused?'

By *all* the circumstances, he meant the deaths. The circum-stantial deaths. Ratface would make out that I was getting away with murder. But I could tell, even at that point, that all this was a ruse. He looked at me like he was getting ready to pull my toenails out with his teeth.

Bodene up.

'Yes, I shall be calling the accused.'

Bodene down.

She couldn't handle a death. The full force of a life in the form of death had never got under her fingernails. Ratface – he looked like he traded on death. Like an undertaker. He could bring a death to life, make a film of it. Draw up a plot and cast the key players. He would know its every geometry. Oh yes. Ratface could handle a death or two.

After a few more goes of the bob-up-and-down routine, Ratface held up items of evidence, piece by piece, and named them in a long slowhand hammer of a drawl, dropping bags here and there and then having to clamour them all together, to make the pile seem more. He piled it, mounded it, spread it and rattled it and made such a racket about it, I didn't stand a cat in hell's chance of getting off.

That was me coming down off speed. My grasp of the situation, my logic, my rationale, all on the plummet. The night before I'd whizzed off into verbal infinity with Irish but now I was falling down, at the same speed, with the same intensity.

And there was Cuttlebert. Late. Running in from the back of the court, nodding, thinking he'd missed the show. DI Cuttlebert. Bald as a badger. A reptilian neck. Diamond-shaped blood vessels. He smiled at me, basking in his suc-cess. Ratface turned around, wondering at all the commotion. With a horizontal palm, he told the plod to calm down or maybe he told the plod that everything was under control. Which indeed it was. But I wasn't.

Chapter 2

'Would you take the stand, Miss Jackson?'

The screw unclasped the cuffs and stood back. I walked towards the witness stand with all eyes following me. I felt them. I climbed up the stairs and strangely, once I was up there, in front of the two mikes, I felt an overpowering urge to sing at the top of my voice. I chewed my lip instead and looked to my feet.

The usher came over, flapping his gown like a would-be professor, a would-be judge or brief or would-be anything so long as he could dress up. 'Would you take the Bible in your right hand and read from the card?' He never said that. He just showed me what to do, placing the Bible in my hand. I think he thought I was deaf, given his enthusiasm for gesticulation. People do this to me a lot. Because of my face. They think it's a symptom of something more profound, blindness, deafness, stupidity. He gave me the card and pointed at the words in large bold type, both glaringly simple and sinister. I remembered back to school, learning to read, trying to get past row four on my reading card. I was trying for it now, trying for the same dignity, but in that strained unwholesome light the air seemed thick with lies. All I could see were hungry crows flapping about my head squawking, ready to feed.

'Mmm . . . You are of Christian faith, I take it?' asked Judge Benkinson, checking his knot before the garrotte, interrupting my flow, the flow of the court, making the woman writing it all down look up, making rustling papers settle like leaves on the calm. He held his pencil mid-bet in a horse-race, ready to tick off the result on his slip.

'Yes, I am,' I said. 'I've just told him that.' I pointed to the usher still holding the card.

Then I turned right round to the judge and gave him my face full on. I wanted him to see it right then, so he wouldn't get a shock later on, at a time out of my control. He looked at me and was immediately embarrassed, which was just how I wanted him.

'Thank you, Miss Jackson.'

The judge wrote something down then. Cocksucker. Smart-arse. Fucking guilty. Fucking ugly, more like.

'I swear by Almighty God I'll throttle that jumped up little get . . . that the evidence I shall give . . .'

Ratface stood up very slowly, looking down at his papers, fiddling with his gown and his ribs, pointing at words on a page but not looking up. He was waiting for Bodene's little speech to waft out of the courtroom. I was standing close to him, above him, looking down. This made me feel like I was on top of the situation. My cuffed hand now free, I had high honour in the dock, hanging loose, looking down to the bench. The furniture layout was contrived just so, to make people like me feel big. I stared down at Ratface's wig, and thought of a horse, showjumping, and still he turned his pages over. He wafted them and wafted them until at last he felt sure that he'd snuffed out the candle of Bodene's good work. He waited for my suspense to balloon and then he set about pricking it.

'So, Miss Jackson, you say that you were under so much pressure that the best thing to do all round was to confess – to provide the investigating officers with a catalogue of myth.'

'Well, I wouldn't call it a catalogue but that's right. I just wanted to get out of there. I wanted to get everyone out. And I didn't confess to the scag. The scag was nothin' to do with me.'

'The what?' said Judge Benkinson, talking to his pencil.

Ratface didn't hear him.

'And, Miss Jackson, did it not occur . . .'

'Did you say scag, Miss Jackson?' asked Benky, a lot louder that time.

'I meant heroin, Your Honour.'

'But did you say scag?'

'Yes, Your Honour.'

'Your street name for heroin, is it, Miss Jackson?'

'Not mine, Your Honour.'

'But you use the term nevertheless.'

'Well, I just . . .'

'Thank you. Carry on.'

Ratface smiled, made a note and carried on.

'And did it not occur to you, Miss Jackson, that to confess to these crimes would inevitably lead to your being punished for them?'

That was my first measure of the depths they plumb to in these places. Benky making out that I was the one who wrote the street dictionary. As if it was me that decided on Top Banana, ace, brill, fab, king or the bollocks. As if me saying scag meant I was married to the fucking stuff. Ratface looked down at his papers again, turning them over, flapping them. He wasn't reading the pages. It was all about creating effect.

'Well, straight after, like I said, I tried to retract my statement but they wouldn't let me. On my way back to my cell, I spoke to the policeman that booked me in and told him that I wanted to retract.'

'Because the pressure was off. That was why you wanted to retract.'

Ratface said it as a statement but looked at me as if asking a question. No . . . he was egging me on.

'Because my confession wasn't true. I made it up. I just wanted to get out of there.'

'Come, come, Miss Jackson. Look, I have your confession here. Written in your own handwriting. You can't even accuse the police of bad spelling, can you?' He was shouting now. 'Because it's your own bad spelling, isn't it, Miss Jackson? It's in your own handwriting, isn't it, Miss Jackson?'

'I didn't admit to the smack, though, did I . . .' It was when they brought the dinner in . . .' I was shouting, bouncing up and down in my box. 'They kept badgering me.'

I swung around to face the judge, but the judge was too busy doodling now, all finished with me, it seemed. I carried on at Ratface, who also wouldn't look at me.

'Listen, you!'

I pointed my finger at him, to get him to see me, like it was me that was in charge. I was high enough.

Ratface laughed. He turned around to look at Mrs Bodene and laughed, to make me look small, bring me down. He was taking the piss out of me . . . I had another go. My problem here was my voice. I tend to overcompensate for poor facial expression by raising the volume. If my face could talk articulately, I'm sure I wouldn't do this.

'Listen, you!' I bellowed. 'People make false confessions all the time. Look in the newspapers. Every week there's a false confession . . .'

'Oh, so that's where you got the idea from, was it, Miss Jackson? The newsssssss-papers?'

'You know what I mean!'

Shouting, bending right over the stand, I was, right in his face, Ratface.

'Quite so, Miss Jackson,' said Ratface. 'I think we all know what you mean.'

He turned over his pages in triumph.

'I think that's all for now, Your Honour.'

And Ratface left a fire roaring round the court.

Bodene beckoned to an usher to bring her a jug of the water but she'd need more than that. She'd reliably informed me that morning that, if we got the confession disallowed, the whole case would be kicked out of court. But Bodene was making it up as she went along. Meanwhile, the court case was going along and now, badly.

'Get back in yer box.'

The usher didn't say that. He just pointed it, the way a ref sends someone off, only he never had a whistle. The police officer didn't cuff me up. A relief. I think he only cuffed me the first time to scare me. It worked. Getting back in my box, on the ground, gave me that rather homely feeling. A safe feeling.

'Stand up, Miss Jackson.'

Everything stopped. The squeaky shoes. The paper shuffles. The heads turned. All heads were on the judge. Bodene looked brave.

'Miss Jackson, you have demonstrated a capacity for both insolence and aggression and consequently I have no hesitation in disregarding the evidence that you have given to this court stating that police duress induced you to make a false confession. You do not appear to be so frail that their questioning would warrant such a breakdown of the headstrong attitude you have most ably demonstrated. You are charged under the Drug Trafficking Act, 1971 with possession with intent to supply the Class A drug heroin. You are also charged with possession of a Class B drug, cannabis. You are also charged with supply of a Class B drug, cannabis. Your bail conditions still apply. The case will be heard in this court which is adjourned until ten, tomorrow morning.'

Bang, bang!

All rise!

Shuffle, shuffle.

The judge walked off the stage and everyone bowed and nodded at his honourableness. Except me. I could feel my make-up cracking under the strain.

Mrs Bodene closed her file. Alan Cunningham didn't even look at me. What to say? You've blown it. You're a prat. You're done for. No, Alan and Mrs Bodene had a few words, probably talking about some case going on next week, probably . . . Alan stuffed his glasses into his snappy glasses case. Then Mrs Bodene and Ratface, learn-ed friends, started talking. They smiled at one another and had a little chuckle about an early morning finish. Perhaps they'd do lunch together. I wanted to get down there and . . . the police officer pulled me from the court. He took me down. There was no need, I'd made bail. He wanted to show me the dungeons way, though. Give me a preview.

'Vivian, you'll have to calm right down. You can't behave like that. What got into you?'

Half a gram of speed – couldn't tell him that.

'I don't know. I think I was just nervous, you know. It's all a fucking game in there, isn't it? Like watching a play or something. Everyone's got all their lines prepared except me.'

'Then may I suggest that you go home and prepare some, using standard English, please. One more false move and you're done for.'

'What about the scag charge? Are they gonna drop it?'

'Let's wait till the morning. See what they offer.'

'I'm not guilty, yer know. I'm not going to prison for something I didn't do.'

'As you pointed out in court, lots of people that *aren't guilty* end up in prison. It's no use just saying you're innocent. You have to prove it. Proof is all.'

'Innocent until . . .'

'Until you make a confession. Round one in the police station and you lost. Round two – we try to get the confession excluded and you've lost again. Round three tomorrow. All you've done today is make bail. You were lucky. Go home, get some rest and, Vivian, make sure you've got your story straight. The truth. Truth shouts louder than lies but lies make more noise. Do you understand what I'm saying to you? And one more thing. Tomorrow. No shouting. No shouting whatsoever.'

It was hopeless. The corridors were crawling with the accused and their relatives. And here was me. Just another nigger on a drugs charge. An ugly nigger too. I made my way out of the place, before the people could stare at me. People in courthouses stare. Outside in the shops they steer their eyes away in long-distance stares but in court, where everybody's life is laid bare, they have the right to stare up front. I thought about my odds. Not good.

'It's not going to be easy, Vivian.'

Ho! Ho! Ho!

When I got home, Bev was in. She'd just scored. First time in three weeks. Her hands and nails were grimed up in coal dust from stashing it.

'I've got a pressy for you here. How'd it go?'

She was scrubbing at her nails in the kitchen, over the sink, tapping her head against a garlic rope hanging from the wall.

'Shit. Case starts tomorrow.'

'Well, enjoy yourself whilst you can.'

With wet hands she tried to open the kitchen window, stretching her body across the sink, slopping flab over too tight jeans.

'You're lucky you still made bail,' she said through her struggle, sounding almost like my solicitor, involved in something more important than me.

At last the window was open and she stood back from the sink, relaxed. She turned to look at me.

'D'yer wanna toot? Your hair doesn't look that bad you know. Different!'

'No. I need to clear my head. I went apeshit in there today. My head's fucked. What's the parcel?'

'Bit of gardening work that's not much cop and some rocky. Wanna spliff o' that? Zero zero.' She wiped her hands down her jeans like she was about to pull guns out of her holsters. Zero zero my arse.

'Go on then. You'll have to lay it on me, though. I'm . . .'

'You still owe me . . .' pointing at me, more accusations.

'Yeah . . . well, when I get my grant . . .' hands in my pockets, tinkling coppers between my fingers.

'Viv, the amount you owe me is more than your grant. I can't just keep giving yer . . .'

'Well, when this is all over I'll get myself sorted, won't I?'

I had no idea how but first things were first and first off, I needed a smoke to cool down the spit turning in my brain.

'Viv. I've told you before how to look at it,' she said, pointing at me, the scolding mother. 'If you *think* you're going to walk, it'll be all the more difficult to cope with when you don't. Yer gonna get banged up. Just get yer head down. That way, you'll try harder in court. You'll slaughter them.'

Bit of moral from me mates, that was. She opened her stash box and took out a blim the size of a pack of Wrigley's, neatly cut.

'Go on then. You can have an eighth. But don't tell Dirk.'

Then she took out a wrap, the size of a razor blade, an

origamied slither of magazine paper, its triangular flaps opening out to display a flat white oblong of powder. Soft grains fluffed as they fell on to the mirror, unbelievably clean-looking for a drug that had travelled, been hidden, bought and sold, bought and sold, and cut and packed and finally, there, there on Bev's mirror, looking for all the world like it's just been sent fresh from the local hospital. Unlike diesel hash. Cheech and Chong hash, I called it.

'Cheers, Bev.'

The silence was cut by the blade, on a mirror that had summer, winter, autumn and spring printed and squashed all across the glass so you couldn't get a clear view of an eyebrow, let alone a nose job. The coke often hid in the skirts of winter and had to be fingered off with a wet tip, ready to wipe the gums. As she wiped, I could see she fancied herself doing ritual in the jungle and perhaps I should have started picking nits out of her hair to complete the picture, but when she wiped the mirror with the arm of her cardy I was back in her front room again. Stoned now.

'The parcel was a lot shorter than we asked for, coz of the drought, so matey gave me half a gram o' charlie to cheer me up.'

Bev was boasting. Half a gram of coke. A treat she said it was. But really, behind the scenes, coke was a password for being there. She hadn't always been like that. Everything used to be natural. Weed and hash and cakes if she was in a good mood, rosy-cheeked and happy clappy, baking in the kitchen. We used to giggle when they said cannabis led on to harder drugs. It does if there isn't any. We used to laugh about that then. We laughed out loud. In those days, that was funny.

I did coke once. I did quite a lot but only the once. At Mikey's place. Headquarters, as he called it. I went to score some bush and left there feeling like a scorched test tube. After I snorted the coke, I waited and waited but nothing. A bit of a rush. Like speed. A freeze on my brain. There was some clarity there and I talked a lot but there wasn't the same hyper as speed, more like the feeling that the speed would rev up any second but it never did. I waited and waited. But nothing. There. I felt embarrassed but I never said anything. After all, I'd snorted about a tenner's worth, I reckoned. What a waste. I decided, just to myself, that the coke was probably cut with something – talc. I'd seen Mikey do that with his whizz but, just as I sat back, feeling slightly sorry for the owner of the coke, everyone congratulated the snotty sniffy bleary-eyed wreck of a man who said he could get as much as we wanted. All the way from Colombia. And pure as the driven snow.

'Well, I'll be damned,' keeping my hands firmly in my pockets.

'Don't tell Dirk I've given you an eighth, will you? He's on at me about money all the time these days.'

I burnt the hash with a lighter. Flakes of softened mud fell from the little brown brick, all along my bed of naked tobacco. (The brown tube of tobacco lying in the white sheets of paper reminds me of me. When I was a kid. In hospital. Me lying naked on hospital white sheets, my burns getting aired. Every time I make a joint, I can see myself lying there.)

'Course not,' I said.

I rolled the wobbly cylinder between fingers and thumbs and licked the seam. I lit the twisted end and lay back on the couch watching Bev do the very same trick only Bev used five papers for her joint, something most of us had grown out of. I wanted to get out of there before she passed me her spliff and I had to pass mine.

'Where is Dirk?'

'Selling the motor.'

'How come?'

'Seen a better one.'

'What?'

'Cavalier.'

'Bent.'

'Spect so.'

'Bit dodgy that, isn't it?'

'Not as dodgy as that Metro. I think someone welded that

thing together in their sleep. You could hear it falling apart even when it wasn't going. Death trap. He's got some biker after it now.'

'Does he know?'

'The biker? It's Mikey's mate. Well, he should figure it out really, shouldn't he? Buying a motor off Dirk.'

'What does a biker want with a motor?'

'Doin' a job, I s'pose.'

'I'm jiggered, Beverly. I'm goin' to bed. Thanks for the blim.'

'Hang on, Viv! You haven't told me about today. What happened? Are yer sure yer don't wanna toot?'

She was dying for someone to gab to now she was all charged up. I squeezed her hand, shook my head and went. I feel guilty about that now. Squeezing her hand.

Chapter 3

After knocking the toot back yet again, I took off for my flat. Just down the stairs from Bev and Dirk's. Dark it was, right at the back of the house. The place stank of damp and must. My kitchenette altar was old but still working. The furniture was dark-green and brown to match the carpet and curtains, though matching hadn't been the intention. Everything had just turned that colour over the years.

I lit the gas cooker for the kettle. Then waited for the whistle. I had to get the dress off. The costume. I couldn't blame all the dressing up on the system, could I? I'd take a shower. I felt for the hole in my nose where the stud should have been. The wastebin was still full of plaits, a writhing mass of black snakes. Plastic hair that should have been on my head, hiding my face.

Only that morning, after coming home from Irish's, did I unplait the final crop. Then I'd sat and unknotted my natural hair, combed it out so much my scalp hurt, and then the headache. Well, I couldn't go to court with plaits in my hair. The judge would see dreadlocks. Dreadlocks meant drugs and drugs meant guilty. Headache.

In the mirror, my hair was back to childhood and my nerves too. First, I had to take the make-up off. Special camouflage stuff it is. Except it isn't. It doesn't. It cracks too easily. And it's a bugger to get off. And when it's on, it looks like it's on. The lumps on my face show through. With my make-up-destroyer cream, I scraped it all off. There, that's better. I felt the scar, a smooth bit, the shininess of it, like plastic, like warm ice. I sneered at the mirror, like the lions do at the camera. Then I sucked harder on the joint. I ran the shower and changed into a gown, waiting for the bathroom to steam

23

up to a warm. I lit the gas fire. It was Indian summer but not in my flat. There was never any summer in my flat, Indian or otherwise. I sat, supped tea and felt a bit of a yarl coming on. I stopped it. I tipped my head and the tears ran back, over the top of my brain.

Normally in the shower I am needled into life, into an assessment of it. I hold my face, the poorly side, under the fiercest forces of the nozzle, and consider myself naked. This is the only time when my face feels like the rest of my body – when water is upon it. When I can hold my head up and feel like the perfect human, the complete person, the naked animal I was born. Especially so, with no plaits in my hair. But it's not just my body that's naked, it's my mind too. I believe my consciousness is fed by tiddlers that sleep until electrically activated by water. Water settles the skin but electrocutes my brain and like some mammal of the sea, when in my element, a bulbous consciousness awakens and rolls over me. Like the soft rays of a red lamp. My mind breathes when there's water all around me. That day, stoned, exhausted and rigid with anxiety, the shower spray fell like water caning marble, sliding off me, not getting through. The phone rang. I stopped the falling water. I stepped out of the lifeless pool at my feet. Dripping on to lino, I stood, waiting. The call wasn't for me.

'Well, fuck off then!'

That's what I said out loud, wet and wired.

I had to think of a story. Over the months, there'd been plenty. When it first happened, there were stories galore. 'You could say this, that, this, that.' I listened intently but in the end, I shelved each one. There was always a flaw. And of course there was time. The case would take a while to come up. The scag charge would be dropped at the last minute. There was plenty of time to make up a good story but now, already, it was the eve and there *were* no stories. The scag charge was still very much alive. How Bodene had the bottle going into that court without a story was questionable. For me it was disastrous but what was her game? She knew I wasn't completely innocent. What was my defence? Me saying *I never did it* which as a mantra feels fine but as a weapon is a custard tart.

It wasn't long before my friends got bored. Not long at all. Surprising really. One imagines one's friends as part of a whole, all intimately and intricately linked into the consciousness of the present. I did. I thought my friends would be with me all the way. I thought we were all sailing the same ship and against all storms, we would row together, as one. This is never so, I have found. Friends jump ship and are happy to watch you drown, from the safety of their lifeboats. Of course, as a child, I should have learned this lesson. I did. But I thought the lesson was for childhood, not for life.

As a child, we ran through fields, fields still hilly with dips for rabbit runs and badger lairs. The narrowest stretch of the river in the whole of the county was to us the crossing of the channel. Stepping stones begged us to go over, whether the water was high or low. When high, still to be seen were half-moon edges of boulders promising a safe crossing. We often slipped and iced ourselves. Our rubber plimsolls slid on shiny stone and froth from the river-flow noised up danger to us as we floundered, from one step to another. We were like fish escaped from the fisherman's hook, wriggling, neither in the water nor out, struggling to get steady, to get back in control. And over the river was Gaddy's farm. And on the far side of the farm, Gaddy's orchard. Gaddy sold his apples to the cider press. Me and Divine worked in the cider press once. Hated it. As kids, we scrumped the apples of the streets but a whole orchard? Think of it.

Edging the orchard, like stalkers, we headed towards the lowest-growing hedgerow, the youngest growth, the weakest part of the orchard wall – a front line of troops, green and sleepy with the hum of fly and the drunkenness of butterflies and bees. The hedge was still quite high and, had it surrounded someone's garden, we wouldn't have considered trying to conquer it. It would have been stupid to mount such a hedge to get into a handkerchief of a lawn. But because we imagined a football pitch of unguarded territory behind, we had to mount it. We would have to charge at it, clasp the hedgerow with hands and knees, throw the whole of our bodies right at it and scramble to the top. Arms and legs would get a right scratching, but it'd be worth it. Three of us. I was first over. First to see it. And look at it! The trees were bulging with it. Redness. Huge football apples shining like bleeding hearts, heavy, full and pumping to death, lying on the floor as blood puddles, around the trunks of the trees for as far as the eye could see. Waiting for me. Us. They were over but Sally was sulking. The skirt of her dress undone from the bodice. Her mother.

'Shut up about yer mum, would yer, and look.'

I dragged her into the full glare of it. I pushed her forward to show her the scene, like it was my scene, my garden.

'Oh Christ!' she said, like we'd broken into the tabernacle itself. 'Oh Jesus!'

'All that time we've been scrumping those shitty crab apples and look 'ere! It's like treasure, isn't it?'

'I think we better go back.'

Tommy was trying not to be shocked. But he was gone on it. This was serious grown-up land. Gaddy down the market seemed a weasel of a man, a bit bent with a squeaky voice. A wimp. Now, looking at his apples, suddenly he was a giant.

'Tommy, I'm not going back without getting some apples. Come on. Don't be a scaredy babby. We can be quick.'

'You go up then and we'll stand at the bottom and pick the best ones. Just shake the branch like mad.'

There were enough good apples on the floor. If we'd picked about a bit, we could have found enough for us to carry home. But I had to get in the tree. It had to feel like I'd really been scrumping. Tommy gave me a leg-up.

I went for the nearest major branch and edged my way along it. I looked down at Tommy and Sally. They were stuffing their mouths with their fingers, looking gormless. Scared. The apples were bristling for release, for to plop, drop and joyride through the air. I was just about to start shaking and looked down to warn them and . . . just where the hell did

26

they think they were going? They were screeching and squealing, high-pitched.

'Vivian! Vivian!'

I figured Gaddy was on his way. I'd hide in the tree and look down on him and wait till he'd gone. Tom and Sal did a Becher's Brook back over the hedge, made a much better job of it than on the way through and then I realised that the high-pitched squealing was getting louder and louder. I looked down to see three massive grey pigs charging the tree trunk, butting it. I could see the teeth on one. It was looking up at me. Like it wanted to eat me. I saw Tom's head over the top of the hedge. Sal must have given him a leg-up. He looked like he was watching a horror movie, glad he wasn't in it. That was the way my friends looked at me, over the coffee tables in the student union. And after weeks and weeks of it, they'd seen the movie so many times they were bored of the script. They'd given me all the stories they could muster and could do no more. Even Tom settled down in his hedge must have found a foothold. He looked up to the sky to watch the crows cackling in chorus, scratching his head, bored, waiting for me to get out of my predicament. Out of my tree.

Since being arrested, charged and, all this time, awaiting trial, I had become to my friends a walking case. With arms and legs and a head. They could sit me down and peek through the contents, rearrange a few things here or there. Or they could nod at me, pat the case on the back, wish it luck and then go. On their summer holidays.

The criminal element of Brimmington, as opposed to the student element, saw things differently. They wanted to know which barrister, which solicitor, how many were at the bust, how much gear, who was leading the drug squad and could they read the transcripts from the interrogation. Had I nailed any of them? Involved them? Dropped them right in it? The people of Brimmington, the crims of Brim, told me to get my head down and keep my chin up. I took heed. I behaved in the way they wanted me to and in doing so, I was accepted. I belonged. For all concerned, including myself, my situation was an hallucination only.

The upbeat faces of these friends became shields. They and only they could blot out the sulks of self-pity that filled the bin of my brain. Their faces wouldn't absorb gravity and grumpiness. Did I ask for pity? Would I plant apple pips in the sand? Their face shields beckoned for me to join them and to cast off the reality, and with the help of a spliff, the demons went away and the days were saved. This I did for four months, day after day. The falling down was slowed, my soul was fed and I fought demons. Mum and Dad were the scariest demons so I never went home for the holidays. I managed a couple of weekends, that was all. They weren't that bothered, they said. So long as I was behaving myself, they said.

I slapped cold juices of moisturiser all over me, rubbing it in good. Now I would shine. I built another spliff and climbed into bed. I turned on the electric blanket so I could get to fry a little. Resting my eyes on the poster of my spliff girl, I copied her, blowing the smoke out, up to the ceiling, slowly, in a ritual train. I was too mature for posters – not too old – too mature. I recognised already the stamp of a student trademark that was trying to buy me. Maybe, in another life, I'd have taken the poster down to keep me more of a mystery, not allow people to make judgements about my levels. But the dappled black damp stain behind the poster, compared to the white-painted walls around, reminded me of the torched skin of an infant. An infant in the children's ward where I had spent so many hours. There, I'd measured burn against burn. There, I was in the top ten.

'Nurse, what's in there? What's in that room?'

'Never you mind. Go back on the ward.'

It was the Chinese nurse. So vicious with the cold-burn spray. She got too close. All the other nurses wafted it on, gently. But the Chinese nurse sprayed it direct, freezing my face in agony, casing it with a white scream. She was mad for fresh air too. Always opening the windows. Like she *so* couldn't stand the thought of a burn, she had to make everything cold. Even herself.

The room with the infant in was at the entrance to the ward. The door stayed shut. It wasn't shut when the boy with no hair was in there. The curtains were open then too. But now, the people went in and out covered from head to foot. Everything closed, clothed and shut up.

'But why does everyone get dressed up to go in there?'

'Shut up and go back to the ward.'

Because I had a bit of a burnt leg they gave me crutches. I didn't need crutches. But it was the least they could do, wasn't it? With a face like mine. I loved my crutches. I went everywhere in them.

People went in and out of the room all morning. There was much kerfuffle and commotion. When lessons were over, I followed our hospital teacher out of the ward and saw it all. The commotion. I saw a man come out of the room and drop his mask from his chin and then immediately cover his forehead and eyes with his hand, like a mask again. He wiped his brow and walked slowly down the corridor. I had to go and have a look. I just had to. The door was slightly ajar so I pushed against it.

The front half of the infant was burnt off. A nurse was in there with her back to me. So engrossed she didn't hear me. She held the baby like a sacrifice, and lifted it into the cot. I saw its white bottom. When it was laid down, I saw its blackened front. No red bits even. From head to foot. She covered it with a sheet.

Mum and Dad brought me new clothes to go home in. A white pleated skirt and a sailor's shirt, with a toggle on. Mum helped me dress while Dad spoke to the nurse with red eyes.

'She was putting her other child to bed and left the baby by the fire, in its blanket. The guard wasn't on. She'd only just lit it. She hadn't finished putting the coal on, she said. Some wood fell from the fire. The baby kicked its way out of the blanket and the blanket caught light. She's only nineteen, the mother. Out of her mind, she is.'

'Where was the dad?'

'At work. On shifts.'

'Tragedy, eh! Damned tragedy, that is.'

Dad liked tragedies. I was a tragedy but he'd grown bored of me, of facing up to me. I was in there for weeks and what can a dad say to his kid when half her face is burnt off. He tried to climb inside other people's tragedies instead. As if to say to me, you're nothing special. You're not alone. See. See that baby. Dead and gone. Here you are, alive and well, and look at that boy over there. He'll never walk again so think on, young lady. Think on. The deeper he delved into their tragedies, the deeper I delved into mine. Dad knew what was wrong with every kid on the ward.

The damp patch on my bedroom wall was the same colour as the baby's burnt skin so the poster of the spliff girl stayed. Van Gogh prints and opening-night posters from theatres in London would have been more mature but I never had the right feeling in my head to shop for such fancies. If I got sent down, though, I'd ask my friends to bring me posh posters in. I'd look cultured. Different from the rest. But I wasn't different. I was the same as the rest. The screws would see a nigger doing time for drugs, whatever posters were stuck on my wall. I sucked my teeth, something I'd been practising, then I sucked on the joint and held the smoke down for as long as I could. It makes a change, a bit of rocky, I thought. Bit of bush would have been all right. Both. Dat wudda bin boss. Cocktail of rocky and bush. Yeah. Story. I had to get my story straight. I set the alarm for 5 a.m. There was no way I could straight think before then. Now smoke, rest, fry and sleep.

I awoke before the alarm went off, as one does when there's something not right. I watched the luminous hands of the clock turn not so luminous, as the light came in through the window. My blood was cooked good. I half dreamed the idea that black people had gravy for blood, cooked blood. That if white people had eaten black people instead of killing them then white people would think like black people because that's where thought comes from. The gut. And then . . . I awoke a little more. I wafted my blankets to circulate some fresh air. Ahhhhh! I thought I could hear my skin take breath. Made me want a cup of tea. I jumped out of bed and snuck next door, to light the gas fire, then jumped back into bed again, waiting for the room to warm up. Story. Ratface. Insolent and aggressive, that's what the judge called me. What did he know?

My trouble was set free on the fresh of the morning, as a spinning top, whirling around my brain at morning speed, the maximum. I held my head in my hands, lying flat on the bed. And then everything stopped. A chill crossed my eyes as a foreboding and when I opened them, I just knew the gas had run out. There was no gas in my bedroom, but I could sense the power had taken leave. The spin had stopped. Metre. Change for the metre. No fifty-pence piece. No cup of tea. No getting out of bed. Dirk and Bev would still be fasta. What about Captain Blaster upstairs? I could hear the faintest tinniness of his radio. Yeah, Captain Blaster would sort me out. I braved the cold air to go upstairs. I never went up to his place much. He kept himself to himself but he had a blow. Blast. Liked his draw. Used to be an alcoholic. Once an alkie . . . He worked for the gas board and I wanted a fifty for the gas metre. I thought on that dull coincidence for more than a moment, a moment more than a sane person would. My world was all dot-to-dot pictures. I drew in joins, no matter how tiny the distance, just in case a picture emerged that might help me.

'Hi, Jack, have yer got a fifty for the metre? Sorry to bother yer at this time, only I heard your radio and I thought . . .'
'Still with us then?'
'Just.'
I wondered whether he slept in that hat.
'Still up for it then?'
'What?'
'Court.'
'Yep.'
'Good luck.'
'I'll pay yer back tonight.'
'Don't worry about it.'
'Cheers, Jack!'
'Don't close the door. I'm coming down now. Take it easy, yeah?'

31

When I walked down the stairs I was fully awake and fully convinced that everyone had buried me. Giving me fifty-pence pieces like it was the least they could do. An eighth of rocky to see me through. I had to concentrate hard. It really was time I got my head together.

I made a cup of tea and jumped back into bed. With a pad and pen I wrote down all the questions I figured I'd be asked by Ratface. And underneath each one, the answers I would give. I did this till the clock said six and then I listened out. Would I hear my door being pushed open and then slotted shut to, like the closing of a safe? I did.

'Hiya!'

Dirk slipped off his dressing gown and climbed into bed with me.

'Mmm . . . you're just like a roast potato,' he said.

It was just what I needed. Well, nearly. I needed a hard cuddle first but Dirk got stuck in instead. Never one to stand on ceremony. Or talk. What you see is what you get. Or nearly. I got what I could see but more. I needed him. That was a first.

I was in bed with the Dirk in need. The one not to be frightened of. The Dirk making, but more often than not taking, love. Once he got going, I didn't mind the ride. He could always bring me up, make me rise, make me feel like I was animal. He could do it in minutes, bring a true bleeding to my senses, a washing together of the waters, in the basin of my mattress.

He never spoke about the case with me, not in words. It was all there, though, in his fierce blue eyes that feared for me. That was good to see, that fear for me. Both unnerving and reassuring. Empathy and sympathy. A sort of reality. Stopped me going mad. When he came to me like that, heavy with pant, covering my mouth with his hand, I was his lonesome queen and all the more attractive – silent. Subdued. Voiceless. I completed him. Bev provided the structure, the padding, the predictable future. I filled in his gaps with the passion. If I hadn't been going to prison, I wouldn't have shared him with

Bev. But at this juncture, there was no point in making waves. Before work, most mornings, he slipped in to see me.

'Good luck,' he said, kissing my forehead.

I knelt up in the bed and massaged his neck whilst he fixed his dressing-gown belt, his back towards me. He threw his curtain of hair back, like a girl, and it hit me in the face. Vosene. Sunday-night baths before school. I hugged him from behind and then threw myself back into the sheets, curling up. He looked at me once more before he left.

'See ya later,' I said.

And he was gone.

I went back to my writing pad with the questions written on. I cross-examined myself, on each question, taking the story further and further away from the truth. But to no end. No one would believe that a man ran in and framed me. No one would believe that I had been forced into a corner by a man I didn't know the name of. The plots on TV look so real, the victims seem so credible but in Brimmington Crown Court they'd be rocking in the aisles, holding their ribs. Over and over I practised my story but when I said it out loud, the facts of the matter tormented me, came at me from all angles as if unleashed by the very idea I was going to deny them. Like a demonic Satan on guard, the truth is always listening and humming. Any astute barrister would detect it, would hear it being rubbed up the wrong way, would feel the heat from the friction, not the air of a smooth and flowing natural vibration.

I put some skins together to make a spliff and then thought better of it. That rocky was quite strong. It might be better to stay straight if I could handle it. I looked to my Buddha. After doing what I did with Dirk, knowing what that would do to Bev, I didn't deserve to get off. Buddha was bouncing off the mantelpiece, telling me so. No, I must stay straight. But then, what if I got sent down? I wrapped the blim up in clingfilm. Later on I'd put that somewhere safe.

When I met Dirk, I'd already been at college for a whole year. Learnt loads. Firstly, that life outside college was a lot more interesting. Secondly, that education was necessary but the education system wasn't. Thirdly, that students bought drugs, by the truckload. And this was early eighties, when drugs weren't even fashionable. Dirk said that education was just a good excuse for a sit-down. He didn't reckon women much either. Didn't reckon we were up to it. We were just there. Half the human race. In his face. And a lot of them in college. Sat down. I was sat in his flat when we first clapped eyes on each other.

GOING TO COLLEGE

Chapter 4

'Hiya. Found us all right then?'

She made it sound like a question. Stupid question. I nodded my head vaguely, politely, and then swivelled to get a good look at the room. There was a body half lying across the couch. Still. A dirty man in a well-oiled denim jacket, his head down, corkscrew curls crowded up into a fuzz and knees poking out of his jeans. Before knees were allowed to poke out of jeans.

'This is Mikey,' she said, loud enough to wake Mikey up.

'Hi, Mikey!'

Mikey murmured something and then suddenly sat up. His fuzz, like a wig fallen down, didn't move with his head. It was possible that we could meet yet not even see each other. He stood up. I did a sly head-cock, to get a good look at him.

'Sorry, I've gotta go. Can't sit round here getting wrecked. Much as I'd like to. Cheers for that, though.'

He offered a thumb of thanks to Bev who stood with hands on hips, glad to get rid. Tucked under his arm was a half-full carrier bag wrapped to a sausage. He pushed the fuzz from his face to give his eyes a way out, his hand plastered across his forehead.

'Bye!' I said. 'Nice to meet you.'

I felt stupid then, because I hadn't *met* him. Eyeballed him, more like. He gave me a smile anyway, a widening of the lips. Bev pointed to a chair telling me to sit down. I fancied a lie-down on the couch really, but I couldn't do that. This was my very first visit.

'Tea?' she said, and then, as if she were in some other film, she pulled a chair close up to the fire, smoking spliff.

With her I watched the red coals die and, with a poker

aimed directly at the most charred lumps, she set them crunching and grunting to ash, to the graveyard of the grate. She was a tired waitress between shifts.

'You'll not find tea in the fire,' I wanted to say. 'Mmm. That'd be nice,' I said. 'Cup o' tea.'

Then a crash, followed by another, then another. Bikey Mikey was falling down the stairs. It took him ages to reach the bottom and he yelled, the whole way down. Bev held the joint to her lips, not taking a drag, as if to do so might break his fall. We waited. And there . . . the bang of the front door. She inhaled and got up. On her way to the window to watch him leave the premises, she passed me the joint.

'He's such a shit,' she said, and as if summoned, I got up and followed her to the window. To watch. I liked it here. Already, I was a member of the audience.

'Why bother with him then?'

'He owes me money.'

'Why lend it to him?'

My head back and forth – first to her, then down to Mikey.

'Because he owes me money. Once he's paid up – that's it. I should never have bothered with him in the first place, but you can't always tell, can you? Scag-heads.'

We watched him hobble down the path. He was carrying a Biggles helmet, the carrier bag stuffed inside it. I don't know what she meant by 'you can't always tell'. Mikey was the dead spit of the last person in the world you'd lend money to. I thought wearing bare kneecaps was admirable but taking scag? This guy was serious. *I*'d never do that, take scag. Too scary. Too much tosh about turkeys and dirty needles.

Bev looked at me and smiled. I didn't know if it was friendly fire or what. I made a mental note to watch my step when I left.

'He does quite a bit of business, as it happens,' she said. 'If he wants to go throwing himself down the stairs, that's his problem.'

I imagined he could feel our eyes following him down the path. He stopped to straighten his back out. He puffed out his chest like he'd just got out of bed of a morning. A pretence of control after making such a dick of himself. Little fall down the stairs wasn't going to have him go jumpy. He stretched his body up and out so his leathered arms filled up slowly like inflated rubber gloves. Then he put his carrier bag between his knees and shook the straps out of his helmet ready to put it on. We still watched him, in silence. He squashed his way through the hedge and was gone. I heard him kick-start the bike and then angry mad revs, over and over. Growls. Our cue to leave the window.

Bev went to the record player and put on Al Stewart, *Year of the Cat*. She piled up cups from the previous sitting on to a wicker tray and asked again if I'd like tea. She was an illegal abortionist. A witch doctor. She was soon back with two cups of steam and no tray. No way had she let that tea brew. Raspberry tea? No amount of brewing would have done for it.

'I hope you don't mind raspberry tea?' knowing damn well I'd hardly complain.

But still, the quietness of our chatter was easy. I passed her back the spliff smoked down to the cardboard. I'd have felt much worse, just stubbing it out in the ashtray. She looked at it and stubbed it out in the ashtray. I settled down, supping sip sounds, viewing the room, feeling quite at home.

'Do much business down the Fayre the other night?' I asked, stuck for a proper, more interesting line of enquiry.

Up until then, I'd bought all my blow from Mo. Mo was moody, his hash was moody and to make matters worse, he was too expensive. I needed someone further up the supply chain. On Fresher's Fayre night, down the student union, I'd been serving at the bar, my dealing headquarters. The bar manager had never known anyone quite so eager as me. Bev turned up to set out a stand and came over to buy a juice. Later, collecting glasses, I saw her signing people up for the Save the Whale campaign – a dead giveaway in her Chinese shoes and rainbow jumpers. I guess she wore that stuff to make her stand out – her face was one of those you see in a crowd. Short mousy hair, uniformly parted like a boy. She had broad shoulders, a flat chest and legs that stopped before the even got started. The fulcrum of mediocrity. Except for her clobber. I went over and had a chat with her. I was a dead giveaway because I was wrecked, eyes slit, wearing Rasta-coloured jumper, plaits without beads and a nose ring. She felt sorry for my scar on sight and overdid her generosity by giving me her address and the promise of some Nepalese Temple Balls. That was what brought me to her house. Temple Balls.

It was easy to spot the house because the windows were covered in rainbows. She'd warned me. I rang the doorbell but it didn't seem to work so I threw stones. Appearing at the window like a trapped ghost, she checked me out and threw down her keys. The hallway was semi-dark. The lino gritty. Bicycles lined the walls like scaffolding. In the porchway, an old Advent calendar was taped to the wall. All the windows were open. That was optimistic. Down the corridor there were steps to blackness. A helmet hung on the newel post like a cannonball. On the bottom step, junk mail and orange peel. Up the stairs I was helped out by a light going on. At the top of the stairs, the carpet was coming away.

'Watch that,' she said. 'Dirk'll be fixing that tonight.'

Through her door I walked into a temple of red velvet and beaming green plants, healthy plants with leaves big and shiny like sunlit dinner plates. There were posters showing the backs of people walking into paradise together. There was a table in the corner covered in a granny-green velvet tablecloth, a whole side of it annihilated by an attack of campaign badges from CND and LCC, Save the Whales, Meat is Murder, Sandinistas and Women Against War. Hundreds of badges. A fire. Red but not hot, not unless I stood close. Beads of Rasta colours hung across the air, everywhere. Wall-to-wall tapes and albums. Hookahs. Stash boxes. African headgear. A huge mobile dolphin in blue and silver. A tree painted on the wall with zodiac signs encased in the fruit. Elephants. Praying kids. Wisdom pictures. Prayer mats. Fucking mad. Mad. Buddha says hi! as I walk through the door. Boomshanka! Wherever you are. Whoever you are.

'I didn't do as well as I did last year,' she said.

She opened a cigar box and took out a small black wooden pipe, the size of an antique teaspoon. Smoking pipes made me cough and the worst thing to do, trying to look cool, is to cough off the pipe. Like at school when you first start fags.

'The Midland Bank did all right,' she said. 'They had them queuing down the stairs.'

'I won't beat about the bush, Bev. I'm after some draw, about a quarter pound if it's about.'

She filled the pipe and put it between her lips, a lighter turned upside-down to fire it. She sucked and sucked, concentration total. To stop the worry working its way up my windpipe, I coughed, preparing my own lungs for the onslaught, clearing a runway for the smoke.

'How much d'yer want?' she asked, choking through the puff.

She passed me the pipe. I took a few conservative sucks, quick ones to build up the glow till it really blared, and then a huge suck. Quite a smooth ride really. She was still coughing off, striking her breast, heaving. I waited patiently. Smugly. I felt a slight nudge to get something off my chest but I smothered that with a strong intake of breath.

'Quarter pound?' I said, exhaling, my voice wavery, my throat a little raw.

'We don't usually do less than half. Get too many visitors otherwise.'

'Well, that's all I can afford. I've just got my grant, see.'

'I'll lay the rest on you then,' she said. 'You can pay me back when you've sold it.'

'Are you sure?'

We stared at one another for an embarrassing but necessary amount of time.

'I know where to find you.'

'What is it?'

'Lebanese.'

'No Temple Balls?'

'Too good, for the punters, Temple Balls,' she said, turning up her nose, like I should have known that. 'That's the Nepalese you're smoking now.'

Bang, bang, bang. She hammered and emptied the bowl of her pipe on the table, getting it ready for another blast.

'If you've got time?' she asked, holding up the pipe to me. Another duel.

Warmed by the fire, we smoked the hash into rushes and streams that curled over and under the bars of guitars and the getting to know one another. As the smoke caught its own weight in the air, a mosaic curtain of blue fell upon the weak sunlight. Through this curtain, I watched her face fall into a place of safety, of relaxation, and I noted just a shimmer of reverence.

It was a mark of respect to have a smoke with your dealer after scoring. Mo told me that. He said that the dealer doesn't want to feel like a supermarket and that the punter should stay a while and share the vibration. Well, I wasn't into all that bollocks but as this was the first time, it made sense to hang around and be studied, investigated.

'D'yer mind me asking? About your face?'

I did, actually. Well, I didn't. I didn't mind telling but there are times and there are times. Some people knew just when. Some didn't. Bev knew. She knew I wouldn't mind but couldn't be arsed waiting. Must have been killing her. Most tokers held off, like prisoners who don't discuss what they're in for. I guess coz I was scoring off her she reckoned she'd paid her due.

'No. Not at all. Jam. I was eight.'

'Must've been nasty.'

'It was. Still is.'

I hate the ones that try to make *me* make *them* feel comfortable. I don't do that any more. Opened my life up no end, that strategy. One of my greatest joys is watching people, seeing how long it takes them to rest, relax, ask me all about it.

'I'll get the blow for you,' she said. 'I'll have to open a new lot, though.'

Like I was bothered, cared, wanted or even needed to know.

'SOK,' I said. 'Whatever. So long as it works. I won't find that out till this wears off, will I?'

'It works.'

The Nepalese certainly did.

'Goes straight to your head, the Leb,' she said. 'That Nepalese creeps up on you but when you're there . . .'

She smiled at me, head-on, with dancing eyes, a hazy vibration falling down from them, to hit her lips with a grin. I was rising up to it myself. Up there. The Nepalese crawled down my back and halfway up my backside. I needed the toilet. A lie-down. A drink. More raspberry tea even. She passed me the pipe and left the room. She came back with a bin bag and pulled out a tablet of hash, the size of a baby blackboard, covered in pink hessian cloth. Using a toffee hammer, she smashed it up. Shards of it crumbled up from the break. From under the table she pulled out some scales.

'You're not selling the rocky any more then?'

She didn't look at me so I knew it wasn't a question. She carried on weighing the hash. Playing Queen Cool know-it-all with her gob but fucking up the effect with her bad behaviour. She didn't know how big my gob was.

'Who told you?'

I laid the pipe to one side and rolled a joint using my own tiny blim, to be polite.

'It's not such a secret,' she said, now looking at me, with warning signals.

Her happy buzz had fallen away now, the force of it gone from her face. From me too. Still inside me, but not showing.

She sneaked a look at me and, 'I know who sells all the gear down the union.'

I laughed and nodded at her balancing the scales. I wanted to let her know she was being a bit slack on security. She didn't get it.

'So someone grassed me up then, eh?' I asked sarcastically.

'You should watch it, you know. Being black, they'll make a beeline for you,' wrapping the gear up in clingfilm.

'What? Down the union?'

'DS. Drug Squad.'

Licking the seal of my spliff, and twisting its wick, I lay back in my chair to examine the dolphin hanging from the ceiling, its flipper somewhat an afterthought. The moment the idea 'Drug Squad' registered, I saw American loons in peaked caps jumping out of helicopters shouting 'Huy! Huy! Huy!'. She passed me a lump of the Leb to look at, so that's what I did – looked at it. Then gave it back to her. I took just one drag on my joint, and offered it up to her. She waved it off – didn't want it. Then her wave stopped mid-air, like she was miming. She jumped, her head alert as a fragile bird. She turned down the music and listened again. I looked to the door and saw strings and strings of tiny dull brass beads. I thought they were beads, but then I focused on just one and stared hard. I saw a tiny slit in it, like the slit in the visor of a knight's helmet. Then in all of them. Then the bells rang out, talking to me, as if they'd heard me looking. My head pinged with the rings. I took another drag on my spliff as a sort of thank-you for the communion. The door opened. A man came in. Tall. Long and long blond hair. Not smiling. With a chin to slice bread with.

'Ah. It's you. This is Dirk. My boyfriend.'

'Hi, Dirk.'

'And you are?'

A molten boulder from my spliff rode down the canyon of my breasts and burnt a hole in my jumper. I slapped at my chest to minimise the damage. When I'd finished, I looked up to see Dirk looking at Bev and then back to me – all worried, he seemed. The shock of my scar didn't faze him at all. He stared straight into it, to face up to it, like a man. He was waiting to be told who I was. And Bev had forgotten my name. She didn't know my name but there she was, chopping up lumps of hash on the coffee table.

'Sorry, Dirk, I'm Viv.'

He walked back out in a huff.

'You'd better go,' said Bev, doing her numbers quickly, counting out loud.

From her mumblings, I tried to figure out her cost price but couldn't. She was too quick. She wrapped my purchase in a carrier bag and I quickly counted the money. She bit off an eighth of the Nepalese – very nice. Thank you. I held back on fifty quid. No point her having it if she wasn't gagging for it. I left her with the spliff and was out of the door.

'See you again.'

'Yes,' she said. 'And soon. I'll give you till Friday before I come looking for you.'

Endings like that can ruin anything.

Chapter 5

Going home, I broke into a trot. All the way down the main road a learner driver purred behind me, and I figured maybe he wasn't a learner driver after all so I changed tack, and zigzagged down the back alleyways, my head full of excitement. I love those times. Padding the pavement with a lightness in my step, with deceit in my mind and the thrill of it spilling out of each nostril with each breath. The stuff of living, of feeling alive, at home. At home it would all change. It was Irish's birthday and I would be expected to act up, be happy for him. Pretend to be someone else. Drown my soul and dress my mind with a social amiable curtain. A bit like stuffing cloth down the mouth of a trumpet, to my mind.

'Will you be joining us tonight?' Vinnie said, washing up, talking down to me, which he shouldn't even *try* to do. He was only five foot two.

'Is Mo coming?' I asked, parking myself at the kitchen table.

'He lost his job today. He wants to make a night of it.'

'Nigger time not agree with 'em down there then? How'd he lose his job?'

'I don't like that, Vivian.'

'What?'

'You saying nigger.'

He was too straight for me, Vinnie.

'How'd he take it then?'

'Looking forward to the lie-ins, I think. I've warned him, mind.'

'About?'

'About the rent. Our Dubliner black belt landlord, or have you forgotten?'

'Jesus, Vinnie. Give the man a chance.'

'Got to keep on top of him, though, haven't we? Just you watch him. He'll blow his wages tonight, I bet.'

'I expect he'll find his money from somewhere.'

'No doubt he will and no doubt you'll be helping him.'

Vinnie turned round at that point. I was writing my name in salt on the kitchen table, the scarred side of my face resting on my free hand, my right hand. Over the years this habit of covering my face has made me ambidextrous. My ambidexterity I see as compensation and smacks of God taking the piss, like making blind people hear good and letting deaf people have eyes in the back of their heads.

'I think I'll ask Roy to come . . . tonight, I mean.'

He turned away again and crashed cutlery on to the draining board.

'That weirdo. Again. I can't make you out sometimes.'

'There's nothing to make out.'

'He's a non-starter, Vivian. I'd have thought you'd have more sense.'

'What's up, Vinnie? Jealous?'

'And what if I am?' he said, chucking the teatowel away and walking towards me. 'What if . . . what if what you really need happens to be right under your nose?'

Right under my nose he was then, just. That's how far up to me he came. I put my hand up, traffic-warden style, to tell him to back off but he just stood there.

'Vinnie. You're too small.'

He pulled back with a wince. I could have kicked myself. Fair dinkum, he was too small but to tell him. Just like that. To tell any Nigerian he's too small is . . . well . . . it's not on. But he was asking for it. *Small* was the kindest word. He was too straight, too scared of his dad. He was too smiley, too false. Too many things.

Mo came in and split the room in two with four cans of lager.

'Where's Irish then?' I asked, as if nothing had gone on. Mo felt it, though.

'You two havin' a row?' he asked, looking at me, since Vinnie never rowed.

47

'No,' said Vinnie, taking a can, cracking it open for his Popeye impression.

I did likewise and was glad of the cut to my dry mouth.

'Irish has gone to spend his mammy's birthday tenner on something he won't feel guilty about,' said Mo. 'Twat,' he spat, at the end of it.

'I'm going for a lie-down,' I said.

'You look pretty wrecked,' said Mo, examining me more closely, his mouth invisible behind his beard, his hair as though he'd been lying down on it all afternoon. He was still smelling of glue.

'I am.'

'Well?'

'Well, what? Jesus, what is this?'

'This,' he said, pointing to his chest. 'This is a man without a job wanting drugs.'

'You've got a blim, 'aven't yer?' I said, backing off from him.

'Yes. But not what you're smoking. What is it? Look at her eyes, Vinnie. Come on, Viv. Out with it. What are you smoking?'

'All right there, Irish! Happy Birtday to yer!'

Irish's hands were full with wok and long sticky cooking utensils, his face beetroot red and his hair redder than that. He was laughing. We clashed our cold cans against his cheeks, as a cheers. He moved away from the onslaught and relieved himself of his packages. Then he clapped his hands.

'I'm cooking tonight,' he said, and we all groaned.

It started off all right. The night. Irish's birthday night. Then, coz Irish had done one, Mo made Vinnie do a yard of ale (nearly as big as Vinnie) which he couldn't finish. Made a right mess. Mo did a full yard and carried on where Vinnie left off. After a few more pints, they were well on their way. I was only half drunk, half bothered. I took advantage of Mo's inebriation to let him know that losing his job gluing man-made soles to man-made uppers wasn't the only threat to his livelihood bobbing along the horizon. As I figured he would be, he was too drunk to care. I rang Roy and with some nudging and Temple Ball talk, he agreed to come out and play. The minute Mo started fighting with a bunch of burly locals over the next go on the pool table, we left them, to go home.

He was all right at night, Roy. The very first time I spoke to him properly, we were as a group, walking home from a gig. About six of us. About six months ago. As we turned into the park, there was a moon hanging, like a giant medallion. I was giddy, looking at it, walking towards it. A big dong. Like a solemn grandfather clock. Sensible. Sombre and sure, compared to us – pissed. Strangely, it shut me up. Roy came alongside and joined me in the hypnotism. We walked as wise men. The silence was stupid so I broke it.

'Is that a spliff?'

'It is.'

'Gizza go.'

'Shall we sit and roll one? Take in some moon?'

I looked ahead to the others. They weren't even looking at the moon. I bet they hadn't even noticed it. They were looking at their feet – like metal detectors.

'Yeah. All right then,' I said, alert.

Alert to his strangeness. He carried a handbag. Not the way the women do, clinging on to the straps as if they were reins on kids. Over his head and shoulder like a traveller. As if the bag held promise, intrigue, treasure even. It was his coat that did for him. Little mirrors all over it, hexagonal ones. Right down to his knees at the front and halfway up his bum round the back. He took it off and laid it on the grass as a spangled island. I sat, with him on my good side. I do that quite naturally now. At school, after the accident, I always had to sit by the window, my face to the sky. The kids left a chair free for me. They didn't like looking at my face any more than I did. Splash, they used to call me, coz you could just make out where the jam had splashed across my chin. After my first graft you couldn't – but they still called me Splash. Made me 'Get Well' cards with 'To Splash' written inside. And Spider-girl. They called me Spidergirl sometimes. Splash, mostly.

Vinnie walked ahead with his back to the moon, shouting to us. We waved him on. Long after, I could still see his head turning back, wanting to be with us. I knew then that he had designs on me. To Vinnie, being small was the same as being scarred. That we were both black reinforced his determination to make a girlfriend of me. Having me as a mate built him up, made him feel taller. Having Vinnie as a mate pulled me down. Like he was the best I could do. The highest I could get. A fucking reminder, in *short*.

Roy sat cross-legged so I copied him. I began to roll a joint. The half of the skin I didn't want rolled off into the grass but Roy caught it, picked it up, deftly, with the fingers of an elf, as if it were a precious coin. I watched him lick his skins together and in a really sickly way, it was like he was licking the very first bond between us. I shuddered off the idea of it. Like I'd picked up the wrong coat at the end of a party.

Sat in the middle of a flat long playing field, lights at each far end, we smoked. The grass could have been a lake, a rink, could have been the feathery quills of a million dying blue-birds, their heads buried in the earth – after a few smokes, it could. A thin scattering of stars draped us, like a coat, like the mirror coat we sat on. The sky was a ceiling falling in on us, a ceiling of crystal points. God's marbles. God's map. The wind rushed across our faces and being so stoned, it felt like the night spirits themselves were out with us, giddy at the moon, playful, their fingers lifting his fair-haired fringe, wispy, film real. Vivid. Tangible. Like kids we were. In Eden, at Midnight.

'Makes me feel giddy the moon – does it you?'

'Yeah, a bit.'

We kept our eyes on it. Like something good on the telly – the true story of a woman sentenced to death, to hang. We watched the noose being put around her little white neck. In the morning she'd be dead.

'Swap?'

I didn't look at him. I watched the spliff exchange and then back to the moon. It was chilly but not bone chilly – more like air-conditioning. I felt trickles of the chill inch in, up my sleeves, down the back of my neck. My skin itched for a connection, for contact. I put my knees up to my chin and hugged myself.

'The lunatics'll be at it tonight.'

'It's not full,' he said.

'Tis. Look! Look at the man's face. The man in the moon. I can see down the back of his throat.'

'It's not full, I'm telling you.'

'And you'd know, of course. You being the local moon expert.'

Which, as it turned out, he probably was. He celebrated full moons and solstices at parties up on Catnap Hill. He danced the seasons in, round camp-fires, with folk who played folk on guitars.

'Why d'yer think that is then? The lunatics, I mean.'

'D'yer know some people can't see the man? The man in the moon?'

'They must be the lunatics then, eh? They say that witches can't see themselves in the mirror – did yer know that? Maybe they're all lunatics too.'

'It's got nothin' to do with witches,' he said. 'That's all a myth. Lunacy is due to water, the most powerful element on the planet.'

''Snot an element, it's a compound.'

'The elements. Wind and water and fire and . . .'

'Yeah. OK, Professor. So what about the water?'

'Water. The body's made of water. Moon controls the tides. Moon controls the body tides.'

'Well, how come some people loon right out and others don't?'

'Ah,' he laughed.

'What's so funny?'

I looked at him properly then. He was tidying up his tobacco tin, putting his lighter in his pouch. I could see him up a mountain, hunting deer.

'You'll only call me a weirdo if I explain,' he said. 'When people like you ask me questions like that . . .'

'What do you mean? People like me?'

'Well, let's just say that you're probably a bit out of touch.'

'Don't mince yer words on my behalf.'

'Don't get snotty. What did you say you were studying? Economics and business?'

I nodded.

'Well, I rest my case.'

'Oh I get yer. Coz I need to get a job when I leave college, that turns me into an out-of-touch capitalist pig, does it?'

'Not . . .'

'Let me tell you something. I don't give a fuck about business and economics. It's something to do. Gets me off the dole. Makes me look respectable. And anyway, I *might* get a degree.'

There was silence whilst we re-adjusted ourselves. We tried to get back to the earlier reverence.

'I wanted to do psychology,' I said softly. 'But me dad wouldn't let me. He said there's no money in guessing games.'

'There is, though.'

'But me dad said not for me. Not looking like this.'

Roy stared up at the moon again. I was waiting for him to tell me about the loons but he just sat there, silent.

'Well, go on then. Tell me!'

'Tell you what?'

'The loons, stupid.'

I pushed him lightly but he pretended even lighter than that, a collapsibility. As if he were made of paper, he rolled to the ground. Then he heaved himself back up again, smiling, letting me know that he didn't mind 'boisterous'.

'I want to hear about the lunatics,' I said.

'Everyone can feel something when the moon's full,' he said. 'Hey diddle diddle, the cat and the fiddle. They just don't tune into it.'

'Hey diddle diddle?'

'Song of the lunatic.'

'What d'yer mean?'

'A true lunatic will sing that song during the madness. They feel it.'

52

What? What can they feel?'

'A connection.'

'Bollocks.'

'The little dog laughed, to see the craft. That's the dog star. The dog star is one of a pair. A binary star. One of the pair of stars exploded to make a white dwarf. That's why people don't feel the moon, coz they're pulling towards the dwarf, trying to pinpoint the movement of truth, instead of just living it. They can't see.'

He was priest-like, mumbo jumboed into missionary madness.

'Everybody should feel some movement, some cascading of the spirit. At the moment, civilisation is stuck in a sort of synapse.'

His joint had gone out so I offered him my red end to re-light it.

'Take the female spirit, right?'

'Roy, I'm bored. Can we talk about somat else?'

'Take your periods, for instance.'

'Roy, for fuck's sake. Do we have to?'

'When you're on your period, do you feel more spiritually connected to the world?'

I felt slightly undressed. As though a veil had been whisked away from me. The secrecy of the blood, maybe. The discharge. In a man's voice.

'Well, I'm not sure that's a goer really.'

I wouldn't look at him dead on. I wouldn't look at the moon either, fearing its brightness right then.

'I'm on the pill and if you're on the pill, periods don't count, do they?'

'The pill isn't such a good idea.'

'For period pains, it is . . .'

'I mean, for feeling the spirit. You don't teach a child to eat and then show it pictures of food. The spirit would starve.'

'The kid would, you mean.' He was dead right. He *was* a fucking weirdo. 'I bet you're into all that Guru Maharaj Ji crap, aren't yer?'

'See. So you think the pill's all right then, do you?'

'I don't see what the pill's got to do with the moon.'

'Well, if you weren't so chemically fucked up, you would.'

'Keep yer hair on.'

The wind was blowing it up with his temper. I quite liked him then. An original. With a mind of his own. I was hoping and praying . . . that he fancied me.

'How come then? Tell me.'

I leant back on my hands, moonbathing.

'Just before your period, the earth speaks to you.'

'Oh give over, will yer.'

Laughing too hard, I was. I'd have to control myself, else he'd know that I was after him.

'See?'

'See what?'

'That's what happens. People laugh at me.'

'And you'd know all about it, would you? Have periods up on Catnap Hill, do you?'

'During your period, the earth gives you power – creative power.'

'Gives me a bellyache.'

'The period is the alarm clock of the planet. A timing mechanism. The longitude and latitude of the human psyche can be mapped out from it, and if women were united, as a collective, the human bond between nations would be terrific.'

'Have you got any idea what it'd be like if all the women of the world came on, all at the same time? If you think there isn't much world peace now . . .'

'You know what they did to them in the old days?'

'What?'

'Gave them hysterectomies. That's where the word hysterical comes from. Hyster means womb in Ancient Greek. When hubby went off to war for months on end, the women went mad. Couldn't cope. So they whipped out the gubbins. No PMT after that. Men are frightened of women, see. Women have the power. In some cultures men send their women away whilst they're menstruating. Don't let them near the temples

54

or anything. We in the West laugh! But even the Christians won't let menstruating women mess about with their tabernacles. Modern form of hysterectomy, the pill, mark my words.'

'And you wonder why people take the piss out of you.'

I stubbed my joint out in the grass. He was on tablets, maybe. He put his hands up in the air, ready to be shot for his words. I smiled at him, as if to say, you're safe with me. Maybe he liked the mothering type.

'I really think you've lost it a bit, yer know.'

'The electro-magnetic energy is almost tangible tonight,' he said. 'Tomorrow, it'll be a real frightener.'

A frizz of energy seized him. Worked him up.

'It's the invisible light, you see. Darkness is leaping with invisible light. We can see it with our heads – we just don't practise. We're not close enough. Not being close to the moonlight is like having a photograph without a negative. Our image of reality is fixed but it steadily decays. Eventually we won't know what reality is. We won't know who we really are. That's why people loon out. They can't fix themselves because they can't see the full picture. We need moonlight to recreate new realities. It's more important than sunlight but not in its physicalness – more in the way we treat it, the way we understand it. In the night, everything is laid bare. It's raw. That's why we're scared when we're kids, not coz it's dark but because the light inside our heads goes on. And we're alone with it. We make things up. We create our own world, one we feel safe in. As we grow up, our spirit matures. The world becomes safer. And women. They get a special gift. They get to mimic the moon and when the moon is full, when the light's turned full on, then she sees. She sees the whole picture and when she sees something wrong, she gets hectic with her PMT – the whole of her body and soul can see. She can see the mess that men have created. Even if it's just in her own back yard, she can see it. And that's why men are scared of her. Of her power to create, reproduce, feed, see. And that's why religions are run by men. They wanted the power for themselves so they took it, illegally. Priestess is a word of the past now. She turned into a witch. Menstruation, instead of being pure and at one with the earth, was made dirty, unclean, at odds with the sacred and the divine. Men. Instead of a sacred well, they preferred the sacred wand. That's why a man in charge will always have some sort of stick in his hand. Some wand of power. A dick extension, they call it now. Now, they fly off to the moon in dick rockets. That, it has to be said, is the greatest irony. Since man stole the power from woman, he lost the true nature of his spirit, and now he has become obsessed with the physical, the material. He hasn't cottoned on to it yet.'

'Roy, I don't give a toss about the moon and the loons really. I've had enough.'

I thought I'd try and bring the conversation round to us, my face. Perhaps, him being so away about the physical, perhaps he'd say that my face didn't bother him.

'Listen,' he said, taking my arm, really going for it. 'The only way we humans can get through the mess out there is through the spirit world. The only real and undisputed method of reaching the spirit world is through woman, through the waters of her body . . . her . . . her cardinal humours.'

'Roy, I mean it. I've had enough.'

I was sulking now, holding my chin up with cupped hands. This woman he was on about didn't sound like me. Then I had a thought.

'Is this why you've got an 'andbag? Do you want to be a woman? Is that what this is all about?'

'The humours are the temper. The temperature really. When the temper rises, the woman becomes incandescent. Full of light. All her humours are drawn up, into her spirit, just as the moon draws the tides . . . every twenty-eight days, she, the moon . . .'

'Roy?'

'Yeah.'

'What do you study?'

'I don't.' Head down, picking grass, back in Brimmington.

56

'I'm a plumber. I used to study philosophy at Oxford but I couldn't hack it. Six months and I'd managed to philo . . . philosloth . . . philosophise myself out of the course, out of my mind nearly. I couldn't see the point.'

'Mmm. My sister went to Oxford. Divine Jackson. Do you know her?' Bring him back down a bit.

'I left quite a few years ago, I'm afraid.'

'Our Divine did this, you know?'

'What? On purpose?' he said, an uninterested expression across his brow.

'No, course not. 'N accident.'

'Oh well, you win some, you lose some.'

'You're supposed to feel sorry for me.'

'So you want pity, yeah?' rolling another joint. 'Sorry. I don't do pity. Like giving a homeless tramp an umbrella. That's what my dad used to say. Give him a house or let him feel the rain. An umbrella makes it look like he's coping. You could get your hair done in plaits. That'd look nice.'

'Your dad *used* to say?'

'Dead.'

'Oh Roy, I'm sorry.'

'Not as sorry as me, so don't pity me and I won't pity you, OK? Get some plaits in your hair – they'd cover the scar a bit, no?'

A long silence. I was in that gap. Didn't know whether to ask him about his dad or just ignore it. He was acting like he wanted to ignore it, but I did that sometimes. When someone got close to the bone. His madness was making sense.

'Money. Plaits cost money. How'd it happen then? Yer dad?'

'Don't wanna talk about it.'

'I'm not asking out of pity. I just want to know. I like knowing how people die.'

'We were fishing on my thirteenth birthday, in Cornwall, on holiday. Four o'clock in the morning. The sea took him. I was catching a fish at the time. Never even noticed. Too busy reeling the fucking thing in.'

'God.'

'God. Yes. The Grand Architect of the Universe. Jesus. The fisher of fucking dads on holiday. I've had it with God.'

'Zat why yer into all this moon stuff then?' I was dead quiet.

'I'm into anything that comes in waves. Anything that can carry me along. That's all there is.'

'What about your mum? How did she take it?'

'Very well. She was trying to divorce him at the time. If he hadn't died, she would have crucified him. Now that's it. I don't want to talk about it.'

'I'm sorry.'

He leant forward to kiss me on the forehead. Was I on for it? No. That was it. Like a seal on a box. Like an ending and a beginning all at once. I kissed him back, tried to get his lips but he quite deliberately gave me his cheek. Still, it felt all right. I've had bigger letdowns. He took my hand and the warmth of his squeeze fed me. Took away the embarrassment of the kiss too. We hugged then, as humans. Not lovers or family or anything like that. We were just two strange humans meeting on a plane. Smoking Manali. Moonbathing.

'Guess what?' he said.

'What?'

'They didn't give them hysterectomies when the men went off to war. I lied.'

'You're such a twat.'

'But I do know where you can get your hair plaited. Cheap. The girl that lives upstairs from me does it. Single mum. Needs all the dosh she can lay her hands on. She does about two a month. They look amazing. You'd suit that – plaits in your hair.'

'I do suit it. I just can't afford it.'

That was the first time I met him and always how I remember him. In the dark. In the moonlight. With a silver-tinted brow and a spangled coat. More lit up than enlightened. He was lifeless pigskin in the daylight. All grey and pasty.

On the night of Irish's birthday, walking home, there was no moon and no stars. Just clouds. I walked tall with a head full of plaits and we talked. We talked about there being no more Manali one day. No more Thai Stick or Sensi. Easier to smuggle in bags of scag than decent blow and so that's what people were doing. All blow would be wholesale in the future, he said. Like he was the managing director of it. It would be more of the same, all of the time. So this night, he was pleased to be smoking my crumb of a Nepalese Temple Ball from Bev. We laughed all the way home, like drunkards ice skating on the rink of our imaginations. Sliding around our own little temple in a whirl.

In the morning he paid me cash on the nail for two ounces of the Leb. I sent him packing before the daylight got to him, before I opened my curtains. Roy wasn't one for hanging about of a morning, drinking coffee. He wasn't one for domestics at all. I always put him straight out the front door like the cat. He didn't mind. As we creaked down the stairs, I noticed Vinnie's door open slowly, just a small amount. He was watching us. I never let on I knew.

Chapter 6

I went back to bed for an hour but not to sleep. I rolled a joint and lay on my back, feeling my scar, the shininess of it. Some bits are so shiny I can feel the contours of my fingerprints ribbing against it. I think of an artist's palette, after he's done with painting the flesh of his woman. He leaves the palette to the side of the easel and goes over to her, to dress her. I am left on the palette. Lumps and twists of creased uneven browns and pinks, in knots down my cheek, a bit on my neck and up around my eye. It wouldn't be so bad if it was all the same colour, all the same level even. I think of chocolate and vanilla ice-cream left to melt, slithers of a chocolate flake freshly layered on top. A dirty splodge when you first see it. It hugs the side of my eye like a near miss or a near hit, depending on how I feel. It takes up a lot of my time, my scar, a lot of my mental energy. In the mornings, I have to grow into it. Less so if I'm spending the day at home but if I'm going out, I have to work at it.

Vinnie came into my thoughts that morning. I didn't want him to. I didn't want him to want me, so after basking in the wonder that at least somebody did, I let the thought die off. The Vinnie and Viv dream sounded OK but I didn't buy it. Like a daydream pools win, just a nook of a chance but first, one must buy the ticket.

I was so much taller than him. Walking amongst the street people, a tiny little black man with a pin head, smooth and shiny, and then me. The scarred woman. I tampered with the idea of him taking my virginity but I cringed at that even. Just the tampering. The theory was fine. The fumbling, I knew, wouldn't be.

When I got up again, I went straight to the bathroom. It was locked. I could hear oceans of water being chucked round the bath. A bath at that hour? Only I had baths in the morning. For some reason men are not ready to be submerged first thing in the morning. There's always something they want to do first. I went downstairs. Mo was up, supping cornflakes like a baby. The first day of the rest of his life worn into his forehead like a badge.

'Who's in the bath?'

He smiled at me. A wind-up smile. No work to go to so he'd work out on me instead.

'Who's in the bath?'

I put the kettle on for coffee, opened the fridge and, 'There's no milk. Yer eatin' cornflakes and there's no fuckin' milk.'

'I was thirsty.'

'There's a tap in the sink.'

'I'll go and get some from the shop.'

'If yer wouldn't mind.'

Then silence whilst he carried on eating. I stared at him, to hurry him up, to get him to finish off and get down the shop, but he never ate any quicker. Then someone came down the stairs. The door opened too warily for Vinnie or Irish. Her long painted fingernails came in first. She was a bit fatter than me but still quite shapely . . . no . . . a bit squat, I thought, once I got a good look at her. Smaller than me but bigger than Vinnie. Brown. To look at Mo's face, you'd think he'd never set eyes on her before. Couldn't believe his luck. He pawed at his own face in a semi-panic. He wasn't sure whether he had cornflakes stuck in his beard. He did. An exotic broken English would have just finished her off but she was from Bradford.

'All right,' she said.

'Hello.'

'I'm Simmi.'

Mo was up on his feet, clearing crap off the table so she could sit down and be seen.

'This is Viv, Simmi. She shares the house.'

'I'd make yer a cup of coffee, Simmi, but he's used up all the milk.'

She looked at me properly then, but turned away quickly, shocked. My hair was still tied back from bed and I hadn't done my make-up yet. She got the full glare.

'I'll go and get some, shall I?' she said. 'I don't mind.'

'I'll come with you,' said Mo, in too much of a hurry.

'Mo, you can't send the girl out for milk when she's only just got out o' the bath. She'll catch her death. Where's yer manners? Sit yerself down, Simmi.'

He was irritated. 'You don't mind going, do you, Simmi?'

'I'd rather not,' she said, thanking me with her eyes, checking the drizzled rain on the windows behind me.

'I'll go then,' he said, glaring at me.

She was in a black dress, red cardy and black strappy shoes. Mo kissed her on the forehead and left.

'You at the college then?' I said, hating conversation first thing in the morning.

I smiled so she could see I had teeth, white pretty teeth. I wasn't all bad. It was just my face and only half of it.

'Aye. Doin' social policy. And you? Are you on the same course as Mo then?'

'Mo? On a course? He got the sack from Dumfie's yesterday. What's he been telling you?'

'He said . . . Oh I can't remember,' she said, lying. 'I was drunk. Anyway, it's nice to meet some black people. Not many about, is there?'

'There's enough,' I said. 'Is this your first year?'

'Aye. Bit of a culture shock, to be honest. Bradford's not as bad as I thought it was, now I'm here. What yer studying? What year are you in?'

'Business studies. Second year.'

'Gonna go into business then?' she asked, slightly incredulous, though I may have been sensitive. It *was* first thing in the morning.

'I don't know about that. Not thought about it, to be honest. You gonna be a social worker, are yer?' (Yawn, yawn.)

62

'Well, if I pass the social policy bit, there's a chance I can do the social work qualification.'

'D'yer take sugar?'

'One, please.'

She was pulling at the rings on her fingers, like abacus beads. Her elbows were on the table and she was looking down, trying to hide her face, it seemed. It was a beautiful face. Too beautiful a face. No need to hide it.

'Where d'yer meet him then?'

'Jollo's.'

'I bet he was well pissed, wasn't he? Oh God, that sounds terrible, doesn't it? I meant because of Irish. It was Irish's birthday yesterday.'

'Sall right,' she said. 'We were all pissed. I didn't know where I was when I woke up.'

'Jesus. You musta gone for it.'

She stood up and dusted herself down as if to dust the night away. An aberration. Here before me was the real Simmi. Then she got busy. Washing things up and tidying things into cupboards, as if it weren't right for her to sit down in a kitchen and do nothing. Maybe she thought I could do with the help. I went to the bathroom.

I heard the front door slam. Mo with the milk. I made my way back downstairs. The fresh air and rain of the morning must have set his memory tape to re-wind. He was waiting at the bottom of the stairs for me.

'What was that you said about scoring last night?'

'I've scored off someone else.'

'Who?'

'That'd be telling.'

'What's the SP?'

'Cheaper than you.'

'How much?'

'Ten quid an ounce cheaper than you.'

'For?'

'Leb.'

'Can you do me some?'

63

'Does Simmi smoke?' I asked.

'No, but she's cool.'

'Oh really,' sarcastically.

'She had a spliff last night but was sick. She'd drunk too much. She's all right.'

By teatime that day, he'd scored off me three times. He still owed his other dealer money, but decided to bump him. There was no loyalty with Mo. He went wherever the wind took him.

Whilst he was toing and froing all day long, getting cash together, selling draw, he left Simmi to clean his room, do the shopping and get tea ready. They were like a real mum and dad already. Five of us at the dinner table. Simmi put the rice in a serving dish, not straight on the plates. Then she served us. We all sat there tugging at imaginary serviettes sticking out of our collars. She asked us if we wanted drinks. Mo sat smiling like he'd just bought a slave. Irish, Vinnie and me kept our mouths shut, enjoying the catering, knowing it wouldn't last. When Simmi finally sat down to eat, we'd all finished. I wanted out, but it seeemed rude to leave the table when she'd only just sat down. Irish and Vinnie were fidgety too. When she was done . . .

'Will you help me clear the plates,' she said to me with a smile, girl to girl, woman to woman, let's-make-a-bond-in-the-kitchen bollocks.

'No, sorry, I can't,' I said. 'Get Vinnie to help you. He loves washing up, don't yer, Vinnie?'

Start as you mean to go on, that's my motto. I went upstairs.

I started reading up on some work but kept getting distracted. My face. Sex. Sex distracted me all the time now. It seemed the wanting of it created the antibody to getting it. If only I could just . . . well, relax. I knew about masturbation but I didn't fancy it. Didn't fancy the idea of touching myself. Down there. Messy. Squidgy. I didn't see the point either. I needed a man. A real one. Roy was no good. Well, he was great for a cuddle but he couldn't do it. Wouldn't do it. There was something wrong with him – down there, I thought.

'What d'yer mean you can't?' I said, the fourth time we were in bed together and I'd stopped being polite, hopeful, patient.

'I just can't,' he said, the back of his head to me, on the pillow. 'And not because of what you think.'

He turned round and kissed me then.

'Well, I'll help you if you want,' I offered.

I tried to touch him but he pulled away both times, made me feel stupid, slaggy.

'You can't. It's not like that. I just can't. Have you ever heard of a shower of fishes?'

'What? What?'

'A shower of fishes. When the fish, from nowhere, fall to the earth in a shower. I'm waiting for that to happen. I want to see it happen. Maybe then, my body will work as it should. Until then, let's just lie together. I like lying with you. That's all right, isn't it?'

And you can't argue with a shower of fishes, can you? Him being a bit disabled in that department solved lots of problems for me, coz it meant no one knew I was a virgin. Everyone that knew us thought we were screwing.

'Are you a virgin?' I asked him.

'No. I wanna go to sleep now, Viv – can we leave it?'

And so I never got to tell him that I was. We just lay together, like brother and sister. He kissed me, though. Not snogged. Just kisses here and there. Fast and gentle and sometimes by surprise. Nobody else did that. That was our intimacy. That was our making love. He could trust me. Who was I gonna tell?

Vinnie and Irish went off to the library, shouting up the stairs to me, did I want anything, books taken back or whatever. I didn't answer. I was hugging my totem pole, thinking. Later on I heard Mo come up the stairs. He knocked on my door but I didn't answer. I crouched down. Didn't want to talk. Sat behind the door opposite my bed, I saw it open. He must have popped his head round to see if I was in. He couldn't see me behind my protector. Then I heard Simmi come up the stairs and I heard a kiss. They were in his room.

'Get 'em off then,' he said to her, really curt. So rude. And so loud.

His door was open. Usually he locked it. The house was in silence. I should have coughed but I couldn't. I was too intrigued. This was Mo in action. I'd never heard anyone in action before. I'd heard grunts from Mum and Dad's room but they disgusted me. Always on a Friday night so it wasn't spontaneous love or anything. Just Dad's right. Dad's night. Mum called it 'a man's needs' when she talked about sex. But it was more like his 'right'.

'Get 'em off, I said, and come over here.'

'It's cold . . . Mo, don't be like this.'

'Last night you said you liked me being rough so I'm being rough. Come over here.'

'But I didn't mean . . . Can't we just sit?' said Simmi, in a little girl's voice, for some reason.

'No. I want you down here. Undressed. Go on. Please . . .'

There was silence then.

'Come here. I'll undo that for you.'

More silence.

'Right. Now get down there. Here you are . . . not like that . . . look here. You can kneel on a cushion if you like. Save your knees.'

More silence. Minutes of it. I was keyed up for noises, egging a noise to come out of their room . . . I wanted to light my spliff but the noise of the match . . . and then they came. The noises. Like sick, like vomit that starts and won't stop. Slurping noises, heavy breathing, out-of-breath heavy breathing, slurp slurp . . . then the weight hitting the mattress.

'Turn over.'

Then Mo getting off – like a train pulling into a station, breaking heavy metal on metal. I imagined the ejaculation and retched. I couldn't hear Simmi at all. Hard breath. I was cross-legged, rocking with the motions, a deep knot, a bolus of uninvited tension balled up in my chest, a kind of warning that what I was doing was wrong. But it was too late now. I was part of it. A couple of kiss sounds and then silence. I felt

66

ashamed. Trapped. My heart beat the rhythm of a lonely animal running through the bushes of the night, away from all it has known, from all it can't be. And then even more shame as my breasts juddered with the thrill. All of a sudden, tears came to me. They shot up from nowhere. Poked me in the eyes and like fallen soldiers, they fell to my chest. I wiped my face and when I felt the gristly hills of my scar, I really wanted to sob. Gasp. I wanted to bawl myself out, get rid of me. The peep-hole girl. The voyeur. The village idiot, sitting on the floor, spying with my ears. Devouring sex I wouldn't have, couldn't have.

I could let any old sod get on top of me if I wanted to. I'd sworn not to do that – let someone empty themselves out, inside me. My mum said that if I didn't love myself, I'd fail. The world is not inclined to take on defective goods. She had a way with words, my mother. The wrong way. Make myself whole, she said. Love myself so much that people out there will think there's treasure inside. And there I was, sitting behind the door, listening to Mo getting off. I chewed on my knuckles for a while. Really lonely.

After the sex, they talked. Simmi asking Mo about his family.

He was always trying to get us to feel sorry for him, Mo. Telling us stories. Trying to compete with Irish half the time, coz Irish had seen gunshot wounds. Seen action on the war-torn front of Derry. Irish had nursed people without arms or legs or kneecaps worth standing up in. Irish told me to go over there if ever I thought I was hard done by. See it for myself. Mo figured he could be more interesting than that. Like it was a race.

'I'd love to live up a mountain in Afghanistan,' said Simmi, talking through her arse.

Mo went the whole hog. He told us that his uncle kidnapped him when he was ten. He'd been walking down the mountain slope one day, minding his own business – this was his Heidi story. 'Not goats,' I said, when he told me. 'Weren't yer minding the goats then?' His sad little face would get all worked up. I didn't believe in this Heidi stuff, yet as he was

67

telling it to Simmi, the story sounded pretty much the same. There was an additional hot sun, a sore foot and some hunger thrown in, but for the most part, the same. Then his uncle brought him to England. When he told her that his uncle was banged up in Pentonville for selling arms and drugs to Afghani nomads (the modern-day variety – instead of camels, British Airways) he revved it out as a full-colour motion picture. That was his Sweeney story. Then came the Oliver Twist bit. The bit that got Simmi, I suspect.

'And what about your mum?'

'Can't remember my mother after living in London all that time. I saw so many faces I can't remember hers.'

'You must miss her like mad, no?'

'I do. Don't all men miss their mothers?'

He had his hoarse voice on, all sad and soft.

'I miss mine,' she said.

I could imagine him lapping up her strokes. I bet she was stroking his eyebrows. He had big bushy eyebrows, Mo, bushy hair too, short at the back but a real hedge of it on top. A tower of firm yellow muscle, a complexion to cream coffee. Him and Simmi in bed together – they must have looked spot on.

'Well, have you thought about going home?'

'Where to?'

'Back to your village, to your mum.'

'But who says she's still alive? The Russians have been in since I left. Anything could have happened. And anyway, I couldn't afford to go back. And I don't just mean money. As soon as immigration find out I'm not with my wife any more, they might start picking on me. It's too dangerous to go home and expect to come back again.'

'So what happened to your wife . . . Mo, you don't mind me asking all this, do you?'

'No. It's all right. I'm resigned to it all now. My wife was a bitch, Simmi. She wanted me to be her slave and when I wouldn't dance her tunes she dumped me.'

'Did you love her?'

'I thought I did. She was two-timing me.'

'I thought you said she was an invalid.'

'Yee-es. They're not immune.'

'I know but . . . well, I can't believe . . .'

'Well, forget it then. You don't have to bloody believe.' Mo was talking in thick accent then, almost Indian accent.

'I didn't mean . . . Oh Mo, I'm sorry,' she said, falling for his twaddle like a trout.

'Come here,' he said.

I was smoking a spliff sat upright now, legs crossed, back against the wall, candle at my feet. Being strong.

'How did she do her face in, Mo? Viv?'

'Her sister did it. Jam, apparently. So Vinnie said. She was only little. About ten, I think.'

'Can't she get a skin graft on it?'

'She's had skin grafts. That's the best they can do.'

'It's awful, isn't it?'

'Well, yes. It is. But she's got such a chip on her shoulder about it. She's so bitter. So hard to get on with. She sees this bloke sometimes – he calms her down a bit. She saw him last night. But he's never around in the morning. Ashamed of her, I suppose. D'yer know what I mean? It must be hard for him not to keep looking at it, no? *I* don't mind it but then I don't have to kiss it, do I?'

He kissed her then, I heard him.

'Mo! Don't be so mean. She's lovely. Half her face is really beautiful. God, it must be awful.' Then a pause. Then Simmi again. 'It wouldn't be so bad if she was a bloke, would it?'

'Why?'

'Well, blokes don't need the make-up and the clothes, do they? Not like a girl. I think that that make-up she wears makes it look worse, don't you? It's the wrong colour, for a start. I looked at it in the bathroom. Special stuff for disfigurements, it says. It's like Polyfilla. Makes trying to look pretty look stupid, I think.'

'Well, she doesn't ever look pretty. She never dresses like a proper woman. Not like you. She's always in trousers.'

When I heard all that – the freak, freak, freak of it . . . the poking in my eyes turned into gouging. Someone was stabbing me in the eyes with knitting needles. Grains of sand ran through my tears and my tears cut at my ducts like glass. I held my breath.

'She doesn't go round feeling sorry for herself, which is a blessing,' said Mo. 'If anything, she's a little bit too pushy.' (Indian-style, he said that bit.) 'A little bit too self-assured. Thinks too much of herself.'

'Well, she can't let herself go under, can she? And she's obviously clever.'

'Too clever, sometimes.'

'She's got to have something going for her, Mo,' said in a little girl's voice, probably stroking his eyebrows again.

I snuffled. My face hurt. Like all the nerves had opened up. The crust of a fresh scud, being rubbed too much at the edges, sore and hot and ready to bleed. And no, I didn't feel sorry for myself out there, where people could see me. But on my own, in my room, that's all I ever did. On my own there was no one to be brave for. I burst then. Burst open. The snuffles, loud. Too loud. I had to breathe. My door opened and Simmi came in, a towel wrapped round her. She found me curled up on the floor, foetal.

'We didn't know you were in here.'

I lay with my head to the carpet, crying to the ground. I cried out through the knuckles filling my mouth.

'Oh God, I'm sorry,' she said. 'If I'd . . .'

I sat up. Arranged myself. But I kept my head down.

'I was half asleep . . . and then I heard you. I heard you talking about me.'

She knelt down on the floor, to stroke me. She was stroking my scalp, between rooted plaits, small strokes, soft strokes.

'Listen, we didn't mean anything bad,' she said. 'I can't really remember what I said,' trying to get me to repeat the worst of it, I didn't wonder.

'It doesn't matter,' I said, wiping my eyes but keeping my head down between my knees so she couldn't see my face.

She put her hand in between my knees and under my chin.

70

Then she lifted me. She lifted my splodgy splash of a face up to hers. Luckily, I couldn't see the keenness of her beauty right then, not through my tears.

'It's a face,' she said. 'It's not all of you, whatever anyone says. We feel sorry for you, that's all.'

I got up and threw myself on to the bed.

'Fuck off and leave me alone,' I said.

I did the Leb out double quick, coz of the price, Bev being so high up the supply chain. Roy, Mo and a posh bloke off my course called Hector – they cleared me out within forty-eight hours. Irish did a bit as well. For the lads down O' Hagan's. I did a few quarters serving behind the union bar at a huge margin. But it was better to deal wholesale than to punters. Less effort. Less risk. When it was all gone, I felt like Mr Marks and Sparks with my first empty barrow of fruit.

Bev was pleased to see me back so soon. Dirk even more so. I saw his blood vessels pop back in when I handed the money over. Deadlines take on a different dread in druggy druggy land. I was more scared of Bev and Dirk than Mr Cranton, my tutor.

Round at Bev's was a new life for me. No bullshit. No ceremony. I was allowed to slip into their circle like they'd been saving a place for me. We smoked spliffs like fags. Gone the childish naughtiness. Gone the dare. Gone the idea we were breaking the law. Spliff *au naturel*. I rolled them a joint, asked could I choose a tape to play, and we were off. Dirk wanted to try out his birthday present – a gimmick, he said. A lampshade that doubled as a bong. The tubes came out of the vase and where the light bulb should go he inserted the bowl of the pipe. We sucked on the tubes and then heaved our heads off.

'I think we'll use it as a lampshade,' he said, and we laughed.

We'd outgrown our smoking toys. The lamp was the last game, the goodbye, the putting away of the roller skates.

Then Dirk taught me to how to play backgammon. The actual board was a round coffee table with the triangular slots carved into it, uneven, amateur but used, worn, homely, comfy. A carpenter friend had made it specially for them. In the nick. Those were the days. Most of the crafts that came out of the nick were matchstick models – picture frames and matchbox holders and for the armed robbers, gypsy wagons. A gypsy wagon begging for a shire horse. They must take ages. If I was banged up for seven, I'd have done a matchstick Concorde or a spaceship – something fast, so fast it broke the sound barrier. It's noisy in the nick.

Backgammon, we played for fun, not money. Dirk said learning to play would help my mind not to get lazy. My mind was past saving after lampshade bongs.

'You erhh . . . into a pound this time? Half a key?' Dirk this time.

'Well, I can still only pay you for a quarter pound so you'll have to lay the rest on me.'

'That's all right. I think we know you well enough. We know where to find you. It won't go above the pound, though. Not unless you pay up front. I know enough students doing badly at college who'd be only too pleased to have someone lay a pound o' gear on them.'

'Fair dinkum. I'm into that. And by the way, I'm not doing badly at college. I do all right.'

'Right . . . I'll sort you out in a minute.'

Then he got double sixes and cleared all his pieces off the board. I sat back laughing. Bev and Dirk made me happy, happy to be with them, looked after. I was a customer. I had a purpose, as well as a face.

It was scary leaving Bev's that night, the street so black and wet and then pools of yellow streetlight up ahead, to make a thriller of it. I was out of my box, paranoid as fuck. I'd never carried such a bag before. It felt heavier than it was. A gang of lads fell out of a pub, cheering and singing at the tops of their voices. Like the troops of the Grand Old Duke of York . . .

they were neither up nor down, climbing the hill towards me. A couple of them throwing up. When I don't want to be seen, which is often, I make myself invisible. I hide if I have to, but if that's not on, then I make myself invisible. For this, I have to concentrate *really* hard. First I walk in a dead straight line, not looking down or up. I make sure that my plaits are in curtain mode. I can work it without plaits but it means bending my head at an angle and that can attract attention – just the slightest suggestion of the body in a state of forced geometry can be bad news. Or swivelling the head, stopping and then starting, looking over one's shoulder, looking down to the ground, up to the sky or as I said, just a slight turning of the head inwards, to the shops maybe. It's not about avoiding eye contact. Or making eye contact. Both of those strategies are no-nos when trying to be invisible. The idea is to disappear. Obviously in a street full of snipers this doesn't work. Best not to go out at all under those circumstances. For a leisurely stroll on the home route, though, gliding seems to work. So, I walk in rhythm. Rhythm is essential. It goes hand in hand with the geometry.

First off, I needed to get my mind in gear. So, I calculated the price of a quarter, on the ounce, the half-ounce, pound and half-pound. I exorcised all emotional cues and turned the danger visual. Purely visual. To cut the rush. There, that was it, my mind was up there and I was riding on air now. Towards the boys. The boys were clogged into one maraud of arms and legs, falling all over the place, getting closer. I glided towards them. It's easy to do this in a shop – to bustle about at the same speed as the crowd, blend in and don't look. Don't think. Don't shed any energy in the direction of the enemy. Sometimes, even if I am seen, the enemy doesn't come over – they're afraid of confronting my vibe. In the street, when there are no crowds or colours to busy up the eye, being invisible is much harder. After exorcising, concentrating, the next step was the emptying. Emptying the mind. The mind must die. No perception. No evocation. No energy. Then and only then could I phase into the atmosphere as one being, separate from earth and thought and light. And right past them I walked. Up and through. Not a crackle. Not a cry or an eye from any of them. Being stoned helped.

For the rest of the walk home, I contemplated just how much of me had disappeared. How much of me had gone. The cutting down. If I didn't watch myself, I'd disappear completely. Getting stoned was the only way to stay in, I decided. To fit into a world of leftovers.

Chapter 7

I was back round to Bev's two nights later.

'Jesus, you're shifting it, aren't yer?' said Dirk, counting the notes, making five-bar gates out of them.

'I thought you were working at the union tonight,' said Bev, rolling a spliff on an album cover.

'I've given it up.'

'I thought yer did quite a bit of blow down the union.'

'Well, I did, but with Mo out of work and Roy, and I've got this other bloke Hector, he does all my college stuff for me – between the three of them, they can shift everything I've got. Last night I had nothing to sell. Four poxy quid, I got, for serving two hundred pints. The rugby team won. Terrific. Horrific.'

'Well, every little helps,' said Dirk, packing his money bag to the seams.

'I'm done with grafting for four poxy quid.'

Bev finished rolling the spliff and passed it to me, unlit. An honour. A sign she really liked me. Yes!

'Fucking barmaid, they call me,' I said, fiddling with the spliff wick, getting it ready to receive its torch. 'I guess they think that's polite, eh? Fucking scivvy, more like.'

I sucked on the spliff and fell back in the chair. After another suck I was on my way. Bar-job talk wasn't what I'd come for.

I passed the joint to Dirk. He held it between his lips whilst he brought out a new sack of hash. He put some tablets on the table.

'You're the worst sort,' he said, stacking the hash into blocks, carefully, like he was measuring them with his eye, just like a brickie, in fact.

'What? Me?' I said.

'You go to college and fanny about. Read some books, get wrecked and then you're off into the world with the rest of them. You'll end up doing fuck all, just like the rest of them. Bang! Suddenly you're one of them.'

He pulled on his spliff so hard the roach stayed stuck on his lip, just hanging there. The effect he'd been creating, his know-allness, was blown. I had a go at him.

'Jealous, Dirk?'

I looked away, to hide my smirk, to let him fix his spliff with dignity. Then I heard him twanging an elastic band round his money bag. I looked to see his eyes narrowed in concentration. In self-glory. The money bag was now tight, full and sealed. He bounced it on the table as a financial finale.

'Jealous of you?' he said, still with his eyes narrowed but aimed directly at me.

I looked into them, to measure their venom. He was having a go at me.

'Eh? Jealous?' he said. 'You're asking *me* if I'm jealous of *you*?'

I wished I'd never said it. I was only joking. Nearly crying now, though.

'I think not,' he said.

He swiped the money bag away, got up and left the room. The jingling bells on the back of the door ended it all. A cutting chill of draught from the door closing de-cosied me completely. Silence. The silence was like the clanging of a lid on a dustbin. A cymbal. I was lost for a minute. I was losing myself again. Not just in thought. Not even in thought. Thinking is like reaching, like trying. I wasn't trying. I was like a toddler, lost, unstable, wandering aimlessly round a landscape beset with pot holes and mineshafts. One strong push from a wagging indignant finger was enough to floor me. I was scared.

I stayed subdued. Calm. He'd pushed me out to a far-off valency and somehow, I had to swim my way back in again. I needed to be still. Let the experience wash over me and move on. I wanted to let both of them know I had a mind of my own and no matter, I'd be myself and be by myself. I would not be manipulated into accepting an unspoken apology. If Dirk didn't have the guts to speak it, I didn't have to buy it. So I didn't laugh at his follow-up jokes, his trying to be kind to me. His trying to make me, make him feel better. I gave him small quirky grins that snapped back to straight-facedness again. I read the back of a few album covers. I rolled joint after joint until he got his Sensi out – his special stash. His very special stash, he said. Bev looked confused then. She didn't see the occasion. I did. I could feel it. 'Occasion' was being ritualised for me, in the air, the smell, the noises, the music. The mood. It was vital. Only something vital could bring me out of my forced melancholy. It brought me out bouncing, on the vibration. Inside my head, a fiddle set to work.

Outside my head, the words of the music became a sermon, a medium between the matter and me. The music said I should bend a new corner. Satisfy my soul. That every little action . . . That I was on a journey to a hole in the middle of the universe. To a secret place. Just because I couldn't see it, *can't you see, do you believe me*, didn't mean it wasn't there. The world is like a Polo mint. I was crawling towards its inner rim, tapping to get through. To live in a world where matter didn't matter. I wanted to crash through and bend a new corner of my life so that my whole view of it could widen. In the hole, there'd be a new world, a new way to live and after a blast on the Sensi, I felt myself being hauled through its sphere by electric suction. Shhhhhhh!

The earth spun around me, a me unhinged, unbalanced and floating. I wasn't 'high'. I never quite understood 'high'. I was out of it. High up where? I almost understood. But even then, high wasn't the right word. It was more 'deep'. I was in deep. Out of the thin superficial wrapping, and into the thick fathomless space. I couldn't feel my body any more. This wasn't toddling, it was flying through force.

Bev and Dirk looked straight at me, in synchrony, the three of us an energy. That helped. Seeing faces. Like shields. Spirits sent to assist me whilst I crossed the passage to the other side, a different side to them. The middle passage. Where only the strongest could survive. As I made my way over, louder and louder came the poltergeist noise of havoc in my brain. To hold on to my sanity, I had to look to my shields for calm, to take away the energy from the knocking, the sound of my unleashed fears. There's no rhythm in their soundings. That's how I knew I was in danger of losing control. Once the poltergeist of fear is set free on the fabric of the senses, it takes hold of a thread and pulls at it, as if to unravel a woolly jumper like a crazy child. I would not have the might, or the energy or the craftiness of God to be able to knit myself back up again. It's a one-way ticket to the other side and all the while over, the traveller must seek calm. Bev and Dirk looked after the calm. They vibed me well. Kept me in touch. Bev came over and sat next to me, squeezed my knee and then sat back, close, touching, with me. It was like we were all in church, our lips buttoned, every movement a reverent one. They checked it, and we smoked on it. They smiled in silence, but stared at me. A psychic farewell for me. I could hear them in my head, saying 'You be careful', and 'You take care'.

People koshed out on the physical can't do this. If the world is a Polo mint, such people are stuck in the mint with no connections to the hole in the middle. The important bit. The bit that can't be measured, sold, packaged. That is the place where people find freedom. Those that are sealed up – they get stuck in the mint, stuck on stuff like . . . say, geography. Oh dear, what can the matter be? Who cares. The race, the human one, cannot be drawn in latitude or longitude. Men that draw such lines are the needle scratching the record. Dinosaur DJ's that won't change the fucking record. Now it was time to get into the gap. That's where it's at. In the silence after the noise. On reaching the gap, I would witness the eclipse, the moon over the sun, the sudden primeval darkness. A cosmic darkness that never ends. That's where I was going. Into the next layer. Into the known but unknown. Into the place that anchors surreality. The connection. The most real connection. And there has to be one. There has to be a connection for balance, to sum up all the parts, to make the earth whole. Perhaps it's always been like that. Perhaps the other world, the under-world, innerworld, holy world, perhaps it was a lot closer in the old days. Matter is just the clog, the obstacle, the seal. There is now a lot more matter.

I slipped through my rim and was at first surprised by the sameness, the stillness. This, I guessed, was just another trick of the demons, to make me feel mad. But I knew I was through because at last, I felt free. I was on a float heading off, with a direction and purpose. Always before, there'd been a stoned aimlessness about my life. But now there was a purpose to it. The practice of freedom. Now I would and could worry about the enslaved masses and seek to instil a charge of liberty upon their souls. This was all very grand and positively ridiculous. It was the demons talking or it was the summit of possibility. It was crass. It was impossible. But for me, it was new. It was a sign that I had the ability to connect from the unreal to the real. It was my energy speaking, not me, not my heart, not my body, and as such, I read the messages as a child might play with its first fairy-tale. An essential morality entangled in myth and subconscious meanderings. The message was a tradition, not a religion. A guide, if you will. But I was through. I was in there. It felt like breathing underwater.

Dirk saw me to the door.

'See ya back here soon, yeah?' he said. 'Not with the money for that, though,' pointing to my parcel. 'Just come back and see us. Whenever you like.'

He said that last bit with his eyes down, his eyelids like delicate veils, silky and fragile. Veiny. They needed a dewdrop kiss to glisten them. I felt us soaking in a wave of our own presence. Then he reached over and took my face. I thought to kiss me on the lips but he took my face, my chin really, like he was going to eat me, like I was something he'd picked off a tree. What he was after was one of those Mafia-style kisses, like they do in the *Godfather* films. He swivelled my head round and kissed me on the cheek. My good cheek. He didn't actually kiss it, to be honest, he just held his lips against my skin and pressed. As if to say that that meant more than a kiss. The pressure, the deliberateness. I didn't look at him after that. I turned away and ran down the stairs. I heard the bells on the back of his door pinging. I was so stoned. So . . . off my face. My face felt happy that night.

GOING TO JAIL

Chapter 8

So it was all down to him really, Mo. He started me off with the dealing. He was the one that made it all feel normal, easy, the thing to do. And I can't take it on board this morning, this particular morning, that it was down to me. That would be negative thinking. That would be going into court with my hands up in the air saying *Shoot me*.

Now it was time to shower, oil my hair, to go ask Bev if she could lend me a couple of quid for the bus fare down to the courts. So's not to dodge the pavement cracks. So's not to show my frizzy head and scar. I didn't have the energy to play invisible. Not first thing in the morning. Not for a whole mile. *Black girl in a spotty dress, with face and handbag*. I should have asked Dirk for the bus fare but I couldn't, could I? Not after morning love. Not after our silent morning awakenings in the mattress. After wiping the sweat from his brow, massaging his clavicles, licking my signature down his spine. After the silence. *Can you lend us some money for me bus fare, Dirk?*

I went to the bathroom to start the shower. Before the steam obscured me, I looked at myself in the mirror. Mirror mirror on the . . . blink. Never a good move at the best of times, that. I sat on the edge of the bath and looked to the floor, under the sink. There was Simmi's box of bleach. A job-lot. I'd sent it on to her, with a letter, asking for help. But it all got sent back. Unopened. My gut was so full and tight, I wanted to sick it empty. But it already was empty. You can't sick out tension. It needs lancing like a boil. I used to see tension as a tendon string, pulled, ready to snap – a tug of war. Now I see it as a mindless child, filling a balloon at the sink, giggling. Turning the tap on, off, on, off. Mindless. Until the critical mass of water is reached . . . when da bubble him burst . . . when the balloon explodes . . . now I see tension make way for shock and watch waves of it bleed out all over everyone. Everyone is Mum and Dad. Waiting for them to get soaked is the worst of it. If I'd pleaded guilty, I would have known what to do. Where to go. How to be. The tension would be minimal and the shock would burst forth, fast and direct as an arrow to cut straight to the heart of my parents who would in turn cut me off. For me, the beginning of a lonely walk through the noise of an angry jungle. Sitting on the bath, behind the bathroom door, counting bottles of Simmi's face bleach, I felt that stabbing in my eyes again. That village-idiot sense of failure. Same old me, sitting on the sidelines feeling sorry for myself. Me, watching life through a fog. Other people's lives. Pity I haven't got any hair to bleach, I thought, trying to make my mind change the subject. Not even under my arms, I checked. No. Like fucking eyebrows.

After the shower, I felt more fortified. I dabbed my make-up on in efficient strokes and was pleased with the result. I was ready for Benky and the barristers. Ready for the bastards. With the towel wrapped round me, I checked some of my cardboard boxes, made sure they were firm. I'd only boxed the small stuff, the ornaments and half-interesting mementoes, my underwear so no one would paw over it. Most of my books and both of my photo albums. Buddha and the totem pole stayed out. Couldn't box the totem anyway. Too big, and Lord knows where that was going. It was my only big thing. My only big possession. I couldn't, no, wouldn't, send it home, whatever happened. My dad'd burn it. See it as the satanic emblem of my downfall. Dirk said he'd get me an attic. Or a lock-up. Pay for it secretly. Whilst I was inside. No room at home, anyway. Mum and Dad had converted mine and Divine's bedrooms into seed-growing rooms, storerooms, magazine-pile rooms, a tumble-drier room. Said we could sleep on the sofa whenever we went home. We hardly ever went.

I was half living, really. Half awake in two separate worlds. The world that went on. And the one about to stop. Bev! Jesus! I forgot. I needed bus fare. Just as I left my flat, I heard the postman clunk the letterbox. The mail landed slappy flap on the doormat, in a pool of damp dark silence. Only in films are people waiting on the doorstep in the sun, waving to the postman who arrives on a bicycle doffing his cap. In reality, he's wet and hurried and pushes envelopes through letterboxes of people he never sees and would prefer not to. He needs the money. The letterbox snapped back closed with a metal grunt, reminding me of prison. The cell door. The being fed by an unannounced uniformed guard. In the tower blocks it must feel more so. Or maybe . . . maybe it was just me, getting the gips about my second day in court.

There were two for me. One from Mum and a postcard from our Divine. 'Glad you're not here but I miss you.' Divine was homesick. The picture showed a young girl sat on the back of a bike ridden by a man smoking a cigarette. They both wore lampshade hats. He looked like he was taking her to market. On reflection, he probably was. Smoke from his fag was billowing into his eyes. There was a Marlboro logo under the stamp. An advert masquerading as a postcard.

I knocked at Bev's door and waited. I knew she'd still be asleep and be mad to be woken but maybe, with me going to court and all, she'd hold off. She answered almost immediately. Red-eyed.

'What's wrong?'

I'd never seen her cry before. She walked away from the door and into the kitchen stamping a well-worn path to the kettle.

'Dirk . . . landed me one this morning, didn't he . . . he didn't beat me up or nothin'. He just slapped me. Lost his rag. I slapped him back. Vivian, I don't think I can stand it any more.'

'What . . . what brought all that on then?'

I was fumbling for script. I hadn't bargained for this.

'He says I'm . . . he says I nag him too much – says I'm . . .'

'Bev, I'm gonna be late. I'm ever so sorry but I've got to get to court. I wondered if you could lend me some bus fare? I'd stay and talk but . . .'

'I'll get my purse.'

She pulled back then. Lips thin and closed. Like I'd cut the rope between us. She felt the jerk of it. I should have been going 'The bastard, the bastard' and she knew it. She knew I wasn't on her side. By the way she swayed, her head still in the jerk, I could tell she couldn't quite believe it. She went in on herself, as if to play jigsaw with it all. We bounced off each other. We whirled around the purse and the coins and a time-check just for good measure, anything to avoid the matter. I was too quick asking for my bus fare. Too slick. She closed her door without wishing me luck.

Well, he didn't have a go at her on my account, I said to myself, walking back down to my flat, playing the bus-fare coins like prayers between my fingers. In my flat, I closed the door behind me and hunched up my shoulders for a cringe. I cringed for Bev. Then I set about myself.

I heated my blim up over the gas to make it soft. Then I played it like clay, making it into a torpedo. Later on, I'd slip it up my backside. That'd get me through the night. I'd heard tell that the first night in nick is the longest and the only way to do it is off your head. Draw's ever so expensive in the nick and I very much doubted I'd have the wherewithal to go buying gear on my first night. Best to take some in with me. To stick it up my backside was a bit . . . well, a bit low-life really, I suppose. I wasn't one for messing like that at all, but then, it had to be done. I'd done it before.

The night I met Mikey the Biker outside the club. Mikey the scag-head. He offered me a lift home, lidless on the back of his bike. He stopped halfway, took off his helmet, shook his hair out and asked me did I want to go to headquarters and do some O.

'O?' I said.

'Opium,' he said.

'Yeah, sounds great. Let's go.'

He offered me his helmet but I wouldn't take it. Last thing I wanted. The oncoming cold air sealed my face up. I was wind-bathing. It was therapy. Just trying to keep my eyes open against the force was a battle. That I could hold my face up to the world without anyone pointing at it, taking sly swipes – that was a feeling I'd pay for. To be carried through the winds by a god, a silent god that would deliver me. Mikey bent forward towards the handlebars. His jacket billowed, his whole body was immersed in wind and helmet and creased leather. There was a huge white spider on his back, that shone like a skeleton in the moonlight – just a messenger from the gods, maybe – but he revved his wrist for me. He was taking me away from it all, to his world. My face was fed by the air rushing it with nakedness, just like in the shower. Just as the water could wash and make it come alive, make it charged, the wind seared it, sealed it, made it feel complete. I gripped the back seat with both my hands and lunged at every corner, every bend. When the bike banked left, I banked right, greedy for the wind. I stabbed the air with my grin, my mouth wide open. I swallowed the wind like a drunkard. And then suddenly we slowed, the fast high hedges closed in to wall us, the gears changed down and like a tape reeling off the final spools we stopped.

'Will you pack it in?'

'I'm loving it,' I said, my smile refusing to register his anger.

'You'll 'ave us over in a minute. Stay with the bike.'

'I like it . . . the wind . . . I like it.'

He pulled at my arms to put them round his waist, his face tired and disgusted. I wanted the ride to go on and on but I wanted to see headquarters too. I'd heard quite a lot about the Tarantulas, the Taras, they were called. The local hell's angel look-alikes. They did a hell of a lot of business but the word was, they couldn't be trusted. Ripped people off all the time. Dirk told me about some bloke from deep down in the country. He came up to Brimmington to score off the Taras, his first time. He arranged to meet them in a car-park. Stupid country boy passed the dosh through his car window. He was rewarded with a shooter in his ear and told to drive off. The Taras hadn't ever shot anyone as far as I knew but they were getting jumpy for it. Would have liked to. To up the stakes a bit. Create action. Relieve boredom. Make some money and run. Lucky for the country boy he was driving a Morris Minor. Anything decent, he'd have been taxed for it.

Mikey was one of their more benign. Their main buyer, since he could add up. When he went off to score up the line, he took minders with him. In my head, I saw the headquarters crawling with them. I figured about thirty of them. They came on so strong, the metal, leather, graffiti, the size of their petrol tanks, the low seats and high risks, the beards, their behaviour down the club, the only club that let them in. The only club I felt comfortable in. Full of low life and artists, junkies and stoners, men dressed as women even. Even Simmi liked it in there coz no one paid her any attention. No one went there to get laid and that made it comfortable. Vinnie wouldn't go there or Irish. Mo went there to do business. No one danced except for the girls. And the men dressed as girls.

So I thought of the Taras as an army. In fact there were only eight of them and one of those was Chasey's little brother who didn't really count. Mind, he could cause more trouble than the rest of them put together. Trying to grow big before his little bones would let him. Scarred for life he was, like me, and that was the great thing. When I arrived at headquarters, a cottage on some heathland, thatched, detached and filthy inside, I was treated as a guest. A cool guest. Coz of my colour and my scar and coz I turned up with Mikey. These people lived in a world of grotesque. Their posters, their attitude, the state of their kitchen. Monster magazines and space-ship fantasies filled their days. And drugs, of course. Their days were nights. Their nights were afternoons. When I walked in with Mikey, not a stir. A head-turn here and there to check I wasn't some enemy, a squidge up on the settee by one, in case I wanted to sit down.

'Foil!' Mikey barked.

'Sempty,' said one of them, kicking a cardboard cylinder.

I followed Mikey into the kitchen – the kitchen was all bluebottles and Pot-Noodle cartons. Whilst Mikey got a new roll of foil out, I asked him about the scag and that. Like most junkies, he thought of himself as a professor. He said we're all junkies. We're all on something.

Back in the front room, he got the opium ready.

''Snot quite the same, though, is it, eh?' I said. 'Fixing scag, I mean. I mean it's not like having a fag or a cup of coffee, is it?'

'No. The scag's a lot better.'

'But sticking needles in yerself is a bit much, isn't it?'

'Bit much for who?'

'Well, look at me. I get a bit pissed off sometimes but I don't wanna jack up.'

'Well, I fuckin' do, all right?' He smiled when he said it, but it was a false smile, it melted too quick. A We-aint-gonna-discuss-my-habit switch-off.

He offered me a rolled-up note and a square mat of foil with what looked like mouse pooh on it. Burning. I smoked up the trail. Breathed in, really deeply.

'I know what you mean, though,' I said. 'Smoking dope doesn't get you right off, does it? Makes you think a bit.'

He looked straight at me. Straight at my scar. He was deciding on my best route through life. Like he was my doctor. Quietly, so the other men couldn't hear, he advised me.

'When I'm wrecked, I see so much it makes my brain hurt. So I do the scag and scuzzy doesn't feel scuzzy any more. I see fuck all. You should try it, might help yer.'

'Uh-uh. Don't fancy being a junkie *at* all.' I said it too loud.

A couple of the men on the couch shifted about uncomfortably. I giggled and covered my mouth in apology.

'And what's that yer doin' now then?' he said, smiling as I inhaled.

'I'm not gonna be an opium junkie, am I?' Whisper.

I had another smoke. Living it up. I took on the pose of fiend, a connoisseur. My hair was all out and the plaits hung down as a symbol of my seriousness, as a trademark nearly. Us playing with the O together, the rolling, the roasting, the tearing of the foil on the table, that was all drama, scene setting.

One bloke was on the floor watching telly with the sound down, big with thick blond hair and a tattoo on his throat. There were two others on the settee, bearded and spidered up, with lots of greasy hair and in another world. When Mikey introduced me, they looked at me with a sort of envy in their eyes, measuring my scar like it was just another tattoo. They wanted a face like mine, like schoolboys want the most stitches, the most broken bones, the most plaster.

'What's the difference then,' I asked, 'feeling-wise, between the scag and opium?'

'The opium's more colourful, more pure. More trippy, I suppose.'

'So why isn't there more of it?' He looked taken aback. 'I don't mean here. I mean generally,' I said, laughing.

'Easier to sell smack, innit? Smack's gettin' big now. Them fuckin' dope smokers think they're at Sainsbury's these days. Don't want this, that, black, weed. Yer can't run a business like that, can yer? You need to nail the customers down. Get them at it. Big demand and easy entry – bingo. The Old Bill can smell the blow a mile off. They could smell the smack if they tried, but they don't bother. A little bag of smack's too much like hard work even though I make more money on it. They'd rather go for the big stuff. Get their photos taken next to a lorryload. They get promoted quicker too. It's a damn sight easier to find a lorryload of hash than a purse full of smack. Twats. Imagine, eh? Imagine if they found a way of detecting just the tiniest grain of scag on board a boat or a plane – the tiniest, tiniest amount of it? Like all they had to do was shine an X-ray light and it showed up. Fuck me. The country'd go nuts. They wouldn't do it even if they could.'

'If they did, there'd still be smugs druggled. Everyone's on for a bribe, aren't they?'

'I suppose we could bribe the people doing the scanning,' he said.

'Ah,' I said. 'If I was in charge, I'd pick 'em out like juries – I'd appoint random scanners. Then the drugglers wouldn't know who to bribe, would they?'

'We'd bribe the jury picker.'

'Not if it was a computer.'

'Bribe the computer man,' said Mikey.

'My mate Roy says it's the government that brings all the stuff in. He says they have diplomatic handbags the size of lorry containers. They want everyone doped up so no one knows what's happening.'

'Is that Moon Boy Roy?'

'D'yer know him?'

'He's my plumber.'

'How d'yer meet him then?'

'Down the club.'

'He doesn't go the club. What d'you need a plumber for, Mikey?'

'Nosy, aren't yer?'

'Was only asking.'

'He's all right, Roy Boy. Keeps his gob shut.'

'Bit of a loon, though,' I said, not taking the hint. 'He lost his dad in a wave – did he tell you?'

'Wish I could lose mine.'

I laughed. After more foil smoking, he pressed a piece of O into my hand.

'Go and stuff it up your bum,' he said. 'You won't waste so much then.'

'Yer should have told me sooner,' I said. 'No point in wasting it.'

He smiled at me. Shy like.

'I thought I'd get you started.'

I thought Mikey was a bit on the smelly side but the toilet smelt a lot. A bare pink light bulb framed the horror of it. There were daubs of filth across the walls. All over the bowl, there was a crust of shit and no seat. Scary. I couldn't imagine Roy wanting to fix it. After ten minutes I was throwing up in it. A really good one, it was. Felt great. Felt animal. Felt not scuzzy at all. Afterwards, I sat in the front room smoking whatever anyone passed me – when I wasn't goofing off. I could have been the bass. A human instrument. Someone to twang. I was sealed up warm, like that kid on the Ready Brek advert. My voice didn't have to try any more. Every air and care just strolled along on, in a hush of contemplation, a freedom. The five of us watched King Arthur and his Knights on the telly. We said it would be us, in this day and age – it would be us to take the sword from the stone. We'd have bikes, not horses. We'd have guns, not swords. We'd have a right laugh. We never said nothing of the sort. We just thought it. I could hear everyone thinking it. Living it.

In the morning, it took me an hour to get out of the place. Turning off the alarm. Putting it on again. Finding the keys to fit the locks. I broke the key-ring in the struggle and all the keys fell off so I threaded them back on again, the penknife, the naked lady and a beautiful silver spoon, tiny on the end of a chain. On the handle of the spoon was a lapis lazuli eye. I wanted it. I was actually thinking about stealing it. I gave up stealing after the scar. Too hard for me to keep a low profile then. But suddenly that stab of greed, of desire, resurfaced and the childishness of it made me laugh out loud. What made that happen? That wanting to steal. Maybe all my childish bad behaviour was only buried, not gone for good at all. Maybe we only learn *how* to shut the door on evil but when we're free to fall, when we're in the wind, maybe then, the door can swing open again. I still enjoyed the spoil of white snow, white paper, white icing. A draught of evil would for ever reek under my door. Maybe now, in this new life of mine, maybe I hadn't been vigilant enough and the door on those well-oiled hinges was opening up again. Did I still want to steal, destroy, hurt? I put the spoon back where it belonged and at last, got myself out into the overgrown back garden. I looked down to the river. A rainbow came out to see me. I swear that rainbow was mine, just for me. It was Sunday and not yet six o'clock. It was country. I watched the rainbow bleed across the sky, like someone was painting it there and then, fresh with morning water-colour. The arc. Was it a reward for not succumbing to temptation, I wondered. Out loud, I said, 'Good morning.' A bird screeched it back to me, like a flute gone mad. I searched the tree to see it lift its head, to see it blow out its solo, but I couldn't find it. Hidden inside somewhere. Behind leaves.

I hitchhiked home then. But that's another story.

When I left my flat for that second day in court, possibly my last day in court, I didn't tidy up or take lingering last looks. I tried to live in the positive half of what could happen, so I left my coffee cup on the table, the bed unmade, the writing pad and pen on top of the gas fire, the dressing gown on the couch. I looked once only before closing the door and shaking my head, shaking some energy into it. And I don't mean physical energy. Walking down to the bus stop rolling the torpedo of rocky between my fingers brought all that Mikey stuff back to me. The madness of Mikey.

The bus was full of schoolkids. I'd forgotten about them. It might have been better to walk and dodge the cracks after all. Then maybe not. I sat next to a black man for protection. I felt him pull away from me when I sat down. I would have got Mum's letter out, but I didn't want to attract attention. I kept my head down, all the way to the town centre.

Inside the court building, Cunningham plodded up and down the main corridor, checking his watch and then going off to speak to one of his client list of low-lifes whenever he could spot one of them. I hung back by the phones. I didn't want to run the gauntlet of waiting throngs who would all turn and stare. Especially the kids, bored shitless. I'd be like a walking telly if I walked through there. Even with so much going on, the pace was fast in the court corridors. I'd have expected the Crown to be more dignified. More slow and solemn. Mad as the magistrates' it was. Justice inside the court was slow and painful but judging from the activity outside the court, it was prepared for in great haste. Between the flurries and flutters and the flapping yapping briefs talking to their peeps, Bodene spotted me. She came dashing over, holding on to her wig, clutching papers to her breast.

'Come with me.'

The place she took me to was approximately five metres away from our original position. Still in the corridor. Still standing up. Still within earshot of an usher.

'The prosecution will drop the heroin charge if you plead guilty to the cannabis supply charge. I've spoken to the judge and he's happy about this. The indication is you'll get around six months. That's good. Under the circumstances, very generous indeed.'

She was ready with pen and open mouth, ready for me to accept this. Perhaps she wanted to go home and do some decorating or gardening or catch up on some other case.

'Mrs Bodene. I'm nineteen years old with a face like the back of a bus. My chances in the job market are nil and in the marriage market probably even less. Now do me a favour and listen . . . I'm not guilty. OK? My liberty may not mean a great deal to you but it's all I have. If that's all the advice *you* can offer, sod off.'

I think I detected a glimmer of a smile, a quiver on her lip. She bit her pen and took some papers out of a folder. She sped-read a few sides and then looked at me again. 'I wish you'd allow me to subpoena Simmi Reza.'

'No way.'

'Perhaps a hostile witness at this late stage would do more harm than good.' She carried on flicking through her pages and then sighed.

'You do realise that, if you're found guilty, he'll really sock it to you. The judge, I mean.'

'Don't threaten me.'

'Miss Jackson, I'm not threatening you. In my experience, this judge is not lenient. I'm merely pointing out to you the likelihood of a longer sentence if you're convicted.'

'And if I plead guilty, a generous small sentence, eh?' This was turning into *Midnight Express* without the language difficulties.

I left the corridor and went down to the dungeons to await being called. They said I shouldn't be down there, that I should go up to the main courtrooms, but I pleaded with them to let me stay. Away from the roving public eye. They weren't dungeons really, they were more like waiting rooms with dungeon windows. They didn't lock my door. One of the coppers smiled at me.

'Chin up,' he said.

Up until seeing Bodene, I'd felt reasonably refreshed after my good night's sleep. She was supposed to be on my side but

. . . well, even thinking that was stupid really. Why should any of them be on my side? Why should Bodene try her utmost on a stupid case like this? All that work for what? A pittance, I imagined. It wasn't going to be easy . . . ho, ho, ho. But still, I wasn't going to let her knock the wind out of me. I was going to have my day in court. I was going to *make* them send me down. I was going to go through the motions.

I got very bored waiting, beating myself up with the bother of it all. I flipped my mind back to Dirk and Bev. Their rows. Their ruptures. Maybe Dirk would finish with her. Maybe he'd visit me when I got sent down. Maybe he'd wait for me to come out. Shit. Maybe if the case went slowly today . . . The evidence. A statement, written and signed by myself. The circumstantial. My head. My colour. My scar. My shit barrister. One thing in my favour. No previous. Major major problem. Angry judge. Mandatory prison sentence.

It was a woman screw that day. Blonde and made-up, chain hanging like the bit of a blinkered horse. She could only look in the direction her head was facing. Maybe my scar was too much for her. Maybe she was taking her job too seriously. Who knows. Even after Bodene's little chat, I was much more relaxed than the day before. It was all upon me now. No point squawking. I had to get into the swing of things. This was a bog-standard straightforward screw. Well, they'd have to work at it. I wasn't going peacefully.

Ratface and Bodene had a cosy little chat. Setting up the goalposts, no doubt. Like kids sent out to play rugger in the rain, they didn't look enthusiastic but they would play just to see who won. Bodene or Ratface. Their little chat was the handshake before kick-off. I was the ball. Here he comes . . . here's Judge Benky now. Looking a bit more spritely today, I thought. Kick-off.

The eventual jury was lined up like two rows of skittles. I might have been at the fair with one of those guns. Knock six down for a teddy! Six down for a teddy! If it hadn't been for my face, I might. As each skittle took position, they searched me out. I couldn't bear to have them look at me, the freak of me. Not like

95

that, like I was an exhibit myself. I looked down to my lap. I needed a distraction. I took Mum's letter out of my handbag. (*Women with white handbags don't go to jail* was my thinking.) I held the letter down by my legs so the screw couldn't read it. Mum wrote big so I could easily make out her writing. It was their twenty-fifth wedding anniversary in two weeks' time and they'd hired out the illustrious lounges of the British Legion (I cringe) for the purpose of celebrating their phenomenal achievement. They would have liked both of their successful daughters to accompany them on this memorable occasion but, as Divine could not afford a passage home, they supposed that they would have to accept and would honourably request the pleasure of their youngest daughter only. Your very poshest frock would be appreciated as also the absence of the nose ring. Please RSVP by telephone to confirm your date of arrival, so that sleeping arrangements for the rest of the family can be organised. (I'd be sleeping on the kitchen floor, I knew.) Hope the study is going well and that the books sent down are useful. Good luck with your re-sits. Concentrate hard and you'll make it into your third and most important year. We'll always be very proud of you. Whatever happens. Lots of Love, Mum and Dad.

That last bit was a lie. That they'd be proud of me if I failed.

The screw told me to put the letter away. Poked me. Then cuffed me.

Right. Jury all sorted. Judge settled down. He could have done with a little pillow so's not to get a crick in his neck. And are there any eider ducks left? I wondered. I don't know why.

'You are charged with possession with intent to supply the Class A drug heroin. How do you plead?'

'Not guilty.'

'Bla bla bla for possession of cannabis. How do you plead?'

'Guilty.'

'Bla bla bla supply of cannabis?'

'Not guilty.'

Eh up! Ratface at the bench. He would like to call to the stand . . . well, he would like to call for a victim.

GOING UP IN THE WORLD

Chapter 9

Mo moved Simmi in. Not officially. She still had a room at some lodgings in a family house, but it was our bathroom she clogged up with huge bottles of hair stuff, body stuff, bleach. She had to bleach her face because she had a beard. Not like a man's, all stubbly. More like down, like baby hair. And it was black. She bleached it to a blond and, mixed in with all her foundation, you couldn't tell unless you were up close. She cooked too. She cooked good. Irish and Vinnie didn't mind her being there, just on that account. I didn't mind another girl in the house. Made me feel more feminine. More normal. Still, he was bang out of order for just moving her in without asking.

Our house smelt like the Bengal Tiger, day and night. She cooked dishes the day before we ate them, the spices absorbed by the ingredients, slowly and in perfect harmony, she said. She fried eggs in butter and made tea in a pan, the milk all mixed in with the tea-leaves. She made chapatis and burnt them on the hob, so they had dark-brown dimples on, like pancakes. Then she wrapped them up in a teatowel. She shopped daily for fresh vegetables and brought ladies' fingers from Bradford. They were just hairy beans really. Vinnie called them something else. She brought big bananas which she fried. I asked her to send some to my dad so she did. Mum and Dad live on the wrong side of the Pennines for plantain, in a village surrounded by stables and steeples, garden nurseries and trout farms. And orchards. Dad hadn't eaten plantain since leaving Nottingham. After I sent up two lots to him, Mum wrote and told me that he didn't like them any more. No more, she said. Sometimes Vinnie cooked up an African stew and Irish made us eat with chopsticks once a week. Mo and me just ate. We gave them marks out of ten after. Not to their faces, mind.

I came back from the phone box on a downer. Roy wasn't home. No answer and no answerphone. He had an answerphone but he only used it when he was in. When he was out, he wanted people to think he was in and when he was in, out. Easier not to have a fucking phone, I thought. Simmi was in the kitchen. She seemed relieved to see me.

'How's the study going?' I asked.

'Not bad. Not getting very good marks, though. Where've you been?'

'Phone box.'

'Oh, I meant to tell yer. I gave Roy a lift this morning. He was getting soaked. I took him down to the station. Said he was going to Oxford to see some mates.'

'Yeah, I know,' I lied.

'He said he forgot to tell you.' She gave me a look. Not nasty but a put-down. Made me feel vulnerable.

'Well, he must've forgotten that he told me then.'

I moved some of her books out of the way and sat at the table. Looking over at her writing, I left a long enough pause to change the subject back again.

'I thought you were struggling a bit. You're worse than Vinnie for swotting, aren't yer? At it every night.'

'Well, if I don't get through this first year I'll be buggered.'

'Well, you can take the first year again or change your course.'

'Can't. Me dad'll do his nut. Anyway, I want to get through it.'

'So you can go and work with your battered wives?'

I looked at her on the snide, picked up a few of her thick texts and turned them over.

'Will they really benefit from all this then? I mean, d'you need to know all this stuff, to have a cup of tea with a battered wife?'

'Yes, you do. And it's not just that,' she said, pulling her books towards her protectively, 'I really want to get through this year. Otherwise . . .'

'Otherwise they'll marry you off. Jesus, you will be buggered then, won't yer? Specially if you marry the wrong one. Yer might become a battered wife yerself then, eh?'

She gave me one of her You-don't-understand-Muslim-culture looks. 'You're just like white people, you are. All you can see are mosques, marriages and Paki shops.'

'Vinnie's mum and dad are Muslims – did he tell you? He says he can marry who he likes. I'd like to be a Muslim, actually. So I could wear one of those . . . what do you call them?'

'Yashmaks.'

'My scar wouldn't be so obvious then, would it?'

'The yashmak's a very oppressive device,' she said, all serious.

'I think it's quite sexy myself. Just seeing the eyes.'

'That's because you're . . .'

'No it's not, Simmi. And anyway, look at you! What do you do, eh? Cover your face in bleach and make-up and what for? That's oppressive. You can't walk out with the face God gave you, coz it's got a few hairs on it. Make-up's just another form of yashmak. It's the same thing. You want men to see you the way men want to see you.'

'And you don't?' she said, high-pitched, getting confused by the argument and pointing at my face covered in camouflage cack.

Then it dawned on her that my problem wasn't just with men.

'D'yer know what my mum says.' Laughing now, she was, to get away from what she knew was the truth. 'My mum says that the women who cover their heads n' that don't mind doin' it coz it means they don't have to do their hair all the time.'

'See. 'Snot oppressive at all. It can free you up.'

'Come on,' she said. 'You wouldn't want to cover your head and wear a yashmak all through the summer, would you?'

'Wouldn't mind, so long as everyone else did it. I've got nice eyes. I'd be doing meself a favour.'

'See, that's what I mean. It's only coz you're . . .'

'I wonder if Vinnie's mum covers her head,' I said, not wanting the truth to catch up.

'D'yer like Vinnie?' she said, putting her pen down, sitting back.

'Yeah, course I do,' I said. 'He's all right.'

'I mean . . . do you *like* him?'

'Oh Simmi, don't you start.'

She laughed, flicked a few pages back to see what she'd written and creased her face up in frustration.

'Not good, eh?' I said.

'How come you don't do any studying? Don't yer care?'

'Hector. The posh one that comes round? He gets all the information for me. I buy it off him. Whenever I have an assignment to do, I just read all the info, listen to a couple of tapes and write an essay. It's easy. I'm not after doing very well anyway. I just want a degree, whatever flavour it comes in.'

'So he sells degrees as well as drugs then, does he?'

'Very entrepreneurial, our Hector.'

'But you're hardly ever there, are you? Don't you have to go to seminars and tutorials and stuff like that?'

'They send me letters about stuff like that, every now and again. To get me to go. It's not compulsory, though. I think they give me the benefit of the doubt . . . because of my face. They think I'm disabled. And anyway, I get my assignments in OK. It's not like I take the piss full time. D'yer wanna cup of tea?'

I was bored. Vinnie and Irish were studying. Simmi was studying. Sod all on the telly.

'There's some lassi in the fridge.'

'I feel like a cup o' tea.'

'It's good, the lassi. You'll like it.'

'Look, Simmi, let's get something straight, shall we? I want a cup of tea.'

She lifted her books as if to set off out of the kitchen.

'Simmi, don't go. I didn't mean . . .'

'You did mean.'

'I didn't. It's just that . . . well, for God's sake. Since you've been here you've taken over the place. The kitchen. The bathroom. The meals. Everything I eat and drink seems to have your name on it. I just want to make myself a cup of tea if that's all right.'

'But you've never tried lassi before, have you?' Like it was a rite of passage . . .

'No, Simmi, I haven't, but maybe one day, when you're not trying to stuff it down my throat, I will. Shall we leave it for now? Now. Do you want a cup of tea?'

'No. I think I'd better go.' Then she paused. Then, 'Back to my lodgings.'

'You know I didn't mean it like that. I like you being here. I just don't want to be taken over, that's all.'

I made her a cup of tea anyway. Peace offering. I knew she'd drink it. I put the mug just out of the way of her books.

'What's that you're reading now?'

She wasn't reading. She was feeling like a spare part. Didn't know how to bounce back in again.

'*Sociological Consequences* of what? Jesus . . .'

'We get tons of it,' she said. Then we have to discuss everything so I can't even pretend I've read it.'

'Don't worry. You'll get the hang of it. I was a bit like that when I started.'

'He doesn't get it.' She was thumbing upstairs, to Mo's room.

'Who? Mo?'

'He just expects me to drop everything whenever he . . . I'm beginning to feel like his bloody taxi driver.'

'Tell him to sod off.'

'I like him but . . .'

'But what? Tell him to sling his hook.'

'He's my first proper . . . yer know.'

'Start as you mean to go on, girl. Don't take any shit.'

I knew he was her first and I knew that's why she was still with him. She wasn't the sort to lose it to some no-mark. Even though she had. Staying with him justified the mistake. I rolled a spliff and gave it to her to light. She looked down at her books and then closed them. She had her hair tied back in a neat little pony-tail and to carry on the relaxing, she slipped off the lacky band and let her hair fall round her face like a helmet, shiny and rounded. She lit the joint and sucked at it, as if sucking poison out of a wound. She reminded me of the way artists paint images of Cleopatra. Poison in there somewhere.

'If your parents are modern enough to let you come to college, maybe they'll let you off the arranged marriage stuff, eh?'

'Uhh-uhh. No way. I'll shame the family if I don't marry the right Muslim. And I'm not likely to find him on me own, am I? In some ways, I don't mind, yer know. At least I'll be living in comfort when I'm married. Wealthy.'

She blew out some smoke, smiled and then said, 'You won't get any help at all, will yer?'

After she said it, she got nervous. She bashed the end of the joint against the ashtray. That's the sad thing really. As soon as people get used to my face, they feel free with their talk – it's not guarded or filtered. But the other side of that means they fall into traps like that one. Then they see my face and nothing else. Instead of getting nervous she should have just carried on with her 'benefits of arranged marriage'. We would have been making progress then. She wasn't that good yet.

'No. That's right, Simmi. I won't get any help, but then I don't think I'll be getting married anyway. I'm not really into all that shit. So.'

Quick as a flash, I put myself in her shoes, a trick I use to stop me feeling sorry for myself. To deflect the spotlight away from me.

'Will yer dad give you a choice, like?'

'Course he will!' she screeched, like a child, as if it were just too utterly incredible the idea that she wouldn't get any choice. 'First off, they show me pictures. Photographs. If I like the look of him, then we invite him round with his mum and dad. I've seen a couple already, last year. Before I knew I was coming to college, that was. In fact, that was when I got the idea . . . of coming to college, I mean. Seeing a future husband in the flesh is frightening. I'm too young for all that.'

She was smiling when she spoke. She liked talking about the strange customs of her Muslim world. She liked being differ-ent, out of her pond. I guess custom was all she had to hang on to, so she milked it. She thought she was exotic. One day she told me that she couldn't touch the Koran if she was on her period. She was smiling when she told me, like it was some kind of gang rule, a gang I'd never be asked to join. This was a particularly lurid rule that she knew would titillate me. I told her that the only reason they had such a rule was because men were scared of women's power. She looked at me like I was mad. Like I was the one with all the phoney ideas.

Just at that moment, Vinnie came in.

'Hi, girls. She's not distracting you from your studies, is she, Simmi? Watch her. She doesn't care.'

Simmi was just about to say no – when it dawned on her that I was. That was exactly what I was doing.

'Get back in your box, Vinnie, and leave us alone.'

Too harshly, I said it, not even looking up at him.

The door closed and he left. I should have run after him, maybe. Because I never, he got even smaller then. And we laughed at him, that uncontrollable stoned laughter from the early days of toking when to see a tragic figure is to see, at the very same time, the comedy of it. The whole of the moon, as they say.

Then Simmi, still in her early days of stonedness, went all serious and silent. I think she was surprised at herself, at her lack of compassion.

'You're horrible to him.'

Then silence again. I snarled up my nose at her. Then I waved my hand for the spliff.

'I wish me dad'd do that for me, yer know,' I said. 'Send me pictures of prospectives. 'Slong as he knew some good-looking ones, mind. Not fat old arseholes. What if yer dad can only get you fat old arseholes?' I half hoped this was a possibility.

Always happy to go back to the peacock feathers of her ethnic landscape. Always so proud. So vain, I thought. She snorted, laughing. No way was Daddy going to get her a fat old arsehole – *that* was what the laugh said. That was a basic rule of the engagement. She gave me the spliff, got up and started chopping onions. I could see her mother in her. I'd never met her mother but she did such a remarkable impression . . . That was tomorrow's tea she was getting on the go. More than a rich Muslim husband, I wouldn't have minded a rich Muslim wife.

Mo came in then.

'Simmi, you want to come over to Zebedee's place?'

I threw Simmi a look of preliminary disgust and she caught it. Made her think.

She moved the weight from one foot to the other and said, 'No, Mo. I don't think I do. You go off on your own.'

I blew my smoke into Mo's face, smiling at the same time. Mo slammed the door hard on his way out, smashing the glass in the front-door window. I heard the trinkets and shards of it fall to the floor. That was the first time there'd been any violence in the house. Like a shot, it was. The first bullet. A change of reality. Vinnie rushed downstairs and yelled that he thought we'd been busted. Mo didn't even stay to inspect the damage. I passed the spliff back to Simmi. She looked a bit scared. Maybe it was just onion eyes – I couldn't tell.

'Now, lass,' I said, 'I'll have some of that old lassi you were on about. And put that pinny away. You're a free woman now.'

She wasn't wearing one.

Simmi, in the house, carried with her an aura of female competence and comfort. Outside the house, she wore a suit of psychological armour to ward off interlopers. Interlopers were white people. Even Irish got some of that treatment. She talked to him as if through a veil, not giving full vent to her meaning, not letting him find the real her. She walked past him in kameez, even in jeans she did this, giving way too much room, too much respect for herself, shrouded in the swaddling of her culture. Black people, of all races and creed, were considered friends, of one aim, of one lot, of one body of opinion, until they fucked up. All others were aliens. I enjoyed playing that one. Aliens. Me not being an alien for a change. I took up this cloak when we were out together. We surrounded ourselves with a mysterious barrier of superiority. Well, it was myster- ious to me anyway. Sometimes, though, because I wasn't a true racist, sometimes I cut the barbed-wire and let white people through, particularly some of my good customers who became friends. Simmi even looked down on Hector and he was colour blind to the hilt. Money was all that Hector was after, money and leadership. All his school reports said he'd make a good leader and he believed them. He was treasurer of no less than three college societies. Getting the share prices, a daily fix. But he wasn't racist. As I pointed out to Simmi, when the whites had gone and she'd managed to find her tongue again, my mum was white. They couldn't all be bad. I put her naivety down to all those kitchens and mosques she'd been sheltered in.

'Ahh!' she said. 'Yer mam can't be that white. In her head, I mean. Getting knocked up by a black man in them days . . . There must have been some black in her.'

'There was.' I said. 'My dad.'

I could still remember how the people looked at us, when we moved into the cottage. Aunty Aggie's cottage, left to us in the will. Dad was all but done for by then. Mining had got into his lungs and his back. Mum had to go out cleaning schools and people's houses, to keep the boat afloat. We moved our stuff in, with a rented van going back and forth three times. Curtains were not twitching. The neighbours were too bare-faced for that. Half of them were stood out in their front gardens. Jean from next door was brave enough to talk to us, to welcome us. And to establish just what sort of black people we were. But she asked Mum all the questions. Mum the white leader, it seemed, as she sat on the fence, gesticulating and smiling and trying too hard to be friendly whilst her kids carried tea chests and Jamaican banana boxes jammed full of button bags and lampshades and bits of past that should have been left behind.

Oh true, they smiled well enough, the neighbours, nosy passers-by who just had to get a closer look. But behind the smiles there was exasperation and misunderstanding, for how could this white woman be one of us? How could she do it? She must have been a whore in her day. For sure. For sure.

There was Mum making all the right noises, all the right hand signals, a PR expert through and through, but still, even with these skills she couldn't penetrate the skulls of those people who wanted to know how she got herself shacked up with a black man. When did it happen? Why did it happen?

Yer got yerself pregnant, yer parents kicked you out and you've been scrabbling about for a living ever since, with yer piccaninnies on yer skirts and nowhere called home to go to. No. I wanted to tell them the truth. Come right out and say it. Fair and square. No beating about the bush. I wanted to flake away the story that the people had made up, digested with their very own fear and brought up from their gullets like vomit, urging out of their eyeballs. No. It wasn't like that. My mum was not a whore, never was. Leave her alone. Stop staring at her like that, looking at her clothes, her hair, the way she moves her legs when she walks. Don't stare. Just stop it, will yer! But they never did. And she never let up. In the greengrocer's, the garage, the church. The people saw past her face but never tried to find the ways and words of the spaces inside her head, as though the inside of Mum's brain was a no-go area, a place they shouldn't enter, shouldn't ask about. Just live and let live, said their faces, when they smiled, gave change, stamped Dad's pension book at the post office. Suckers on society.

We never saw Mum's knees. She wore little pins in her ears as a gesture to her femininity but nothing would ever hang down from those lobes as such a trinket would invite cat calls from across the green. That would be the proof of her looseness. There was nothing loose about my mum. She was tight-lipped, tight-arsed and tight-fisted with her feelings.

There was Mum being sensible. Scarves, mackintoshes, shoes, woolly tights, high collars and values and morals to suit. But still, this PR trick didn't get through. Almost like the people saw her as an act, a performance designed to distract them from the reality. The reality was that she was shacked up and married to a black man and what white woman does that, did that? In them days, eh? Look! Those kids aren't in prams. You could understand it nowadays, there's more of it about. It's almost acceptable, though Lord knows, you wouldn't wish it on your own kids, would yer? It can't be easy, whatever anyone says. It don't seem right somehow. Them days . . . well, she must have been a fallen woman. Musta been.

God! How tall she walked amongst them – their sniding in the grasses, their bellies stroked with the surface slime of earth that should have long ago been trodden in and done away with. For such people couldn't climb up and be at one to one. Couldn't let their prejudices bleed out to the ground to be trodden in and done away with. They couldn't do it because the old stuff was rooted firm and deep within them. Snaked in their guts.

Dad didn't arrive till the third trip and by then the whole street was waiting for him. He was anxious and tired. Worn out. The van parked respectfully like a hearse. Our driver got out and ran round to open the door for him. Even before Dad stepped down, his spirit was wafting up the street. A silence descended as we waited for him to pass judgement on our new home. What were the neighbours waiting for? A big bulk of a man with his finger on the pulse, his shoulders broad and threatening, cocky, lazy and arrogant. A dirty mac and a hat. An umbrella? Dad arrived in a big black coat, much too big for his frame but warm. Yes, he had a hat. To keep off the cold. He'd never got used to the cold. And an arm to hold him up as he wavered and walked in tiny steps towards the house. A broken man turned up and the neighbours turned off. That was too boring for them. Back to the telly and . . . those kids need watching. There's no sayin' what sorts they'll be attracting to the area. The new health authority hadn't sent an oxygen tank and Dad was anxious. Breathing very badly. He didn't even look up at the house. As if on a conveyor belt for broken bodies, broken down, he plodded on to the front gate, up the front path and through the door to sit on the chair he'd sat on for nigh on seven years now. Dad's chair, next to the fireplace. And when I sat on the packing cases in my new bedroom, I broke down. The family was breaking down in my mind. We could never build it back up again, in this strange red-bricked silence. But in the next room, Divine had found her cassette tapes. She blasted out Aretha Franklin, to build the house back up again. A little respect. Respect. A little respect, please, for the ladies. Out of my window, a tree. Three sparrows hopped upon it, in rhythm, one after the other, one, two, three. It seemed like an omen.

In those days, I blamed everything on white people. Because round there, they were all white. They hated my colour and they hated my scar and before long I hated them. All of them. Everything was down to white people. History. Slavery. Mum wouldn't have any of it. She was sick to the back teeth of the slavery story. She said the only slave we had to think about was her, since she did all the skivvying and got no thanks for it. Ever. I said that she didn't know what it felt like to be the fourteen-year-old descendant of a slave with a slave master's name. Our Divine agreed. And she was doing her A levels then. She went one further. That was her trademark. Going one step beyond. She said Jackson was as hurtful as Sambo. She said if names were to follow her about all the days of her life, she'd let people know that her name was not *her* name. I followed suit. I still looked up to her then.

She called herself Divine SN Jackson. SN for slave name. X was self-flagellation, she said. It was too silent, insignificant. Malcolm hadn't tried hard enough, she said. SN, on the other hand, would have to be explained. It was loud, unpoetic, messy. SN was disturbing. And it was. It disturbed everyone. I became Vivian SN Jackson. Divine said that to ignore the pain of our heritage, to ignore the fact that we had lost our true names, our culture, our families, was to let the white people believe that they had done right. It was to let them forget too easily. She fed me this stuff with more passion than any of my schoolteachers could ever muster.

I checked in history books and saw nothing of what she was saying, save the odd section on seventeenth-century trade. There, there were references to slaves, but honoured only with a few lines of text, explaining the 'now understood' abhorrence of a trade in flesh. Willy Wilberforce and Boswell. The goodies and the baddies. Oh, and not forgetting the rather loud introductory accounts of how it was all down to the Africans really. It was the Africans that did most of the selling. They sold themselves. The Europeans only moved in to improve on distribution. No blame there then. The cruelty inflicted upon those that took the passage? That was because they considered the Negro as stock, not human. They weren't in their right minds then, were they? Profit was a greater draw than humanity, than nature, than morality. No change there then.

In the books they would have me believe that slavery was just a bad law that needed correcting. Nowhere did I find an account of how the souls of all those enslaved Africans were remembered by the Europe that sent the ships to Africa. Nowhere could I find a British apology, a monument, an anniversary for the souls of my ancestors. Adding SN to our names was the least we could do. We lived the idea for months. It separated us from the world, even Mum and Dad. To imagine the pain of the slaves was to reduce my own. The pain on my face. Divine had shown me a diversion, a way for us to share something. A way for us to grow up with ourselves. It was a big open secret.

Dad just laughed at her, when she told him. He laughed his head off. That's why I followed suit. We got our names changed on the registers at school, on our library tickets, on the netball fixtures. Everywhere. 'Why?' they all said. 'In case you've forgotten,' we said. 'Lest we forget,' we said. 'We think England should remember.' Dad tried to make Divine look stupid when she was deadly serious. The battle was on. It felt like every day she'd find something else out about England and then come home and blame Dad for it. She said he was weak. They all were. The West Indians. They were conned into becoming modern-day slaves. She told me that they queued like the Jews to board ship ready to be taken over to their so-called motherland. At least the Jews saw their enemy coming. At least they felt him press down on their souls. At least they had some past to hang on to. The West Indians were blind, said Divine. So ready to undertake yet more forced labour, a forced labour clothed in the English-language notion of need. Robbed of their past they couldn't see where they were going. And when they got here, they were beat. She told Dad that he'd been too weak. That he should have sussed it all out. At that point, even I thought she was getting a bit above herself. It was all too close to home. She was blaming Dad for everything. I stopped using my SN. She'd gone too far, I thought.

They tore each other to pieces with their words, until at last Dad shut up and our Divine was left ranting to the air. Then she gave up. Dad tried to re-establish his stranglehold on the family by repeating the same old mantras and neither of us dared argue with him. Not out of fear. Out of not wanting to see him fall down any further. We could strip him of his pride, we knew that now. But who wants a dad stripped, shamed, beaten. We let him have his way. He said neither of us knew which side our bread was buttered and to get on with our schooling since education was the only gate open to us, given our colour. Given my scar. (Thanks, Divine.) He said that England might have lost its manners but it was ram jam full of education. Wall-to-wall carpets of it, he said. He wished he'd had the chance. He said for us to go out there and do some thinking of our own for a change, instead of fighting battles already lost and making more for to come. He got so breathless with trying to make us see – we just nodded at him in the end. Said yes, Dad in the end. And when we did anything bad, besides all the other punishments, it was that look in his breathless face, his eyes tied down with worry and fear for us, the sadness, the disgrace – it was all that, that did for us.

When we were kids, Dad used to talk about the slaves. I guess because we couldn't answer back then. He said that slavery wasn't down to white people anyway. He said it was down to the gun. When we came home crying and creating about kids calling us names, or men calling Mum names, he sat us down, in front of the fire, and made pictures in the hearth with the coal.

'See this 'ere? This is di earth,' he said, holding up the coal. 'Your daddy's been out all day chopping up earth so the people can keep warm. We're turnin' the earth into fire.'

'Fi-ya', he said, his accent strong when he told us fairy stories.

'The fiya god shows us ow to do this, see? And it was the fire god who gave man a gun. The fire god was jealous of the water god, see. And so he gave man the power and the swiftness of the bullet. Man forgot about the Lord of all tings. What's this?' he said, and with a jerk of his arm, quite suddenly, without us knowing what he had in his hands, he threw a great chunk of coal into the fire, old coals falling on the hearth, as surprised as us, it seemed.

'This is a cannon ball smashing down the castles,' he said, and chucked more and more coal on then, small bits and big bits, picking them out of the bucket and throwing with a face that wanted to kill. 'The people were feared for their lives – that cannon was a monster. Real. Alive. Bang, bang, bang. The men who made the bells to ring in all the steeples?'

He donged the tongs against the coal bucket. Dong, dong, dong.

'Of all the churches across the world? For all the peoples? Those men stop making bells. They make the cannon machine instead. So lowwwwd!'

And he stood up and threw a whole bucket of coal on to the fire.

'Those cannon balls move faster than the word of any water god. The tide was high. The people moved on. With the blast of da cannonball. Those bell makers did not know the knells dey rang. The people laid down their hearts and souls – to the gun. They laid down their souls to the knights who had such a gun. They forgot about theya church. That's why I go to me church and call up da Lord for to bring the light back again. Those people? They were blind to the glow o' da light around the steeple. God's steeple. From that day to dis, dey've been blinded. By the power – o' da gun. They saw riches, spices, jewels. They saw only slaves in Africa. The African man kep' slave fo' 'imsel' but na never mekkim die, for how can he work if he dead, if he no fed, if he no play with da chillen, eh? The white man care for nowt but 'em numbers. And slaves for him were numbers. Not men. For they was blinded by the fiya, by the gun, see! They didn't see the people livin' nicely der. Just blinded, ya see! Just lika when you are blinded by da sun. That was the time of the wantin' – not the needin', see! Whatever the colour o' da people, they succumb to the gun. When the children a call a yer names? You remember. They are the dying breath o' the fire god. The las' smoke of his chamber. Only water will dampen him. Right now, the smoke is in yer eye and make yer cry. But one day, the fire god will make it up with the water god. Until that time, sticks and stones will break yer bones and names will follow ya aroun', all a days o' yer life. Now – y'ask me why I call yer what I call yer?'

As if we were in the heart of the blacksmith's forge, the heat from the fire would burn up our shins to warn us of the gun. Dad's spit on the hearth sizzled in distress and disappeared before our very eyes. The earth god dug deep into his lungs and came out of a night, in his choking heaves. The wind god creaked into his back. It came under the doors to make draughts to crick in his neck and I got to thinking then that all the gods were bad. All of them.

'Names. Names, my children, are very import-ant. The one ting my grandaddy say I should never forget.'

Dad was called Winston. He told us that in Scotland, in Edinburgh, there's a clock that instead of donging fires a gun, every day at one o'clock. In the castle, it is. He met my mum in Scotland, when he was in the army. Her name's Grace.

My mum wasn't white when we sat and talked that stuff by the fire. And we weren't black. We were all orange and ruddy and hot. The flames licked our cheeks and we looked like ghosts.

When Mum was wheeled in to the headmasters and the shopkeepers, the policemen and the priests . . . then she was white. She was white and wrong and sad and strong and both me and Divine were fierce in our love as we watched her walk through parted aisles of staring eyes, asking her just how come she'd sunk so low. Mrs Jackson.

'Simmi, change the record will yer? You're decades out of date. My dad says that bad vibrations always go home. They boomerang right back at yer . . . right in yer face.'

'And so you don't care about your slave ancestors then, eh?'

She sneered when she said it, like I was the letdown for the whole of blackdom.

'I don't Simmi, no.' I was angry then. 'I don't give a fuck about slaves. I'm more worried about my face than my race and so would you be if you were me.'

(I was pointing my finger in *her* face.)

'Real scars don't come in colours, Simmi.'

'Now that's just you feeling sorry for yourself,' she said, waving my finger away, still stalking the high ground.

'That's just you talking shit,' I said. 'And maybe, when you've had a bit more education . . . maybe you'll learn about what size and colours the *real* bastards come in. That'll wake you up.'

We had loads of those. Race conversations. Bored me rigid. Same old claptrap every time. Licking wounds so much they were sore all over again. And although she'd never marry a white man, whoever she did marry would have to be good-looking. Her brother had photos of good-looking women sent over from Pakistan. Young girls, some of them. Thirteen and that. As soon as her brother found a nice one, they were going to ship her over. Like a slave. Blew my mind, that did. She'd be good-looking too, Simmi said. 'Fair', she called it. Now there's a laugh. Beauty and justice in bed together.

Simmi said it wasn't about skin colour. It was culture, she said. She only waved the culture flag when her colour argument dried up. Like then. A disgrace to my race, she said to me once. To my face. Laughing. Telling me I couldn't help how I was, could I? And that was the funny thing. She tried to make me feel that my view of the world was scarred – because my face was scarred. She wanted to take my eyesight off me as well. My arguments were invalid. And sometimes I felt like an invalid. No good. Crap. When I was on my own, that was. I never let anyone see me like that.

I guess I never understood Simmi's culture thing. To me it was just another stick in her arsenal. She had looks, brains, her married life plotted out for her and now this culture. This belief in extended family tradition, extended family order, extended family pride. She walked tall with it, her shoulders stiff as an ironing board, her back unbendable. This culture thing was something else to be jealous of. It engulfed her like a baby's swaddling clothes, as though, from the cradle to the grave, she would always be rocked to sleep, safe, comfortable in the knowledge that, from all sides, she would be kept in a state of belonging. I was jealous, sure, but I was angry too. Surely feeling so secure, being so cosseted, having it all, surely she shouldn't have felt the need to look down on me, attack me, make me feel smaller than I already was? I didn't want pity but even less so contempt.

Bev was more like it. Not quite 'it', where I think 'it' really is, but more like it. Not so many games with Bev. No having to talk about people with a prefix of white or black. Bev took delight in taking me under her wing and that was why it wasn't quite 'it'. She had that in-built arrogance of the rest of the world, thinking that, by treating me better than normally, she was doing me a favour when really she was putting me down and keeping me there. I didn't mind, I was used to it. I just didn't buy it. And also, I got the feeling I was doing her a favour – making her feel better. Like I was giving her something to do. She used an aura of charity, that minute yet detectable vein of arrogance – she used it as a cover for her own inadequacy. An aura vivid and suggestible enough for me to feel comfortable, absorbing her but not suffocated by her. She gave me room to breathe, to move about, grow.

In her dodgy car, she took me off to big parks with lakes in, out in the country. We went for walks, just to pass the time. I was never sure how innocent these walks were. I had the feeling she was checking up on her stash really, making sure it was all as it should be. Then again, being an environmentalist (first-class degree with Hons), it could have been just how it was, Bev out green-bathing. She was dead against sunbathing. Ozone mad. She said I had stuff in my skin to protect me – melanin. I told her to shut it. Skin wasn't my favourite subject, as well she knew.

There was a long silence. Awkwardness.

'Bev,' I said.

'What?' she said, sulkily, bit miserable, head down.

'You've got a big green monster of a helicopter stuck in yer hair and just about to tunnel its way down your earhole.'

She shook her head violently and the insect flew off and away.

'What was it?' I asked, coming up close to her, to make her feel relaxed again.

She stopped and turned towards me.

With a serious look and squinty eyes, in a Chinese accent she said, 'That was a grasshopper, my child – now go walk on the rice paper and roll me a spliff.'

Smoking spliff, I looked down into the lake.

'My lake,' said Bev, like it had her name on it.

The wind busied up the surface of the water and so busied up my face. You couldn't see my scar then. I smiled. I went and sat by a tree, named and classified for me by Bev. Given a history by Bev. She knew the tree well, she said. Had sat and meditated there, many a time, times when the world was against her. I wasn't interested in tree names or their dates of birth. I pretended to listen. Roy was into all that stuff. Trees. He said tree blood was magic water, sent from the god of truth. Sometimes, he was a bit over the top.

I examined Bev's face. She wasn't exactly pretty but there wasn't anything out of place. Some make-up would have put her eyelashes on the map but Dirk, she told me, didn't like fussy women. She loved him but didn't like the way he took over the air, the atmosphere. Willy-nilly. Just like that. And that affected everything else. They'd been together, living separate lives, for six years. Joined at the hip by the rent book and the weighing scales.

After that day in the park, I grew up a bit. I got mad when people got nervous about my face and I got mad when they forgot about it. I couldn't have it both ways.

Chapter 10

Bev invited me to a dinner party. Now Simmi and I were such good mates I asked if she could come too. We weren't really mates, more symbiotic. I diluted the impact of her beauty. Ugliness should enhance it but, just as in the tropics, where nature hides her colourful secrets beneath a blanket of plant and leaf, I sheltered Simmi. Camouflaged her. Distracted attention away from her. Alone, we were a target for the scan of a tracking pupil. Together, we busied up the eye of the pink-skin people so violently they couldn't rest their eyes on either of us. They moved on and we moved on. Simmi and I needed each other. We weren't mates.

Simmi's evenings had been shaved down to study and cooking in the kitchen, sex in the bedroom or making coffee for Mo's punters if she dared go into the lounge of an evening. I reckon half those punters came round just to get the treatment. She fell into making tea and titbits unconsciously and for to please Mo, I suppose. But when we were alone together, she went feminist. Said he was bang out of order. Said she wasn't his skivvy. I swear I could swing for her sometimes. What she said and what she did were two different countries. So, I thought a night off would be good for her. Also, I'd get a lift in the motor and dodge the rain showers. Dodge the street people. I wanted to arrive at the dinner party the way I imagined one should – not like some geographer on a field trip, stopping off for a bit of tucker. Bev said she didn't mind Simmi coming but could she be trusted? Well . . . she was supposed to be a law-abiding Muslim girl, so obviously not, but since it was Bev doing the asking.

Mo flipped, didn't he. Chucked all his teddies out of the pram. Said he wanted to come.

'There won't be enough chairs round the table,' I told him. I'd never been to a grown-up dinner party before so I assumed a table plan. Hats, maybe. He started creating then, saying Simmi couldn't go.

'And who do you think you are?' I said. 'Her dad?'

'I'm her boyfriend, for God's sake, and I don't want her to go.'

When he was angry, his accent got really thick, like everything inside him was coming out of his mouth. He raised himself up over me.

'Who are *you* to come between a man and his girlfriend?'

'Doesn't sound quite right that, does it?' I said. 'Man and his girlfriend . . .'

His face fumbled in embarrassment. He thought I was taking the piss out of his English. *Man and his girlfriend.* He knew it didn't sound right but wasn't sure why.

'Get a grip of yourself, Mo. This is what women do these days. She's exercising her rights. Every time you jump into bed with her, you do the exact same thing.'

'You know what you are, don't you?'

He was gruff now, his neck swollen, all the anger clogged up inside it, vibrating. He pointed death-wish fingers at me.

'You are no better than the white trash out there, with your filthy mouth and filthy habits.'

'Filthy habits? What are you on about?'

There was a drought on at the time. Mo was out of money, draw, friends, it seemed. He wanted Simmi to drive him round town to look for some draw. He wanted to come to Bev's to get an introduction. Take over my end of the business. He wanted to rule the fucking roost.

'That man you have round here. What are you? Some sort of prostitute? Huh? You come here and speak to me like . . .'

'Mo, leave her alone.' That was Vinnie. He pulled Mo away from me. 'What's going on?'

'She's interfering. That's what's going on.'

'Vinnie, listen to him. He's slinging mud coz he can't get his own way. He's pathetic.'

'What's the problem, Mo?'

'We're going to a dinner party and he can't come. That's his problem.'

'I'm thinking that Simmi's going out with her, not me.'

'Well, she is tonight so get yer head down.'

One thing I had on Mo was a voice. When he was trying to get words out, I talked over him. I made every effort to squash his voice. My voice was louder than his, confident. British. He spoke in hushed concentration. Like an Afghani Sasha Distel. When he was angry, he needed the words to come out quick and sharp but they just weren't sharp enough. He was left wide open then.

'Simmi,' he said, all quietly, politely. 'Will you give me a lift into town? Before you go?'

Simmi looked at me, as if asking for permission. Mo bit his lip in exasperation. She was still looking at me.

'What are you asking her for? See, Vinnie! Look at them. Who are you going out with? Me or her? Whose car is it? Yours or hers?'

'Get back in your box, Mo. You're making the girl nervous.'

I was laughing by then. Vinnie frowned at me. Mo couldn't say stuff like that. 'Get back in your box.'

'Listen, you two. I have got a mind of my own,' said Simmi in a nearly-bursting-into-tears voice.

Then Vinnie piped up again.

'What about the four of us go out one night, eh?'

He had hold of my arm now, smiling up at me.

Out of synch, as always. I looked at him like he was sick. So did Mo.

'What? A foursome, you mean?'

'All right,' he said. 'Only an idea.'

I was surrounded by idiots. I went for a shower. After a couple of minutes I heard tapping on the bathroom door. I prayed it wasn't Vinnie. It was Simmi.

'He won't speak to me now.'

'Good. Fuck him.'

'Can I stay in your room tonight? Otherwise I'll have to go back to my lodgings and . . .'

'Sleep on the couch.'

'No. I don't want him to get me. And I wouldn't anyway . . .' Ashamed at what she'd said. 'Not with Vinnie and Irish in the house.'

'What d'yer mean?'

'Well . . .'

'Don't bring Vinnie and Irish into it. You're scared of him, aren't yet? How can you be scared of *him*?'

'It's just . . .'

She didn't want to admit it. I passed over it, let her think about it.

'Pass us that towel, would you?'

I dried myself and set about plaiting the end of my hair. I'd do it in a pony-tail, I thought. Make myself look posh like the woman in the After Eight adverts. Simmi sat on the loo and had a go at her nails with an emery board.

'Well, you'll have to sleep on the floor then.'

'That's all right. I'm used to that. I sleep on the floor at home.'

'Why?'

'When my cousins come round we give the kids the beds. Mind, at home it's not so bad. We have these big heavy quilts to lie on, so it's like lying on a mattress really.'

'Well, tonight yer on the carpet, my dear.'

'Thanks.'

Just as we were leaving, Simmi called Mo for his lift, but he didn't answer. So we left without him.

He'd been drinking a lot lately. Simmi said the smoke made him paranoid. The drink made him careless and catty, though. He was doing pubs big-style so Simmi stopped going out with him. She still bedded him but wouldn't go to the pub with him. She hated pubs. To be honest, she didn't suit pubs. Her going-out face was too beautiful for the pub. She wore jewellery on every part of her body that would take it, including the nose. It was only a stick-on imitation diamond (copying me, I said, but she put me down with her culture blanket) but well over the top for the Pig and Whistle. She was exhibit A in there. Glass case and all. If she'd worn a sari she might have blended in more – would have come up to people's expectations. In her jeans and tight bright jumpers and shoes high enough to paint the ceiling in, she was something of a turn. For Mo, a handbag. He went off to play darts and left her sat there for the locals to gawp at. At the end of the night he picked her up again. So she stopped going, stayed in with me and got stoned. Sometimes we'd go to the club and he'd turn up later on, leching and smelly. By then, his accent mixed in with his alcoholic slur made him unintelligible. He was going downhill fast.

So this night, we left him sulking in his room, and went off to our dinner party, in the luxury of the car. The anonymity. The lifting up from the streets and the feet of the masses. The warm air. Music. Comfort. Control. Like queens, we were. We purred our way through the streets, out of town, first to where Simmi's lodgings were. When she got back in the car, she was reading a letter, chewing on her fingers.

'From me mum and dad,' she said.

'Bad news?'

'Mmm.'

'What?'

When someone's holding bad news, I first of all prepare myself for the worst, then work backwards, depending on their expression. This wasn't really bad news.

'What?'

We were down to something like Dad's got to wear a hearing aid.

'Imran, my brother, wants to come down. See how I am.'

'When?'

'They don't say. They're just letting me know.'

'Don't yer like him then? Yer brother?'

'He's all right. Bit Bossy. Bit like Dad really. He does like to practise at being Dad. He used to be a right rebel when he was about ten. Now he's gone right the other way. He's lovely though. Earns loads of money.'

'What does he do?'

'He's a plane engineer. Fixes planes. It's funny coz he did that when he was a kid. Loved it. You know them plywood things. He loves stamps as well.'

'Stamps?'

'Stamp collecting.'

'Jesus, Simmi. That's almost sick.'

'Me dad's been a stamp dealer for years. Imran does it to keep up with him, I reckon.'

'Sounds like our Divine. She's been practising grown-upness since she was eight. She'd never do that, though – come down and check up on me. She wouldn't give a shit.'

'Well, he's not exactly checking up on me. He's coming to see I'm all right. When he came down last time, he went back and told Dad I needed a car. So I don't have to walk home from the library – late at night. All those white boys out there, see . . .'

She was laughing when she said that, glad they were all so stupid. She stuffed the letter in the glove compartment. I stared at the glove compartment for some time. I was jealous. At home we didn't have a car. Dad was too sick to drive and Mum wouldn't learn. The thought of going home for an Easter holiday of catching buses to town with Mum appalled me.

'D'yer fancy coming to Paris?' I said. 'In the Easter holidays. I fancy Paris in the spring. We could ride down the avenues with the wind in our hair. Yeah!'

I opened the car window to get the effect.

'To see your sister.'

'Well . . . sort of.'

'OK then. I've never been to Paris.'

''Cept we won't go and see our Divine. Well, not straight away.'

'Why not?'

'I've just told you. She's a grown-up. We just go to Paris, bum about till the money's run out and then go and see her.'

'All right then.'

'They'll let yer?'

'If I say we're going to see your family. Don't see why not. What about my brother, though?'

'What about him?'

'I'll have to go back to my lodgings, won't I? Move all my stuff back in and that?'

'Tell him you're busy. Doing exams and that. Get him to come down after the holidays. Tell him you've got tests. Like at school. Not exams. Tests. Then next term you can find somewhere else to live, no? We could get a place together, eh?'

'I'd like that,' she said. 'I would. I think I'd prefer it – if it was just us.'

'Me too,' I said.

'I'll ring home later. Put him off.'

She was all cosy-looking then. She whacked up a jazz tune on the cassette and played percussion on the steering with her fingertips. We *were* friends really.

Then we stopped off at the offy for a bottle of wine. Neither of us had a clue about wine.

'Is it red meat or white meat?' the man asked.

'She doesn't eat meat,' I said.

'What? Doesn't eat meat? What sort of a dinner party's that?' Simmi wasn't convinced.

'Are you sure? No meat at all?

'No. She eats cheese and stuff.'

'So what colour wine then?'

'Not white,' said Simmi, arrogantly. Curt.

Although I didn't see, I bet she gave him the slit-eye as well.

The shopkeeper sneered at her. 'Red it is then. We don't do Paki wine, I'm afraid.'

'Eh, you!' I said. 'That's race discrimination!'

My face was wide open to him. My pony-tail bravery had turned into nudity.

'What's your game?' he said to me, as if I had no right to speak, let alone join in.

'I was just saying that that's racial discrimination.'

'What? Telling her we don't do Paki wine? Well, we don't. Or would you like me to? Is that yer point?'

'Forget it. Just give us a bottle of red, would yer. Cheapest you've got.'

When I got outside the shop, Simmi was wrenching the gear stick out of the bowels of the car.

'How you can even *think* about giving him money!' she said, treading way too hard on the accelerator.

'Coz he said Paki? As you keep pointing out, you are from

124

Pakistan.' Then, under my breath, 'Even though you've never stepped foot in the place.'

'I heard that.'

'Well, what the fuck are you on then?'

She was on the wrong side of a residential bendy road, doing fifty.

I thought I'd done my best with the man, to be honest. I'd let him know he was on thin ice. That's a result in my book. She wanted sanctions. Well over the top. I used that offy quite a lot for skins and fags and late-night munchies. She always wanted to take things too far. I wanted the silence to stop. Car silence is acute. Even with the tape blaring. I rolled a joint. Then had an idea.

'And anyway. When we're smoking Paki black you don't go all funny, do yer? You've heard me say Paki loads of times and never said a dickie bird.'

'It's the way *he* said it.'

'What, like Pakkkki? Like the way you said "Not white".'

The silence continued, the air thick with it, irritating, like the repeated growls of a moody dog. Maybe there'd be strokes and waggy tails in a minute. But maybe bared teeth. I wanted to clean up the mess, for that was what the man had done. Left a mess on us. Even though I'd stood some ground with him, I hadn't stood it all. We should have left that shop all giggly and girlie but no, we let the situation knock us down. We fell together, privately, in the car. We weren't riding round the streets as dinner guests any more. No. Simmi had turned those streets into white people's streets. Lined up with white people's houses. We were driving past as visitors, with contractual permission to be there. In silence. And the truth was, that that shopkeeper wasn't on about black hashish wrapped in red seal. Prone to cause headaches if smoked in large quantities. He was on about the Paki shop half a mile down the road there. The one that opened on a Sunday when he wouldn't. And of course, he was on about the wine. I gave her the spliff. It was between her lips when my arm stretched over with the lighter.

'Doesn't Pakistan do wine then?'

'I think you'd better shut up,' she said.

Chapter 11

Bev's flat was blessed with the fumes of a thousand candles and burnt soya-meat lasagne. The candles were placed around various demons which turned out to be deities. Simmi picked out Shiva and Ganesh as long-lost friends. Friends of friends, she said. And, 'How come you've got such a big Buddha?' In Dharma speak, size doesn't matter. But Dirk and Bev didn't want the fat man sat alongside the mother-of-pearl stash boxes like he was some kind of mantelpiece filler. So he was speaker-stand filler swinging from the rafters, glaring down on us all. Reminding us. Big wisdom from east. Big madness from west. Bev bought up the signs of this philosophy like they were just that, road signs showing us the way to go on. Between the summer and winter solstices she wended her way through England's earthy festivals like some demented islander, round and round in circles, picking up signs of hope for to hang on the living-room walls. Worse than that she'd recently covered the windows in maps of Britain, the fifty-second state, coloured in with the stars and stripes of America – the Demon Reagan, as an emperor, sat on the toilet in Ireland, burning bodies on a toasting fork. Dirk was angry about that. The windows, I mean. The neighbours. Weren't rainbows bad enough, he said.

After I'd introduced Simmi, Dirk took the cue to play some Indian music. It twanged in the background like hopelessness, like it was homesick, disorientated. Competing with the twanging was a jingling sound coming from a man in sarong and headband. He was recently home, confused, suffering a serious dose of *gone native*. Simmi was confused too. It was paining her face, trying to sort out all the religions.

'Have you got a statue of Mohammed?' I said to Dirk.

I fluttered my eyelashes a bit and gave him a secret smirk. This was how we had our fun. At Bev's expense, I might add. Me and Dirk were on the same wavelength. We picked up the vibes as they happened. Bev only understood vibes afterwards, after she'd had a think about them. That's like listening to the news instead of being there watching it happen. I think she could only be in one person's head at a time. Dirk smiled back at me, uncorking a bottle of wine, his eyes tearing straight into me. I'd begun to fantasise about him. Squidgy masturbation was worth the mess, I realised, for a good fantasy. That's all he ever would be, a fantasy, and that made the masturbation more productive. When I tried to fantasise about Roy, nothing happened. Just an achy finger. A bed wet with spit.

'Simmi's a Muslim,' I said. 'I'm sure she'd like to see a Mohammed if you've got one.'

I looked around for a possible contender.

'Mohammed doesn't have statues,' said Simmi, looking about, making sure, just in case. 'Mohammed doesn't have a face. Nor Allah.'

'We don't think God's got a face either,' said Dirk, trying to keep up with the latest, no doubt.

'Could have fooled me,' I said.

'What's all this then?' said Simmi, her arms in the air like Jesus.

'Come here,' said Dirk, taking her by the arm. 'Come over here a minute.'

He took her to a framed embroidery on the wall by the door, more like a mini-tapestry. Yet another present from a friend in jail.

RIDING RAINBOWS

Each line of the poem was written along each colour band of the rainbow, the last line on to the landscape, a hillside. Would have got shut of six months bang-up, easy. As Dirk read it off, he looked back at Simmi's face, every other line, smitten.

Over the Arc I ride
On water slides of colour
I leave the sun behind
Tis the wind that gives me power
To ride to the end of the rainbow
And follow the Arc beneath
To circle the rivers, the rocks and the earth
To stand on my own two feet

'Everyone has an aura, Simmi. All different colours. Like the rainbow.'

He put his arm round her shoulders and turned to face me, like he owned her, like it was her turn for some . . . I was rolling a spliff sat at the kitchen table.

'We believe that God's face is nature,' he said, smiling his cheeks at her, ready to take hold of *her* face. As though her face was something he could pick off a tree.

Simmi was trying to get away. He was too close, far too close.

When we arrived, Simmi took to the stairs with one idea – to get the night over and done with. I prayed the stair carpet was fixed. She was too mad to be warned about it. It was fine, tight to the top. When Simmi got sight of all the candlelight, her tenseness from the car disappeared. Her lips nearly smiled. Stood at her side, watching this transformation, I was a messenger from the gods, because that look on her face was as if she'd been transported, taken out of herself and yet caught unawares – as if she were feeling the charm of the fun-fair for the very first time. The glory of it all shone across her face and made her forget. She spun about on excited feet agog at the gallery of curiosities. When the sitar began to wail, I noticed her shoulder blades widen, her body open up. The perfume from newly lit joss sticks acted as a potion, calming, it sealed up the last gaps to the outside world. She behaved and was treated like an Eastern deity but was all the more honoured, since she was alive and kicking. If I'd asked God to architect an environment that she could feel restful in, that made her feel welcome, this was it. And there was Dirk, right on her, in her face, still holding her arm. Her shoulders went narrow again – in on themselves. And then he picked up the vibe. I saw it travel from her to him, his sheepish grin narrowing now. Her aura was smacking him right between the eyeballs. He hooded them in embarrassment. Caught out. Caught out trying to get too close. Most girls would have put up with it, out of sheer politeness. Not Simmi. She was good at knocking out vibes.

Anyone else, I'd have worried. Worried about what Dirk and Bev thought. Whether they thought my friend cool enough, intelligent enough, entertaining. With Simmi, the other way round. She had power. She didn't use it as black art, for gain or influence. She used it to keep hold of herself, her direction. I was worried Dirk and Bev weren't good enough for *her*.

The man in the sarong jingled into the kitchen for a glass of water. Bev poured him one and he jingled back out again.

'He's a bit confused,' she said to Simmi, with her nose scrunched up in pity.

Simmi held her stomach and covered her mouth. And then we all laughed. Simmi laughed. She was relaxed again. It was all going to be all right. Saved by jingle bells.

The guests. There was a man called Julian. A lecturer in operational research. Probably end up teaching me for a term, he said. After a brief description of what operational research was, I made a mental note to change my options at the earliest opportunity. Nothing against Julian at all, but he didn't sell his subject terribly well. There was a woman called Bernie who drove buses for a living and had done for fifteen years. She took over from her mum who drove them during the war. She was skeletal, tiny. She had a special contraption for putting on the driver's seat to reach the pedals, she said. Her mum made it for her. Her mum drove her on to those buses. She was interested in astronomy and was toying with the idea of college. When I pointed out there wasn't much call for astronomers in Brimmington, she said so what? I began to explain but she was talking to Simmi by then. I twiddled my thumbs. Jingle bells twiddled his. More deliberately than me, I thought. If I started on him, he'd start. I'd get verbal holiday shots from India. With passion. I left him rocking to the sitar and busied myself with the roll of spliff. A couple, recently returned from Morocco, never turned up. The dinner party was for them, actually, but they weren't to know. Bev wanted to chummy up to them since they'd brought back a parcel and, being first in line, the potential profits could have been enormous. So really it was a business dinner that never quite came off. Dirk told me all this when he called me out on to the landing.

'They've gone to London. I knew they would,' he said. 'Bev thinks she can run their fucking business for 'em now. They wouldn't split the load besides a bit o' tops, which is for me, so all I managed to get was some oil. How yer fixed for some o' that?'

'What d'yer mean, Dirk, oil?'

'Hash oil.'

'What do you do with that then?'

'Well, you can slither it down a fag, cook with it. Whatever you like. It's good. It's *very* good.'

'How do they do that then? Make oil.'

'It comes from making the hash. After the weed's been pressed.'

'Mmm . . . how much?'

'On the street it'll go for a tenner a gram. I'll do you 14 grams, for a hundred quid. If you clear that lot you can have some more.'

'Dirk, I need to score. I don't wanna be faffing about with a fucking hundred quids' worth of *what*? When are you gonna score? Properly, I mean.'

'Fuck knows.'

He took my wrist and squeezed it, a grip, a hold, almost as if he were my doctor imparting bad news, as if he were trying to help me out on some journey. Or maybe he was just confirming we were still close, still good mates. I figured that last idea. He thought he'd come across more sincere if he stood close, touched. Like he did with Simmi. He didn't fool me with his insecurities. Having to cling on all the time. I pulled my hand away from him and stood back.

'This is all we've got,' he said, trying to read me, trying to suss if I was away about him or just his oil. 'Take it or leave it. Anyway, have a go first, before yer start knockin' it. Bev made a cake with it – well, it's more like a biscuit really.'

'For after dinner?' I asked, fiddling with my hair, thinking of the After Eights.

'No. It's the starter. You'll feel it come on, in an hour or so.'

Bev presented her creation at the table with some majesty and we all laughed and clapped. On the plate, there was a huge gingerbread man without ginger, she said, and no face. She didn't have time to do a proper face. I saw her shrink back in her chair after she said that. Dirk saw her too. No one else did.

'Simmi, I wouldn't if I were you.'

She was just about to take a huge bite out of its leg. We were all sat in the kitchen, listening to Steve Miller now, each of us with a limb on our plates. Dirk with a head. Bev with his chest. A crumble of a tummy still on the baking sheet. Jingle bells offered his leg back up to Bev, holding it like a priest would a host.

'Why not?' said Simmi, taking the bite.

'Coz you're driving, soft arse. You don't know how bad you're gonna get.'

'Oh I see. I'm back to being a bloody taxi again, am I?'

'I didn't mean it like that. You know what I mean.'

'Well, I'm eating it.'

'OK. Don't say I didn't warn you.'

'You can get a cab,' said Dirk.

I frowned.

'Don't be such a miserable cow,' said Bev.

'I'm not, it's just . . . well, her boyfriend Mo, he's a bit . . .'

'Leave Mo out of it, would yer?' said Simmi, taking control. 'I don't tell you how to go on with Roy, do I?'

'Roy?' said Bev. 'Roy the plumber?'

'Her boyfriend,' said Simmi. 'Hasn't she told you?'

131

I got mad then but I didn't show it. I didn't want Bev to know about Roy coz I didn't want to lie, to say we were fucking when we weren't. But I calmed myself. I was grown-up. We were all grown-ups together and grown-ups don't talk about fucking their boyfriends like kids do.

'You kept that quiet, didn't yer?' said Bev.

'Well quiet,' said Dirk.

'She keeps him locked up in a cupboard, don't you, Viv? Gets him out for bedtime. That's the only time we ever see him.'

'That's probably all he's good for,' said Dirk. 'And I have to say, I'm surprised at that.'

Sneering, he was. Didn't look at me when he said it. Who gave him the right to wade on in and slag off my boyfriend?

'What's it to you?' I said, with a snarl in my voice but staring straight at him.

He cowered at the sight of me. He bit his lip and sucked it in, keeping something back from me. As if he wanted to tell me something but knew he mustn't. Not there anyway.

'Nothin,' he said.

'I didn't think women approved of sex objects', said the operational researcher, thinking he was funny, trying to lighten up the mood.

And then the whole fucking table looked at me, laughing, and in their heads they were imagining what it would be like to screw me. Me with the face. They were nudging each other at the elbow, like I was some snotty twelve-year-old lad who'd just learned how to wank (I had) and been found out. The operational researcher gave me one of those Well-there's-someone-for-everyone looks, his head tilted to one side and then back to his lasagne. He was feeling jolly proud of himself, I could see. Proud of being part of a society that even now, in the age of glitz and glamour, lets ugly gits like me get laid. And the sad fact was, I wasn't getting laid. Never had been laid.

Of a sudden, just then, it happened. The whole idea of it. Getting laid. Dirk screwing me from the other side of the table, tearing into a bread roll like he was peeling my skin back. Opening me up. The whole idea of it was physically repugnant to me. I knew then, just then, that I didn't want my body to couple. The suffocating, slurping – the soggy sweaty breath of it all. I would keep my happiness to myself and ride on essence, not give myself up to a body that wanted me. For who would want me? Someone that would want my mind. Someone who could see through my mask. They'd fall in love with my mind, the only pure part of me, and then fuck it. No way.

I shifted about in hot temper, harassed, uncomfortable. Lost, really. And I refused to smile back. I gave them the vibe to leave off. I pulled my hair out of its pony-tail and let it cover my scar. I used the hair to wipe a few tears that broke loose. Truth was, I was quite stoned before the biscuit took hold and when they did that, took the piss out of me having sex, I went in on myself. Normally I can look out. But there was wind in my ears, conch-shell wind. And their faces poured into me, through a fish-eye lens.

Simmi was unconcious three hours later. And heavy. She wasn't going anywhere.

Conked out with her gob wide open, spread-eagled on Bev's couch – that picture had me laughing in Mo's face when I turned up without her. He wiped his nose with the back of his hand. Like he wasn't sure which expression to give out. He thought the worst, obviously. He'd been waiting up to apologise to her. His dick must have had a word with him.

The next morning I woke late with a head-banger, having drunk wine on the stonedness. Daylight appeared as a warlord at the window, smashing his way in. It was Saturday. Hector had come round with some info for my essays. He was waiting in the lounge whilst I acclimatised myself to being vertical. Out in the street, an engine had been running for ages, irritating me. I coughed. I'm a Pavlov woofer for running engines. I found my sunglasses and looked out the window. A post office parcel van. The post office man was sat on a wall yapping to a woman across the street. She still had her dressing gown on. I thought that a bit rum of her, as Simmi would say and there was Simmi now, parking her car. She locked the car and walked away from it wistfully, like she'd left part of herself inside it. It was easy to see the dread in her face. She always seemed to be trapped, Simmi.

The postman and the woman stopped their face-to-face banter to follow her. He shook his head. The dressing gown tightened her cord. Simmi rang the bell. I ran down to answer it and Hector came out the front room, briefcased. He was imitating his dad, I could tell. When Simmi saw him she lifted her eyes to heaven. I laughed at her but she wasn't in the mood. She headed straight up for the bathroom. For to clean her panda-black eyes, I expect. I told Hector about the oil but he wasn't interested. He said students wanted lumps of stuff, not test tubes and straws.

'Would they like biscuits, d'yer think?'

'Oh yes!' his face all bright and chirpy.

'Don't get excited, Hector, I haven't made them yet.'

He hmmmphed. I took the papers and books from him, paid him and let him out. I hated giving him cash but I couldn't force him to take the oil. I was desperate for the info. The essay was well due. Before he left, he invited me to a party. I shook the books at him.

'Do you think I've got time to fucking party?'

He laughed.

It was a huge essay to pull off. Not a normal one. They called it an assessed essay. There were two of these assessed essays per year and they were supposed to be five times longer than the usual. The result could mean the difference between getting an honours degree or an ordinary one. No big sweat but I fancied honours. The brackets around the Hons made it look . . . well, serious, I suppose. Like royalty had a hand in it. (Hons.) I opened one of my books and the words flew off the page like missiles, hitting me straight in the eye, making me blink, making my eyes water. *Inflation, elasticity of demand, money supply, labour supply, depreciation.* I chose labour supply. Adam Smith says that wages follow the amount of work available so keep them down. Keep them down and make them think they're lucky. Arsehole. And then I heard an almighty thud. I twitched to hear more. Nothing.

I got a vial of the oil out and shook it like a chemistry teacher, a pen in my mouth. Then another thud and Simmi crying, I thought. I went on to the landing.

'Simmi,' I shouted.

Mo's door opened and he stuck his head round it.

'What d'yer want?' he said, the jailer.

'Simmi. I want Simmi,' I said.

'Well, she's busy', he said. 'What's that? What's that you've got there?'

I was trying to look round him but he distracted me.

'Oh it's oil,' I said. 'Hash oil. What's all that shouting and banging going on then?'

'Viv. Why don't you mind your own business for once?'

So there wasn't a lot I could do. I went back to my essay. Then the front door bell went. I was trying to get my head into a short-loan book entitled *Who Owns the Means of Production?*. The answer to that question was about four inches thick with no pictures of whoever it happened to be. I heard someone come out of Mo's room and then I heard it being locked. I jumped up, opened my door and saw Mo going down the stairs. I knocked on Vinnie's door and went in. He was asleep. His books all over the floor as usual. I knocked on Mo's door. No sound. Simmi wasn't talking. I heard Mo tell the visitor that he had nothing. There was nothing around. Mo wouldn't go for the oil. I knew that now. Do it in straws, Dirk said. Twat. I felt a bit ripped off somehow. I'd do a bit of work and go back round there. Get Bev to help me make some biscuits.

It all went quiet again. Music. I made coffee, tidied my drawers, counted how many pairs of socks I owned. Took a few plaits out – I was due for a re-plough. My work table was immaculate. Simmi and Mo must have made up. Silence. Work. Then the door bell went again and I did in the end ask Mo if he wanted the oil.

'What d'yer think I am?' he said. 'A fucking chemist?

As I suspected. Then I heard him locking his door and running down the stairs, top speed. Then Simmi screaming. She woke Vinnie up and me and Vinnie met on the landing in a panic. Simmi was locked in and Mo had gone out.

'I'll get something from the shed,' said Vinnie.

'Hang on there, Simmi. We're going to break the door down. Hang on.'

She went quiet. Vinnie came back with a long metal stick with a wooden handle. He put it between the jamb of the door and pushed.

'Give it 'ere,' I said, taking it off him.

I did the same, just beneath the point where the lock engaged, and then I threw my whole body into the force. Vinnie was shadowing me throughout, as if he were helping. I never said anything. Bugging me, he was. After a couple of goes I was through.

She was sat on the end of the bed. Head down. Snuffling.

'Vinnie, leave us, would yer?'

'Right,' he said. 'Shall I make a cup of tea?'

'D'yer wanna cup of tea, Simmi?'

Like we were kids, in the playground. *D'yer want a drink of water?* In soppy voices.

'No thanks.' Snuffle, snuffle. 'Have you got a spliff, Viv?'

Spliff, Viv! Spliff, Viv! 'Course I have, my dear. You wait there. No. On second thoughts. Come with me. Come into my room.'

I sat on the floor by my totem pole and rolled the spliff. I didn't look at her coz I don't like people looking at me when I'm crying, so when I leant over to pass her the spliff and saw the black grapes under her eye . . .

'You been doin' your homework or what? Look at the state of yer.'

'Give us it,' she said, waving for the spliff.

'Simmi, did he do that to you?'

'No, I did.'

'Jesus, Simmi.'

'Me dad . . .' She snuffled . . . 'Me dad does this to me mum.'

'Oh God, Simmi. I didn't realise.'

She dissolved. Her whole chest of complaint was brought up. I sat on the bed and put her head on my lap and rocked her.

'Jesus, Simmi. I didn't realise.'

After a few minutes, she quietened.

'Look,' I said. 'Let's get out of here. Let's go round to Bev's. She's good at this sort of thing. I need to go round anyway. Come on. Buck up. Wash yer face, get yer coat and let's go.'

She couldn't find her keys. I looked out of my window. Her car was gone.

'He's nicked yer car, Simmi.'

She didn't seem that bothered. I think she was glad he was far away.

'Come on. Let's go.'

I gave her my sunglasses.

I must say, walking round to Bev's, I felt great. We looked great. Kind of weird, Simmi with her sunglasses on, me all tuckered up in khaki pants and big black boots. People actually looked scared of us. Simmi walked with her head in her chest.

'Chin up, Simmi. Face the world. I do it all the time.'

She smiled then. Still kept her head down, though. I was the leader for once.

'You should report him,' said Bev.

'Yeah. That's what I said.'

'They don't do nothing for domestics,' said Simmi. 'Believe me. I know.'

'For the car then. They'd do him for the car.'

Simmi smiled. Then went all serious again.

'He knows I'll be at my lodgings. He'll come round and get me.'

'You can stay here,' said Bev. 'In fact, the bloke downstairs is moving out. You could move in here if you wanted to. I'll ask the landlady. I'm sure she won't mind.'

'No thanks,' said Simmi.

'Yes please!' said I, the idea a great idea.

Simmi looked worried then.

'Why not?' I said to Simmi.

'My brother wouldn't like it,' she said.

'Well *I'd* like it, if that's all right with you, Bev. Is it one bedroom or two?'

'Just the one. And yes. It's fine by me. The landlady'll be pleased not to have another junkie moving in. He never paid his rent for weeks, apparently. He's only going now, coz his mum's dead. Left him a load of money. He's going to London to jack it up. The landlady's cool. She's seen it all.'

'Simmi, you could stay with me whilst you get yourself sorted. We could find you a place later.'

'Can we go to France?' she said, like it was a completely new idea she'd just made up.

All that talk about France in the car had been a dream. She'd had no intention of getting some wind in her hair.

'I can't go home to Bradford like this. Can we go soon. Like tomorrow?'

'We can go Monday. When I've handed in me essay.'

'Stay here till then,' said Bev. 'Sleep on the couch like yer did last night.'

'Can I?' said Simmi. 'That's really kind.'

'She flitted a look at Ganesh, I noticed. And then off she went to the police station.

'I hope you're not grassing anyone up,' said Dirk, coming into the kitchen just after Simmi left.

We just smiled at him. That warpath woman smile that men can't read.

Chapter 12

The THC of cannabis, the bit that works, is absorbed by fat very rapidly, Bev told me. No chemistry – just directions, please, Bev. So the hash oil was mixed with the butter. The amount she suggested didn't seem like much and anyway, I wanted rid of the stuff. So I poured the lot in. Too much, as I later found out. Making hash biscuits was a lot more me than writing essays. I shaped the biscuits with a silver gingerbread-man cutter. Dirk watched telly throughout. He came in once to tell us to keep the noise down, wiped his finger round my mixing bowl and sucked it, right in front of me. Staring at me. I thanked him for the dinner party, for something to say, really. To make a noise. Silence seemed to follow him about these days.

He touched my shoulder and said, 'That's all right.'

He completely ignored Bev and I got the feeling that she thought he was being nice to me, because he pitied me, pitied my face. I also got the feeling that that wasn't the case. In actual fact, I knew it wasn't. I know pity. I look for this stuff. I can spot pity a mile off.

When the biscuit men came out of the oven, they were hard and green. Leaf green and burnt black at the edges. Their currant buttons down the front were like bullet holes and their faces how you'd expect them to look after being shot in the chest three times. They were scary. I called them the Madmen. I put them in a flour box that Rose gave me, clear plastic with a red lid on. It was full. So a carrier bag as well.

Looking into the box as if looking into a fish bowl, I asked Bev why they were so green.

'Why d'yer think?' she said.

And no, she wouldn't taste one. Said she had chores to do. Like me. Still with an essay to write.

Simmi came back from the police station and ate up all the scrapings. She didn't want to think about that eye of hers. It was sea blue now, as well as purple. This made the rest of her face look like an arty-farty black-and-white photo, like all the healthy brown had been sucked out of her, leaving just a darkness. Secretly, this amused me. The police were on the look-out for her car.

On my way home, I rang Hector. He said he'd be right round. Said the Madmen would make his party go with a bang. He wanted me to go and I really wanted to but . . . No. I had less than thirty-six hours to produce an essay that should have taken me six weeks.

When I got home and got down to it, I felt quite woozy. Stoned. The butter must have absorbed into my fingers. It was hard to concentrate on labour costs and innovative invest-ment. When Hector came for his party supplies, I didn't entertain him with his usual cup of tea. An in, out job. One pound fifty a limb, I told him to charge. And three quid for the torso.

'The head? And how much for the head?'

Fuck off, Hector.

I wanted to sleep but I couldn't. I had to get on. And there was Irish coming in with Vinnie. They looked pissed. Pissing it up in the afternoon now. After they came in, the door bell rang three times. It was like a fucking train station. I needed peace and quiet. When Irish knocked on my door I told him to fuck off and locked it. I felt bad after. I heard him go into Vinnie's room. The music got louder and I realised just how much shit I put Irish and Vinnie through when they were doing their studying. Which was most of the time. And never on a Saturday teatime like me.

I was exhausted. I convinced myself that, if I got my head down for just a couple of hours, then I'd wake up refreshed and with the help of lots of coffee, I'd be able to work through the night.

At eight minutes past eleven I awoke to see two uniformed policewomen stood at the end of my bed. One of them was holding the metal stick we'd used, to break Simmi out. I was confused for a sec.

The commotion through the house was fantastic. There were at least fifteen of them charging around. I was told to get off the bed and face the window with my arms up, just so all the neighbours could see me? I've no idea. I saw a dog in the garden sniffing, leading a policeman around, up a tree for a piss.

'Right. Turn round.'

It really did feel like a game.

I haven't got it. It isn't in me pocket.

'Name?'

'Full name, please.'

'Is this your room?'

'Does anyone share it with you?'

One stood asking the questions, the other one walked about lifting things up as she'd seen done in the detective films.

'We have reason to believe that you are involved in offences relating to the Dangerous Drugs Act . . . bla bla bla . . . is there anything, before we start, that you would like to draw our attention to that may be contrary to the Dangerous Drugs Act . . . bla bla bla . . .'

Then they proceeded to bomb the place. These people were crazy, in charge crazy. The only thing to do was to stay calm. See if it calmed them down a bit. It never. The calmer I was, the more mad they got. All the fear I'd ever had of them evaporated in the comedy. It felt like being raided by a bunch of badly bred schoolkids from a neighbouring school – without the fighting. Messing things up and looking for the treasure. The sane intelligent response to all this was to stay calm, polite and still. Set an example, if nothing else. This attitude completely threw them.

All the roaches they put into huge plastic bags. Each bag was signed three times by three different people. I was very awake. The bed was stripped and the blankets and quilts piled on to the landing with everyone else's. Every bank statement was looked at, every cheque book checked. The lampshades swung, the doors banged with draughts and wind and the policemen and women couldn't hear themselves think so they screamed at each other. And at us. The longer the search went on, the more frustrated they got. One of us had to be witness in each room they searched.

I was taken to the kitchen. On the way I noticed a plod in the bathroom with his hands in the toilet cistern. In the kitchen, all the drawers were lifted out of cupboards and left upturned on the floors. Cutlery was thrown in the sink. There was a man outside with rubber gloves on stuffing things up the drains. I certainly learnt a lot. Like where not to stash gear. All the kitchen cupboards were emptied one by one, and they treated the food as filth, making wretching noises and vomiting sounds, like kids. They picked up chillies like they were dog turds. When they opened a big long tin, an old Christmas cake tin, they got a full shaft of a draught of a Bombay duck. An old one. That put a lid on it.

'Fucking wog food. Smell it! It's fucking disgusting. How can you lot eat this crap?'

They took the bag of rice from under the sink and carried it upstairs. Were they mad? They emptied it in the bath and sifted through it with a stick. Looked like a stick.

One older policeman felt particularly peeved.

'Jesus. Trust me to get a wog's kitchen. I could catch somat in here. 'Ere, Jim, look at this.'

He was showing Jim a bag of frozen whitebait, a particular favourite with Vinnie who liked to dip their heads in chilli sauce. They looked at me as though I weren't human. Then it was the spice cupboard. That completely threw them. Every little jar.

'What's this?'

'What's that?'

'What d'yer use that for?'

'We could look them up in the cook book,' I said with a sarky grin.

'Why can't you lot eat proper food, eh? Look at these things, man, they're growing hairs.'

'They're ladies' fingers,' I said.

'Button it,' he snapped.

'I was only saying,' I said.

Then, the tea and coffee cupboard and there, in the cupboard, the Madmen. Green and evil-looking, staring out of the plastic box.

'Oh for fuck's sake, Mick. Look at these.'

He was showing them round to all the policemen, laughing and looking back at me like I was sick. I was crawling up the walls but they couldn't tell. If they'd taken the lid off . . . Then a policewoman took me back to my room. There were three men already in there, taking up the floorboards. Another policewoman tapped one of them on the shoulders.

'Can you leave us to it, lads?'

'Right. Sure,' said the men, turning to look at me on their way out – an empty professional glare.

The door closed behind them.

'We're going to have to strip-search you.'

'What?'

'Strip-search. You remove an item of clothing, one piece at a time, and hand it over to my colleague. She'll check it to see that you're not concealing anything, whilst you remove the next item. OK?'

'What?'

'You do understand English, don't you?'

'Well, yes, but . . . when would I . . . ?'

'Just do as you're told. Start with your jumper.'

Starting with my jumper, I felt very naughty. With a few words of sympathetic encouragement from my observers, I could well have fallen into the trap of trusting them and getting upset with myself, for bringing all this trouble, all this bother to the house. But they stood stony and slightly bored even. Like I was nothing to them. Like all this bother was no concern of theirs. I would do whatever I was told to do. I would do it because I was nothing. Not guilty or innocent. Just part of their job. I don't like being overlooked like that. Down to my bra and pants, I stopped.

'Bra,' said the one with the pad.

'There's nothing in my bra. I didn't know you were coming, remember?'

They stood absolutely still, rooted to their reason. I looked into their eyes, searching to see if they were enjoying themselves. I couldn't tell. Still stony-faced and staring straight at me, they waited for me to carry on stripping. When I was a kid, I used to get ambushed by the council-house gang. They used to make me strip, so they could see my scars.

These policewomen were just doing their job. Glad they didn't have a body like mine, face like mine. But they knew I wasn't concealing anything. Just as sure as I knew I wouldn't let them get to me. That they could do what they were doing was something they took for granted and I took for bloody cheek. I knew what they really wanted. The thrill of the kill. There were no drugs so what else could it have been? I handed the policewoman my knickers and she told me to drop them on the floor. She wasn't going to soil her hands. I stood with arms folded under my breasts so that my nipples torpedoed them with loads of don't-give-a-fuck and they hated it. They never got what they wanted and there was nowhere for them to go now. There was no thrill, no kill. I'd removed the police and reduced them to women. Just women. They got flustered then, getting their little forms and their pens sorted out.

'Get dressed,' one of them said, shoving the pile of clothes towards me.

'Do I need to sign something?' I said, making no attempt to cover myself.

'Get dressed,' she said again, walking past me, looking down on me and then out of the door, leaving the younger policewoman to battle with the shame.

God, they were easy. When I had to sign her form, I moved right up close to her, still topless, so that she was smothered in embarrassment. She scarpered then.

Half of the floorboards still hadn't been lifted and checked but they were too bored and tired to carry on. They gave up. Their total find consisted of two hash pipes from the lounge and bags and bags of roaches from all over the house.

'Sign here, please. Roach in ashtray in bathroom.'

And scales. They found the scales under the sink but there weren't any weights. Couldn't find them. Bugged them.

'Where are the weights?'

'You're getting warmer . . . no, cooler . . . no, warmer.'

Four hours, they were with us. When they left, they didn't even close the doors behind them. The front door was swung back on itself, the light from the hall shafting the pavement. After Mo, after Simmi, after that, everything felt so very very *after*.

Vinnie made us all a cup of tea. Irish rolled a joint. We were all gagging for a smoke. My knees jumped and jerked as I waited for the spliff. There was no room to elbow-pose on the table because it was full of kitchen innards, from cupboards, drawers, boxes of domestic juices. Across the chaos, the sombre faces of Vinnie and Irish practised twitchy smiles, in response to one small joke after another. I felt guilty. I was waiting for one of them to suss this and then ride across my guilt with the whip of it. But they never. I was shaking too much, I suppose. I put some papers together and beckoned to Irish for his blim. Vinnie took it off him. He got up and came over to me, knelt down and put his face close to mine. He took one of my hands and squeezed it. I squeezed it back again. For to hold on, I suppose. I needed something, someone, to hold on to. And as I say, I felt guilty. He pressed the blim into my hand, got up and went back to his seat. Irish watched it all thinking Vinnie and me were having a private party. The silence was comfortable, like balm.

I figured Mo the grass. It felt right. Then I realised that that was my first thought anyway. The moment I'd set my eyes on the wake-me-up policewomen. In my dream I'd seen Mo or someone like him, sailing down a river in a canoe, dressed up like a Michelin man. I was in the water naked, wailing and waving at him to help me. Then I woke up.

At seven o'clock Sunday morning, I sat down to write my essay amidst the rubble of my room.

At eleven o'clock Sunday morning the front door slammed and we were all summoned to the lounge, by the Dubliner. The landlord.

'Where's da Paki one?'

'He's Afghani and he's not in. We were wondering the same thing ourselves.'

'Well, perhaps you'd like to pass on a little message to him then. You's to be out of this house in one week. If you're not out, I'll throw yers out.'

'You can't do that,' said Vinnie, in his best English accent.

'Errh, Mr Brophy, if I could just have a word wi' yer?' said Irish, trying to pull race. It worked for getting us into the place, perhaps . . .

'There's no need, my man. I've made up ma mind and yous are to be out by the end o' the week, the lotta yer.'

'But you can't,' repeated Vinnie, who still hadn't got over the bust properly, his eyes clogged up with sleep, red, as if he'd been crying.

He wouldn't be smiling his way out of this one. I felt guilty. I at least had a place to go to.

'Oh, I can't, can't I? And who's, which of yous is going ta stop me? You!' he said, pointing at Vinnie.

Vinnie looked smaller than ever then and he turned to Irish for help, to get him to do or say something. Irish, in a T-shirt, muscles bulging, moved closer to the Dubliner.

'Back off there, young man. There's nuttin' you can do so be good and start packin', will yer? I was mighty upset to find out I'd rented my house to a bunch o' drug dealers. If there's one thing I can't be doin' with, it's teevin' little drug dealers. D'yer hear me?'

'But they never found anythin.'

'Oh so it's all a mystery to yer, is it? A big mistake? Well, save yer stinking breath coz I'll not be needing it. So pack yer tings and be gone. And don't expect yer deposits. Yer deposits won't cover what yer've put me through, I'll tell yer that for nuttin.'

Poor Vinnie.

The Dubliner went out of the room and into the kitchen. Then carried on screaming.

'And yer can clear this shit up an' all, yer bunch o' feckin' hoodlums, yer.'

Then he was gone. Front door slammed shut. Through the hole in the glass, I saw him walk the long path with his head down, his hands in his mac pockets. He looked disappointed. I almost felt sorry for him. At the gate he looked back at the house. Like the house was everything he'd worked for and we'd ruined it all for him. And then I saw Roy. He was carrying a plant, quite a tall plant. The Dubliner was still at the gate and Roy, stood next to him, was indicating he wanted to get past which brought the Dubliner to his senses. Roy had his spangly coat on and he must have just washed his hair coz it was thin and flying about all over the place in the wind. The Dubliner took one look at him, his plant and his bracelets, and started laying in to him. He grabbed the plant by the pot, pulling it from Roy's arms, but Roy resisted. It looked like a show. The Dubliner wasn't giving up, though. He was going to have that plant, there was no two ways, and as this registered, Roy gave up the struggle. The Dubliner flew backwards into the hedge, the plant and its soil all over him. Roy walked up the path, looking back in astonishment. I felt really sorry for the Dubliner then.

'Who's that mad bastard?' as I let him in, helping him to brush soil from the spangles.

'The landlord.'

'He thought I was bringing drugs in. Said he was gonna get the law on to me so I let him have it. It was your birthday present, actually.'

''Snot till next week, me birthday.'

'But yer won't be here then, will yer?'

'Won't I?'

'Yer said you were going to Paris.'

'We got busted last night.'

He covered his mouth.

'And . . . ?'

'And nothing. Let's get some coffee and go upstairs. I'll fill you in.'

'Yer know, I always thought there was something funny about him.'

We lay on the bed together, me on my back, him pressed up against the wall like an ironing board, rolling a spliff.

'In what way?'

'Just a bit shifty, that's all.'

'Now you say.'

'No. I can tell with people. If they're not on the level. First off they think you're not on the level. They come at things from the wrong angle then . . . it doesn't feel natural. Doesn't flow.'

'Is he like that with you?'

'Yeah. He thinks I'm stupid. Coz of my clothes. And my bag. And coz I won't sit with his cronies in the lounge talking shit. He's always holding something back . . . there's never that feeling he's just riding along with the tide. Always trying to get something on me or off me. Do you know what I mean?'

'What was the plant, Roy, my birthday plant?'

'Adam's Needle. It's a type of yucca. I figured it'd look good in here. Next to your totem there. Jesus, Viv. Imagine if they'd got you. Have you thought about that? What it'd be like. They hate goin' away empty-handed. They'll be ready to have a right pop at yer now. Do you . . .'

'Don't, Roy. Not now.'

He leant his head over towards me. He touched my cheek softly, my good cheek, and then kissed me. Full on the lips, for about six seconds, his lip in between my lips. A proper kiss. I opened my eyes, so I could see it. His eyes were closed. His blond lashes were batting up and down in a fury. He looked a bit sissy to be honest so I closed my eyes quick in case he caught me. The image of Siamese twins joined at the head flitted through my mind. That's what it felt like. It felt like I was stuck to him. I pulled away. Tried to make light of it.

'I wonder if he's taken it down to the cop shop,' I said, really

148

cool. 'The plant? The Dubliner? They'll think he's a right dickhead. They could give it to Mo. Keep him company while he stews in his cell. I hope they keep him in for the whole weekend.'

'I'm glad you're going to Paris,' he said.

I was not glad. I wanted to stay now. And I didn't want him to be glad either. Was he glad coz he didn't like kissing me? I looked him in the eye and there was a want there. He did it again. Kissed me. This time I put my back into it. I grabbed his arm and pulled myself up to him, like I was getting ready to eat him. He pulled away. Shit!

'Shall we get into bed?' he said.

'No,' I said, too quickly.

'Is something wrong?'

'No,' I said, my eyes filling up for no reason whatsoever.

Well, there was a reason. I'd changed my mind again. Perhaps I did need to be fucked after all, to feel the full force of me, the whole of me. Perhaps then, I'd feel all in one piece.

'Shall we wait a while?' he said, stroking me.

I nodded involuntarily.

'Let's wait till you get back from France. We'll find you a new place and make it right. My place isn't right for us, is it?'

I nodded again.

'Then we can get stuck in, eh? You've got work to do now, haven't you?'

My big chance. My big chance of a real boyfriend and I was fucking off to Paris. I wanted to ask how come he felt better. Had he suddenly been cured. Where were the fish? The shower of fishes? I figured, just the mention of his problem might bring it all back on again. Draw energy to it. Might just lose him the nerve.

'You need to get away from all this,' he said. 'Have a rest. Did you write and tell Divine you were coming?'

It took a few seconds for me to absorb this normal talk.

'You must be joking,' I said. 'She'd write back and tell me not to bother. She won't want me there. I've already found somewhere else to live, by the way. Bev's place. There's a flat going.'

'Is that such a good idea?'

'Why not?'

'Bit hot there, isn't it?'

I sat up and swung my legs round, my back towards him.

'Jesus, Roy. I'm hot.'

'I don't like that Dirk very much.'

'Why not? He's all right.'

I rubbed my eyes in sheer exhaustion.

'He thinks he's . . . oh, it doesn't matter. I guess it's coz he doesn't like me. Doesn't reckon me.'

I thought about that for a while and tried to count on one hand anyone that did like him. Then my head came together.

'Listen, Roy, you better go. I've got this essay to write. And I don't want the spliff, so take it with yer.'

'I thought I'd help you clean up.'

'No need. I'll be packing up tomorrow. And I'm getting my hair re-plaited. For fuck's sake. How am I gonna fit it all in? Tell Elsa I'll be round about ten, will ya. And how's little Shula?'

'Coming on in leaps and bounds, as they say, bounding down the stairs, that is. What time are you coming?'

''Bout ten.'

'Well, when I get out of me pit, I'll come up and keep you company. Keep the kid off yer.'

'Brilliant. Sounds like I'll need yer. See ya later then.'

'Right.'

'You look pissed off.'

'I was gonna borrow my mate's van and take you up to Siren's Cliffs. For your birthday. D'yer know it? Over near the borders. I've got some acid.'

'There's no way I'm taking acid . . . with you . . . on a cliff. But get the van anyway. That'll come in handy – for the move!'

'Fuck off. Get Dirk to move you.'

I raised my eyebrows to him.

'You don't like Dirk at all, do you?'

He kissed me again. A few short smackers, like he normally does. As he walked to the door, I stared at his bum and wondered whether it'd be hairy. In the split, I mean.

Then Vinnie knocked on my door.

'Vinnie, I've got work to do. I can't talk.'

He came in and closed the door behind him. Like he was planning on staying for a while.

'Did you hear what I just said?'

He went to the window, folded his arms and took a deep breath. Drumming up courage. I could have really done without this.

'Now,' he said. 'Now, don't you think it's time you put a stop to your activities and got on with your studies?'

'I am,' I said. 'Look at me.'

'I mean total. Not just one day a week. Look, if you need smoke, I'll buy you smoke, but I can't bear to watch you throw your life away like this. That Roy. He'll cause you nothing but trouble. It's all trouble, Vivian, and you know it. Please, now. Come to your senses.'

It was a speech he'd been rehearsing.

'To *your* senses, you mean. I'm not you, Vinnie. I'm not anything like you.'

'Irish and I are to take a flat together but if you like you and Simmi could come too. We'll look for a flat for the four of us.'

'I'm moving into Bev's.'

'Vivian, give up this nonsense.'

'Vinnie – fuck off . . . Vinnie, I'm sorry, all right?'

I looked up at him but he wouldn't catch my eye. Still staring down, stroking his chin.

'Me and Simmi are off to Paris in the next couple of days. I'll send you a postcard, eh?' my voice high-pitched, trying to make it all light.

That did it. He slammed the door behind him. Everything was cracked. Everything was after.

The next day Simmi came back in her car. Upset again. Mo was an illegal immigrant, it turned out. The Sweeney story was true, after all. At the more benign level, he was wanted for using false national insurance, and then on a more serious note, for conspiracy to sell firearms. We wouldn't be seeing Mo again. Served him right, I thought. Shouldn't have grassed us up. Simmi didn't think he deserved deportation. She said the Old Bill were just picking on him. That was her problem. Common sense for the common people didn't include her. She was of another world. So she sat supping coffee, snivelling guilt. I told her to think of her mother. To look in the mirror and think of her mother. She'd done the right thing.

I wrote home for some money . . . to top up the train fare to Paris . . . I hated doing it because they weren't well off, but neither was I after shelling out for a deposit on the new flat. Mentioning my birthday diluted the scrounging. Mum sent fifty quid and four pages of won't it be good when I leave college and get myself a proper job. Dad has got his very own oxygen tank. Latest model. Divine is doing very well for herself in Paris. Here's her new address. Mark Mum's words, Divine has set me a good example. She hopes I'm strong and Dad hopes that I'm being a good girl. I detest the idea of being a 'good girl'. How about 'happy girl'?

GOING TO JAIL

GOING TO LAW

Chapter 13

I felt quieter today. More like a lady. Every time I got my hanky out to dab my nose, I saw Ratface cringe. He thought I'd be the same dickhead that turned up yesterday. Thought he'd win on attitude. Government attitude. Law attitude. Posh attitude. My attitude, my style, my personality only served to lay bare my case, expose my nerve, my contempt and my conviction. We were not on the same side. Even if the court was dismantled, the nets lowered, the umpire called down, even then . . . me and Ratface were not on the same side. He was at the peak of all that is British. Only a few people make it that far. That kid in school. The one that can't do sport. Wears glasses. Gets his mum to pick him up and drop him off. Comes top. Bores the teachers rigid coz he knows everything and more. The kid no one wants to be. The kid that pays the price for being clever. Ratfaced is how they turn out. He looked up at me with a winning grin, the look you give a fly just before the swat. He swatted with his pen, holding the baggy sleeves of his gown up, so he could write with speed. I sucked my teeth. He heard, looked up and caught my smirk, hidden behind my handkerchief. My winning smirk. You think you're gonna win do yer, Ratface? Well, I'm going to show you just how wrong you can be! Dab. Dab.

Today there is nobody in the public gallery. The jury, though. A right crew. All tired and religious-looking. Some with pens and pencils out, making a day of it. Some sipping water which I could tell they didn't want. Cup o' tea? Just the job. No chance.

The only problem I had with Bodene was that she wanted to be a Ratface. She was batting for the right side on this occasion but how long would it be before she took the king's shilling?

How long would she hold out? Maybe the Crown wouldn't have her. Maybe she wasn't good enough and if she wasn't good enough for them, then she wasn't good enough for me. I'd like to see her CV, to be honest. See her form. For all I know, she might be planning to throw the game. Maybe she was taking the king's shilling after all? If I was to tell her that I was guilty and then insist on pleading not guilty, she'd refuse to represent me. But, if I tell her I'm not guilty with all the sincerity of a priest (and this is what I've done), she's allowed to tell me to lie, to instruct me to plead guilty, so the judge can get off for an early lunch and the crime figures look good. Until now, I wouldn't have believed such a malarkey went on. The only one who wants me to have my day in court is Ratface. And that's because he's so fucking arrogant, he thinks he's won. Bodene is so worried she's lost, she'd rather I declared. That way, she gets paid for doing nothing. As I said, the king's shilling. Ratface and me had more in common than I thought. Until being made to worm it, at the feet of the great and the good, I could never have had such a view. If you're bang to rights, you should get some rights, real rights . . . not be put up for sale in a marketplace of justice waiting to see if you're crime's worth getting dressed up for, whether anybody can be bothered to deal with you. *Get up. Stand up.*

By dragging everybody into their costumes, for a day, two days, or even three – for that I would pay dear if my gamble didn't pay off. As for the judge, caricatured to play his part to the letter, at least while the case was going on, I could thank my lucky stars that he was two centuries and a half removed from the truth. He wouldn't spot the truth if it rapped him on the napper. When he got round to sentencing, though, this detachment from reality would work against me. He'd be in his element. Sticking to the letter of the law, he'd perform his stunt of authority with such predictable accuracy . . . such dedicated precision, that already, I could see him . . . I could see him coughing before he wrote down the length of my sentence. Judge fucking Benkinson.

Mind, at least for today, I was getting my act together. I could play the vibes round the court. They didn't intimidate me any more. After all, I'd had a little dress rehearsal without the jury watching – the chorus. It was all beginning to make sense now. I was reminded of our school plays. Every year there'd be a production, sometimes Shakespeare, sometimes a Gilbert and Sullivan. I never actually took part in these things. Well, I wouldn't, would I? No parts for me, were there? Mrs James said my scar would be too distracting but I could help with the scenery if I wanted. Or wear a donkey's head. The early rehearsals were always done in school uniform. No costumes at all. No chorus either, just the main characters. The magistrates' courts are something like this. The early rehearsal procedures are so deadpan. The drama is completely excised in favour of process. Procedure goes so fast in magistrates' no one gets to finish a sentence, let alone a paragraph, and the clerk, he would liken himself to the executive director – he decides which characters perform in the main act and which don't. In our school rehearsals, this was true also. Mrs James was always besieged with would-be film stars . . . mainly because, the week before the performance, all afternoon lessons could be missed and, during evening rehearsals, the boys got to be in close contact with some of the most beautiful girls in the school. There was never a shortage of players. Mrs James's decisions about who was in and who was out were based on firstly talent, which there wasn't a lot of, and secondly previous. Only the first-years had a hope of being surprised.

In the magistrates', if the crime is small, petty, common, the criminal is dealt with much the way Mrs James dealt with her bit-part actors. She hardly recognised them. Indeed, the boys often used to swap parts without her noticing. The more meaty parts were monitored more closely, assessed for authenticity and then given a tick or a cross, depending. The more meaty parts in the magistrates' were dealt with much the way the bit parts were, from what I could see. It's just that the actors in the magistrates' never quite knew what play they were starring in and consequently weren't up to giving their best performance. The executive director could spot this and so gave them a cross.

Now that I'd made my Broadway, I was far more aware. I now knew how big the swell of evidence could get. I'd begun to understand the archaic language. The superfical conflicts were a ruse. I was now keyed into the play within the play. I knew how to get Ratface on the go. Me being myself, that was a no-no. Me believing that all this stuff was for real, well . . . he'd slaughtered me. It was time for me to be someone else. People do it all the time, don't they? Now it was my turn. My command performance. My royal gala.

When the police take the stand in court, all done up in their uniforms, they act like they're in charge. They come prancing in like they're doing the world a favour. Full of smiles and ready to bed themselves in for the day. They belong. They know the rules. They whoosh into court with a wind of responsibility and triumph. Up the steps like they're about to receive a medal. The WPC puts her hat on the side, since she's not about to get smacked round the head in the court-room. Her hair is shiny, clean and coming away from its bun in a feminine tease. Ratface gives her a grin to settle her in.

I'm surprised they do this. Let me listen to all the evidence laid against me. It means I can change my story to suit. It means I can pick my way out of the mess. The evidence is in her little pocket book.

'Could you open your pocket book to the date when you first met Vivian Jackson.'

She took the book out of her bag like a schoolgirl about to reveal the contents of a secret diary, the pages within the proof of her lust, of her life. The court was ready to hear it. They, like the school-kids, were eager for a story. Unlike the kids, the people of the court were not giving off false smiles, all the time inside their minds, ready for to pick up on an inaccuracy, a fantasy, an inconsistency. For here was an agent of the state, a pretty one too. Perhaps, though, perhaps she clung to the book too possessively to pull it off. Perhaps someone as young and as malleable as her didn't have the words to report the facts objectively. Perhaps she wasn't old enough to be in charge of a tiny little notebook, to put her name in the front cover and fill all the white space with biro sentences that would prove to the world she knew how to do her job properly. Mind, she wasn't the sort to bully a prisoner. Just one look at her told us that.

'WPC Henley, besides Exhibit C, did you find any other heroin or related paraphernalia on the person or premises of the defendant?'

'We found a used syringe in her dustbin.'

She said it like she'd been dying to say it.

'Did you find anything else in that dustbin? Anything of relevance to this courtroom?'

'No.'

'No? I think you must have a short memory, WPC Henley. Weren't there some photographs in the dustbin also?'

'I didn't think they were relevant.'

She was twitching a bit already. Unprepared, obviously. Thought she'd only be going through the motions at most. She thought she'd be in the staff canteen by now, catching up on her paperwork.

'You didn't think they were relevant. Could you describe the photographs to the jury, please.'

'They were pornographic photographs of young girls, poorly developed . . . the photos, I mean, Your Honour.'

Your Honour looked over his glasses and confirmed his understanding. He needed to be told. That was the funny thing.

'And do these photographs belong to the defendant?'

'No.'

'How do you know that?'

'Well, she's . . . well, we tested them for fingerprints. All the fingerprints on the photographs belonged to the previous tenant.'

'Did you test the syringe for fingerprints?'

'Yes.'

'And.'

'There weren't any.'

'Did you find *anything* else in the dustbin that belonged to the defendant?'

'No.'

'What did you find in the kitchen cupboards?'

'Nothing.'

'What? Nothing at all?'

'Completely empty.'

'Why was that, WPC Henley?'

Stone the crows. Bodene had done some work after all. Rooting about in dustbins, no less. No. Surely not. I looked at her nails. Definitely not. Only the police would stoop that low. Oops! Judge is getting jumpy.

'Mrs Bodene, is the examination of the contents of the defendant's kitchen cupboards absolutely necessary?'

'Your Honour, since my client is charged with intent to supply a class A drug, I am determined to establish, for the sake of the jury, that the evidence presented in court today, far from incriminating my client, actually and more substantially absolves her of the crime of which she is accused.'

'Yes, I know you're trying to do that, Mrs Bodene. That's your job. Just get on with it, would you!'

Bodene didn't seem particularly fazed by this rude interruption. I half expected her to sit down and sulk but instead, she got into the swim. Which gave me an idea.

'So, are you prepared to accept that the syringe found in the defendant's dustbin did not belong to the defendant but rather to the previous tenant who had, only a week earlier, moved out?'

'Well, it could have been his but . . .'

'Thank you. Let us move on to the defendant's custody arrangements. Did the defendant at any time during the period whilst she was in custody make any effort to make a complaint about the treatment meted out upon her?'

'No. She did not. No such treatment *was* meted out on her, that's why.'

Plod began to flick through the pages of her book, pretending she might come across something to discount this. No.

All done. Nothing in the little book about it. So. No complaints were made then, were there?

Ratface grinned. Bodene scribbled away on her pad. Cunningham read papers. The jury, I noticed, was bored. One of the women cocked her head to one side and gave me a little smile. She wasn't listening to the policewoman. I could tell that much. My screw was all ears. Maybe one day she'd be allowed to take centre stage and let rip. WPC Henley was in oratory mode now. Reading out of her book like it was a poetry reading. With that much conviction.

I should have been hanging on her every word but Mum and Dad's wedding anniversary was still crucifying me. He'd be alone for it. Dad. My two uncles would be there but Dad would want me there. Some colour. Some family colour. There was no way our Divine could make it. Right then, all our lives were wrapped up, mapped out and biroed into the pocket books of the police.

No press in the gallery today. A better show on in some other court, perhaps. Still loads of people writing everything down, though. You'd think they'd get a tape recorder in. Save them the bother. My dad says that once you start writing things down everything else gets forgotten. I didn't really get that. Until now. Bodene and Cunningham were comparing notes. Bodene chewed her pencil. She was just acting. There was nothing to think about, concentrate on. Nothing to focus on with a mind's eye for detail. We'd scraped the barrel already. The dustbins at least. I noticed, too, that the judge was open-chested to the WPC. Not like he'd been with me. He looked down on me. With me he closed his arms around his papers. For WPC, he pulled himself down, to get on the same level as her pocket book. To see it all from her angle. It was a foregone. Just a matter of time. People like me have to be dealt with.

I squidged up the torpedoed rocky in my pocket. I'd like to have dropped it there and then. Swallowed it, I mean. A waste, though. It would have to be stashed for later. Plugged, as they say. Later on, I'd smoke it on slow release. My torpedo would blur the edges of the prison days to follow, take the clatter off the gates for me. Take the vile out of the uniforms. Make the bed I would be sleeping on not real. I looked hard at the profile of my screw. She looked more like a traffic warden than a policewoman. People should know who they are before they don a uniform and become someone else.

I'd get a kicking for my face in prison, no doubt. I wouldn't blend in very well, I knew. The make-up would be a joke. They'd laugh. They'd stick my head in the slops. The idea of it. The fear of it. All of it mounted up in my brain as the pretty little policewoman gave the court the evidence to prove that I deserved everything that was coming to me. Dad, sitting down, clutching his stick, breathing hard. Breathless. Disgraced. Mum, sitting across the visiting table, crying at me. The wedding anniversary. I was the bruised fruit of their loom and here were the flies, buzzing away on the badness. Maybe that's why they call the Old Bill bluebottles.

Bodene wanted to have a look at that pocket book. She wasn't taking the plod's word for it. Hand it over. Hand it over. The book was passed round, pass the parcel, till it landed there in Bodene's hand. She flicked through the pages like the mother that would like to read the schoolgirl's diary. Bodene knows just how much a vivid imagination can upset the balance of things. Bodene knows that what one wants to happen isn't necessarily what should happen. Bodene knows that schoolgirls are notorious for not wanting to accept the state of affairs as they happen to be. She stops at the appropriate page.

'And can you tell me, WPC Henley, can you tell me why, if, as you have said, under oath, you wrote this incident up in your pocket book on the very night it happened, why is it in different ink to the notes you wrote earlier that day, but in the same ink as the notes that you wrote two days later? Can you see? Shall I show it to you?

'Oh I see, so you forgot. You *didn't* write it up at the time after all. It must have been later. Well, let's go over things again then, shall we?'

Bodene was spraying out fly killer. WPC hugged her hat, like it might shield her. Ratface, on rapid fire, wrote and wrote and I had the feeling he was writing up notes for some other case, for some other court, for some other life to ruin. I guessed he was the sort of bloke who'd sold *into* the system. He wasn't prosecuting for the Crown to pay off his mortgage, even I could see that. He would never save up for holidays or feel the financial pain of school fees. Here was a guy who'd had money enough to avoid all this. He could have become a yacht-maker or a tree surgeon. Anything he liked. Career prosecutors (and Ratface was most definitely one of those), they must, in usual circumstances, be bought off, be paid to think that they're doing society a favour. But here was a one-off. Here was a man who *believed* he was doing society a favour. A man who didn't need the money. What kind of bastard wants to prosecute the masses proving police fictions to secure his convictions? *Dieu et mon droit.*

GOING ON HOLIDAY

Chapter 14

Simmi said she felt funny wearing sunglasses when it wasn't sunny so I wore mine, to give her a bit of moral. I wore a hat too. Bev gave it to me. Big black rim of a hat. New plaits. Nose ring. I was slim as a pin in tight black jeans and raring to go. My scar was fading away.

Simmi packed white high-heels in case we went dancing, when we got there. Paris. In the spring. We had fifty quid each for a week's holiday. And she thought we'd be going *dancing*? When we started to hitch, she was all thumb and smiles. After forty minutes of sitting on a hard rucksack on a hard shoulder in a hard rain, she was all moan. Convinced no one would pick us up because we were black. I told her, if she carried on like that she could go home.

At last a car stopped.

'Dover?'

'Get in,' said the man.

Simmi bent down, ready to climb in.

'Dover?' I asked again.

'London, actually.'

'Simmi, get out.'

'But . . .'

'He's going to London.'

'Well, I can go to Dover, if you like.'

'That's a bit out of your way, isn't it?'

'I can go that way. No bother.'

The man saw women's bodies with voices.

Simmi was still climbing in. I had to drag her out by the hem of her coat.

'But he said . . .'

'Forget what he said. We're not going with him. He's a perv.'

The man drove off. Simmi took off her sunglasses to watch him, as though he were our last contact with civilisation. She'd rather have been in the car with him than on the kerb with me.

'Even though he was a perv?' I said.

'Yes,' she said.

'That pissed off, eh?'

'Yes,' she said. 'Don't ever drag me by the coat again.'

She wouldn't talk to me for an hour.

The lines across her forehead disappeared when we got a really lovely lorry driver, a jolly dad of a lorry driver with football stickers across his windscreen and a flask of stewed tea. When he gave Simmi a go on his CB, she was back in primary school on a day trip. That was the first time I'd seen her grin like that.

After two more lifts we arrived in the lorry park at Dover. There was a group of dads with their shirt-sleeves rolled up, fags hanging from their grins, all trying to squeeze some summer out of the sharp spring night. There were ships in the background, blocking out the vastness of the sea, making it look like a big puddle. The sun was yellow and weak, still undisturbed by the grey puffy clouds bouncing and rolling towards it. The wind blew the hair from the heads of the dads, revealing baldness. Sign city it was. 'Departure', 'Arrival', 'Passenger', 'Freight', 'Passport', 'Customs'. All happy-holiday stuff. Simmi, when she saw the group of men, wanted to go to the toilet.

'We haven't got time.' I said it like I was the teacher.

'I've got to, I'm dying.' She said it like she was the kid.

'Well, don't expect them to wait for you. They're not going to stand there all day.'

She smiled a wide manic smile, as if to say *God, this is exciting*! It wasn't. We marched off to the dads and stood a few feet away shouting our requirements, me pushing Simmi forward. She was the face and I was the voice. We were overcome with offers. I chose the safest-looking one, a small one with glasses and grey hair, a plaid shirt and a big watch. I whispered to Simmi and she pointed at him. He walked towards us. We might have been choosing a slave. Simmi shifted from one foot to the other, humming.

'Hello, girls. So you want to go to gay Paris, huh huh huh!'

Driving the lorry he made me think of the woman at the dinner party. The one that drove the buses. He sat on a cushion and worked the engine like a round-the-world yachtsman, sailing by his hissing gears, looking all about him, out of each window, bending forwards and sideways, turning his wheel through the wind of so much information. The engine pumped power and know-how, defying nature, a multi-ton machine being guided through narrow concourses and bollards that sat like party hats placed there by officials, who watched the whole game with some intensity and arms folded. There was so much weaving to do, ramps to negotiate, all with braking distances that were impossible. But the little man, swivelling round his cabin, heaved the monster through and brought it to rest in an iron cave of carbon monoxide. Engines roared as if cross about their containment. There were men jumping in and out of their cabs but we sat silent, waiting to be told what to do, where to go, when we'd be free to roam the decks.

Before our driver got out, he gave us vouchers for food and wine in the restaurant. Our first free meal. Simmi just nodded and took the vouchers off him. Like she'd paid for them. I thanked him double.

'The food's not that much cop, yer know. That's why I'm giving yer the vouchers. Don't get too excited, m'dear.'

'Better than being poked in the eye with a sharp stick,' I said.

Simmi flinched, all scared, like I was giving the man ideas.

Soon, we were in the boat proper, walking the carpeted decks, shiny and plastic, new-looking. Once on board, I felt captive. The passengers were fellow prisoners, mumbling and stumbling their way round the ship in shoals. This was the beginning of a disaster movie. We escaped from the prattle of the proles and went top deck to check out Vera's cliffs, over a spliff, of course. There was still a fair bit of blue left in the sky.

Wistful white dreams in puddle shapes hung like sadness over the top of the chalk. England stood still and unmovable. Like an oil painting behind glass. The cold air was like a cool glass of water on my skull, still tight with newly ploughed plaits. Wind-bathing, I was. The deck was a disappointment. No waves crashing over the side. Or men in dickie bows waiting to romance me. Or sun to beat me. I said a little prayer for the Elephant Man.

'Take your sunglasses off. Get some wind on yer face.'

'I wonder where he is now?' she said, not taking off her glasses.

I think she was crying.

'He might be on a boat,' I said. 'Like us. Or d'yer think they put 'em on planes, in handcuffs?'

'Planes,' she said. 'Out as fast as possible. What should I do with his stuff? What should I do? It feels bad doin' this. Nothin'. Goin' on holiday. I feel bad, Vivian.'

'Sell his stuff and forget about him.'

'It's not that easy.'

'Simple,' I said.

'Bit mean,' she said. 'He wasn't all bad. Wrong sometimes, maybe, but . . .'

'He was wrong, full stop.'

'No, but I let him, though, didn't I? I let him get that far. I was out of my depth. I guess I didn't want to be on my own. I'm not used to it.'

'You've got me now.'

'I know. I think you might be right. About forgetting.'

'Don't forget what you learned,' I said.

'Should'na nicked my car, should he?' she said, bucking up a bit.

'Shouldn't have beat yer up, yer mean. Get your head round it, Simmi. You grassed him up because he hit you, not because he nicked your car. Remember that. And after grassing me up, as far as I'm concerned, he got what was coming to him.'

'You always hated him. Didn't you?'

'I wish I'd believed him. His Sweeney story. I liked him for that. Shame his attitude was all to cock, eh?'

'Well. All over now.'

She took off her sunglasses and wiped her eyes. The tears were streaming. I think she was thinking about her mum, not him.

'Eh. Come on. We're on our holidays. Let's yell our good-byes to England.'

And we did. We let rip. A couple of passengers alongside tutted at us. We laughed.

On our way back down to the lower decks, a couple of charging boys stopped in their tracks to examine me. Head twist, the lot. I dived at them with my hands in the air, making monster noises. I did that for the Elephant Man.

We didn't have money to waste so I wandered around the ship looking at the sea through the windows. Boring. People queued for money. Perfume. Coffee. Anything. Queuing to relieve the boredom, I bet. I knew. A ship full of punters carrying shiny plastic carrier bags. Eventually I settled down on a semi-recliner to read *Cosmopolitan*. Simmi followed me. Everything I did she did. She read my *Cosmopolitan* after me. I slept or tried to. Woke up to see those horrid boys again, creeping up on me. I was supposed to play with them at that point. Take it all in my stride and do monster moves to entertain them. But I don't like horrid little boys. They were sniggering, doing ghost noises, trying to get me at it. I told them to fuck off and pulled my hat down over my eyes, like you see men do, posh old men sleeping in the sun.

I thought about the stupidity of sailing away from the first fuck of my life. I imagined, after a few more snogs, that I might fall in love with Roy. He was used to my scar now. I was used to his loony stories too. In fact I'd started telling a few of my own. Porkies, actually. I called them dreams. To keep up with him. To let him know I wasn't just some college kid, going through the motions. He said he liked my latest dream best of all.

'The world is a what?' he said.

'A petri dish. Those little dishes that they have in the science labs at school? For growing diseases on.'

'Yeahhh.'

'And we're the bacteria. The culture in need of a cure.'

'And how we gonna cure ourselves then?'

'We run off the edge of the dish and set up camp on the other side. The people on top won't know anything about it. They'll be so clogged up they won't notice that there's glass in between us.'

'So what good's that? Being on the other side?'

'Well, in the dream, the glass dish was like an eye, like a lens for to see through. Them on top used it as a bowl to fill up. So it all got clogged up. Serious consciousness needs wind and space. So the light can get in.'

'Who goes over the edge first?'

'Ah!' I said. 'Some people have always lived underneath. They're the weavers. The ones who chuck out the cosmic strings.'

'You've really thought about this then, eh?'

Laughing at me, he was. As though I didn't know what I was talking about.

'I mean strings of molecules from the elements.'

I had by now decided that for any theory to sound even half viable, it needed some science speak to give it a leg-up.

'We grab hold of our string and follow it. Most people can't find the string in all the confusion. If you grab hold of it, you can feel the vibration. The string guides us out of the confusion. We feel pulled towards nature, towards reality.'

'Wouldn't it make more sense if there was a hole in the glass? An aperture with laser-light strings shining through it, or across it even. Like on a guitar. We'd need some light or sound to recognise the strings.'

He was trying to steal my dream.

'But that takes us back to Polo mints, doesn't it? No. A hole is too vulnerable. Some bright spark would stick a door on it. Like a door to a temple. To the holy of holies. They'd try and seal it up. We have to have the guts to go over the edge. Not jump off it, like the nutters do. Go under it and hear the spirits buzzing. They're not spirits really. They're charges. Electric pulses moving really fast. The buzz is like the vibrating wings of a bumble bee. Well, in my dream it was. In my dream I could see the sparks firing signs to each other. The wind keeps the sparks alight, see. Fire is a gift as well as a curse. My dad told me that. So.'

'But surely if we all go off the edge and live underneath, there's a risk of the culture problem being mirrored – on the other side, I mean?'

'No. Matter doesn't matter there. It doesn't have any power until we give it power. The spirits that make the break from the material world already know how not to give matter power. That's how they get their freedom. That's the edge they have to go over. They need to have guts. When there are enough sparks, the energy will be strong enough to push the dish into a spin and turn it over. And the dish ran away with the spoon. Remember? We need lots of spirit to do that. Lots of fire, energy. Maybe it's like osmosis. Maybe first of all, we have to break through a membrane of global consciousness – to get to the other side. There must be a magnetism that eventually pulls us through.'

I knew the theory was too complicated but it got him going. Held his attention. Only someone clutching at straws would listen to my cosmic theories. That was Roy. However, I wanted him to clutch me, not my stories, my lies, my straws. I didn't give a toss about theory. I wanted practice.

'After the flip, the culture falls off the underside of the glass. In clumps. Because it's so heavy. And listen to this . . . I looked up the word for the heaviest element in the world. Coz it's all about matter, see. The heaviest element or matter is called osmium. The mother of all matter. I think that's the key. The elemental equivalent of the heavies – the people that are infected right to the core. We should call those people osmic. We're cosmic. They're osmic. They use osmium in electric lights, yer know. And pen nibs. Apparently this stuff really stinks when it's heated up, but more importantly it attacks membranes with venom. I think it's all connected. *Os* – wise . . . I looked up some os's in the encyclopaedia. There was osprey. That's a fish-eating eagle.'

'I know.'

'I thought you'd like that. And there's osier. A plant. Its leaves are used for basket weaving. It must be all connected, don't you think? The weaving and that? Then I wondered about the Latin – coz *os* is for bone, isn't it?'

'*Ostia* means hole or holes.'

'Does it? Well, there you go. Bones are full of holes, aren't they? And what about . . . what about . . . maybe it's to do with shape, yer know? Bones and holes. Rods and cones. Maybe inside the dish it's all to do with sex and underneath, it's all to do with seeing. I even thought . . . and I know this sounds stupid . . . you know, in Chinese whispers, how all the message gets fucked up, the more people repeat it, well, what if, instead of light being to do with enlightenment, what if it originally meant light and not heavy? It was just a thought.'

'No one'll go underneath if there's no sex there.'

'But there is. It's just not the bones and holes sort of sex. It's electric sex. It doesn't matter what the physical make-up is – it's just sex. But with foresight. Osmosis. Do you think there could be spiritual osmosis? You know. Consciousness osmosis?'

'Then those underneath would rise up to those in the dish. Like sap in the trees. There'd be no flipping, just a slow dawning.'

He was trying to steal my theory again. Trying to fit it into his own stuff. I wasn't having any of it.

'No. We need to get to the other side. After a spiritual exodus, the dish would flip and we'd be on top, living on the arc. We'd feel the wind up there for sure. It'd make the fire inside us roar. We'd only use fire for balance then. That's what we need, don't you think? Anyway, my mission statement is . . . we're doing mission statements at college . . . my mission statement is "Less osmic – more cosmic".'

'Good dream. Good dream.'

'D'yer reckon?'

'Yeah. Better than the one about the Polo mint. I like the culture bit. That works quite well.'

I tipped my hat up to take a look at my surrounding shipmates. To see if anyone was looking at me. Everyone was pretending to sleep. As you do.

Chapter 15

Sat in the cab, driving out of the boat into Calais, I felt like a stowaway. We'd spent next to nuppence and now we were in France. Mad. But Calais docks made me think we hadn't travelled far at all. We never spoke our disappointment to the driver. He was taking peas to Spain.

'Why? Don't they have peas in Spain?'

'Obviously not.'

'How long will it take you to get them there?'

'About two days, maybe a bit more. I've a couple of stops beforehand.'

'Fancy doin' that, eh? Spending two whole days taking peas to Spain. That's mad.'

I was staring straight ahead but I saw his head swing sideways to stare at me. He thought I was taking the piss. I had to tell him to keep his eyes on the road. I pointed at the juggernauts heading straight for us, looming up like monsters in a widescreen 3D movie. As though he'd planned his every move, he picked up his CB mike and rattled something off in code. Simmi looked at him and then at me, worried. She thought he was up to something. I touched her leg to relax her, and then snuggled back in my seat, ready for a varied foreign landscape that never materialised.

When he'd finished nattering, I asked, 'Is it all right if I get my head down, please?' pointing to his bed behind the seats.

'Aye, yer can that,' he said, glad to be left with shimmering Simmi. Shimmering to him. Sweaty really.

I asked her to wake me up in Paris – joking. Well, it was about time she did some work. Somehow, I'd turned into chief travel agent, her asking me the ETA, the weather, the exchange rate – I got to thinking I wasn't doing my job properly if I didn't know all the answers and now, heading along the motorway to Paris, I figured it was time to clock off. All she had to do was talk to the driver and stop making faces at me. I was glad to get her off my back and lie down on it. I never slept. I just wanted not to talk, not to make up conversation. After a few minutes, when the air had settled again, she turned round and thumped me a dead leg. I just laughed at her, rubbing my leg hard to make the pain go away. Then I must have slept coz when I woke up she was talking to some bloke on the radio – an Italian. Flirting with him. In that short space of time, she'd acquired a French accent.

The driver dropped us off at Gare du Nord, in the madness of all the traffic going home from work. The daylight was almost spent. I spotted the 'M' for the Métro station and we ran towards it, excited. Then I stopped.

'Shall we have a spliff before we get into the thick of it? I'll get the tube map out and we can decide exactly where we're gonna go.'

I needed a spliff before the confinement of the underground where people would stare at me, at us. Being stoned separated me from all that. When I'm stoned, I'm on a different playground, the rules are purely sensual. From there, I can watch people. The balance is redressed. They can't watch me because I'm stronger on the spliff. I see, hear, and think in concentration and the noise of all the input doesn't leave room for being watched, for being judged. I watch people and they fidget. My eyes are trained to take in their every thought, idea, their preoccupations with their oh so small lives. The readers are the worst. They're in another world. I can't get at them.

We found a shop doorway and put our bags on the ground. In the shop window there were baths and sinks with psychedelic patterns round the side. I didn't think they went in for baths in France. The road was jammed with cars and trucks, headlights coming on like early evening predators getting their torches out. There was absolutely nothing to say that this was France, except words. The picture was identical to England. Simmi was sulking, lip out, banging her back against the shop window, looking at my spliff, and you'd think we were down and out in Brimmington, she had such a gob on. I thought it was the disappointing landscape making her heavy but no.

'I wish we could go to Divine's tonight.'

'Well, we can't. The deal is three nights on our own, three nights at Divine's. You agreed.'

'Yeah, but we don't even know where to go, do we? We might be on the streets if we don't . . .'

'Simmi. Calm down. Don't panic. It's Paris. Not Hong Kong. We're a hop, skip and a jump away from a Marks and Spark's. There's nothing to panic about.'

'Well, I'd rather we got on with it than standing round doorways doing drugs.'

And then she was off, pulling my arm, knocking my half-made spliff into the air.

'You stupid cow . . . what d'yer think yer doing?'

A group of boys, near-men, were upon us. Not smiling. They'd come up quiet behind me. Simmi must have watched their every move and only realised they were after us when their trainers veered *en masse* at the very last moment. I turned round to see them all smiling, in a north, south, east, west arrangement of Queen's 'Bohemian Rhapsody'. One of them had a knife out. If I hadn't seen the knife I'd have shaken his hand. They were hee-hawing in French, talking really quickly. I picked up my bag and tried to run after Simmi, who was now halfway down the road. They caught me easily. North with the knife had me by the scruff. He was African black wearing a thick purple bandanna round his forehead, and in the centre of it, a red heart burned with flames of fire and drops of blood. Simmi managed to run across the road, a dual carriageway. She stood on the central reservation waving her arms about. The other three boys followed her, slowly, like they knew they'd get her eventually. No need to rush. North dragged me into the road, oblivious to the traffic. I felt my denim knees brushing against the car bumpers as I trailed behind him, led by my throat. The disorientation was fantastic, the foreign shouts, foreign cars. Foreign. Foreign. The cars queuing at the traffic lights edged forward, inch by inch. The boys ahead navigated between the bonnets and the bumpers, towards Simmi who had now climbed over the central reservation to get to the other side of the highway. She was spinning out, not understanding the direction of the traffic because ahead were major crossroads, and behind were major crossroads. It was, in fact, slap bang in the middle of a major crossroad.

I came to my senses a little because North, constantly shouting at his mates, arm around my neck, was treating me like a prisoner without a chance. I tried to elbow him in the stomach but he blocked me easily and took off my hat, laughing. I dared to turn my head round to look him straight in the eyes but he was laughing away from me, laughing at his mates getting stuck between bumpers in the road. Shouting. Waving my hat about in the air. Only strategy could help me now. With my rucksack and his knife, violence was out of the question.

'*Laissez-moi*, you fucking bastard,' and stuff like that, I screamed.

Stupidly, I wasn't scared of his knife. I didn't think he'd use it. Not with all those people around in the cars. The queued-up cars had gone through the green lights and now there was a new lot, waiting on the red. They must have seen us. *I* saw them. I saw drivers look at me and then turn away, no doubt put off by the gleaming blade, pricking my throat. I thought of men shaving. The drivers might have been witnessing a regular teatime execution. Edging closer, bonnet to bonnet, green light up and they were gone. I became a lot more worried then. When I realised there'd be no help.

I saw Simmi run over to a taxi and get in it. I couldn't fucking believe her. Where did she think she was going? Sat in the back of the cab, she patted the taxi driver on his shoulder and pointed at me, and then to the lads who were hovering just a few feet away. The taxi driver checked the plot and got out of his cab. He opened up the passenger door and started dragging Simmi out. Simmi wouldn't come. Simmi held on to her seat and kicked at his head. The knife was still at my neck but not pricking my skin any more. Looking down, I could just see the gleam of it resting on my collar. North pushed me forwards along the reservation to get parallel with Simmi's taxi. I still had my blim in my hand and so I held it up for him to see.

And then I did my monster thing. I swished my head right round so he got the full whack of me. His shock on seeing my face – his shock both gladdened and saddened me. He put my hat back on my head and put his hands in the air. He flicked his knife inwards. I was crying now. Tears of joy, in fact, but to him, sheer desperation. He smiled and I noticed he had two front teeth missing. I bit my piece of hash in half and offered it to him, like a biscuit to a dog. He was laughing now. Shaking his head. He couldn't have been more than sixteen. I pointed over to Simmi still fighting with the cabbie.

'*Laissez la femme – laissez la femme.*'

What could he do with us? We weren't fancy tourists, or women of the world. So no thrill. No kill. No easy conscience and no option but for peace. He called his dogs off and in seconds, they all walked backwards away from us, North walking amongst the traffic like an expert herdsman. Their eyes were on us all the way. Simmi was in tears at the foot of a lamp post. I ran across the road dodging the traffic to get to her.

'Come on, Simmi,' I said, like a mum, wiping her hair in hard strokes. 'Come on. They've gone now.'

She was howling. I looked round for a café or . . . and there were the boys again. Heading towards us. Walking quickly but breaking into a canter.

'Come on, Simmi. We've gotta go. They're coming back.'

We picked up our bags and ran.

We turned left at the crossroads and ran and ran, me pulling Simmi's arm all the way. She couldn't run as fast as me but knew she had to, knew she had to lift them legs higher, girl! Higher! Faster! This was sports-day running. A shock to the system. We ran past a hotel and I doubled back and dragged

Simmi into the doorway and then round the revolving doors. Just inside, a small Chinese man. The foyer looked like the entrance to a Chinese temple, all pearls and glass, columns and white carpets. The Chinese man caught us as we fell in, looked at us with some amusement and then promptly ejected us, pushing us back into the revolving machine, back out on to the streets. It was like being flung out of a space capsule.

The boys were coming down the road on each side, about a hundred yards away, combing the side streets for signs of us. We carried on running. We dodged down the side alley of a big department store and out on the other side, to another main road. Then we calmed our pace. I looked ahead and told Simmi to break into a run again. I saw a woman entering a house, up some steps. In appalling French, we asked her the way to a hostel.

We pointed behind us, whimpering, 'Les garçons! Les garçons!'

She could see we were terrified. I kept turning round, as if frightened they might come upon us any moment. Though I knew they wouldn't. The woman beckoned us into her house. By the time we sat down safe, I really was gagging for a spliff.

She was a schoolteacher and looked like one, long blonde hair with lots of facial expression. Miming with sound. She treated us as her little charges. She spoke good English but I didn't speak it back. I couldn't find the energy to want to. Simmi was bursting for it. I told her to button it till later. Wait till the woman went to bed. We had bread and jam and orange juice. The woman's breakfast, but she could see we needed it. She'd get more breakfast in the morning. I had a shower as a ruse for a spliff. Simmi just had the shower.

On the wall of the lounge, boxy but light, there were shelves dotted with white porcelain pieces, wheelbarrows and cats, mainly. The woman cleared the shelves and then unclasped the structure from the wall. The shelves pulled down to make a bed in the centre of the room. After settling, Simmi talked over the incident again and again and by the end, she was laughing, like a child, almost glad it happened. Almost. There was a flush about her, as if she'd broken through some barrier that might have been there, but had always eluded her. Real life, perhaps, life without the grille of the playpen. Her expressions were new. Her curiosity genuine. That was it. She was more humble.

'Can we go to Divine's tomorrow?' she said, weak and childlike, enough excitement for one holiday.

It was difficult getting my head round our Divine. She'd maimed me. For life. I was sentenced to the prison of the freak whilst she went off with her Oxford honours to live in Paris, and took life in her stride. How was I *supposed* to be with her? My mum and dad instilled in me, or tried to, a lifelong duty not to blame her in case she got a complex about it. I did love her, you know, she was family, wasn't she? I had to love her. But my top soil didn't speak words like love. The top of my brain didn't love her at all.

'No. We've been through this, Simmi.'

She sighed and settled down to sleep.

I couldn't sleep. I was in shock. Until then, shock was all a bit sissy to me. Suffering from shock? Well, lordy lordy. Life's full of shock. Shock to me was just a few notes down the pleasure scale of surprise. But that night I was introduced to the quiver of the difference. Shock isn't *a* shock. Shock is an unwelcome visitor in the deep seas of the mind. Reality is reconstituted as imagination without the discipline of fact behind it. It is a rogue fish in the lake of the brain. The Shockness monster comes to mind immediately. There must be a section of the brain that acts like a lock in a canal. When shock wants to visit, the lock is opened and the lake of the mind fills up to give passage to ideas that pour in, unrestricted, from all the tributaries of possibility. And shock got me that night. Over and over I thought of what might have happened, what did happen, what could have happened, what should have happened, what they might have done to me, what he did to me, what he wanted to do . . . over and over each scenario raised my pulse rate – beat a rhythm so cracked, turned my stomach and my body over and over in the bed. Simmi woke up and shouted at me. Told me to stop fidgeting. Why didn't I go and have a spliff in the bathroom? She was exhausted. Pack it in, she said. Pack it in.

I didn't suss that it was shock waves rolling me about because, like I said, I'd never understood that *a* shock is wholly different from Shock. So I never said anything to Simmi. I didn't complain because I didn't know what to complain of. To tell her that, all of a sudden, I'd come on a bit wimpy and couldn't stop thinking about what had happened . . . well, that sounded too sissy by half. I was sweating. Cold. Sick. But at what? There was nothing wrong with me. My whole body was perfectly intact. There is no focus in Shock.

After Divine did my face, I lay unconscious in a hospital bed for three days. When I came round, I was shocked but not in shock. My brain must have dealt with it before I woke up. Three days after that, I collared a boy. He hobbled into my room on crutches, just to look at me. I got him to bring me a mirror. Then I went into shock. I remember it now. But it wasn't reconstituted past shock, it was Dreading-what-was-to-come shock. It was re-imagining the faces of my best friends, Yvonne and Shirley. It was the snarled-up faces of the boys and the spits from the Bailey sisters when I walked past their street. All of them would stand on the corner and jeer at me. For weeks that shock swam round my brain. I stopped talking.

The French bed that pretended to be a shelf in the daytime took on the air of the sinister right then. As if it might be all arranged that we would be got at, that someone would arrive at any moment and lay claim to us. The woman, the strange woman that just took us in – in the morning she'd go out to buy some bread and jam and come home with the soldiers. She would give us up to the enemy with the ease of a Nazi sympathiser. And then I wished that I hadn't smoked that spliff in the bathroom after all.

In the morning we said our thank-yous and goodbyes like good little children, except Simmi meant hers and we went upon our way with a packed lunch of croissants, not finished at the breakfast table. I binned mine. Simmi looked at me.

'You have no sense of honour.'

I looked in the bin, confused.

'They're too dry.'

'It's food, isn't it? You should respect food,' she said.

'Oh go on. Give me a starving African. Get them back out the bin then, Gandhi.'

She was sullen. I wanted a happy day. I wanted to walk and dream and loll through St Michel. Be spotted for a model and find myself on the front of a French fashion magazine. That's how hard I wanted to dream, that first sunny morning in Paris. And here she was, with a gob on about frothy croissants.

'It's nothing to do with starving Africans. At home, we are taught to respect food, especially food that has been given to you at a time of need. It's holy.'

I ignored her. Told her all about jumping over barriers to ride the Métro for free. I'd done it in London. She loosened up a bit then. Nothing holy about jumping over ticket barriers. I pretended French when she spoke to me and, fed up with it all, she answered me in Punjabi. I said she wouldn't get far in France spouting Punjabi. She wouldn't get far snivelling round lamp posts either, I told her. That shut her up. I took turns on her. Geeing her up, to get her mad, then telling her something lovely, something interesting, to get her back on my side. I wanted to get her at it, because she was shitting herself now she was out of her pond.

When we got to the Notre Dame, Simmi asked me where the mosque might be.

'A French mosque?' I said. 'Are you mad, or what?'

'We've got mosques in Bradford.'

'What, with big domes and that?'

'You don't need a bloody big dome for a mosque.'

She said it in a mix of Yorkshire and Pakistani – 'bloody big dome'. When she talked about Muslim stuff, about clothes or her mum and dad, her accent chucked up with bits of Paki stuck round the edges, to authenticate the information, I guess.

184

Like she had to change skin and all. I don't think she knew who she was really.

'Well, I'm not going off looking for mosques, Simmi. If there aren't any in the guide books, they're obviously not up to much cop, are they?'

'Oh, I see, we come and see your church . . .'

'Precisely. Look at it. Boring as fuck, isn't it? Let's go and get a coffee. Sit by the Seine, eh?'

I couldn't see the Hunchback's bell tower. I wanted to look up at it and give off some bell vibes. Say a little prayer for him. And the Elephant Man. And I got to thinking that they could have met. In another life, maybe the three of us could meet up and give it licks on the bells. The bells. The bells. I said a prayer, but not a God prayer. A prayer to the fire god, it was. To the spirits.

Because of the crowded tiled floor that blocked off the space of the grandness, I couldn't take Notre Dame seriously.

'Nice windows, Simmi?'

'They're OK,' she said. 'Not bad.'

Like she'd seen loads. And loads better.

'Here look, there *is* a mosque,' showing me the guide book. 'And it's got a dome.' I raised my eyes to heaven.

In France we didn't look normal. We got looks. We weren't normal because of our black faces and knapsacks, because of my scar and plaits and Simmi's hennaed hands and sunglasses. We weren't fit for an anorak advert in a French camping magazine.

At the café, we took ringside seats, as close to the river as we could get, but we still couldn't see it from our tiny table. I fancied I could have the river flow past my feet and almost dip my toes in but there was a road between feet and river bank, and along with the morning smell of pâtisserie came the choke of exhaust. Cough. Although I couldn't see the real river, the artists sitting to the side of their easels, dreaming, had all done a pretty good job of their own.

Chapter 16

'Let's go to the Moulin Rouge, eh?'
  'Sex stuff?'
  'Yeah. I wanna see some prostitutes.'
  'What for?'
  'See what they look like.'
  'Slags.'
  'French slags, though.'
  'Yer sound like a fella.'
  ''Snot that. I just wanna see what they look like. It's s'posed
to be like Amsterdam, yer know, the women sitting in the
knack and hanging out the windows.'
  'They don't.'
  'They do! Bev told me.'
  'Come on then.'
  There wasn't a tube stop called the Moulin Rouge. Or one
for the Eiffel Tower which was even more stupid – not that we
wanted to go.
  'It'll be like Blackpool,' I said.
  Looked like Blackpool on the pictures anyway. Big metal
tower. Wow! When we came out of the Métro, what a
disappointment. We couldn't go asking people for the sex
places. It wasn't even midday. On the Boulevard de Clichy we
looked every which way for signs of debauchery and deca-
dence, but it all seemed normal. Till we got in deeper. Walked
in further. There. The debauchery was in the detail. The
women, up high, were indeed hanging out of windows, in
bras and pants and suspender belts. Like live caryatids. Some
wore corsets like that woman off *The Beverly Hillbillies*.
  'Freeze yer tits off in this weather, wouldn't it, eh?'
  'They don't look that bothered, though, do they?'

'They're out o' their minds, that's why. Who's gonna wanna screw at this hour o' the morning?'

'Him. Look at him there.'

We laughed.

The street was clogged up with a knowing silence. Like weather put on hold. The night could easily be imagined but the sun creamed the scene into a film set for us, props in place, shops ready to open, ready for action. Snap. Dildos and vibrators. Movies and Moulin models everywhere. Live and plastic. Coming to you. I wished we could've got rid of our haversacks, walked and ambled with our hands in our pockets, looking up and down the buildings with a swively head instead of having to make neck-breaking effort. Simmi got accosted by an old man with no leg and two sticks, hopping right after us . . .

'Let's go in here.'

A sex shop. Live sex shows.

'Is there a show on? Can we have a free look?'

The place was wallpapered with photographs of breasts and more, the more you looked. The man, behind his counter, was tidying up his filthy books and sex aids. Young man with blow-dried hair. He was rearranging the gift-boxed vibrators like a newsagent sorting out his Easter eggs.

'You want to see?' he said, flashing his eyes at Simmi.

'Yeah, we do,' I said.

'What? What would you like see?' Grinning.

'Sex. We want to see some live sex, please. For free, though. Yer not busy, are yer?'

'No. It is quiet. There is no live sex this morning but I'll let you have a look in here.'

He walked over to a little kiosk, bit like those you get your passport photos done in.

'Sit in here and I'll put machine on for you.'

We both budged in and sat down. The seat wasn't wide enough to get really comfortable. We felt really on holiday. Like on a ride. Then the pictures started flashing past. We sat engrossed at first, but each picture got progressively worse, more bloody-looking, pink and squelchy, and the positions of

the women . . . and the animals . . . you know the sort of
thing. It all got really sick. I couldn't watch. I kept hiding my
eyes, a kid watching a horror movie. Simmi lasted longer than
me, and then she gave out a warning of rising vomit. I fell out
of the machine laughing, tripping up and falling over myself,
like it was the fastest ride I'd ever been on.

'Come on! Let's get out of here.'

We were giggling, ready to carry on the laughing as we fell
into the street. We got to the door. It was locked. We pulled
and pulled at the door. The man wasn't there. There were
curtains at the back of the shop, red velvet curtains, and he
was behind them. Locked in his shop surrounded by blow-up
dolls and dildos. We got really scared then.

We wouldn't go to the curtain. The curtain said *Behind here
you'll find horror* and our bellies were just about full of that
and would stand no more and we thought that maybe behind
that curtain they were doing the very same things we'd seen
them doing in the pictures and obviously we thought they'd be
wanting us to join in and coz we were black they'd think that
that was really special and that we were just tarts anyway, and
skint, and as all this raced round our heads as we turned to the
glass front door, we banged our terror to the streets screaming,
'Help! Help!' loud and long.

The young man came out from behind the curtain laughing
at us, sucking on his gold-chain necklace.

'You want to go now?'

He was ringing the keys as bells, like a teacher at the end of
playtime. Simmi and I were wallpapered to the door, trying to
go through it, like ghosts. He walked towards us and we
cuddled, huddled together. He opened the bolt at the top of the
door, put his key in the lock and let us out. When the sun hit us
on the street, it just added to our shame.

We skedaddled off back to Notre Dame then, back to the
shallow end with the proper tourists. From Notre Dame, we
could find our bearings again. We could watch the dancing
ladies. I threw them some money. A man sat on the grass,
playing a guitar, looked up at the women as if they'd floated in

from some world beyond him, as if they'd go back there any minute and he had to get his fill. They were all right but they weren't that good, so I figured he was in love with them. The sun jingled his dream into theatre. They bowed for him and danced about him till he stood up, to follow them. They all danced off down the path.

'Let's follow them,' I said.

They seemed magical to me, those people.

'I'm hungry.'

'Simmi, look! Look at her dress. She's beautiful. She's got bells on her feet, look.'

'Can we get some food? I'm starving.'

'Let's follow them and we'll get some on the way.'

We had to run to catch up. Soon, they stopped again so we sat on a nearby bench to watch them. The guitar player must have spotted us from earlier on and he came over. Davy, his name was, hitching his way round the world. Had come all the way from Australia.

'Yer lying bastard. You 'aven't hitched from all the way down there.'

'No. I got a ticket to England, but I've hitched all right since then. See her?' he said, pointing to the purple chiffon dancing in a frenzy now, up and down, like a dying swan dying fast, again and again.

'Yeah.'

'She's just come up from St Tropez. I was down there a few weeks ago. We've just bumped into each other again, now. The world's just a fucking playground, yer know? The same people meeting up all the time?'

'She's good, isn't she?'

'She's very good. Made a fortune down south.'

'God. What's it like, eh? Fancy dancing yer way round the world. I wish I had the bottle to do that.'

'It's nothin'. Yer don't need guts. Yer need faith. When you're travellin', yer God goes with yer.'

'Leave me out, Jesus.'

'No, it's true. I ain't no Christian or nothin'. I been on the

189

road for near a year already and I tell you, some of the jams I've been in . . . I could'na got out of any of them if there had'na bin someone looking out for me. She's the same there. Jessie. She says the same thing. But you gotta have some soul, yer know? Yer gotta give something and live. I do this, see . . .'

He twanged his guitar.

'You've got a string missing,' said Simmi.

'I know. After today, I should have enough cents for a new one.'

He began to roll a cigarette.

'D'yer want one o' these?' I said, offering him my pack.

'Taste o' crap, those things.'

'D'yer wanna put some o' this in then?' holding out the hashish.

'I surely would. Watcha! Now there's a . . .'

'I'm hungry.'

'Simmi. Stop mitherin'. Why don't you . . .'

'So you're Simmi and your name is . . . ?'

'I'm Viv. Vivian. Everyone calls me Viv.'

'Viv and Simmi, eh? Simmi, there's a shop just down that street there. Sells wine and bread and stuff? Zat what yer after?'

Simmi looked at me.

'Go for it then,' I said, impatient with her.

I wanted to get into Davy. The travellers. He looked at me like I could be with them, one of them. Didn't bat an eyelid at my scar. Like he'd seen worse, been further, done more, more than I would ever know, scar or no scar. All he had in the world was what was in his little bag, haversacked to his shoulder blades. A bag the size of an Amercan mail box, those they have in the street at the end of their front gardens. I thought of all that belonged to me. Still in tea chests in Flat 1, underneath Bev and Dirk's flat. Ready to be arranged into a lifestyle, into my new home. My totem pole in the fireplace. Black bin bags full of clothes I never wore. I wondered whether, one day, I would carry *my* life between my shoulder blades. Simmi wouldn't. Not ever. Her bags and boxes filled the hallway, the kitchen, the boot of her car. She still hadn't found a place to live. The night before we left, she packed her holiday haversack high-rise. I had a word with her. She was glad now.

She came back with bread, cheese and wine.

'Simmi, what yer doin' buyin' wine at this time o' the day?'

'Well, he said . . .'

She stopped. She was looking at Davy.

'Well, I thought, when in Rome.'

'How are yer gonna open it?' I said, all cocky, nose scrunched, sure of myself.

'No worries.' Davy said.

After a few glugs, some bread and cheese, a couple more spliffs and a lie-down on the grass, we were truly on holiday. Out of it. In spring. In Paris. Maybe Davy liked me. It was spring. It was Paris. For once I felt like I had treasure inside. Jessie said she'd teach us to dance. Her mate had gone off to work some 'plass'. Everything had a 'plass' in it in Paris. 'Plass' de this and 'Plass' de that. Simmi didn't really want to do the dancing but I told her that, to dance now, would prove that she was truly on holiday. To dance would be to embrace the freedom of the spirit. I didn't say it quite like that but that was the general idea.

'Nobody knows you,' I said. No one will take the piss – it's just you and Paris and the sunshine. And five minutes of being yourself.'

After another swig on the wine she was up for it. We started with some waves of the leg, in and out and around, pivoted. Then the other leg. We all stood in a line and followed every movement of our leader. Then the purple chiffon pranced off jumping high in the air, lifting arms to the sky. We danced right after her, sailing on the freedom, on the new air that brushed against our faces, jumping as high as we possibly could, me throwing my hat in the air in triumph. Really into it, we were. I remembered the very same dancing around, in vest and knickers at school. The same feeling, only this time with sunshine, with wine, hashish and unrestricted freedom of movement. The tourists saw us as a sight, a sight to see, as Paris know-alls, Paris lovers – and I loved that. Being part of

Paris. Not watching it but being it. Then, all of a sudden, Jessie danced off into a sprint.

'Jesus, look at her go,' I said.

We both stopped and saluted our foreheads, pretending more sun than there was, pretending she had more flight than she did, but after a couple of seconds, the flight and our plight became real.

'Look, there's the other girl. Her mate. They're running off together.'

We turned round to walk back to Davy, and he was gone too. And Simmi's shoulder bag, her money and passport contained within it. I patted my coat pocket to check my own house was in order. I'd kept the important stuff separate and close. Like they tell you. In the Girl Guides.

'Fucking great,' said Simmi. 'You're fucking great, you, aren't yer?'

Nearly in tears. Using swear words that didn't suit her and blaming me for leading her up the garden path.

'It's you that got the wine, remember.'

'It's you that rolled the spliffs, remember.'

There was a hiss on the word 'spliffs' as if the spliffs were the root of a nagging worry. Since the bust, I'd noticed her wavering on the spliff front. She'd been far less enthusiastic about rolling joints. When she said 'spliffs' like that, she betrayed herself. She wasn't a proper toker.

'What now?' I said.

'We've had it. Instead of fucking about with those bloody bastards we could have been looking for a room. How much money have you got?'

I was low. Too low to listen to her giving it one.

'I was gonna give him some money, yer know. So he could get a string for his guitar. The bastard.'

We sat back on the bench where the friendship had started. Behind it was a wastebin. Simmi checked it. Her bag was in there, but no passport in it. No money. No carnet.

'Well, they won't get far on yer passport. And anyway, from what Davy was saying they've done Europe.'

'They'll sell it, stupid.'

'What, to someone that looks like you? They'll have their work cut out.'

'They'll swap the pictures . . . listen, Vivian. We'll have to go to your Divine's now. Today. Please.' Whingeing.

It was like Divine was pulling at us to go there. After being light as air, dancing with the purple chiffon, nothing could be as heavy as we were, broke and spent on the bench. And I wouldn't be able to spliff up at Divine's. And the people. As they walked past us. They looked at us as scum, the French in their clean mackintoshes and shiny shoes. The Americans, chained down with camera wear. The Gendarmerie suspicious, nearly accosting us, but probably on their way for something to eat, couldn't be bothered.

'Funny, isn't it? How one minute, the world is full of possibilities and the next, you're being dragged back down to the misery zone. Like we're not supposed to get high. Like we'll always be pulled in by that magnet of doom. D'yer know what I mean?'

She did. She had it worse than me. She didn't answer.

'Eh?' I said, patting her on the knee. 'Don't worry. It's not the end of the world. Where would you rather be? Passportless in Paris or cooking rice with yer aunties?'

She laughed a bit then. Her eye was a lot better. You could hardly see the bruises at all now. That pissed me off.

We went over to look at all the paintings and the painters, while we thought about what to do. The painters wanted Simmi to sit down and be done. After it was established that *she* was supposed to pay them for this honour, we ambled back to the Métro. She was much cheered by then, though, because the painters said she was beautiful. As they did to everyone, I suspect. Though, they didn't lie to me, obviously.

'What are you doing here?'

As if I was some recurring skin disease. Which I suppose I was.

She had a towel round her head and already I was thinking maybe she was going out and we'd have the place to ourselves. I hadn't seen her for almost eighteen months.

'I thought you'd be pleased to see me.'

She didn't see Simmi until I pulled her into view. That stumped her. Jesus, what a sight! I swear if our Divine didn't look the spit of Mum on her best behaviour. Completely false.

'Hello there. You'd better all come in.'

Like we were a football team.

The plan was to make Simmi look as grown-up as possible so I made her put more make-up on, before we arrived. In Divine's head, all my mates were still in their school uniform. With Simmi done up like a tart, Divine was done up like a kipper. It was great. Simmi was more woman-looking than Divine would ever be. Perhaps this wouldn't be so bad after all.

'Well, you could've rung,' she said, so politely, I could hear the words slitting her throat.

She was ahead of us, climbing spiral concrete steps past very well-looked-after front doors with mats outside.

'Thought we'd surprise you, didn't we, Simmi?'

I was to get much mileage out of this situation. Simmi didn't answer. She probably realised she was about to become a fence for me and Divine to talk over.

'What time did you get into town?'

Because Divine had to be on her best, I was well placed to tell a few porkies. Simmi was a woman, a grown-up. She couldn't call her a liar.

'Couple of hours ago . . .' I said.

At the top of the second landing, the door to a flat was partway open. The room inside looked like a chess board. Then I couldn't believe it – we were on our way in there.

'Take your shoes off,' said Divine, slipping slippers off with ease, then removing her towel to show short hair, cropped hair, not a hint of relaxation.

'Actually, something really terrible's happened . . . Divine.'

My words were lost to the ground as I struggled with my bootlaces. Still, I was convinced she'd heard me. She was ignoring me, as usual. Knowing I was lying. Knowing we'd been in Paris for more than two hours and knowing there was no way she'd be my first port of call. Simmi had her shoes off in a tick and by the time I got into the flat, they were both knee deep in politics. We shouldn't have come.

There was an overwhelming feeling of space in the flat and not because it was big. There was sod all in it. The walls were covered with white shiny stuff flecked with slivers of Japanese letters and umbrellas floating down to a graveyard of letters and umbrellas, a frieze around the bottom of the room. There was no couch, just black cushions on a white-tiled marble floor, a floor flecked with yet more Japanese typography. I gave a sideways look to our Divine. Was she out of her mind? There were a couple of tall black tree stands with ornaments on, busts and naked men. The centrepiece of the room was a black coffee table with no legs standing on a black fur rug. Around it the cushions. There was a huge bean bag in one corner and it was there that I wanted to park myself. But it was out of the way, out of the social centre of the room which was pointed out to me by Divine – round the frigging table.

As a teenager, she put net curtains up in her bedroom and she never had posters on the walls. She bought ornaments for her windowsill – instead of going down the pub. And she was clever. Very clever. In France collating reports from advisers doing research on effective pesticides for staple crops in Francophoney African Countries. That's how she put it to Simmi. Simmi went on about British Empire stuff in Africa and already I was uncomfortable, sat with aching back at the coffee table. Our terrible ordeal I was supposed to be reporting on was getting less and less terrible by the minute. I was losing the passion for telling it. Shattered, I wanted to lie down. I wanted Simmi to pack it in. She'd done her stuff now – shown how grown-up she could be. Now it was time for food and wine and to settle down with a magazine and leave them to it. No telly. Didn't matter. Would've been in French anyway. I stood up.

'Well, come on then, what's this *terrible* thing that's happened?' when it was finally noticed I was not contributing.

She'd waited all that time. She *had* heard me at the door after all.

'That's what I was going to ask *you*, Divine – what in heaven's name is this place all about?'

I was gaping wildly round the room, holding an ornament picked up from a stand.

'We got mugged,' said Simmi. 'Twice.'

Smelling a rat Divine turned on me.

'Twice?'

Coming over to look me straight in the eye, lashing it out cat-style.

'I thought you said you've only been here for a couple of hours. Some going that, isn't it?'

I turned defensive by instinct, habit, Divine tapping away on my anger hotspot, a spot she knew well.

'She means there were two of them. One of them tried to get my bag but I wouldn't let him. They got Simmi's, though, didn't they, Simmi?'

Simmi nodded, looking back and forth to Divine and me, like a goalkeeper, getting ready for a save.

'Yes. That's what I meant,' in her poshest voice. 'There were two of them.'

'What did they take, Simmi?'

Simmi wanted to tell her all about the black men at the Gare du Nord since that was by far the best story but that didn't happen, did it, Simmi? I said with my eyes, to warn her. She'd have to give it welly about the girl in purple chiffon and then chip in with a lie about my bag being pulled off me by some heinous thief. My bag looked like it was full of muddy football boots. No one in their right mind would try and nick it.

'Oh my passport and some . . .'

Then a woman came out of a room from behind us, a room I didn't know was there, a white door in a white wall. We all turned to look at her. Japanese, tall, slim and used to carrying her beauty around. She was yawning. She had hair you'd have surgery for. Loads of it.

'Errhh . . . Annique, this is my sister Viv and her friend, Simmi.'

Annique made tea.

Chapter 17

In geisha-style, Annique arranged four bowls on the table, smiling in a way that was both simple and complicated. White bowls. Then four spoons, tea-caddy spoons. I felt like I was back in my wendy house, the preliminary polite silence, the playing with my spoon. Wouldn't be long before the play-acting stopped. Taking turns, we sat cross-legged, then knees tucked up, then champing at the bit, riding on our heels. The teapot poured urine water into cups too cold and grey for anything but sugar lumps. No handles. Dressed in a long black T-shirt, tight black leggings and on toes dipped in blood, Annique flowed in and out of us like tide lapping against rocks on the beach, rocks she knew she could engulf later on, when the family matters were out of the way.

'So you thought you'd just turn up expecting me to look after you for the week, eh? Without bothering to ring . . . or write?'

Simmi changed from kneeling to sidesaddle and as she did so, knocked her bowl of tea over the table. So I didn't answer. I wanted instead to bathe in Simmi's embarrassment. And smirk. Simmi caught me and gave a silent snarl. She too wanted the family matters out of the way.

Still a geisha, Annique wouldn't let her porcelain face crack at any of this. She wiped the table and re-filled the bowl with tea. Earlier, Divine had been in the kitchen with her, mutter-ing. I couldn't hear any of it. Divine slagging me off, I supposed. I guessed she'd already told her mate all about me, sketched me out in pencil faintness, inserted the scar story, relieved herself of the guilt of it and then built up a frame of her younger sister obsessed by facial disfigurement even though the family had bent over backwards to point out to me that my disfigurement was physical and life in all its true glory cared little for looks. She would have pointed out to her friend that I had never bought such a story and had labelled it a Christian whitewash.

But now I'd arrived, the paintbrushes were out and Divine was sploshing away, colouring in, like those painters down the Seine, doing as much as she could to get Annique to see the light, shade, shadow and central theme of our relationship. Me, pondlife parasite and jealous of a sister who had survived and thrived, having scaled the walls of the British establishment as well as, and this would be the most important bit, spending her teenage years on a guilt trip because of what she had done to me. She had punished herself and punished herself but to no avail because I still hated her. She had foregone boyfriends and make-up. Just for me. She had locked herself into her studies, so that I could not be jealous of her. But she got no thanks for it. I still used her. Still made her pay for her crime. And now Divine is all mended. She has rid herself of self-hatred. Pity was now in her court, in her CV. She was the one to be pitied, praised and respected for the way she had managed to overcome her difficult sister.

Annique looked to me and then to Divine. She was waiting for a cue, to rush on in, to close the wendy-house door behind us and create a warm, intimate session round the table.

'So, you're from Japan then?' I asked, ignoring Divine and setting off into pastures green.

It wasn't usual for me to ask people where they came from. Better to wait and be told. Sit and guess. Put odds on. But since we were sat in an oriental theme park, I felt more than justified.

'Vietnam,' she said, paddling back into the kitchen.

I thought of helicopters then. And tents. And paddyfields.

'I asked you a question,' said Divine, steering me back to her own tiny world. Repeating herself.

Back came Annique, with a tray of bowls and in the bowls, rice and vegetables. Simmi seemed more relaxed than me – I guess she thought I was the one who had to do all the work. Still. Out went Annique again.

'Why didn't you ring?'

This was the brim of Divine's politeness. Any minute her cup would be full and she would overflow. She was no good at this stuff. Not with me anyway. When I went to her graduation, after just an hour she was poking her finger in my face and dragging me round the grounds by my cardy, like I needed reins. But not now. Not yet anyway. Simmi, I guess. The unknown quantity. Or maybe she was someone completely different when she was with Annique who now returned with serving spoons and no meat to go with the food.

'And you, Simmi? Where are you from?'

Annique and Simmi locked eyeballs at that point so Divine, considering a duet between ourselves, leant over the table to ding my bowl with her spoon, tinkle, tinkle, tinkle. She wanted a separate conversation but still, I ignored her. Simmi was talking. I looked at Simmi and then back to Divine. Simmi's talking. Don't be rude, said my eyes and bare-faced cheek.

Simmi calculated her answer carefully, I noticed. Her parents were Pakistani, she said, almost asking if this was OK.

'Oh, so you're a Muslim?' said Annique, emptying rice into our bowls.

Simmi was debating what should have been a reflex answer to that question.

'Christian?' asked Annique, getting impatient at Simmi's formless, clueless face.

'No, Muslim,' said Simmi, 'but not a very good one.'

There. Now that wasn't too difficult, was it?

Silence. Except for me battering the crockery. Everyone else tinkled. I crashed. They nibbled. I chomped. I could feel Divine embarrassed, her eyes trying to rein me in across the table. I carried on trowelling the food to my mouth. There simply wasn't enough of it. I dripped hot sauce over everything, so the chilli heat fed me, fed my mind, distracted my senses from the echo of my belly. I could see why Divine had lost weight.

'Do you cook, Divine?'

This wasn't just conversation. I was investigating the palatability of an extended stay.

'No.'

'D'yer get take-aways?'

'No. Annique cooks. Is that a problem?'

'No!'

My cheeks bulged. I turned to Annique.

'I didn't mean . . . I was just thinking . . . Annique, it's lovely, honestly.' Swallow. 'Must have taken you ages to chop all this veg up. Must get you down, that.'

Too much. I said too much.

Annique said, 'Merci.' She liked to cook.

Simmi tinkered with her bowl, trying to copy the way Annique held hers. She loved all this ethnic stuff, Simmi. I wriggled uncomfortably. An armchair would have been welcome. My feet were snoring, my back twanging with the stretch.

It was the first time she'd got me on her own. Divine washed and I dried.

'Divine, I didn't know you were on the phone, and no, we weren't going to do that . . . were we, Simmi?' shouting loud.

'What?' shouted Simmi.

'I was just saying.'

I stood half in the living room and half in the kitchen, shining my plate as I shined up my story. I announced my lie for all to hear so that everyone got their story straight.

'I was just saying we weren't gonna stay here for the week. We were coming here first to get some advice, weren't we, Simmi? And then we were going to book into wherever you thought best.'

(My voice was turning into a story voice and I saw Divine's shoulders rise in a half-hackle, coz she knew my story voice.)

'But we can't do that now, coz Simmi was holding all the holiday money. Weren't you, Simmi?'

I stacked another shiny plate on to the counter.

'I've got two hundred francs. That won't get us very far, will it? And Simmi lost her passport too, remember. We were scared Divine, weren't we, Simmi?'

Simmi's affirmations got weaker with every count.

'Well, there's nowhere for you to sleep here. Have you got sleeping bags? You can go to a hostel.'

Divine was running both taps, cleaning out the sink, getting done with me, it seemed.

Annique piped up then, in strong French accent.

'We have bags for sleeping,' she said. 'In the closet, no? Re-mem-ber? From campy?'

'I'll go top and tail with you, Divine, and Simmi can use the cushions on the floor. She likes sleeping on the floor. Does it all the time at home, don't you, Simmi?'

I got the feeling Simmi wished she hadn't come.

'Well, you can't top and tail with me, I'm afraid,' said Divine, wiping her hands.

'Why?' I said. 'You're a lot skinnier than you used to be.'

'Yer just can't,' she said, gripping the sink as if to stop falling down, like some harassed housewife, she was, and me the kid going one step too far.

Then she walked round me, not even looking at me. I followed her body out of the kitchen and then noticed, just then, only one white door within the white wall. Only one bedroom leading off this flat. And then it all came together. Her and Annique. I was so dense. So fucking dense. Full of purpose, I strode into the centre of the lounge and looked straight at Annique accusingly. She was licking two Rizla papers together.

A freak wave. A jigsaw being completed on a speeded-up video. A sudden season with all the trimmings, summer falling out of winter, autumn out of spring, the fruit, the leaves, the bonfires. Foreign France. Oriental fragility. Divine, like a stranger but complete. More complete than I had ever known her. More controlled. I came up for air and was engulfed again and again by all the ramifications. The silence was dinned to a clatter by Divine stacking the plates in the dresser, shaking by the bones, it seemed. I was so many things. Embarrassed coz Simmi got it at the same time as me. Sad, coz I wanted my sister to be normal. Amused because Mum just wouldn't believe it, any of it. And angry. Lastly angry and this monster hung around for a good five minutes. That was how long the silence lasted as the information criss-crossed between us, the idea of it, the truth of it, the shock of it and what I was going to say about it. All done in complete silence. I stood next to the dresser with my arms folded, nearly crying. I'd been made a fool of. Simmi wouldn't even look up.

'I think you'd better sit down,' said Annique.

She asked me whether I smoked, holding the lump of hash like it was some sort of consolation prize. I wanted to tell her to fuck off and walk out. Be on my own, back in my bedroom, in the land of not knowing. Budding trees and April showers.

'Yes,' I said to Annique, on my best behaviour.

'I didn't know when to tell you . . . whether to tell you,' said Divine, at last sitting back down at the table.

'Do yer smoke spliff as well?' I asked her.

I could only take so much.

'Sometimes. Not as much as Annique. I'm doing a lot of editing at the moment. There are so many colloquial terms for so many publica . . .'

'I didn't ask for your CV, Divine. Stop ranting.'

Snapping. Punishing.

Simmi was still head down, embarrassed. I had to get my head together, handle it better.

'What yer smoking?' I said to Annique.

'Moroccan? You like?'

''Sall right. 'Snuthin' special.'

Sulking. My eyes burned. Then filled up with liquid. A slow-fill washing machine. When they were full, water drops squirted out like I was a Tiny Tears baby. Silent tiny tears. I never ever leak like that. Sometimes, in bed, at night on my own, I give my eyes a bit of a wet just to complete the day, just to bathe myself in my own liquid and to wipe my face of it all, as if wiping those tears is bringing on a new chance, a new attempt to be strong. To cry in public is not an option but an uncontrollable reflex. Water pouring, but not at my command. Why? Because life was becoming more complicated. Was it that simple? The tears splashed off the table and must have been seen by all. The huge silence that grew in the room was only there because all three of them were inside my head, all of them trying to figure out what I'd do next. Would I storm out shouting? Rail up in anger? I, like them, didn't know. The suspense of the silence mushroomed further. My brain, my mind, wasn't big enough to hold it all in. I was about to yarl out loud. The final surrender. The ultimate embarrassment. The letting go.

'This I think you like.'

Annique patted my arm and showed me something, the hashish, I guess, but through the blur, I couldn't see sod all. I didn't want to wipe my eyes – that would be too belittling. Then I heard movement. And a door close. There was absolute silence. They were out of my head and out of the room. I wiped my eyes and looked up. I was alone with Annique.

Still jittery, I avoided her gaze. Having half the audience disappear was a help. I didn't care what Annique thought about my crying, about my weakness. Who was she anyway? Some dyke that had corrupted my sister. What was she going to do now? Convince me that it was all for the best? What would I say to Mum? I wouldn't tell Mum. What to do now? Now my mind would be invaded by images of Divine kissing a girl, a woman. And what else did they do? Me. On my own. It made me more on my own than ever. Cheers, Divine. Annique passed me the joint to light. Usually an honour. I didn't feel honoured. Bought off, more like.

'Divine tells me it's your birthday today. You have been quiet?'

'Don't like birthdays.'

'How old have you?'

'Twenty.'

'There is good reggae band tonight. We take you there?'

Well, it'd beat sitting round the Japanese table in our socks. I decided, for now, to be on my best behaviour.

'Yeah. That'd be nice, thanks.'

The least offensive action to take. Well, of course, every-thing'll be just fine, won't it? Getting down to the beat of the reggae sounds. That'll bring us all together, won't it? That'd be nice, thanks. I repeated it to myself, in my mind. I was against it. Those words didn't even belong to me. I was cheating. Not being true to myself. I now knew why people hid behind politeness and manners when faced with something, someone they didn't agree with. Such people infuriate me. To fall back on that code of civility whilst inside roaring with fury. To implement that ritual, that barrier to truth, is to disarm the argument, make the opponent impotent. It is a refusal to get out of protected waters, but worse, to let anyone in. I played polite. I played for time. I played the white man, as they say.

I didn't fit in that flat. I couldn't see how our Divine thought she fitted in any better. With everything so black-and-white and us being brown, we trashed the colour scheme. Annique with her white porcelain skin and black slinky hair, sticky arms and legs. She was part of it. Divine was fuller than that, more bulbous, round, more flesh and brown. Now, if she'd been blacker . . .

Divine showed me some wedding photos once, of one of her college mates from Oxford. A wealthy girl who married a Ghanaian. There were black men in dickie bows either side of a huge fireplace, smoking cigars. They were taller than the whites. There were more blacks, outside, drinking champagne around the garden urns, their colour not blending with the grey and the granite, but next to the flowers, there, there the black people shone, brought the colours of the flowers out to a peak. There was Grandaddy's portrait on the stairs, dull and demure, looking down on the blacks milling about his mansion. Grandiose blacks, highly achieved, buckets of integrity, intelligence and generosity, but . . . well, I hate to say it . . . Grandma, still alive in her wheelchair, didn't look all that chuffed. The only ones beaming truly were the bride and her parents. The groom looked a bit poorly, I remembered.

I'd stared at those pictures for ages. Thought about the blacks not fitting in, for ages. The pattern spoiled. The fact of the blackness. Not the baggage that comes with it. Just the black. The colour black amongst white memories and impressions, in their chairs, seats and systems. No. It wasn't the baggage. It was just the black. Just the damn colour. Messed up people's heads, that. And you could see the extended family in the photos, with their heads messed up, uncomfortable in the family line-up. I could almost hear the stilted and forced conversations between Uncle John and Abidaya, Abidaya, trying his damnedest to make himself fit, fit for office. In the night pictures, everyone was pissed. They were all happy by night-time, just bodies grinning cheese. Divine should have draped the flat in flowers and pictures of blood-red sunsets. Scarlet scarves and shiny red ornaments to blot new seams into the landscape. She'd have fitted in fine then.

'You are shocked, no?'

Annique pulled her cushion closer to me, sitting lotus. She was used to it, I could tell.

I gave her a numskull look. As if Divine wasn't minority enough, Oxford, an *anglaise* in Paris, Jamaican, black, and the brains on her! And now she wanted to be a fucking lesbian. Just to rub it in good. Maybe a disease next, to round it all off, something really debilitating. She used to think she was a sickler when she was little coz she couldn't jump hurdles or run for the bus without passing out. It was her semi-circular canals, the doctor said.

'Well, actually, I expected our Divine to go for a suit in a bank, to be honest. She's always been mad for a house and kids.'

Time for attack, I thought.

'Bank suit?'

'Office man. I thought she'd marry an office boy. Company director sort of chap.'

'And now you think she's done badly, yes?'

It was all that angelic butter-wouldn't-melt stuff. I wasn't buying it. She was too catty-looking for that. And anyway, I didn't really give a shit about our Divine. It was how it all reflected on me that mattered. Me, with the scar. See her . . . her over there . . . with the scar . . . see her . . . she's got a lesbian sister in Paris. Weird. Dead weird. As if life wasn't weird enough. Why couldn't Divine just be normal? Be something I could be proud of? Pride.

'How long have you been . . . yer know?'

'Lesbian?'

'Yep.'

'Since I know me. Since I feel me.'

'Well, our Divine's different. She doesn't know what she's doing. A late developer, you could say. She was never very trendy as a kid.'

'You think she doesn't love me?'

I didn't answer her. What a thing to ask me. Asking me to dive in deep when I was only skating round the sides . . . testing the water, the ice, the threshold of hate versus nice. Love? What's love got to do with it? Surely this set-up proved neither of them could find love. They'd found each other and decided to *call* it love. How long was our Divine gonna keep this up? Was she gonna bring happy Jappy home for Christmas? I didn't think so. Annique played xylophone on her lips with her fingers, as if testing the tune of the words that might fall out of her mouth. She played with light fingers for ideas slightly off key, and pressed heavy impressions to the teeth for the thoughts she really believed in. I was glad Divine had left the room. I wasn't ready for a head-on. Or Simmi. I needed to get my bearings. Annique must have guessed that. I offered her the joint. I'd hardly smoked any of it – still sulking.

'You keep. I make another.'

I had the feeling she was trying to hide something from me. She wasn't looking at me head-on either, as if she was after appeasing me. She should have done. She should have stared me out. But then, maybe she didn't really care what I thought. Why should she? She owned Divine, the flat, the food, the space between us. She was setting up to do a presentation and I didn't like it one bit. I like spontaneous information full of all its natural lies and hidden agendas. Not presentation, to be swallowed whole, tight, glib and shiny with polish. Closed up.

'No. I don't wannit.'

I forced the joint back on her.

'Listen, Vivian. I wanted to tell you something because Divine says she cannot. She feels silly. She says you will ridicule her, cause a disturbance. Misunderstand her, maybe. I didn't want to do this but I feel I should help her. This is not me, truly, you have to believe me. I think you too shocked but Divine insists I tell you. I hope you forgive me, that is, if you take it badly.'

I didn't answer her. I wanted to feel her squirm for a while. Make her more nervous than she was.

'Perhaps,' she continued, 'it is best if Divine tell you after all,' and she turned away from me then. Threatening to keep me in suspense, she was.

'Listen. If you're asking for her hand in marriage, then it's me dad you should be talking to, not me. Don't lay all your shit on me.'

'Divine told me that you were the only person she would ever be able to tell about us. She says she'll never be able to tell your parents, no matter what.'

'Well, at least she's not completely lost her marbles. So what?'

'What? Sorry?'

'*What do you want to tell me?*'

That shook her a bit. Made her more nervous. She put the joint in the ashtray and clasped her hands together, head down.

'I am going to live in Vietnam for a while. I have contacts there and I have some money.'

'And you're taking our Divine with you? To Vietnam?'

I sat up, smirking.

'Yes. You think bad, yes?' holding her breath, dripping butter from her shiny lips.

'I was thinking about my dad, actually.'

My back couldn't take any more strain and uprightness. I lay across the floor and stared up to the ceiling. It was all done out in galaxies, the planets in silver grey, little balls and flying saucers all over the place. I closed my eyes to the madness of it.

Then I realised – just that small puff, just that couple of tokes on the joint – I was completely wrecked. I looked back up to the galaxy and saw the vastness of the world in perspective, in relation to my ignorance. I was proud that our Divine lived in Paris and had a first-class French degree. I wasn't gone on Vietnam. Lesbians. Japanese wallpaper. I wasn't really sure what to think now. No bearings whatsoever.

The tide rushed round my bouldered body. Me. A blob of a boulder, fashioned by the endless comings and goings of the same old water, coming in and going out, smoothing me down over millions of years. Or maybe I was flotsam and jetsam. Sounded nicer than being a boulder. Flotsam and Jetsam. If I ever have cats, that's what I'll call them. 'Discuss the benefits of economic stability in the framework of a global market-place with reference to the technological innovations of the last twenty-five years. 3,000 words maximum.' Ahhhh! I was off my head. Two tokes and I was gone. And jealous. I was actually jealous of our Divine.

'I'm stoned, Annique. Tired too.'

Chapter 18

D'Envers was busy with the bustle of colour and blacks when we arrived. Black music shops beat it and food shops coloured the streets as mosaics within grim and grey stone. When we came out of the Métro, the full bustle of it all shocked us, the vibe a vivid dream compared to the dull thud of the tube, the scraping of the tube through the tunnel, like a huge industrial pipe cleaner. In D'Envers there was a teeming mass of energy that reminded me of the fair, the smell of the food and the laughing. The squashing and all the business of heading for some prize. In primary colour.

Tourist Paris, compared to this, was wrapped up. Blind to the energies. In tourist Paris, people were skating over ice, it seemed. Ice skating aimless pirouettes on a greyed-out Christmas cake of a capital city that would never let the icing melt, never give access to the inner centre, the recipe that built the cake, tier on tier on tier. Sure, the researchers, the academics, the politicians, I guess they thought they had the recipe for Paris. I guess they thought they were sucking on the fruit. But really, they were riding in glass-bottom boats. Glass-bottom boats whizzing over the ice of Paris. Paris in *beaucoup de* tinsel.

Out of the Métro, Simmi was at first jumpy. Because of the Gare du Nord experience. So was I, a bit, and both of us were ashamed to be feared that another bunch of blacks would accost us. So much so, that when we set off to find my sister's road, we did it with nonchalance and confidence, hoping that everybody would smile at us and welcome us into their community. But I still looked over my shoulder.

That night, when the four of us left the flat to go to the reggae band, Divine and Annique were on guard. It was dark.

Those that coloured the day were resting now, the shops shuttered, the streets paved with empty boxes and cigarette packs. Those out at night were harder to pin down. Annique said that, on the black side, there were terrorist infiltrations from North Africa, Morocco and Algeria mostly. On the white side, junkies. Plenty junkies. They all needed funding. She said it wouldn't be long before the junkies became terrorists or the terrorists junkies but, whatever happened, everyone would pay. And not just with valuable things like money, she said. Valuable ideas would be lost too. She hoped for less paranoia in Vietnam.

'There's loads of smack in Vietnam,' I said.

She just laughed.

As we walked, our pairing changed. Simmi coupled up with Annique, and Divine at last had to confront me, alone. We'd grown up so much during that past few hours. I saw her as a child again, from a mother point. Suddenly, I was older than her. She'd gone back to the girl she was before she did my face. Her short hair and big earrings. Her eyes rolling uncontrollably, it seemed, seeing for the first time. First time I'd seen them look out rather than look out and judge. She'd plucked her eyebrows too. That was Divine trying for style, style she'd never tried for before. Like she was climbing out of old skin. She was shy. A virgin recently opened up. Opened up my world no end, seeing my sister like that.

'So then. Do you love her?'

I wanted to giggle after I said it. For once, I was on the higher moral ground. If it'd been me turned lesbian, Divine would have kicked off and told me to get off the wall. She would have warned me about drawing too much attention to myself. I wasn't going to do that to her. I was going to make her skin crawl by pretending to be really grown-up about it.

'I think so,' she said.

'Well, best yer make yer mind up, our Divine, if you're off to Vietnam. Be a bit late to change your mind once you're in the paddyfields.'

Silence. She linked my arm. Right at that moment, I had the

feeling she didn't want to be thinking about boat people and poppies, helicopters and heat. She wanted to live in the new world we'd just created. Her secret out, me accepting – all of it must have been a dream for her and she needed to live it as long as she could. What point to talk about her future when there were still these vestiges of her past she could create? Mould. Make as happy as she could. She would like this moment to separate from all other moments. And it dawned on me then that she must have felt homesick a bit. A lot. She was brave, Divine, and I'd never known that. We stopped. The other two walked on.

'I'm really pleased for you,' I said, which wasn't true at all.

I was more scared for her, but I felt it was the sort of thing she wanted to hear.

She hugged me and then cupped my face in her hands.

'Happy Birthday,' she said, kissing me.

I let her play big sister for another moment and then shook her off.

'What's this place we're going to like then?'

'This place' was a derelict church full of smoke and dreadlocks and thumping speakers. A gas. In there, we all became ourselves, dancing, smoking. We thought our thoughts on spiritual islands and danced together in a tribe, passing a splendid love ball between our legs and over our shoulders. We stared past each other but inside ourselves, really letting ourselves go after a couple of hours. And the men. There were men in there to grace temples. What was our Divine thinking of?

The night firmed up the bond between the lot of us. Boxed it off. No funny business. We walked back to the flat making each other laugh. We played soldiers walking on the knee-high walls and then chased each other. Back in the flat we were all family. The lot of us.

'She's told you all about it, hasn't she? How she did it?'

'Yes,' Annique said quietly, letting me feel some of the pain that she'd absorbed from Divine, letting me know that she had indeed heard all about it. 'Yes, but you tell me how you feel about it. Now. Not when you were young. How do you feel now?'

She poured me a glass of wine. It tasted like acid.

'Well, now . . .'

I paused. Because now had only been for about four hours. Now was in France with a lesbian sister off to Vietnam. Now was nothing like yesterday.

'Now, I realise that it's all mine. My face is all mine. Until now, part of it was hers. I think I'll get on with it better now, to be honest.'

I smiled at Divine.

'Remember,' I shouted to Divine.

I was animated. Excited.

'Remember that time down the playing fields with Dad?'

'Oh no. Not that one again. Do we have to?'

I turned to Annique to tell her the story. For some reason I wanted Annique to like me. Probably to cancel out all my previous bad behaviour.

'Listen to this, right. I used to think Divine did my face just to get me back. Coz me dad went mental with her. We were down the playground with him, right.'

I was in my element, if in fact we have one – an element of our own. I believe we do. I was in mine, that night, with my sister, telling stories about when we were kids. Before my face.

'He was stood on the sidelines talking to some woman. Me and Divine were on the roundabout and I was spinning it round really fast. The idea was for me to spin it as fast as I could and then yell out, "Fastest!" She was supposed to jump off then. I did, when it was her turn. So I screams out, "Fastest!" and she's clinging to the bars for dear life. She just wanted the ride and there's me spinning her round like some fair lad on the waltzers. So, when she wouldn't get off, I grabbed hold of her cardy and pulled her off. She went flying. You should have heard her scream. You'd think I'd ripped her head off the way she went on. Me dad came running over and saw all these little white things in the tarmac and then he started screaming. "Her teeth! Her teeth!" "Dad," I shouted. But he was gone. Carrying her in his arms. Terrified, he was. Me mum always said he was crap at looking after us, didn't she?'

'All the way to casualty he told me to keep me mouth shut.'

Divine was covering her mouth, remembering.

'So it wasn't till he got to casualty that he realised she hadn't lost her teeth at all. She'd been eating Polo mints. I can't believe you let him get all that way without saying anything.'

Divine was laughing now. Really happy.

'I was too scared to tell him,' she said, rubbing her cheeks.

'Too scared to go down the garden and tell me dad about me face as well, weren't yer?'

'I was, yeah. I thought he'd kill me. I thought I'd killed you. When he heard you scream, he just kept shouting, "What's the matter? What's the matter?" I'd wet my knickers. I was paralysed.'

Her face went serious again.

'She had to tell him in the end,' I said, looking first to Annique and then to Simmi. 'Go on. Tell 'em. Tell 'em what happened.'

They all went quiet then. They didn't want to laugh any more. Divine didn't want to tell. It was still an unhealed wound for her. And for me. But I was trying to heal.

At bedtime, lying on cushions on the floor and the lights out, I sighed long and loud. I was glad by then, glad I'd seen Divine and glad she was more than glad to see me. She'd got something off her chest. She'd been given a snorkel. Simmi heard me sigh and asked what was up.

'Nothing,' I said, trying to sound more cheerful than tired.

'Vivian.'

'Yeeess . . .' I said, expecting her to say something profound or sympathetic.

Sarcastically she said, 'I think they make a really nice couple.'

I jumped up and smothered her in cushions, punching her. I

heard our Divine shouting from the bedroom, telling me to pack it in. She had to be up in the morning. And so did Simmi. She hadn't changed that much.

Simmi went with Divine to the offices, for to sort out the stolen passport. Divine's French and bureaucratic know-how would ensure as smooth an operation as possible. I slept on. Gathered up the cushions that Simmi left free and hugged them as if a body. I thought about Roy. I was going to let him do it, when I got back. Now I was sure he wanted to. I didn't fancy the arse off him or anything but we were friends enough. It wasn't like just letting anybody do it. I didn't crave him. I craved it. I wanted someone to do it to me. And soon.

Next time I opened my eyes, Annique was pouring coffee at the table. In silk. Hair wet and shining like a mirror. Glinting at me.

'Ye gods. My neck's stiff,' I said, trying to get up.

'Sit up and drink. Divine is out.'

'I know. I heard them leave.'

'You have a plan?'

'Sleep.'

'It is late now. I see your neck is hurt. I give you massage?'

'Can you do it? Proper like?'

'That is my trade. My job, as you say.'

'Divine said you worked in the leisure industry.'

'How you say? Emvarrass?'

'Embarrass.'

'Divine is embarrassed of my work.'

'That doesn't surprise me. She's always been a bit of a prude.'

'You want?'

'Yeah. Sounds great. Do I just lie flat like this?'

'First shower and I get oils. Then I roll my work bed out for you.'

'Oh, lots of kit then?'

'Just a few things.'

'Shall I roll a spliff first?'

214

'Oh no. The massage will relax you. No need for weed. Be natural. Leave coffee till later.'

After the shower, my neck felt fine so I didn't really need a massage but curiosity . . . and well . . . I'd never had one before. She'd changed. She wore a cotton cream sleeveless dress that nearly touched the floor, down the centre small black buttons for effect and a small lace attachment, just below her chest. It was more chest than breast. She looked thin and clean and beautiful. The bed was laid. A mini-train-track of a bed, wooden slats rolled flat across blocks. Looked uncomfortable but wasn't. I lay on my front. She put music on. Al Stewart. *The Year of the Cat*. She rubbed her hands in oil and took my feet as a whittler might begin to shape a new block of wood, squeezing them tight in on themselves, getting the weight, the shape, fleshing out the sole. Felt soppy at first. Pressing my sole. I'm not one for tickly feet and was as still as stone as she faffed about, awakening, it seemed, the South Pole of my head. The smell drifted up to me, the smell of burnt flowers, sickly but moreish. I couldn't get enough.

Then it hurt, in my calf muscles, pain digging into feeling spaces I'd never felt before. I bore it. Flinched first off but after, when I had the measure of the pain, I bore it. Up my legs. My eyes sailed down the wallpaper with the falling umbrellas and Japanese lettering. I counted out their curly sticks, buried in tangled heaps at the bottom of the walls, like scrap. Like bodies. Like concentration-camp bodies, disjointed and piled up, and now she was at the top of my thigh and her lesbian status took on a new dimension for me. She was enjoying this, the little cow. She just wanted to see me with no clobber on. She kneaded me. She kneaded those thoughts too and they rose to the surface like waste. The towel was taken away. I didn't object for my conscious will was waning. Being kneaded out of me, like sweat or bad air. She worked my buttocks. I was gone now. It felt wonderful. My body an element, my skin buzzing and bright from its very own light. I had a beginning, middle and no end in sight. All my nerves meshed together, talked to each other, in easy language, in flow. My head dropped flat. To the bed. Eyes closed. Body hypnotised away.

'Turn over.'

Again she started at my feet. I was back in my galaxy instantly. Like a babe after suckling, changing breasts. When she got to the tops of my legs an overpowering sexual urge engulfed me and I felt embarrassed. I wanted a sexual feeling, between my legs. My mind diverted to that thought and that thought alone and I could see why Divine liked all this. Who wouldn't? No wonder she'd got everything mixed up. The poor girl was confused. Her hands were so close. I so wanted that woman to go with me, all the way, all the way inside me, because every nerve of my body wanted that ultimate melt. But she was controlled. She left for my waist and guts and was up to my breasts and there, I was at it again. I fought with my sex to get me back to my galaxy where everything was of air, higher than sex, than the wanting of sex, the wanting so low down and fixed and distracting. Like stars that never move. I won. I got back up. She worked my body as to train a mischievous child. At last in relent, in peace and then in touch. And then to my head and then she really blew me away.

I can't actually remember what she did to my head, physically I mean, coz like I said, I was gone, travelling in a chariot riding through blackness. Honest. I'm not kidding. I was in some sort of perambulator for a short while, and then as you might let a balloon go, a balloon of inert gas that just rises fast, that was how I was jettisoned into the ether. Not going up or down. I was being dragged in somewhere. I remember the whole of me being turned, 360 degrees, as a planet. I was a planet and first I turned to see my sun but I couldn't look head-on. It was too violent. And then I turned to my moon. Then everything stopped. I was face to face with my moon. It was vivid yet colourless. The moon was colourless but around it, its sea was a deep dark blue, a black blue. I was there. I was in there. Not like dreaming. Every inch of me was in there. Every part of my body was in my planet, humble before my moon. It didn't speak to me, or flash or behave in any animate manner. It recognised my presence and this then made me recognise my presence. There was a wind, but not a blowing. A sound, an inner roar all around, a roar of silence that was almost tangible. Like being inside a sea-shell. It was a visit to the gods. A bathing, a cleansing, an enlightenment. Soon, too soon, my consciousness caught up with me, and for a single second I thought of fear. I don't know why, just a sliver of it quivered me to an outward flight. I felt her fingers behind my ears.

'You sleeping?' she said.

She laid the towel across my body. I kept my eyes shut. I was back. Back on the rack. I felt slightly sad, appalled even. I wasn't one for airy-fairy nonsense but I couldn't deny what had happened. The moon. My moon.

I opened my eyes and watched her put her bottles of oils away in a tiny wicker basket. Like she'd just given me a shampoo and set.

I wanted to tell her . . . all about the moon but just as I began the doorbell went. I was dressed now and drinking coffee out of the huge pudding bowl. No frothy croissants. Just bread. And jam. Cheese if I wanted. I just drank from my bowl. Filled it twice.

Annique answered the door to a couple. Man and woman. French. White. The woman looked a bit caved in. Bit ill, I thought, grey. Neat, though. Neat jeans, shiny shoes, a flashy anorak still with its bobbles on the end of the cords. I'd have bitten mine off first day. Very clean. The man, in black, was more animated. Jittery even. He put some books down on the table, patting them and saying stuff. Pretending he'd read them, no doubt. He didn't shut up. Rolled his sleeves up to give it licks with a French tongue that sounded like the soup was boiling over, spitting and spluttering away. No wonder his girlfriend looked so worn out.

When the introductions came, I smiled as an actress for there was no need to be genuine. There was no way I could communicate as an equal so I took the place of an ornament, that would sit and watch and listen but not contribute. I liked that. The passivity. The not being required to laugh in the right places. I liked listening to the flow of the French, the sound of it expanding and contracting like someone playing havoc with the volume button. Every now and again, I smiled, to let them know I was happy to be ignored entirely. Then I put on a sort of victim expression. Of course, these people didn't know whether I was happy or sad, intellectual or stupid. I think they thought I was ill. They looked at me with a mix of empathy and sympathy cleansed and sterilised by distance. I began to make up poses for myself. The sound of their voices became like swaddling. I fell away from the atmosphere. But then the volume went up again and I'd be back there with them, my head jumping from face to face, sound to sound. When off guard it would happen and bring me back to the room with a jump. Marcelle was speaking to me.

'You like Paris?'

'Oh yes. Very nice.'

'And Divine, your sister. It is good to see her?'

'Oh yes. Very nice.' A curtsy smile. A slurp of coffee.

I go to my bag and find a magazine. I don't go back to the table, I lean up against the wall in the corner, where most of the dead umbrellas are and there is a bean bag and a lamp that stays on day and night, because the flat is dark, day and night. I have relieved the guests of their need to include me and me of my requirement to smile. But I don't read. I think of my moon. And I am tired. So very tired. And a bit of me wants to cry but I have no idea why. I want Simmi to come back and I know I don't want to stay in that flat another day. It's too small and too French. And Annique knows. She knows that I would have let her make love to me. And thank God she never. Losing my virginity to a woman would have been cheating.

Chapter 19

The minute Simmi and Divine got through the door, I burst into English. Was the passport sorted? Was it a hassle? I was glad to hear the sound of my own voice. Simmi said, as Divine had predicted, the French would not make it a problem for her to leave the country. Divine had burst into French and Annique. The multi-chat went on for some time and me and Simmi would have gone on longer if a silence hadn't jarred against us. I turned to look. Divine had shrunk back from Annique. She was tasting bitter, in her mouth, in her pout. Wronged. It was the massage, my massage. What had Annique said? A spike of jealousy flitted across Divine's eyes, watering them. I went back to talking to Simmi but had lost the thread and much as I tried to pick it up, to lilt on, in rhythmic chatter, so more and more did the distress of my sister impinge on my performance. The smell, the touch of Annique's fingers running over my nakedness still lingered, a light bulb in afterglow. The difference between memory and sight inside. This image can be confused with guilt too, and that's how I read it, then, looking at Divine. Preposterous, yet that image, memory, sight inside, wiggled its way into my words to make them stop, splutter and start up again like a car without timing.

Simmi tried to egg me on, her face nodding at me as if I were in some race.

'Come on, girl . . . let's have it then. Get it out.'

I stopped starting in the end, and as one should, when danger looms, I went towards the bubble. To pop it.

'Eh, Simmi, Annique gave us a great massage. Ask her to do you one. It was something else. She's very good.'

And then I turned to Divine.

'It *was*, Divine. It was wonderful. No wonder you're so taken with her, she's . . .'

Then I stopped. Tripped up. Like walking in the dark. I didn't know the words for the rest of the way.

'I'm surprised she lay still for you,' said Divine to Annique, walking away from me, to the kitchen.

'She was fine,' said Annique, balling up her torso, wrapping her arms around herself, embracing herself in defence, like we did as kids, pretending that someone was smooching us. 'Though she has many tensions.'

These last words trailed from her lips like bubbles from a lost and aimless fish.

'Divine?' I said.

'Yes.'

I followed her into the kitchen, so we could feel togethery, for everything to be all right. But running out of words, and of politeness, I got to the point.

'Divine, I think we'll be leaving today. If you could lend us some money?'

'Can't.'

She was oh so quiet. Wincing as she spoke.

'You must have some money.'

She stopped dead still, as a mime, and then spoke, with part venom, part self-control.

'Savings.'

I spoke loudly, to let the other two hear just how miserly my sister could be.

'I'll send it right back to you. When we get back to England.'

'Yeah. Sure you will.'

Softer then, she was, busy with her hands, the sight of her bony shoulder blades cutting in to me.

'Come on, Divine! There's no room here, is there? We'll drive you mad.'

She folded her arms in frustration. Trapped in the kitchen. Audience in the front room. Divine was back to having to play the nice big sister and she hated it.

Then I had an idea. I moved towards her and quietly said,

220

'And what shall I tell Mum and Dad, eh? Do you want me to say that I've seen you or should I just leave it?'

It was a bit below the belt, that. Raising up the ugly spectre of Dad's head. Still, the question had to be asked, the strategy discussed, though to bring it up then, whilst I was trying to cadge off her, it was as I say . . .

'Sometimes you can be a little bitch, do you know that?'

Nice sister checked out. Wax meets sun.

'Divine!'

'Don't come the little twirp with me.'

'Oh for God's sake, Divine. Every time you have to put your hands in your pocket, you go off on one. You're just tight. That's your problem.'

'And you're just a taker.'

She turned round and looked straight at me. Same height as me but her face was more angular. All my features melt into one another, like a series of soft rolling hillsides. Divine had monuments set on her face, high-rise nose, walkway cheeks, a waterfall of a chin. She lifted her chin up to me as she got stuck in, her eyes, mascaraed and narrow, like the closing of the drawbridges.

'Mum wrote and told me about you cadging all the time. They're on pensions, Vivian. They can't afford to be bailing you out. When I was at college, I managed. I wasn't scrounging all the time. But look at you. You haven't changed one bit.'

She turned away from me again, pouring coffee into a filter machine, making a mess as the grains dissolved into spots, all over the counter. Mess really stood out in that kitchen.

'Oh. I see. Back to that now, are we? You being the good girl, sat in every night.' I started to sing, 'The queen was in the counting house, counting out . . . Remember?'

'Don't start.'

Snarling, she was. She thought she'd got rid of me, living in Paris. Thought she'd pulled the net over but there I was, buzzing about in her kitchen. I shrank back from her a little, the outburst too charged up for me. Annique and Simmi were stunned into silent embarrassment. I figured Divine would suss this and calm down a bit but she got worse, spitting.

'I thought when you left home it might knock a bit of sense into you.'

She went all high-pitched, her voice bouncing off the glass cupboards and crashing into the windows.

'You've only been here for five minutes and you're asking for money.'

'Divine, we got robbed . . .'

'There's always something. Always some story.'

Banging the cupboard doors, looking for the cups that hung on hooks, just underneath. Even I could see that.

'Forget it,' I said and stamped out of the kitchen.

I went to my bag and zipped it up, the zip snagging every centimetre.

'Come on, Simmi,' I said. 'We're off.'

Simmi looked worried but nervously got up.

'I've taken the day off work for you,' shouted Divine.

'Well, you better get back there then. You don't want to lose a day's pay on my account.'

And again, I was nearly crying. This was too much. Too much crying altogether. It wasn't out of a need to, or even out of frustration. I think something was opening up inside me, a box that had been closed for a very long time.

'Vivian. Come with me.'

Divine came out of the kitchen, grabbed my hand (that made me feel better) and headed towards the bedroom, the boudoir, as I thought of it. *La chambre*, she called it. So soft – *chambre*. I followed her through. It was bigger than the lounge. Funny. White. All white. No lace. Nothing fancy. White squares of bed and cupboard and floor. Huge pillows, square ones. White cheesecloth duvet cover. Walls white. The only colours were the clothes and the jewellery. And the books and the perfume. They were marketing victims of the perfume industry. The pair of them. Two whole dressing tables laid out like altars. The mirrors flashed back, white on white. Long pencil mirrors embedded as silver shards

222

round the walls. Divine stood out in relief, like she was floating off. The whiteness calmed us. There was a feeling of being abroad of ourselves.

'Listen,' she said. Snivelling. 'I *will* help you. I only get mad because' (now she really was snivelling) 'because you never fucking change, do you? You're always on the scrounge and –'

'I can't help it, Divine.'

It was the first time she'd sworn since we got there. This was real Divine. I put my arms around her.

'What is wrong with you, for God's sake?'

'Nothing.'

Full-blown attack of jealousy. Of being out of sorts. Divine liked routine, order, respect of her privacy. Then her little sister turns up and peels back the layers.

'Doesn't look like it,' I said, with my arms folded, watching her dither in front of me, surrounded by white. The truthfulness of a white she couldn't hide behind.

She took a tissue from a box that was on a low stool by the bed. There was a book on the stool too. Descartes, whoever they were.

'Don't tell Mum and Dad, will yer?' after she'd wiped her face and could look at me head-on.

I was flicking through the pages. All in French. Gobbledegook. I looked up to see her hanging on my answer . . . Our Divine. Scared. Mind, she had reason to be. Dad'd go apeshit. What Divine didn't realise was that I was the last person on earth to tell Dad.

'Divine.' I hugged her. 'Your secret's safe with me.'

She moved away from me.

'Do you like her? Annique?'

'Yes. She's very nice. Divine, are you sure you know what you're doing? You're fucking up Dad's plot, fine-style . . . Vietnam . . . with a girlfriend . . . you seem a bit subdued to me. Are you sure you want to go?' I never gave her chance to answer. 'Can I just go and get my fags and that. I'll roll us a spliff.'

It all reminded me of home, of the nights when we tired of

223

Mum and Dad's arguing. We stayed upstairs, in friendship at first, but then we'd soon find something to row about. Money usually.

Back in the lounge, Simmi was getting undressed. The massage rack was back out. Annique was really sticking the boot in. Rubbing oil into her hands, like hand cream, like she was about to operate. Simmi turned to face me. She looked scared, worried.

'Just getting my blow,' I said, moving round the room as one would in a church, whispering.

I didn't want Divine to come out and see them.

When I got back to the bedroom, she was on the bed, patting it for me to join her. We lay as a mirror to each other, arms supporting our heads. We really were back home, talking, the familiarity. I couldn't see any of the room then, only Divine's face and in it, Mum's. We spoke quietly, as if to keep it in the family.

'I'm not sure I do know what I'm doing, Vivian. But then, I'm not sure of anything any more.'

'Oh don't go all morbid on me, Divine.'

'I ought to be close to home really, near Mum and Dad. His breathing's bad now, you know. I'm quite worried about them. I thought it'd be a doddle getting a job . . . what with my degree and everything but – well, there are plenty of jobs if I want to be some lackey. All the good jobs I can't get. Can't even get interviews. A lot of them said I'd need an MBA to really make a difference. There's always something else, isn't there? They want blood.'

'They?'

'The system.'

'But what about the job you're doing now? Dad thinks you've hit the jackpot. I never hear the end of it.'

'A French school-leaver could do what I'm doing. They do. And anyway the contract's nearly over. Glad to get rid, I think. I think they wished they'd interviewed me before I came. They saw my name, an Oxford first and references sent by fax. I got the job.'

224

'You're being paranoid, Divine. You've always been paranoid.'

I offered her the spliff. She knocked it back.

'Oh go on! Have a spliff with yer skin and blister.'

'I came here fresh as a daisy and full of the joys but on that first day . . . I'm not fucking stupid, Vivian.'

She turned the spliff between her fingers. I held the light towards her.

'What yer lookin' at it like that for? You don't have to, if you don't want to.'

'It's just . . . well, since I've been smoking this stuff . . .'

'Oh here we go.'

'It's like I can't kid myself any more. I was so uptight before, wasn't I? Now I see things. If I smoke more, will I see more?'

Asking me like I was the doctor. She took an almighty drag off it. She was like that, our Divine. If she did something, she went all the way.

'Well, I guess it comes down to whether you want to look.'

'It's not a case of wanting. More a case of needing to know.'

'Know what?'

'Everything.'

'For example?'

'Well, why things are like they are. For black people, I mean.'

'You're not still on about the fucking slave trade. Having a spliff's s'posed to make you forget about all that shit, Divine.'

'Listen to you. Just listen to you. You're so . . . so sodding desensitised, aren't you?'

'Thankfully.'

I took the spliff from her.

'Even though you know it's happening, you can sit there quite happily and do sod all about it, not even want to think or talk about it.'

'Divine, there's no point. What good's talking?'

It dawned on me that it might be wise to talk, at least until Simmi got back in her matching boots and sweatshirt.

'That's what makes me depressed. And when I get stoned it

makes it worse, coz I see more and more. Though sometimes I'm not sure that I do see. Maybe I just can't handle being stoned.'

'Is it her?' I said, nodding with the joint towards the front room, creating a barrier between us and them. 'Getting stoned is supposed to make you happy, relaxed. It's fun. Is she turning you into a commie? She's been getting you at it, hasn't she?'

'Vivian, listen to you. You sound like some Tory twat from Oxford. Commie this, commie that. Fuck communism.'

'Well, I think you're being a bit pessimistic, to be honest, Divine. Life's life. We had a good night last night, didn't we? That's what it's all about.'

'Yes, but now I know stuff . . .'

'Live for the day, Divine. Do what the alkies do. One day at a time.'

'That's what I used to say. What I used to be like. And I tried. I tried for the best. But now. Now I've seen them at it. Jesus. It's like one of those suitcase conveyor belts at the airport. The same old baggage going round and round. Seeing each other off and welcoming each other home.'

'Divine, what are you on about?'

'All the same people, the Law, the City. The money. I bet there's only a few hundred of them, the ones that control it all. The invisible hand, they call it. And then there's the armies of educated dickheads crawling up their backsides. Some of my mates even. Well, I can't' (she gave me the spliff), 'I can't. It's not in my blood. Mum said it'd be hard, but not this hard. And do you know what? I don't blame the blacks for not trying any more. Not one bit.'

I was bored of these stories, these depressions, sadnesses, hopeless cases. There must be a conveyor belt for them too. A huge one. I didn't welcome such stories home any more.

'You can't waste your life moaning just coz you met a few nobheads at Oxford, Divine. You're like those people that give up smoking. You've gone right the other way, 'aven't yer?'

'I'm getting older, Vivian, that's all.'

She stood up.

226

'*Really* grown-up now, are you? You and your fancy flat in Paris, sitting on your backside all day long in some fancy office, feeling sorry for yourself. You don't know you're born. And with your brains, you fuckin' ought to.'

'With my brains I can see what they've built on the backs of sixteen million blacks. I see them totting up third-world debt over lunches down at the embassy. I see too much, Vivian.'

'We can't do this, Divine. We can't go back in history and start calling the odds all over again. We'd be back to the Norsemen and the Danes . . . Stony ground doesn't let water in. It's famine territory.'

'So just get on with it. Is that what you're saying? Other things are more important to you, though, aren't they? Maybe it's not that surprising you don't care.'

She was losing her temper, blowing air fast out of her nostrils. Because I was trying to make light of her depression.

'No, listen to me, Divine.' I was up, sitting up, plucking theory from the stars. 'Fuck the Danes and the Norsemen for now. And the Jews and the blacks. Now then.'

I wanted to let her know that I do think. She was behaving like the rest of them, thinking all I ever thought about was myself. Just seeing my scar.

'What if one part of the human species mutated, you know, like some animals do? And then they kept inter-breeding. Now look at the white man. Little groups of them went off on their own, didn't they? All over the world. They took guns and germs everywhere they went and destroyed half the planet. They bred with themselves. OK, they raped half the planet too but they didn't own up to the kids, did they? They didn't let mixed blood rule, did they? No. They kept themselves to themselves. They decided they were superior and interbred among themselves, to keep things that way. Well, we all know what the *inbred look* looks like, don't we? You see, it wasn't just physical germs they spread across the planet. Their psychological germs are just as powerful and unfortunately, no one as yet has managed to identify and eradicate them. They're like bacteria growing on a culture dish. Unchecked, they grow and mutate, unhindered. The white man is one big germ factory. And look what they're doing to the planet now. They've based their entire culture on what was achieved by a load of psychologically infected dickheads. The white race is unbalanced. A mutation. Unhinged. They're all off their rockers. And like all nutters, they think there's nowt wrong with them. They're mutants. It's sod all to do with politics. That's a red herring. It's in the genes, I'm telling you.'

'What's this? Reverse fascism?'

She said it quietly, like she wouldn't mind believing in my theory for a minute. Just a minute. Just for the fun of it.

'My mate Roy, he knows about the moon and the stars and stuff like that. He says that soon there'll be a big watering of the planet – not real water. He means a watery sensation. A flood of consciousness.'

'Boyfriend?'

'Sort of,' I said, remembering the kiss right then.

'And what does he do?'

'He's a plumber.'

'Well, that explains his flood of consciousness then. If he was a mathematician, he'd have the world drawn out in numbers.'

'Oh yeah! I forgot. He went to Oxford. See! They're not all at the airport.'

'He went to Oxford and he's a plumber?'

She scrunched her forehead up.

'Yeah,' I said, sticking to my guns.

She gave me a little smile. A knowing smile. Like she was glad I was screwing a plumber, a clever plumber even. Screwing someone. She didn't have to worry any more. She blew the relief out of her nose. Her sister was getting laid. Another landmark.

'But they have been pretty thick when you think about it, haven't they? The whites, I mean. And loud. Make loads o' noise don't they? Like kids.'

'Noise?'

'Yer know. Everything they do, they shout about it. Write it down. Make TV programmes about it. They're killing themselves with it. Couldn't pick out the truth even if it was out there. The way to go is to treat *everything* as background noise, Divine. That invisible hand you were on about is the hand of the wankers. We did the invisible hand in economics. The true power, they call it.'

'They can't all be bad,' she said.

'What, white people? No. Some of my best friends . . .'

'You know what I mean. And anyway, blacks carry on just the same. When they get the chance. Until they reach the glass ceiling anyway. That's the official term for it now, by the way. We're banging our heads against a glass ceiling.'

'Well, funnily enough,' I said, 'the glass ceiling links in quite well with my petri-dish theory.'

'Your what?' she said, spluttering.

'Nothin.'

'Petri dish?'

'Actually, Divine. It's not a glass ceiling. It's more like a floor. A floor made of mirror glass. A two-way mirror. All those bastards riding round on it are just looking at themselves. By staying underground, under the glass, you can see them at it. If you're up there and you don't see your face in the mirror, you're in trouble. You have to get out. Go under. On top they always make out that going under is the wrong way to go. They make so much noise about it, everyone believes them. But noise isn't truth. Truth speaks volumes but it doesn't make a noise. It makes music, rhythm. Suddenly everything slots into place. Those people riding round on the mirror don't understand anything, unless it looks like them. I'd rather stay underneath where I can see them. Where they can't see me. I don't want to be obsessed with myself. I don't want their disease. I'm not saying white people are the enemy – just that they're a bit poorly. Look at what they've done. Look at what they're doing. A dad, a dick and a degree and you're in charge. You've just said so yourself. Then an invisible hand appears from nowhere to wank them off. Hey presto! It can happen to anyone these days. In the beginning it was the whites but now everyone is vulnerable. Some blacks get it bad. They live for what they wear, what they drive, whatever money can buy for them. It's a disease.'

I curled up on the bed, safe. Home. Pleased our Divine was down, beaten, demoralised. Horrible, I know, but her being like that made *my* life more valid. If I'd told her everything about my petri-dish theory, she'd have laughed at me. The cosmic string stuff and the weavers and the sparks. She doesn't like spirity stuff. Cosmic stuff. She says mumbo jumbo makes black people look stupid.

'And what's more, Divine, every fucker with an ounce of common knows all this. Do you know what they're doing now? They're freezing their dead bodies so they can come back to life again. If I were them, I'd stay dead coz if they ever wake up, there'll be a queue of people sat outside the freezer with axes, ready for them. Don't talk to me about lost dreams, Divine. Get used to it. Get yer head down. There are no fucking dreams these days. The establishment is set up to kill dreams. That's their job.'

I rolled another joint.

'We're still slaves really, aren't we?' she said.

'Fuck off, Divine. I'm bored of this shit, I really am. Go to Vietnam and start a revolution, why don't you. Or get on with a less complicated life. Enjoy it, Divine. That's the secret. Enjoy life for what it is. Don't get bogged down in it all. People *know*, Divine. One day there'll be a big wave and all the people who refuse to budge, they'll be bashed against the rocks. They'll be floating round the world as jetsam and flotsam. Flotsam and jetsam. That's what I wanna call my cats. What do you think?'

'Mmm.'

'Can you imagine what me dad'd say? He thinks you're a hop, skip and a jump away from the Foreign Office. If he knew you were running off to Vietnam with a dyke . . .'

'Yer won't tell them about Annique, will you? And don't call us dykes. It's horrible.'

'No. I won't. I won't tell, I mean.'

She pushed her hand through my hair, separating my plaits in layers, like she was peeling me back. I let her. Only coz I was on holiday. Normally I'd have told her where to get off. Then she stopped.

'Divine, why *are* you with Annique? Not because of her massage, I hope.'

'Leave it, Vivian.'

'Is she the first?'

'Yep.'

'Don't yer miss . . . yer know . . . ?'

I thrust my thighs.

'We get round it.'

'Get round it!? Round it?' I laughed. 'And what about kids?'

Chapter 20

It should have been Annique and Simmi packed off together. So I could be alone with my sister. So we could spend some time not having to behave ourselves. Be ourselves. But Annique had caught Divine in a trap, as some exotic game. Divine clucked and pranced about the place with wings clipped. Even now, stood in the hallway, Divine stood back, as though Annique had her on a lead and that was as far as it would stretch. To the doorway. I couldn't get the measure of the woman, Annique. She spoke in furniture language, did we want milk, go out, massage. Oh, and by the way. We're off to Vietnam. She did the facial pictures of passion, compassion, empathy and sympathy, but there wasn't any there. The real Annique she kept hidden. Maybe that was the language barrier. More a veil than a barrier, I thought. Reality meshed over. I'd need to know her longer to get that veil off, yet she'd managed to strip me down in less than twenty-four hours. Divine needed me for longer so I could get her to the end of her sadness. So she could still recognise herself by looking, seeing, remembering me. In a few months she'd be in Vietnam wearing khaki, a red bandanna and a peaked cap, cocked to the side. She'd have a cigarette resting on her big bottom lip and lose herself completely. I remembered the man in the sarong at Bev's dinner party. And the bells rang in my ear. I felt a gush of mourning.

We booked into La Rondelle, a really cheesy place with running water and privacy. The next cheapest place was dormitory-style. I thought Simmi might refuse to stay at La Rondelle, but running water and privacy were high on her agenda too. We slept fully clothed.

I lay on my bed and closed eyes for a smidgen of privacy.

Before I fell asleep I puzzled over my two-way mirror sliding with mutated humanoids suffocating. It was a bit far-fetched, maybe. The theory lacked that academic finesse that Roy always lent to his meanderings. I wanted something more earthy, more realistic. More credible. After a toke on the spliff, rolled by Simmi for once, a whole series of nightmares rolled out of my imagination, ranging from white people selling bits of their bodies off to one another (arms and legs), white people licensing their blood so that blood-donor agencies turned into copyright engineering centres, right through to designer cannibalism, to assist with reincarnation. When Simmi offered me the joint again, I refused. I was scared of what came next.

We went out after, me wearing the money belt that Divine gave me, stuffed with francs. I felt like James Bond. We did some postcards and the lightheartedness of the afternoon relieved me. At last we were doing normal stuff. Off we went to the Pompidou Centre, on Divine's instructions. I figured it'd be over-the-top cultural claustrophobia but when we got there I was glad. The building was ugliness. Divine had said that at the Pompidou Centre everything that is normally inside a building is outside. The stairs and the air pipes. The plumbing stuff. Its guts wrapped round it like manacles. Serpents. The soft touch of the idea massaged me. I felt a shifting of perspective, like being in a very dark room for some time, and then someone coming in and moving a huge ward-robe away from the window. Not because I could see a few pipes – because of the idea.

For me, the rest of Paris, the bit I had seen, was the exact opposite of the Pompidou Centre. In civic Paris, everything was hidden away. Its history, its people. True, there were plenty of giant arches and penile towers, wide rivers of concrete dotted with trees and buildings so serious they were frightening. True, the people sat out on the pavements supping coffee and Calvados but all of them, the buildings and the people, looked to me like they were pandering. Putting up a front. As if this church here, that tower there, each monument were a substitute chargé d'affaires. Each street ended with a masonic punctuation mark – a landmark of power. And it was all front. The slick and the suited reading newspapers in a spring wind as the world walks by – all front.

The French were good at it. Secrets. But scrape off the top layer and there are hideous monsters writhing about in the dark, hiding behind the scenery. Maybe that is Paris. Maybe the art of dressing the city so elegantly and leaving reality gasping for breath beneath is what draws people. The great cover-up. Because everyone is at it, to be there doing it must make it feel right. Behind the fashion, chomping cheeks chatter out suspicion to run like oil, to lubricate the boredom. Adrenalin to liven the game up, crinkle the cosmetic. Suspicion to heighten the *frisson* beyond the common caution. I think it was *that* that made Paris buzz, frizz, made people dizzy. I thought about all this because of Simmi's white high-heels and our night out.

Simmi went into mourning when she unpacked the dancing shoes. She sat on the edge of the bed caressing their pointed toes like a child not big enough to wear them yet. So, on our first night away from Divine, I agreed to *dress*, as she put it. Just with that hair of hers, those eyes, she could get away with a straight black pencil dress and be up to the nines. She needed to be told, again and again, that people were staring at her beauty not her Pakistaniness, though I guess, to be honest, this was a ploy. Just so she could hear all about her beauty again and again. I might have fallen for the same bath myself had I the right kit. I wasn't fat. That was my main plus. When the men whistled, she turned round. Not me. I could only get away with feeling beautiful, not being it.

After spending some time with her I realised that Simmi's beauty was a dam to her own flow, held her back. Simmi took stares from men as stares of hostility. In Simmi's mini-universe, this standoffishness meant just one thing – anti-Pakistaniness. I disagreed. I said they were scared of beauty. Most men are. It's the opposite of what I get. She said that coming from a different culture had taught her to protect herself. With dignity. Taught her not to mistake admiration for equality. She was so much deeper than me in many ways. I didn't expect it of someone so beautiful. I, like the men, could only envy her. She was trying to teach me to rise up. She said those men weren't interested in her culture. (Of that there was no doubt.) Away from home, she wanted to cling on to it with both hands. She defended herself from the stares by standing with shoulders back and chin up, a stalk of pride running right through her centre. She looked even more beautiful when she did that. The men became more 'hostile' in her eyes. I suggested it might be an idea to lie down on a metaphorical feather bed and bask. Just bask in the glory. Slumber through the adoration. Just enjoy it.

This particular night, after café-hopping for a couple of hours (we found one café that served us the most splendid broth of vegetable and mutton. We could only afford the soup, but the African French girl who served us kept filling up our bowls and re-stocking the bread basket. We ate our fill for just a very few francs – but even better than that, the whole of it tasted wonderful!) we made our way back to our flea-pit via some cobbled alleyways, Simmi clomping like a horse. We passed a terraced building, four or five storeys high. The ground floor was pumping out music and slits of orange light were coming from the curtain edges. The occupants of the buildings either side appeared to be out, or asleep, which was unlikely. There were no lights on anywhere except in the La Maison de la Musique, which isn't what it was called. On the wall to the left of the front door was a metal plate, a brass one, like for the chiropodist, or the solicitor. 'Le Club International'. We imagined inside there a cultural soup. We hovered, undecided as to whether to ring on the brass doorbell. We tried to peep through the curtains. We muttered to ourselves that the place felt right to us, was part of our destiny. We'd been brought that route just to fall upon what would be an exhilarating end to the evening. We were trying to squeeze out the last bit of toothpaste.

Then we heard a car pull up. A suited gentleman jumped out of the passenger seat. The car was long and shiny black, an important purrer, a creeper. He was upon us quite suddenly, the car away down the alley. We began to stumble off, smiling at him with our turned heads, so we could get as much of an eyeful as possible. He called us back and spewed out a volley of French. He could have been a solicitor or a chiropodist, that type. Steely.

I interrupted him. Pointing my finger wildly, from Simmi and then back to me, I shouted at him, to make sure he could hear me, which of course he could since we were upon him like hungry schoolchildren.

'*Nous sommes anglaises*,' I said, waving my finger back and forth, determined he would understand me.

He jerked backwards because we were in his space but also in some surprise since we didn't fit his English template.

'*Vous êtes anglaises?*'

'It's always the same talking to foreigners. They always want things repeated, no matter how hard one tries.

'*Oui, nous sommes anglaises.*'

We were stood slightly back from him now, weighing him up and acting more ladylike. He was training his eye down Simmi and then back up again.

'You want dance?' he said, wiggling his hips a bit, looking pretty stupid.

We looked at each other and smiled back our appreciation.

He rang the doorbell. We were being vetted through an eye in the door and then we heard the bolt being pulled back. Simmi's high-heels were going to get a showing now. Of course, imagine, super slim legs, beautifully brown, white high-heeels and a black dress tempting the knee. Wouldn't you want to show off? Fat mane of black shine, face for film and elegance oiled with pride. A magnet.

Inside the door, there was a reception desk with a girl sat behind stroking a poodle perched on her lap. She looked like a poodle herself and should have brushed out the over-tonged curls in her hair just a smidgen more. We let our gentleman sort out the language and arrangements and then we were asked to write our names in a book. We were in.

We walked through tables of people to the only table left. There were disco lights and music in full swing but the wooden dance floor was empty. The punters sat back and eyed the floor as if it were an ocean, waiting for some monster to appear out of it. I might have been watching some ritual in an ancient fishing village. They were entranced. Some of them had dogs and we decided that this was a French obsession, dogs. Passion, they'd call it. We knew the French liked poodles – who doesn't know that – but taking them out to the disco? Men with big dogs. After the man sat us down at the table he told us his name – Henri Pont. Then he made drinking-out-of-a-glass signals, so we nodded at him and said *oui oui, merci, merci*. He went off to sort it all out and we both lit fags.

The people in the club weren't talking to each other very much. They weren't very happy at all. Not like down Maple Street on a Saturday night, where, in any club, there were groups of lads jeering and jarring and pouring liquid down their gullets, laughing. None of that there. These characters had been plucked out of the novels. Zola grotesque. Kafka-esque. Big-bearded men. Feminine men. Deluded, huddled and miserable men. Men with curly, wiry hair and men all white, hair, skin, pallor, expression. There were a couple of women with hair piled high like pantomime men. Everyone was sat down.

That they didn't pay us any attention was an anticlimax. That was always the paradox. Attracting attention was as much a drug to me as being able to blend in and not be noticed, as to be invisible. We expected faces to take sneaky snapshots but I never caught anyone at it. They were too engrossed in waiting, stroking the dogs, flicking ash into ashtrays and waiting. For the monster to come out of the dance floor. We then thought that maybe they were waiting for someone to start the dancing. Maybe the French were just shy.

Our man came back with a cigar and no drinks. We screwed our faces up at him, like he'd got the game all wrong. He lifted his arm and with outstretched palm he told us to stay calm, to hold our horses. Then he pointed towards the bar. We hoped, well, I did, that he wasn't suggesting we go and buy ourselves a drink. It was easy to see that drinks weren't cheap. The bar was almost empty, the punters as sober as . . . Then a waiter appeared, but not in waiting costume. He brought with him a bucket of ice and a bottle of champagne. My heart sank. Simmi grabbed my hand across the table and as if volted, I shunned her. We were in the shit now. We didn't quite know what shit, but we knew we were in some.

He poured three glasses and then, at last at rest, he sat with his legs crossed and stared at Simmi. She hit me with her knee under the table. An English pop song blared out from the sound system and I looked at her, nodding towards the dance floor. Here was the chance to show off those nice white shoes of hers. She nodded in agreement. We could talk in private on the dance floor, which we did. We bobbed about like ducks in mating season, eyeing the punters at the bottom of the dance floor, staring sternly at us. It never occurred to us that, from one table to the next, they probably didn't know each other from Adam. To us, they were all in on it, all staring. All still, all sitting and all French. Bob bob.

Then the music went quiet and we waited just those few ticks of the second hand it takes for the next record to home in on the ears to decide. Was it good enough to get away with a few rhythmic side steps and a glib smile? It didn't have to rock. Things like 'Bat out of Hell' would have been out of the question. A George Macrae track ideal. The seconds ticked on and nothing. Then an almighty bellow of cymbals and trumpet music and rather than go straight back and talk to the man with the champagne, we preferred to think if we stuck it out that we'd get the hang of the rhythm any second . . . any second now, and then the room came alive. At last we were entertaining them. Two dark foreigners getting our hips round a brash clash of what must have been a French hit tune. We gave it our all, writhing, because the beat was slow to rise. Maybe others would get up to dance now.

We were so busy watching the expressions of our audience

that we hadn't noticed the woman who must have come in from some doorway to the side of the dance floor. When we turned round to look, it was her tits that first threw us. Just there, right next to us, bouncing about. The audience were trying to look round us because we were in the way now. If only it could have been a dream. But there was more. She was leading a dog around the dance floor like she was at Cruft's. A setter, it was. This got us off the dance floor pronto. We didn't look up, even after we sat down. We just stared at the table and sided glances to each other. The man leant forward to speak to Simmi but Simmi stared back mute, in shock. The champagne was by now so expensive we couldn't raise it to our mouths. We had to get out.

The dancing lady sent a chiffon scarf into the orbit of the audience and a few men jumped up to get it. The excitement in the audience accelerated. A verrrhhhhh of momentum bounced round the room, threatening a finale of frenzy. There were claps and clinking of glasses. The bar was serving fast and thorough now, the waiter back and forth as if on skates. The loo was on the way out. Our man was watching the stripper, smiling round his cigar. I tapped his elbow and did a powdering-my-face signal. Amused at my optimism, he bit his lip and pointed us in the right direction. We fell into the street in stitches, bent double, rolling aimlessly down the cobbled alley, laughing like drains, almost hyperventilating.

We liked the Pompidou Centre and kept going back. Like that club, everything was out in the open. It was a stab at the truth if nothing else. Going up the escalators it felt like I belonged to the Centre or it to me, a contract between us. The portraits inside, the sculptures, the massive canvases of purple mist shouted at me, their authors shouted, told me in plain English that they were not free. That they were not rid of the manacles of control, ambition, habit. The people outside, on the concourse, juggled and ate fire. Mexican men made a racket, stood in a circle playing maddening tunes, on drums and banjos. The mimers, men and women, stood in stone and peasant dress – all of them it seemed eating from the breath of the Centre. I felt a real Paris there. Some say real Paris is in Lafayette's underwear department. But it's not. It's in the underpants of the beggars of the Pompidou. In those pants, there be life, a sailor would say.

We sat and listened to a 'Streets of London' guitarist, since he was the most painless on the ear and least well attended. I rolled a joint and ran through my white mutation theory, once again. I ran through it to get the measure straight, before the calculations and doom theories descended upon me, stoned. I never told Simmi about it because I figured she was racist enough. I had the feeling she would have embraced the theory too enthusiastically and I needed to examine it objectively. And there was Davy and the dancing girls.

'Let's go after them.'

'No, Simmi. I don't think so.'

'But . . .'

'But what? They'll have spent the money. Sold the passport.'

'Just to look 'em in the eye then.'

'What for?'

'Just to let them know we know.'

'They know we know. Maybe karma'll get them, eh?'

I turned away, bored.

'Maybe *we* are the karma,' she said, enthused.

I wanted to sit calm with my thoughts. The idea of confrontation appalled me.

'Go on then, Simmi. You go and be karma.'

I got up and dusted myself down.

'I'm off. I'm gonna go and see the painters.'

'Artists,' she said. 'They're called artists.'

'What's the difference?'

'It's like calling a writer a typist.'

'Or a musician a . . .'

'A . . . A . . .'

'Or a poet a . . .'

'A . . . A . . .'

We laughed.

The upper deck on board *Shining Sheila* on the way home was padded with anoraks and we walked amongst them, weaving our way between four-a-breast families protecting each other from going overboard, perhaps.

'Why Vietnam then? Why's she going to Vietnam?'

'The weather, I guess. I think Annique's father's got something to do with it. Bit of a commie, by all accounts. They're going to live in some paddyfields – start a co-operative or something. Simmi . . .'

'Yeah.'

'What did you think of Annique's massage?'

We were looking over the side of the ship into lifeboats that looked perilously ludicrous. The lifebelts shone up at us like Polo mints and it crossed my mind that even if one wanted to go underneath the glass – even if one wanted to live in the underworld, you'd still need a lifebelt. You'd still need to hold on to something. Beyond the ship, seagull waves rushed away from us to a huge black cloud that had the sun shining behind it, a black jewel, dangerously powerful. She took a long time answering.

'Was all right, wasn't it?' eventually.

'Did you feel anything, though?' I asked impatiently.

'Relaxed, d'yer mean?'

'Well, yee-ees.'

'What d'yer mean, feel anything?'

'Did you feel anything weird?'

'I didn't do it with nowt on. She wanted me to. I didn't think it was right, her being a dyke. I had the feeling she just wanted to get an eyeful. Did you do it naked?'

'Did you ask her for the massage or did she suggest it?'

'I asked her. You told me to.'

'Yeah. So I did.'

'Did you think she was trying to . . . you know?'

I walked away from her, turned and shouted, 'A little bit.'

Now that I knew the truth, I think I would have liked our Divine a lot earlier and a lot more.

That big black jewel of a cloud I was on about got closer. It emptied itself out all over the ship. I emptied my stomach and more besides, in all the loos, over every wave to Dover. Is this the body mimicking the sea? The body fluids urging their way out of the skin, out of the stomach, out of the mouth to be free with the sea? I couldn't even 'think' my way out of the sickness. All of a wobble, a half-spin in a washing machine, back and forth. My inside body on its travels, leaving skin and bone behind. And on my knees, I cried into the toilet bowl. I cried for the Elephant Man. 'I'm not an animal. I'm not an animal.' And yes! These were real tears. Not the stabbing screech of pointed power-drill tears behind the iris, my eyes crying with cystitis – burning water piddling out of clogged ducts, stinging me. No. These tears of sea sickness were the proper tears that I cried as a child. Before the accident. Medallion-sized tears. From a well full of tears. They rolled into my eyes and fell out like storm water. Down my face. Soaking wet and generous, painless tears.

GOING TO JAIL

GOING TO JAIL

Chapter 21

Thinking about Mum and Dad's wedding anniversary brought on a daydream. It's hard to concentrate on court procedure, even if it's proceeding in your direction. It's boring. I can't be more illustrative than that. There are good bits that have you on the end of your seat, but so much toing and froing in between, the mind wanders. To Dad on this occasion. I'm imagining the worst. Tragedy always wants to revel in itself. When I was a child, when I first noticed and felt the keenness of a desert-red sunset, on the floor of the sky, so glorious and so final, I would have bathed myself in blood to be part of it. To get into the sky. For me, it's the same with tragedy. That keenness. To withstand it, I need to revel in it. So I couldn't help but imagine my dad ruined, almost dead. After all, he was on trial too. I imagine he comes to see me.

'This is needin' some paint here, Vivian,' he says, examining the cracked gloss on the front door.

The front door is the best bit of the house and as he walks down the hall this dawns on him. Before reaching the stairs he turns to look at me and wraps his mackintosh round him tight, as if to keep himself clean. Then he taps his hat, as if to keep himself whole. Even though he's old and slow, he's still big and, as I follow him down to my flat, he grows.

'Cup o' tea, Dad?' I say, in a voice too high-pitched.

'Let's be truthful here, Vivian. I have not come all dis way to be en-ter-tained. So let us dispense wid da niceties and hear what it is . . . what it is that you have to tell me.'

In three minutes Dad can reduce me to tears, to the size of a peanut. Shored up in a chair, stroking his moustache that has strands of steel weaved into it, he stares at me, his beady eyes begging me not to make him sad but knowing he's going to be.

My mouth is full of howl but I control it. I won't let it come out. He starts to tap a rhythm on the arms of the chair. Waiting.

Leaning forward in his chair, his mouth manipulated into a horror caricature, in a hoarse whisper that yells gravity he says, 'For what?'

And that's the fracture. That is the measure of my disrespect.

'For what? For what? For what? Tieving? Tell me it's not tieving.'

'Dad . . .' heading towards the door. 'Dad . . . don't go. Let me . . .'

He looks at me as if I am his twenty-five-year marriage gone wrong. Which is taking it too far in my opinion but that's my Dad. If he knew what our Divine was up to . . .

'Dad, listen . . .'

And then he leaves. He creaks out of my flat with his shoulders to me, all bouldered and lonely, miles from the sea. He doesn't limp but in my dream he does. In my dream he is heavy and lame. He's so much bigger than me and so lost from me. He has to leave me, alone. He leaves me as he used to do, when he marched me home from school. Him in front and me behind, keeping up, keeping back and out of his way. At those times, more than any other time, I wanted him to hug me. Like now. But he stopped doing that the day I stopped stealing. The smack that he gave me stung and the stinging pain has grown ever since. It has grown with my knowledge of hypocrisy. The real me was the me that Dad didn't want and so I've grown into a shape that he can't recognise.

I follow him down the stairs.

'Dad, if you hang on I'll ring you a taxi or . . . Dad! Dad!'

He walks slowly down the stairs, out of the front door and bangs it shut. I'm surprised he doesn't go the whole hog and tear his shirt. Maybe outside the front door, as the wind lashes his mackintosh away, maybe he's doing just that. *The Jazz Singer*. He watched *The Jazz Singer* seventy-two times on his Betamax and I just know he's been waiting and waiting to play the dad part himself. What he doesn't understand, after seventy-two times, is that that part of the film, where the dad tears his shirt, is the stupid part. But my dad loves that dad. He wants to play him. So, I re-thought my dream and brought him back from the front door, back up to my flat. He sets off again. He holds his hat to his chest and bows, as if in prayer. Then he puts it on, reverently.

We're just outside the door to my flat when he turns to me. He grapples with his lapel to get to his shirt. It's his faded check shirt that I gave him for Chrismas.

I cry out, 'No, Dad. No. Don't do this.'

He tugs and tugs at the shirt until I hear it rip. I see him gulp the phlegm of his grief and I hear his snuffles. I see the teardrops fall and he backs away from me, into the darkness of the hall. I'm no daughter of his.

This kind of thinking is not good in court. It's wearing.

'You did what?' said Benky, screwing his glasses on tight. 'I can't see the science of it,' he said. 'Is there any evidence to say that this method is effective? Could the contents of the . . . of the vagina . . . be released in this manner? I find that hard to believe.'

'I was only doing as I was told. And it was only the once.'

I kept my head right down. Bodene kicked in again.

'The defendant says three times. Three times in total. May I remind you that you have already lied . . .'

'Objection, Your Honour.'

'Sustained.'

'I didn't lie. I was confused.'

'You have already demonstrated just how confused you were on the night in question – confusion so profound it prevented my client having access to a solicitor. Given that you can't remember how that omission of procedure occurred, why should we believe you now?'

'Because it's true. It was only the once.'

The jury leant forward for more story. Everyone was by now in the swim. They understood why we were all there, what the rules were, what the hell was going on. They'd got used to the dull bright. The squeaking shoes were part of the paintwork. The barristers were opposing directors of a *soon to come near you* movie. No, it went this way. No, it went like this. She did this. No, she didn't. She did that. All the jury had to do was to decide which film they liked best. The police-woman was coming up with the best script yet, unwittingly. Ratface's plot was slowly disintegrating. The jury had begun to like Bodene. She was humble. He who comes humble leaves satisfied, my dad says.

'Your pocket book doesn't show any signs of confusion, does it, WPC McCarthy? Very neat and tidy. Numbered paragraphs even. Everything seemed to be perfectly straight in your mind whilst you were writing down your notes, but now you're in court and the pressure is on, it appears that you are confused.'

Ratface smiled down at his papers. Bodene was ripping off his script. The script he used on me. This game was not chess. It wasn't intelligent enough for chess. It was more like draughts. And Bodene was picking up crowns by the dozen.

Boy, did she look embarrassed, the policewoman. She was almost naked in the stand now. She would like to have covered her breasts with her cap. The men in the jury were undressing her. Giving her some of her own treatment. The story was getting juicy. 'Bout time too, said the face of a juryman, settling down with paper and pen. The press were writing it all down too. Everyone was writing something down. So many words, so much writing. Now the judge was at it. He was writing it down. No memory, these people.

This dressing-up malarkey. With power in their pockets, they don't think they look stupid, but they do. I can see them. The emperor's clothes and all that bollocks. They must look in the mirror and see Olde England in all its Glory, in its wig and gown. The very same wig and gown that dressed the man who consigned my father's ancestors to a lifetime of slavery. The very same costume and they're *still* not too embarrassed to wear it. If I could see some practical use for it, I wouldn't be so base about it. But I can't. And I've tried. I have also tried to accept the whole construct as a deep vein of fabricated tradition and so not shed much energy towards it. The costume is not important. But something inside me tells me that it is, that this bunch of clever clogs know something I don't. It's a trick. A judiciary dressed in the garb of the magician, to pull off some blinder. They may look like wallies to me but there was method in it. Somewhere. The police who considered these jesters the ultimate arbitrators of the law looked up to them, respected them, called the judge 'Your Honour' and bowed down to him every time he threw them an eyeball. A string of magic circles meshed. And I wasn't in on any of them. Lord help any poor soul that comes before this lot and thinks it reality.

I took some lipstick from my handbag. God, it kills me just saying it. My handbag. And a small mirror. I applied gentle strokes and tilted the mirror to show up the good side of my face. I patted my hair and homed the mirror even closer to my face, to ensure that at least a couple of the jury noticed that I was trying to improve upon what couldn't be improved. Because I wasn't practised, the lips seemed bigger after a coat of a paint. Made me look like someone had thumped me. I thought about Bev then.

The policewoman was set free, out of her box. She dismounted a lot more slowly than she got up there. A lot more thoughtfully. Lots of paper-flapping and coughing. Had the jurors been saving up their coughs? The ushers had a bit of a flap and busied themselves with the important break in the ceremony. They flapped. Just what did they think they looked like? All they did was open and close the doors. The rest was just one long snivel. A grovel at the gavel. Nodding at the plod, just politely, not ritually. They might as well have been at the pictures showing people to their seats with a torch. Come to think of it, I could have done with an ice-cream right then. Oh yes. I was feeling a lot better today. Plod had got a right kicking. Get on there, Bodene! Pump it. Oh God. DI Rochester. Ratface would slobber over him.

Just as I said. They knew each other's lines, off by heart.

Hell-bent on heaving me off to Holloway. Bodene was more in the swing of things now, though. It was almost as if, like me, she needed to hear all the evidence to get the measure of the depths, to get the outline and their colouring in, before she could define, before she could etch some reality on to the artwork. After the Old Bill finished sketching out their scenarios, she got up and etched some realism. Loud truths.

'Detective Inspector Rochester. Did the defendant at any time admit to using heroin?'

'No.'

'Did she at any time admit to handling heroin?'

'No.'

'Did you suggest to the defendant that, if she admitted supplying cannabis, the heroin charge might be dropped?'

'I did not.'

'Common practice, surely? When the evidence is scant for one charge, you attempt to secure a conviction on another less serious charge?'

'That's not what happened on this occasion.'

Bodene had a nerve. Here she was, in court, slagging off the Old Bill for doing to me exactly what she'd done to me that very morning. What the fuck was going on here?

'Then why, Detective Inspector Rochester, do you suppose that the defendant denies both the heroin charge *and* the charge relating to the supply of cannabis, yet she readily admits to possession of cannabis? Why has she, in her supposed confession, admitted to supplying cannabis to a character she describes at length but in such vague terms it would be accepted, by the jury at least, that this character was somewhat devoid of concrete attributes?'

'Objection, Your Honour.'

'Sustained.'

'I, for one, Detective Inspector, don't believe that such a character exists. If, as you say, she was not intimidated by your practices but merely wanted to admit to the lesser offence of supplying cannabis, why did she not substantiate that truth, with fact, with substantial evidence? To give her story some metal, so to speak? Why did she not supply you with the names of her customers?'

'To protect them, I suspect.'

'Yet the only persons who were found to have cannabis of the same low-grade type as that found on the defendant are now dead, are they not, DI Rochester? Would they have needed her protection?'

The jury gasped. Honestly, they gasped. As though it was the cannabis that caused the deaths, not the heroin. What the fuck did Bodene think she was up to?

'Yes, but there were others, obviously.'

'Obviously? But you didn't see fit to question the defendant about those others, did you? Why is that? Why, on the transcripts of your interviews, are there no questions enquiring into the names and addresses of the people she sold cannabis to? She says in her confession that she sold a lump of cannabis to a man she doesn't know the name of, who she met in a pub on a large estate that has lots of pubs that all look the same so she couldn't be exactly sure which pub it was. Not very specific about it, is she?'

'Well, she'd admitted the offence after all. There's only so much time and money to spend on cases like this, Your Honour,' he said, looking up to Benky for support.

Benky was clearly impressed and intrigued by this line of questioning. He too wanted to know why the detective had not seen fit to enquire about the victims of my cannabis-selling enterprise.

'So, the victims of her alleged cannabis sales were of no interest to you? Even though it was quite possible she may have sold them something even more dangerous than cannabis, perhaps? Something like heroin, perhaps? You weren't interested, though, were you? You knew the defendant was not a heroin dealer. You wanted a result, didn't you, DI Rochester? However innocuous that result might have been. You got a confession to an imprisonable offence and that was enough. Isn't that the truth, DI Rochester?'

DI Rochester looked flummoxed. After all, that was his job.

'Oh but then you did go after one other suspect, didn't you? A Miss Simmi Reza?

'Yes.'

'Best friend of the defendant, is she not?'

'Yes. So I'm led to believe.'

'And, what did you find on Miss Reza's premises, in the way of drugs?'

'Nothing.'

'Not even a roach?'

'A roach? A roach? What are you talking about, Mrs Bodene?'

'Your Honour, the end of a cigarette that has had cannabis in it.'

'Do please refrain from these colloquialisms. Carry on.'

'Not even the end of a cannabis cigarette, Detective Inspector?'

'No.'

'So the defendant's best friend wasn't a customer then?'

'Not that we can prove.'

'Objection, Your Honour.'

'Sustained.'

'No more questions, Your Honour.'

Half-past three and still me to go. I was free for one more day. Things were looking up.

'Your Honour. Perhaps we could start taking evidence from the defendant and finish off in the morning.'

Judge looked at his watch. It was hanging from his belly. It looked like he was looking at his willy. Seeing if it had a discharge.

'Well, if you think it's worth it,' he said.

He obviously didn't think so. The screw unclasped my cuffs.

I was on. Up there. Still under oath. No. OK then. Right. Here I come.

'And is this a postcard from your sister to yourself?'

Well, of course it is. It says 'From Divine'. It says 'To Vivian Jackson'.

'Yes, it is.' Dab. Dab. 'Could I just have a drink of water, please?'

'Of course. Oh, I see, your jug is empty. Could we . . .'

Get that fucking usher on the move. I'll have him up and down all day if I have my way. If he wants a piece of the action then he's got it. I'll use that swell in his gown later on, to blow the wind out of Ratface's performance. I'll go to the loo and fuck up his finale, the speech where he folds his arms and rocks back and forth on the soles of his feet . . . I'll . . . I'll . . . I'll

'And did you eventually go to Vietnam?'

'No. I couldn't. The police confiscated my money. And our Divine was so poorly – I was worried out of my mind. We thought she'd die.'

That was one hell of a lie. It floored the jury, though. I could see a couple of them having a dab. Eh up. Hang on. Judge Benky's woken up.

'Is that an American serviceman in the background of this postcard?'

'Yes, sir, sorry. Your Honour. My sister is assisting with the rehabiliation of ex-forces families. The ones that couldn't live in America for one reason and another. Also, she has the extra task of helping the research department in the economic development unit. They're sort of teetering on the verge of becoming more capitalistic in Vietnam and my sister is giving them a helping hand. She got a first in French from Oxford, sir. Sorry, I mean Your Honour.'

He wanted to poke my eyes out, I could tell. No, he was smiling rather kindly, I thought. Maybe he'd put my initial performance down to nerves. First-time nerves. It gets better every second.

'And, Miss Jackson, did your sister survive this illness?'

Bodene was really milking it.

'Objection, Your Honour. This line of question has abso- lutely nothing . . .'

'Sustained.'

Too late, smartarse. The information is in the public domain. You'll be remembered as the story interrupter. The jury were dying to know if my sister was all right. I gave them a bit of a nod, a wet sort of nod, to let them know. Dab. Dab. I could see they were concerned. I was knocking them down like skittles. Six for a teddy! Six for a teddy!

'And where exactly did you get this money from, Miss Jackson?'

'From my friend Vincent.'

'And where is Vincent?'

'He's in Nigeria. Poorly.'

Saying that Vinnie was poorly threatened to tip the balance just a teeny bit too much. There were far too many poorly black people knocking about my story. Coupled with a face like mine, I was in danger of alienating the jury, all happy, healthy and white. It was time to gee myself up. Make myself look more credible. More 'not poorly'. No more dabs for now then.

'Oh! If you're interested,' I said, 'I have a postcard from my sister here. It came this morning. She's doing very well.'

I held it up for Ratface to see. He looked at it. The wanker. Somehow his script had gone all wrong.

Bang! Bang! We'll adjourn till tomorrow.

All rise.

I was back in my box. We waited for Benky to stand up. It wasn't easy for him. Bit of lumbago there, perhaps. Then, at last, he was ready. The ushers were ready. The barristers were ready. Then they gave it to him.

The nod.

Tomorrow we'd be sailing with the wind behind us.

GOING OVERBOARD

Chapter 22

When we got home from Paris, Dirk and Bev were having a row. I could hear what sounded like books being thrown at the walls. Then rhythmic bursts of high-pitched screams gapped by silence. Like a needle scratching a record. It was Bev scratching out her record of misery. The quiet sectors were Dirk being calm and sarcastic. Then another scrawp across the vinyl from Bev. Till at last there was peace. Simmi looked at me all worried.

I went through the post. Most of it was junk. An airmail letter for a Mr Kipling, whoever he was. Nothing for me. When we got inside my flat, though, I found a series of notes written on pieces of green paper. The first was written in bold capitals. 'URGENT URGENT URGENT'. The fifth and last weak and in joined-up writing, 'Vinnie's not well.' Simmi was sat on a box reading a letter from her brother, collected from her lodgings where she hadn't lived for months. He was coming down tomorrow. She panicked. Vinnie being in a mental hospital didn't compute for her. She had family news, news so new it went straight to her heart, like a defib. Action was compulsory. She went off to look for bedsits, lodgings, anywhere respectable. Anywhere but where the boxes of her life sat, in a flat underneath the drug dealers.

When it was quiet, I went upstairs to phone Irish and Roy and to get some draw off Bev. I was worried. I didn't want to run in on a row but then how long would it go on for? A month? As I lifted up the phone, I heard their door open. Bev came out.

'Bev! I'm back. Sounded like you were having a biggy. Who won?'

'He did. As usual. Did yer have a good time then?'

'Yeah. Great. Have you got any draw?'

She sighed. She looked tired. Then she bit her lip.

'I can do you a bit,' she said.

'I'll come in after making this call.'

And then I turned away from her, to make a private space for myself round the phone. As I dialled, my ears noticed her still there. I turned back round to see her look at me. There was a want in her eyes. She wanted to talk to me, tell me something. She looked vulnerable, not the Bev I'd come to regard as my banker and stock provider. Maybe I should have offered her my flat, some space, but my head was too tuned into Roy, into the idea of us spending the night together. I didn't need Bev right then. As if I'd made this quite clear, she turned away and went back to her flat.

I called Irish first to get myself comfortable with the phone. Not that phones are a problem for me. Oh no sirree! Phones are Top Banana. But still, there's a swim to get into, a level to find. I do the phone with my left ear even though I'm right-eared. It's that ambidextrous thing again. My body is divided into hemispheres. I like the phone so much, I often imagine having no face at all. Like being on the radio but for ever. No one knowing what I look like. Having to take me at face value, as they say. Face value! Does such an expression have its roots in suggesting that language is a more valuable currency than face talk? It's not true. People can't really hear properly if the face doesn't talk properly. Oh it's all very well if there's a bit of kit like a radio or a telephone to blame. That's fine. Ugly faces can't compete on that level, though. An ugly face speaks a language all of its own. Brain talk is instantly devalued.

A lot of well-meaning people fall into the trap of convincing themselves that what matters is the soul, the spirit. That what matters is not what a person looks like. These people have gone beyond themselves. They've read somewhere not to judge a book by its cover and in their heart of hearts they know this is right, but the judge still sits. This, for me, is the big lie. The biggest hypocrisy of all. Naked emotion, dressed in intellect to cover its private parts, will not, cannot, make love

258

with what it finds repulsive. I see such emperors everywhere. When a stranger's eye roves around my head and refuses to meet my eye, I see that judge delivering his verdict before hearing any of the evidence.

My face is half dumb. When I speak to a person, a stranger, it can't articulate a completely natural expression. It tries but, after doing so, even before my skin muscles have rested, the message I have sent out is being misconstrued, misunderstood or just plain missed. It's like trying to control a stutter. When I'm not trying for control, my face thinks for itself. My face can think all by itself, without any help from me. It has a personality of its own. Lately, I've noticed its acceptance of tears, of being wet, hot and sticky. It used to balk at this. It used to refuse, as a child might refuse to wash its face. As soon as my eye muscles contorted themselves for a good squeeze of the juices, my face would straighten again, the muscles would hold firm and the tear taps turn themselves off, tight. But now, as I get older and become more of a woman, my face has begun to feel the benefit. It's as though it wants to increase its repertoire. I play with my tears. I spread them over my scar and make them stick to its most shiny bits, the unfeeling section. This part of my face doesn't think, it just hurts. To spread tears across it gives it a sense of humanity. In my own little way, I try to make my scar live with me.

When I'm wrecked, my scar, no, my whole face, is alive and unhindered. The only reason I'm not wrecked all the time is because I can't afford it, but if I could, and I was, my face would become my friend and take on a life of its own. It would take more risks. When I'm straight, I have to control my face, for its own protection. Out in the street, I'm in charge of a monster. As I've said before, plenty of times, it uses a lot of my mental energy. People with a face, a full face, don't realise the power they are blessed with. That sounds basic, doesn't it? But it's not as basic as you might think. A face isn't all nose, gob, frown and chin. That's not the face. How we manipulate all the parts together, in recognisable patterns, that's the face. And half of my face can't do it. Strangers think that that's me –

that that's all there is to me. I walk around with a Siamese twin on my head, a me that can't be separated from me and can't do anything for itself. Unless, of course, I'm wrecked.

Because half of my face can't speak the right lingo, I understand now what the voice of the face is for. It's not just handy for direct speech, like a broad, broad smile or a confused brow. The most important sounds it makes are for punctuation. The face paints in the capital letters and carriage returns of our dialogue. It shouts full stops. When people first meet me, I see their mouths fill up with exclamation marks. Only after I've put them at rest can they put brackets around my scar. Once relaxed, they begin to use more subtle delimiters, like commas, or if truly brave, they'll listen to me a while longer and see the need to use a question mark. Success is when they can see me as a full sentence. Ultimate success for me would be the sophisticated use of grave and acute accents for an absolute but subtle change in effect. To have my face read as a book would be even more useful, truthful. Not a book cover, a book, the book. Using my face, I would like to express italics, their cringing narrowness. I would like to speak in bold type to indicate my seriousness. Use dashes to give me some space. What if I could contort my face to produce a few . . . so that I could change my mind mid-flow of conversation, of consciousness. I can do none of this at present. Not with strangers. Strangers are still another country. I let them gulp down their exclamation marks and I don't look them in the eye.

They won't look me in the eye because the eye, I've learnt, is much more than a ball with a hole in, to let the light through. It's a mapper, a template drawer, a pattern cutter, and above all it's an information gatherer. Since the strangers can't read my face, they prefer not to look. They stare from afar but never look to find meaning in me. This, I can't bear to see. When I was a child, with my eyes, I drew templates, cut patterns, gathered information. Before the scar, I did. Now those templates have been ripped up and the patterns cut on my understanding don't have any meaning. They're all jumbled up in my head like bits of a broken pot. I find it difficult to gather information because I can't distinguish from disinformation. So for a lot of the time, one of my eyes is shut down. I'm half blind. I can see where I'm going but not what will happen to me, when I arrive. If I did . . . if I looked with both eyes, like I do sometimes . . . sometimes I see so far and so much, I'm glad it's only sometimes . . . when I see with both eyes, the light that rolls in gives me two images. What people look like, and then, what I think they're thinking. If I did this all the time, my brain would shut down. With one eye, I look but don't see. There's no coordination, no mapping of image against reality. I just see the furniture, the mechanics. If I didn't get wrecked so much, I wouldn't think these things. The phone is my power tool. By using it on my left ear, I'm giving it my best shot.

Irish said he'd be right over. I put the receiver down. I stood in quiet contemplation, finished off my spliff and prepared myself for Roy. I'd like to say that virgin pools of sex seeped between my toes and rose up to bathe the space between my legs. But they didn't. I would like to say that my mind was away to the sound of a welcoming kiss from him, an opening, a suck. But it wasn't. I was fifteen years old, calling my first boyfriend, asking him to come out to play. I was shit scared.

'Ehhrrr. I'm waiting on somebody, actually. I ehhrrr . . . I'll come round later if that's all right.'

He sounded irritatingly casual. And impatient.

'Yeah. OK. I've got a bit of a problem, though. Well, not me. Vinnie, actually. He's in the mental hospital.'

I spoke with a panicky voice, to camouflage the real cause of my panic.

'The ministry for lunacy finally caught up with him then, eh?'

'Sorry?' I said, recognising a softening in his voice, a chance he might mellow a little.

'Nothin'. An old Scottish joke. What's happenin' then?'

'I don't know. I'm waiting for Irish to come round and fill me in. I didn't know you were Scottish.'

'I'm not.'

'I'll probably have to go up to the hospital. Could you come round about nine? I should be back by then.'

Close the deal. That was my thinking. I had to know.

'How was Paris?'

'I'll tell you later. I had a great dream. Petri dishes and Polo mints combined.'

Fuck Paris, I thought.

The bells on Bev's door chimed my entrance into the jarring silence of their empty world. Full of tat. Full of pictures of this and that, and the pair of them sat there, empty and dull.

'Any photos?' asked Bev.

'In my head,' I said.

'So how was your sister? Was she pleased to see you?'

Dirk's head was grim. He was fixing something metal, a green plate, rectangular, about ten inches long, five wide, with lots of mini-skyscrapers in bronze and silver all across it. A metal city built on metallic green grass. His long fingers were deft at pulling the baby buildings off and sticking them back on again. Like grown-up Lego, I thought. He poked into the buildings with a tiny screwdriver and my mind went into the Land of the Giants, imagining all the little people inside the little metal boxes, standing at the windows watching Dirk destroy them with his huge metal wand.

'Divine. She was fine. Bit weird. What's that yer up to, Dirk?'

I wanted both of them to talk. To be normal, and calm. Bev wanted to use me as sticking plaster over the tension.

'It's a semi-conductor board. From a computer. The bike shop's closing down so I'm having to look at new ways to earn a living. Freddy's starting up a computer business and he says he could use an engineer. All right? Does that answer your question now?'

'You can't just do that . . . turn into a computer engineer. You have to go to college for that stuff.'

'What, like *her*, you mean,' he said, sneering at Bev, seething.

262

He stood up and threw the board on the table, all the people in all the buildings dead now. I cringed a bit.

'Don't be telling me what I can and can't do.'

'Dirk, I was only saying . . .'

He rolled a joint in silence. Bev offered him the one she was smoking.

'I'll smoke me own, thanks,' he said, sulking seriously, it would seem.

No way was I a guest any more. I was living underneath them now. Under their skin, it felt like. Bev got me back on track.

'Well, was she surprised to see you then? Divine?'

I wasn't sure whether to tell them. Whether to keep it a secret. It didn't feel like a secret.

'She was the one full of surprises. She's gay. Living with this woman from Vietnam. They're moving out there together. Before last week our Divine was your typical hard-working Christian genius. You can just imagine what it was like for me, can't you?'

Dirk stopped what he was doing and looked at me with a big smirk across his face.

'A dyke eh? Your sister?'

'There's nothing wrong with that,' said Bev, like a grown-up, making out that it was just dead normal. Making us out to be dead childish.

It might be dead normal but it's not when it's your sister. I was with Dirk on that one.

'You wouldn't say that if it was *your* sister, would yer?'

'I would,' she said, weighing a lump of hash. 'That's an ounce there. That's all I can do for now. And you've got me wrong there, Viv. Each to his own, I say. If you're pissed off with your sister, that's your problem. Not hers.'

'I know,' I said. 'It's just . . . it just feels weird, that's all. I try to imagine them doin' it . . . yer know . . . together . . . I mean, what do they do? I wanted to ask her but I couldn't. She's changed. I can't talk to her properly any more.'

Dirk looked back at me in sympathy. Bev's doctrine on

freedom was too wide for us. We checked each other and made friends. With our eyes. Then he made friends again with his eyes. And again. I didn't get it.

'You wanted her to tell you how they did it?'

He laughed, alive to the turn in conversation.

'Well . . . yes,' I said, knowing damn well how they did it.

'She's mad, isn't she?' he said to Bev. 'What if I asked you what you got up to in the sack?'

Bev gave me the joint. I kept my eyes on Dirk. In his eyes, I could see he was doing just that. Imagining me.

''Snot the same, though, is it, with lesbians?' I said, aware of my being undressed, my pubic region hot.

'No, it's not,' he said, sitting back in his chair, big grin across his face. 'But I wouldn't mind watching.'

'Typical,' said Bev. 'And I'm surprised at you,' she said to me.

'Well, what about me mum and dad?' I said, to stop them bickering. 'They'll go apeshit.'

'Well, they don't have to know, do they?' said Bev.

'Well, I . . . Can I pay you for this when my grant comes in?'

With no draw to sell, Hector home on his holidays and Mo back on his mountain in Afghanistan, I'd be skint for a week, till my grant came in. I couldn't ask Mum and Dad for any more money.

'You still owe us, remember.'

'Yeah, I know, I'll sort it.'

'So don't tell them. Your mum and dad.'

'As if,' I said.

Dirk went all cold again. He rolled another joint.

Maybe I just imagined him doing that stuff but whatever, it felt real to me. There was something hanging in the air between us, something he turned on and off when he fancied, almost like a tease on me. He knew I'd received his message loud and clear and just as I tried to get the measure of it, he turned it off, as though nothing had happened. That's what it felt like. But again, I was unsure. Maybe it was just the thought of getting a very real Roy that had heightened my senses, brought the fantasy of Dirk closer to reality. This last was the more concrete explanation, I decided. Before going back downstairs, I rang Roy again, my sex screaming at me now.

As I slotted the coins in, I heard his answerphone kick off. Then I heard Dirk's door bells ringing. I turned round and it was him, coming towards me, his long hair shielding his face. As he got close to me, he pulled his hair back behind his ears and smiled. Another tease.

'Roy, are you in . . . Roy, pick up the phone.' Silence. 'Roy, it's me.'

I was sounding desperate. I watched Dirk's bum go down the stairs. He was ambling. Strutting. He was driving me fucking mad.

'Roy, are you there?'

I was actually praying to God that he'd pick up the phone. I don't do that often. I mean, call up Divine Intervention. But I did then. Even when I'm in deep shit I don't do that. I never ask God for anything. At this moment all I wanted was for Roy to pick up the phone. No big deal. Very small prayer. But I begged God to answer it.

'Vivian? What? What do you want now?'

'Roy!' and a sigh, a pause, to get my conversation sorted out. 'Roy, I hear there's a bit of a drought on.'

'Tell me about it.'

'I just got an ounce off Bev. Have you got anything?'

'I soon will have. I'll see you later.'

'OK. Will you be getting personal or *more* than personal?'

I heard Dirk slam the front door shut.

'Viv. Don't be so gobby on the phone. And get off it. I'm waiting on a call. I'll see you later.'

'Nine?'

'Nine. Bye,' irritated.

I put the phone down and knew I'd probably lost him. It would be hard to inject romance into that attitude. Well, tonight it would be anyway. Maybe, I thought, maybe when I saw him, all that would change. I was, by then, glad I hadn't brought him a present from Paris. I was glad I at least had a

265

kiss to go on. He *had* kissed me. It was real. It was worth following up. It was my best lead yet. Think positive.

Irish turned up on a pushbike. The hallway seemed to attract them. There were two there already and nobody ever seemed to ride them.

'Yer can take that bike home with yer when you leave,' I said.

'Uhhh??' looking at me like I was mad.

'So come on then, what's happened to Vinnie?'

His back was all hunched up when he got off his bike. His arms were bowed out, like a crossbow, and his hands picked his pockets as if any second he would pull them inside out, to empty out their emptiness on the eye. Like all he had left was his body. His ginger beard and hair were still holding the raindrops from a shower, like dressmaker pins, their bobbly heads all shiny. He was enriched for that, as if sprinkled with silver. Sad, bewildered even, he wiped his forehead with the worry of a grown-up and then dropped his fingers to rub his eyes like a tired child.

'The day after you left for France, I came home late with a girl. He was in the garden, digging up the flowers. Bollocky, he was, in the middle of the night. I thought he was tripping out on something. Out of his head on something. "Vinnie, what the fuck are yer doin'?" I shouted. He just looked up at me and carried on digging. Then he started eating the soil, stuffing it into his mouth, showing me how much he could stuff into his mouth. Then he spat out, 'The earth, it's all to do with the earth. The earth. The Lord giveth and the Lord taketh away.' Stuff like that. He was raving, panting. His eyes were sprung out of their sockets. I told him to get inside but he wouldn't. Well, I couldn't leave him out there like that so I grabbed hold of him. I picked him up with a bear hug. He was screaming his head off, thrashing about like crazy coz I had his legs off the ground. I didn't know he was that strong. I was feared he'd wake the whole block up. Then he swung for me with his elbow.

266

' "Look at that there!" he said to me, pointing, getting up off the couch and pulling me under my bald lamp bulb. "Me eye's only just gone down. Look there! Look at that!" It seemed perfectly OK to me. Nowhere near as bad as Simmi's had been.

'A police car drove past us and saw us throwing fists. They got out the car and overpowered him. Jumped all over him. I was trying to tell them that he wasn't well but they wouldn't listen. They cuffed him and threw him in the back o' the police car. The neighbours were up then. In their dressing gowns. I had to follow him down to the police station with some clothes but they wouldn't let me see him. Vivian, it was something else. I was scared for the lad, I truly was.'

I didn't want to hear all that. I'd hoped for a suicide attempt. A bog-standard suicide attempt. I could understand that. I was disappointed rather than sad. It felt like he'd let the side down. Not the blackdom. The side of common sense. Vinnie was too small. Going mental was going under.

'They had him down the general at first but he's up in Seemar now – yer know, in the centre?'

'Yeah, yer said in yer letter. Can we go and see him?'

'He thinks he's the Son of God. The next Jesus Christ.'

'Don't they all.'

'But he really does.'

Irish passed me his spliff.

'He's been taping his conversations with God. He really believes it. He thinks he's been sent down to earth to do some job but someone's put a device in his head to stop him. He says someone's trying to control him and the only way to fight them is to be true to God. And then he says he's been talking to the bloke himself. God, I mean. Like it was his fucking dad or something. It's frightening, Viv. It really is frightening.'

That coming home was a falling down. The lifts in the lorries. The flat not lived in yet. Roy not signing on the dotted line, on the phone. And now this. Vinnie. Attention-seeking again.

When we got to Vinnie's centre, we were shown into an

association ward where, if you didn't smoke you'd want to, just to fit in. Women sat staring into nothing, inhaling, like machines. Fluted silver ashtrays centred tables, like guiding stars. A tinny radio drew the line between calm and panic. Men walked quickly, then slowly. They walked around us and came up to us, asking us for fags. They thought I was one of them, kept pulling at my arm. They bowed in deference to Irish. Coz of my scar, I suppose. Any place I go where there are people fallen, I become one of them. Mental. Criminal. Poor. Thick. Ugly people are all these things.

There didn't seem to be anyone in charge. Irish wandered off round the screens to see if Vinnie was playing cards in the quiet corner. I stood, trying not to look fazed or scared, feeling homesick already. The longer we stood there, the braver the patients got, coming up to get a really good look at me. At last Irish came back and said Vinnie was probably in his dormitory.

He was lying curled up in his bed sulking. Fully clothed. He smiled a bit when he saw us but didn't lift his head off the pillow.

'My father's just left.'

'Yer dad?'

I was surprised. Up until then, his father was a photo representing mission control.

'Got in from Nigeria yesterday. Didn't say much.'

Irish went off to get some coffees. I sat right up on his bed, really close to him. Poor Vinnie. He was worn out. Wouldn't look me in the eye. Just stared at the bedside cabinet, eyes manic. Like he was tied down by something I couldn't see. I wanted him to know that I didn't see him as sick. I didn't want an act. He didn't have to perform.

'What d'yer mean he didn't say much?'

'He just said I'd get over it.'

'Well, he's right.'

'Told me to pull myself together.'

'Are they giving you drugs?'

'Yeah.'

268

'And?'

'And they pin me to the bed. Wipe me out.'

'Irish says you've been chatting to God. Not a good sign that, is it, Vinnie?'

'I *was* chatting to God, but I can't feel the feeling any more. It's like I've been buried. When we were talking, it was like I had a direct line, yer know?'

The whites of his eyes were wincing and wonderfully beautiful, animal. He didn't look at me for more than a couple of seconds before he buried himself into his pillow again.

'Vinnie, sometimes if things are on top of us, our brain can't cope and we go off on one. It's only a phase. Maybe you did speak to God, maybe he talked back but who the fuck's gonna believe you? No point in going on about it, Vinnie. They'll throw away the key.'

'I taped it. The last time he spoke to me.'

'Vinnie, come on. Take it easy.'

I stroked his leg through the blankets.

He sat up suddenly. Shoulders back in warrior pose, eyes blaring. He looked ridiculous. I sat further away from him, slightly alarmed. I figured he might swing for me if I denied God one more time. It was a cue for a cockerel. He bent over and opened the drawer of his bedside cabinet and took out a tape.

'Play that and then come back and tell me that I wasn't speaking to God. I got a bit stuck on the numbers but if I'm left in peace, I'll get there. I'll work it out. I'll work all this out if it kills me.'

I was quite curious as to just how mad Vinnie was, so I took the tape and popped it into my pocket. As I did so, a ginger-bearded skinny rake of a man came up to the bed. He had pink corduroy trousers on and a blue chequed shirt out of some cowboy movie. His ears were pointed and flappy and as if to face up to this handicap, he'd shaved his head. His head kept nodding. He got hold of Vinnie's feet and started cranking them, like they were Vinnie's starter motor.

And then in a really high-pitched voice, 'Come on, Vinnie. Back to the lounge. Telly's on now. Vinnie! Telly time.'

Vinnie got straight back under the covers. I could see his torso shaking.

'Listen, mate, he's not well. Leave him for a bit, will yer? Maybe he'll watch telly with yer later on. Off you go now.'

'Excuse me,' he said, hands on his hips, 'I'm the nurse in charge here and Vinnie has to go into the lounge. No lying in beds.'

No wonder Vinnie was shaking.

'Vinnie,' I said, patting him nicely, 'Vinnie, we better go to the lounge, eh?'

He didn't budge.

The nurse just stood there, impatient, like he was waiting to mop the floor. I noticed then that he had lines, not wrinkles, lines of fold down his cheeks to his chin, suggesting that he was once chubby, once filled those cheeks. He was only about thirty.

'Can I have a word?'

In his office he leant against a wall with arms folded. He knew the cell structure of every brain in his charge (he would like me to believe) and would treat each brain according to his own wisdom along with the drugs prescribed by the doctors. This unofficial agreement that I believed everything he said to me was not signed by me, and would have to be re-negotiated if I were Vinnie's relative, but I wasn't a relative and so I wasn't important and so he leant against the wall, with arms folded against the idea of having to explain anything whatso-ever to me. Or even having to look me in the eye, which is something I would have thought he'd be up for. I guess he saw me as a potential victim. Work. Vinnie had stabilised. That was his mantra.

'Wonderful,' I said and left him there.

I stood in a corridor waiting for Irish to say his goodbyes. I spent my time spotting patients, as distinct from doctors and nurses. The lack of white costume made the place more sinister than ever. It was like alien spotting. I looked for certain tell-tale signs but when I thought about these signs in relief, in isolation . . .

Wandering about aimlessly – that's me when I'm confronted with what they call a hypermarket.

Not able to walk in a straight line – that's me every night.

Walking too fast – me walking the main drag of the economics department at college, making sure I don't get spotted.

Walking with too much purpose – me going to the bar, home, for a smoke.

Walking in a dead straight line – me going to the bar, home, for a smoke.

Jabbering – me after being in the bar.

Not jabbering at all – me stoned.

Tidy – me at five years old, first day at school.

Untidy – me ever since.

Only in combination will these behaviours be called symptoms, I decided. Jabbering and walking in a dead straight line, for instance. That's a sure sign. Untidy and wandering about aimlessly. That's OK. That's called being homeless. Walking with too much purpose and wandering around aimlessly. That's subtle.

I looked for people with nervous tics. Unfair, I know.

The consultant psychiatrist wore a suit and tie and headed up a train of sycophants who hadn't quite mastered the art of how to walk as fast as their leader yet still look calm, unruffled, cool. Outside it was April and 65 degrees. The earth will cook, Bev said, like a huge global bowl of soup. It was too hot for a tie.

They pumped Vinnie with drugs to give the staff an easy life. That's what he said. They had no interest in his message. No interest in the babbles of his frantic state. They wanted calm. He told them that, if they wanted calm, then they should take the fucking drugs, and I agreed with him. Especially after speaking to nursey. I put my hand in my pocket to feel for the tape and when I found it, I squeezed it. As though to give Vinnie a squeeze of encouragement.

Back home, I made some toast and contemplated all the unpacked boxes. What I should have done was set about them. But I was too tired. Hadn't even sat down properly since getting home from France. Simmi blagged the longest sleep in the lorry that brought us all the way from Maidenhead. Cow. I set up my stereo to play some music. I found some blankets and wrapped myself up like a sausage roll.

At last, at long last, I was alone. The utter freedom of it. Completely and utterly delicious. I rolled round in the bed and looked up at my new walls. That was the first time I saw the wallpaper properly. The wallpaper that looks like the burnt skin of the baby. I unravelled myself and put Vinnie's tape in the tape recorder. I sat next to it, with crossed legs. Like I *really* was going to hear a God conversation.

Then Simmi came back. She'd have to sleep on the floor. In the other room.

I stopped the tape quickly.

'Did you find a place?' I shouted.

I wanted to get the conversation over with, do my bit and get back in my own space.

'Yes. Down on Rutherford Street. Top-floor studio flat. Tiny, it is. No idea where I'll put everything. D'yer wanna cup of tea? How's Vinnie?'

'I'll tell you tomorrow. I'm off to sleep.'

'What's this note for then? On the door, for Roy?'

'To tell him not to knock. To come straight through to the bedroom.'

'I'll be moving my stuff out in the morning.' (Alleluia.) 'Imran's getting here round lunchtime.'

'Right.'

'Don't suppose you want to help me?'

'Right.'

'You're so fucking selfish sometimes.'

I turned the tape back on. I'd had five days of Simmi. Enough was enough.

Vinnie coughed a bit at first and then said, 'I hear you. I feel you.'

I looked at my watch. It was ten to nine. I'd rewind it when Roy came and play it back to him.

Then silence. I listened hard in case I missed anything. I wondered whether this God of his had a voice. I knew that people with schizophrenia often heard voices but I didn't know if they could *do* voices as well. Another thought slipped in too. Dad once told me about the obeah men in Jamaica and how they could get demons to live inside people. Could make people possessed. He said that women possessed often spoke with a man's voice so I half wondered, if God was a woman, which I liked to think she was, would Vinnie do God in a woman's voice?

'"Duality."

'What do you mean by "duality"?'

Vinnie was using his own voice for God. In other words, he was truly off his trolley.

'"Duality is a habit of human consciousness because it is one of its earliest developments."

'What do you mean?'

It was the *real* Vinnie asking all the questions.

'"You choose one or the other. One is wrong and one is right. Polarity."

'One is good. One is bad?

'"The human chooses that which is better."

'But what is really meant by better?

'"Better is a measure. That is all. Better is one step after what is. Better is your empirical measure of how well your desires are satisfied. Desire is the conduit of progression and conversely regression. It is one of many gifts and it is one of many curses."

'I don't understand. What do you mean by desire?'

I didn't understand either so I rewound the tape and played it again. Stop. Rewind. Play. Stop. Still no wiser. Play.

'"Desire is having the *want* part of the brain stimulated."

'What stimulates the *want* part of the brain?'

I wasn't concentrating enough. I rewound the tape and played it back again, to get back into the flow.

'What stimulates the *want* part of the brain?

' "Desire! The need to survive."

'How does one find out what one wants?

' "By . . ."

A long pause. God was having a think about that one.

' "By knowing what is beneficial – and then comparing that with what already exists. You make much of the concept of choice."

'What do you mean?

' "The opposite of no choice." '

'D'yer wanna cup o' tea?'

'Simmi, will yer leave me alone?'

'Was only askin'. Who's this Mr Kipling?'

'Simmi, for God's sake.'

' "When choice has no benefit to the species, then there is, on another level, no choice. What point of a vibration that is not beneficial to survival? Yet such vibrations are now chained in energy reactions, creating a fabric that is growing and meshing in power across the globe. You cannot predict your critical mass of self-destruction. You are taught in numbers, not pictures, yet pictures are more an aid to survival than numbers. Have you seen a picture of the power crushing the planet?"

'So you think we're heading for self-destruct?

' "Not at all. Those who know me won't self-destruct. Those who don't, will."

'So it's all down to belief? Belief in God. How come those that believe won't get crushed?

' "Imagination is the key. Those that believe are not crushed. Never crushed. They do not cling on to the fabric."

'I think we'll always be in duality. We believe or we don't believe. That's duality.

' "To imagine oneself out of the fabric is to join with the many million and one ways of nature. To fix oneself firm on to the fabric is to enter the maze of choice, of stop or go. Left or right. Wrong or right. Soon, the people will stop this."

'Why?

' "Because it's boring. Some humans have already stopped but they wander the new world as the early nomads wandered the desert. As the nomads who walked the mountains of ice, unable to understand the concept of a human race. They were one with the earth and they understood it, its breath. These days, you are in the same environment, only reversed. As a mirror, if you will. You have powerful connections with your human race but you do not understand the earth. Its breath. Those that wander in the spiritual wilderness know it, but are few. They are the teachers. After one, a child learns two. Off and on. You have computers. The off energy is no greater than the on energy. They only create as they work together. Humans know that duality is only a physical reality. It is not a spiritual path. By following such paths, as filings to a magnet, all other paths continually ignored are closed paths. With magnetohydrodynamics, you are getting closer to the truth of matter. Do you know the science of electricity?" '

Stop. Rewind.

Stop.

Vinnie worked too hard. That was the top and bottom of this malarkey.

Play.

' "Those who have sought a new path have found a new freedom. Those that insist that there are only two paths are relics." '

'So this is what enlightenment is all about? The New Age?

' "No, it is not enlightenment. It is knowledge. Age, the counting of age, will lose power. New does not mean better. Your people have forgotten that, just as they have forgotten that old does not mean poorer. Soon, there will be a different spectrum where the confines of what you presently understand as time and space will neither be crucial nor restrictive. That is the next step. It is a big next."

'How big?

' "Well, some spirits are ready. Every thought they have is woven into the spectrum that harnesses the spirit of survival. There's a need. There's a demand. It's very big. Soon, you will feel a shifting of consciousness among the people, an acceptance of their responsibility to be true to themselves. There will pervade amongst those willing to accept this knowledge the buzz of a communal spirit. The volume will be turned up, slowly but surely. The physically powerful people will try to search out the source of this buzz. But with what? With their lights? Their lights will not find the invisible. Those who make rules for the mirror of their own reality – they will find nothing. Only themselves. All their vibrations will bounce back in their face, like echoes. They will be lost in the valley."

'How long is all this going to take?'

Quite, I thought.

' "You are as a bird pecking at the entrails after the feast is over. God or your concept of what God is, what I give you, is free of charge. Priceless, as you say. This force is invasive, its energy all-pervasive. It is the opposite and the sum of all the energy of all the universes. This energy stays free. It is the greatest glory of your universe. Your concept of time is outdated."

'So you're not God then? You talking to me?

' "Everything that is imagined is possible. Everything that is possible is imagined. From your state of chaos, will come the expurgation, a diminuendo, a decrescendo. God is a word. Your word. The word. A word that has no word, no sound, no physical form. A spiritual vibration that balances the forces of nature. You can't turn it off. On earth layers, there is a wave of imbalance at this present time. Due to noise. The noise is magnetic and cracks the bubble of individual serenity. It tries to silence the word of God. It will pass. Another layer of the universe will be unfurled. This layer is ungovernable by mankind yet it belongs to mankind. It is impregnable but vulnerable. It is a curse and a gift. The meek? They lie in the trough that will receive the peak of this next vibration. They will stand on the mountain top and view the valley as a battlefield. After this vibration has been revealed, serenity will be restored. The face of nature is the face of that which you would call God. Just the face. It smiles and it cries. Those who look under its skin and yet not in its eyes will fade and froth to bubbles in the skies. To rain that will water the earth and replenish it. Now is the time to look into the eye. In the past, the truth was too bright. But for protection a spiritual shield will aid you. A crystal. Like what you call a sunglass." '

That was the end. The clunk sound of Vinnie turning the tape off and then another clunk, turning it back on again. He did a little cough and then stayed silent. After a couple of moments another clunk sound. Then just the sound of clean metallic tape. I turned it off but could still hear a buzzing noise. I traced it to just under the windowsill. On the sill was a pile of untidy net curtain. A bee was trapped in it, buzzing like hell to get out. I could see it struggling. I opened the window wide before freeing it and then I ran out of the room. I waited a few moments and then went back in. I listened hard. Nothing. It had flown away into the night.

I felt angry. I didn't want to admit to being half mad myself but a lot of what Vinnie said was like looking into the mirror of my mind. Now, out in the open, it was all just ranting. Ranting and raving. All the stuff that went on in my head, Vinnie had brought it out. He, in his madness, called it God. It felt like my underwear was being hung out to dry in front of strangers. In Vinnie, I could hear how stupid I'd been. But at least I knew I was stupid. At least I knew I lived in the wrong spaces. At least I knew I was doing it. And that's probably what held me in check. Vinnie was gone on it. He wanted to drag it out and make it shown, known, and now with it, all my inner dreams were blown. The ineffable was smashed into a noise. A fucking tape of it. As if there wasn't noise enough. And his magneto what? Typical. Some science to make himself sound clever. Typical Vinnie. 'Aves of the same plumage circumnavigate in the same proximal vicinity.' He said stuff like that. He liked to make big words out of little ones – but not to show off. He thought it was necessary. He thought it made him more powerful.

If Vinnie had said all that stuff down the pub, as thoughts, just his own thoughts, none of this talking to God nonsense, he might have got away with it. As it was, he was meddling, meddling too far into his brain and coming up with . . . what was it he said? That was the problem. He believed in himself. He believed in this stupid God of his.

I rolled a joint, turned all the lights out, lay down in bed and heard, not listened, to the tape all over again. It was nine-forty-five now. Where was Roy? I listened to the tape as a mother to a child reading its first book. That's what he was doing. He was re-living that intensity of childhood when every living moment is pregnant with the unknown. Like at night, when the light of the mind goes on. Vinnie's mind light was blaring. Most of us manage to bury it, shade it, opt for consensus, take control, but then maybe, for people like me and Vinnie, the light comes back on too often.

I swam around my subconscious as half-fish, half-human, half submerged in the massive universe, and then every other moment I hit upon something, a bit of common sense, a memory, the sound of Vinnie's voice. I could have done with one of Annique's massages. That would have got me off. The spliff wasn't getting me off at all. It was my third one and I'd put loads in. I was getting less stoned by the second. I felt my face. The gnarled lumps of gristle holding it all together. I hated the feel of it. Hated it. Hated it. Hated it. That's why Roy hadn't come. I tingled with tears. I tried to dive back into my head to get away from it all. From everything. From everything that was wrong. I heard the front door slam shut. Then nothing. Then the sound of a motor bike. Sounded like Mikey. He'd be leaving empty-handed. Bev wouldn't shell out her last bit of draw on him. I thought about Dirk again and got my finger out.

Chapter 23

The long sleep murdered Paris, my memory of it, to just concrete and people. In contrast, my memory of Divine was quite a thrill. I hadn't quite got to grips with the feel of her. The nerve of her.

'Vivian! Come on! I know you're awake. Come and meet Imran.'

I awoke around lunchtime. For the third time. All morning, I'd considered the idea of being awake. All morning Simmi had been moving the bags and boxes of her belongings into my consciousness. The thought of helping her kept knocking me back to sleep again. More awake now, I considered my hunch. Was Roy sat on a big bag of draw? Was he dishing it out to all comers, in a frenzy, in a drought? If I was right, then I'd have to get round there sharpish. Maybe that was why he hadn't come to see me. Doing too much business. Not that I'd be able to sell much draw anyway. Not with the students still at home, chomping away on their Easter eggs . . . but if there was to be an ongoing drought, I should get some stock in. I could raise my prices, too. The mathematics of it all woke me up completely.

'Vivian. Come on! Or do I have to come and drag you out.'

She was trying to make out she was in charge. That she was the dominant one. Since she'd behaved herself with our Divine, I decided to return the favour.

His eyes rested like marbles on the ridge of his sockets, slightly tilted downwards. They protruded out of his head, big and round like black moons. These eyes would not allow or own up to any emotion, but I could tell they were trying to reach out, as if they wanted to escape the body they were contained in. A body of self-containment. There was no way through to Imran, except via his mother, possibly. The beauty of his head was ruined by a pink nylon shirt and a vest clearly visible beneath it. His navy-blue crêpe tie dangled like a flag and so too each leg of his half-mast kegs, flapping even when he stood still as he was now. And then white socks. The full house. There was no mistaking where he came from. This was a stamp collector of the highest calibre. An out-and-out straight, so straight he might snap. His eyes saved him. His nose led the way. A Roman nose heading straight for straight roads that all lead to Rome. Quite the opposite to Simmi. Boy. Girl. Straight. Round. Simmi's face was a roundabout. And her head. And her life.

Imran stood up as soon as he saw me. He'd been warned, obviously. His body didn't flinch but his head did. When we were introduced, he gave me one of those smiles that I knew was a lie. That generosity of good humour would not last. I knew it and he knew it too. One look at my new flat told him all he needed to know. The carpet torn and ragged at the edges, the brown-green stains of the ages, the dirty smoked walls baring scars of pictures that had once tried to brighten the place up. I was low life. And then my face. The nervous grin he gave me did not hide well enough his absolute and unnegotiable disgust. We laughed and joked briefly, nervously, our common thread, Simmi connecting us for just less than a minute. He laughed at her stressed-up attitude to study. To my mind, this wasn't funny at all. Because of Vinnie.

'Would you like some tea?' I asked him.

'Please. And some food if there is any. I'm starving.'

One look at his face told me he wasn't taking the piss.

'I've got a tin o' beans. Nothing else. I had to scrounge some bread from the neighbours last night coz I haven't had a chance to do any shopping yet.'

What the fuck was I on? Sounding off like a housewife.

'Forget it,' he said, sighing heavily.

She dumped him on me. She had to take some books back to college, do some shopping and make some room in her new studio flat, so her brother could sit down in it. She asked me to pick out the last of her things from all the boxes and bags and to keep him company for a while. I really needed to get off to Roy's, but still she wasn't back. Thank goodness I had something to do, bags to empty, shelves to fill. Though, even that was tricky. He watched every jar, every book, every piece of my belongings come out into the open with what seemed to be growing disapproval. He kept tutting but when I looked, he wasn't looking at me, revealing the underclothes of my life.

Unnerved, I spent most of the time in the bedroom where he couldn't see me, judge me, scorn me. She should have been back ages ago. It seemed rude to leave him on his own but I was ready for rude now. More than ready. He sat in the only chair not heaving with carrier bags, reading a book about the global marketplace. His eyes were particularly appealing with his glasses halfway down his nose. Almost like they were getting somewhere. Imran was and behaved like a refugee from the 'nice' world, uncomfortable in these new surroundings, no homely cues to comfort him. All tidy and done up, his tie was a neat seal-up of his nature. A package, tied up. One of those packages that you know not to bother opening. He didn't need company. Not mine anyway. Then the doorbell went. At last. She was back.

'Vinnie! You're out. I was coming to see you later.'

'My father got me out.'

'But are you . . .'

'Can I come in?'

'Simmi's brother's here,' I said, letting him past, putting him in family mode.

'Vinnie – Imran. Imran – Vinnie.'

Imran did that thing that tall blokes do to small blokes. Felt sorry for him with his eyes and then disregarded him instantly. Head back into the global marketplace.

'I was just making some tea – Vinnie?'

Vinnie shook his head.

'Wouldn't mind a smoke, though,' he said.

I warned him with my eyes, looking over to Imran.

'There are some fags on the table over there.'

Vinnie was shuddering. Nervous. I was worried. I didn't want him spouting out God in front of Imran. I didn't want *anything* in front of Imran. Except a book and a cup of tea. Christianity could be tolerated – God on a tape recorder was far too dangerous. Simmi had a fucking nerve dumping her family shit on my doorstep. This was supposed to be my flat. I was supposed to feel free.

I passed a cup of tea to Imran. He didn't flinch his eyes from the book. Taking the tea from me in silence was to tell me that the contract between us was finally over. I think another man in the room knocked the final nail in.

'Imran.'

He looked up at me, ready to give me the piece of his mind that was bothering him. No Simmi. Nowhere decent to sit. Not a chapati in sight.

'Imran, Vinnie and I have got to pop out. Will you be all right here on your own for a few minutes? Till Simmi gets back?'

'That's fine. She shouldn't be long.'

He looked at his watch as if he was timing her.

'Right then. Help yourself to . . . to tea.'

He turned over a page, and didn't say goodbye.

After running upstairs to tell Bev that the blow she sold me was worse than crap and finding no one in, I finally got myself out of the house into a sunny but freezing day.

'How yer feeling now then?' I said to Vinnie, still pulling my coat on, outside the front door, outside Imran's earshot.

'I feel like a smoke.'

He was wearing an anorak, for Christ's sake. It looked like someone had had a bicycle pump to it. And it had a hood.

'Vinnie, I really don't think you should smoke, you know. You have been a bit . . .'

'Yeah, well, maybe some smoke will stop my head spinning round.'

'Well, the smoke I've got won't. I can assure you of that.'

'Where are we going?'

He zipped up his anorak as if to stop the future getting at him. As if to go into battle.

'To Roy's. Listen, Vinnie, I need to score, I'm skint. It'll be an in-and-out job, OK? Then we'll go for a drink. You can tell me all about it. And I really don't think you should have a smoke. Didn't they put you on some medication? Drugs?'

'I'm not taking them. They make me feel like a zombie. But when I don't take them, I'm flying about all over the place. That's why I fancied a smoke. Do we have to go to Roy's?'

He gave me that look again. Like I was stabbing him.

'I need to get some stuff, Vinnie. We won't be long. Fucking Simmi. Dumped that brother of hers on me and then fucks off. He's not exactly a laugh a minute, is he? What tablets did they give you? Any good? Would I like them?'

'Largactil. One, six times a day.'

'Largactil?' I said, shocked. 'That's just kosh, isn't it?'

'My father told me not to take them. Says I should pull myself together under my own steam. He's worried my head won't be right for my exams. What did you think of my tape?'

'I thought it was a load of bollocks, Vinnie.'

'What, all of it?'

'D'yer still think you were talking to God?'

I stopped walking to look at him. His head was down, the hood of his anorak peaked in newness between his shoulder blades. He put his hands in his pockets.

'Take half a tablet, Vinnie. That might do the trick.'

'I want a smoke.'

'Vinnie, forget it.'

Vinnie wasn't pretending to smile any more. His silence was noisy. Usually he'd fill in the silences like kids fill up cups with play water. Not today.

'Your hair looks nice,' he said.

And then more silence.

'You'll meet Elsa at Roy's maybe. She lives upstairs – the girl that does my hair. You'll like Elsa, Vinnie.'

Now. There was a possibility. She wasn't very tall, Elsa, and bringing up a kid on her own was hard. She was straight, like

Vinnie, and bursting with common sense. Which was just what Vinnie needed right now. Perhaps, and I could sort of feel it, perhaps this visit to Roy's would be a turning point. Elsa and Vinnie.

From sunshine to a shower. A snow shower. Nearly hail but not quite, softer. Summer and winter in one hour. Vinnie held his hand out to it and then looked at me, disorientated.

'Yes, Vinnie. Snow.'

'Crystals,' he said, holding out his palm, collecting them to wet. Oh boy!

He linked arms with me. I didn't like it one bit but to reject him, his arm, was too cruel for words. He needed something to hang on to and my arm seemed to be it. Preposterous really. There had to be someone else. I asked him about his dad.

'He's fixed up a bursary for me in Brazil. That's if I get my finals. Some research for an oil company in Nigeria. If I get through that, then I get to take over half of my father's business in Lagos. The consultancy side. Lots of money.'

'But you don't like Lagos, Vinnie. You've told me that plenty of times.'

'I have to honour my father's wishes. I have to repay him.'

'And that's what's doing your head in, isn't it?'

'No.'

'What then?'

'I don't know. I don't hate Lagos. My mum's there. If my mum wasn't there I would.'

'Are you worried about the exams?'

'Of course.'

'Vinnie, have you got any money?'

'Loads. My father made a deposit yesterday. It has to cover my flight home, though. I can lend you some for now.'

'Well, I wouldn't mind. Do *you* mind?'

He perked up a bit then, coz I'd given him a job, I suppose. Because I needed him. I waited outside the bank whilst he went in to withdraw, and I felt like a scoundrel, to be honest. As though I were taking advantage. I couldn't see how but that's what it felt like. The passers-by looked at me in a way that confirmed it.

The door opened as soon as we rang the bell. Elsa. Hair shaved off like Vinnie's, big earrings and a mole on her chin. She was holding Shula in a near stranglehold, the child struggling until she saw me. Her face was covered in chocolate and she grinned chocolate teeth at me, remembering me. Remembering the stories I told her whilst her mother pulled at my head, planting plaits in deep.

'Chooo . . . Choooo,' I said to her, tickling her tum, glad of a childish grin, right then.

'I thought you were the ambulance. The police,' said Elsa, repositioning the child on her hip. Only then did I see she'd been crying, that she was grey. Disappointed.

'What are you on about, Elsa?'

She walked away from us, down the hall.

'Shula found him. Take a look.'

Her eyes were verging on resigned now, the clambering child taking up her energy.

'What?'

'Take a look.'

'Roy?'

'Dead. Green and dead. Drugs.'

Now she was giving off a told-you-so look.

'Roy?'

I went in. She'd got it all wrong, I knew.

He was in his vest, arm hanging off the bed, syringe on the bedside table, bag of smack next to it, lemon, spoon, the works. And a lump of the black hash, same as mine, all crumbled up but not used, as if he already knew it wouldn't work. Then I saw Mikey's coke spoon with the lapis lazuli eye, staring back at me from the carpet, winking, it seemed. I picked it up and squeezed it into my palm as a pebble from the beach. And then I stared at him. To take it all in. It was easy. Easier than I would have thought. His eyes were closed.

It was a stop. A halt. It was after the horse had bolted so it was calm. He didn't look dead. He looked green but not dead. He looked like Roy. I opened the curtains. Then he looked dead. I closed them again. Vinnie was still stood in the hallway. I felt for Roy's pulse. He wasn't dead cold but not warm enough for life either.

'Vinnie, come here.'

'No.'

'Help me get him on the bed properly.'

'No.'

When I moved his head over, sick came out of his mouth, a trickle of black sick. God, he was dead. The hum of Vinnie and Elsa talking in the hall sounded like flies over the demise. I retched. The room was full of Roy still, but his body cancelled it all out. I shouldn't have been there, looking. It was death's time to hang around, that was the feel. I was disturbing the death vibration. Not welcome. This body was not for live consumption. Not for memory, as if Roy had been interrupted in his passage from this world to the next. As if I was ruining something for him. The pictures on his walls were of shipwrecks, their ribs like carcasses on the rocks. Ghostly in the half-light. In death's time, no time. Still time. There was a hook in the air making the pulse of the day excessive, more than was required. All that was required was to rest on the one note of a human heartbeat. And I was on that note, stood next to him, staring down at him, wondering. Had I sensed that this was going to happen? The thick air of the room full of gloom wanted to expel me and I wanted to go. Go. Get out of there. Think upon it all later on. Just shift. He should have come to my place last night and broken me in. He'd still be alive now. Instead, he'd rouletted with a metal swish that found the pocket of death to rest in. And there he was, stranded. Gone.

Huy! Huy! Huy!

'Just stand where you are and don't move. Name?'

'Vivian Jackson.'

'Address?'

That's the problem with policemen and their questions. Every question points to a direction that leads on to another set of circumstances that you really don't want to consider. Like Imran in my flat with half an ounce of black on the mantelpiece. This wasn't going to be easy. I had six hundred quid in my back pocket and a dead in the bed.

'Address.'

A policewoman came into the room and took off her cap, in that *heading-a-murder-inquiry* way. The taste of death was reeking the place out. The police were sucking off it, oiled by it. I was just what they needed. Someone to make the engine roar. They were going to burn me up. When the ambulance men came in, I told them he was my friend. He was Roy. My friend. Through sobs I had to say what time I arrived, what I was there for, what was in it for me. Through sobs I struggled for clichés to give me time to think. Too young to die, a repetitive truth that hit home and then wouldn't let me think. A truth that made me sob till my sobs sounded so false I sobbed myself to a quiet, which made the police suspicious because to them, I shut up like a record going off, like a tape being stopped. Like I knew what I was doing. Which I did. I did know. I just couldn't be me, that was all. Shaking fingers filled up my mouth. I stamped the ground to feel my feet. I liked the police being there. I liked not being responsible. They brought me out of death void. They gave my eye something to rest on. But I couldn't hear them. I couldn't hear a thing.

'I've got her address,' echoed a policeman.

The policewoman reached for his pad and he gave it to her. Out of the room she went. I watched them carry Roy out, sausaged up in a roll. Gone. Gone. I heard them questioning Vinnie outside. Not the questions, just the shouting. For Christ's sake, leave the man alone.

'We've got an address here, sir.' Another echo, then another.

'Just now, sir. They say just now.'

Plastic bags. All the officers were equipped with plastic bags and in four separate clean wallets went the contents of my pockets. The drugs, the money, the key to my front door and the spoon with the lapis lazuli eye, an eye that now looked like it was frozen open, in the palm of my hand. They took it all away in a swift emergency, as if it might lead them to a new death, a new situation. As if it was alive. Maybe they were on a roll. That's what they were after. A roll. I decided not to answer any more questions for the time being. There was too much shouting going on in the hallway.

'Oy. You. Out of there, I said. Stop being a cunt of a nigger and get out of there. Pull him out, Sergeant. Just pull him out. He's as high as a kite, look at him. Now move it.'

I heard Vinnie cry. All the time I'd known him, I'd never heard him cry. Imagined it enough but never heard him. He was crying out loud. Elsa started screaming. She was really giving it what for.

'You tekka yer hands offer my chi'. You stay away from me. Away. Away . . . You can't do dis to me. You leavin' me now. It's nothin' to do with me . . . you leave me now.'

And then one long belly scream that calls the children from the wilds. Hers was being carried out of the house by a policewoman. Another policeman blocked Elsa's path after her. Shula never made a sound until she got outside. Then she kicked in.

'Come on, now. Let's get them out of here. Come on. Round 'em up. Where's that other girl? Get 'em out. Move it. Get the dogs in. Let's clean this place up! Come on. Move it.'

I was the first to be taken away. I was put in the back of a police car. The policeman put his hand on my head and squashed me down into the car. I wanted to turn round and heave him one in the stomach. But I was too scared for wisecracks and heroics. I saw Elsa being reunited with Shula in the street and there was Vinnie . . . they were all being put in the back of a van. Two police officers in plainclothes stood with hands on hips, watching everything.

A policewoman got into the back seat with me and shared out the handcuffs. Once they were on and the doors locked, we were off. Down to the station. Roy's body went on ahead. We caught up with him further on up at the traffic lights. No lights flashing on the roof or sirens wailing. He didn't even get a decent march out of the place. That would have been fitting, some sirens wailing. I was wailing.

I'd never been in a police station before, not even to claim lost property. I figured pleading guilty straight off was the most sensible course of action to take, since I'd been caught fair and square. What was that? Fair cop, guv? It'd be a while before the next spliff.

Up the steps to the station reception, doors unlocked, and then up to another desk that was nearly as tall as me and would be taller than Vinnie if they brought him through, which I knew they wouldn't coz he didn't have anything on him. I was scared now. Dead scared. The sergeant took my name and address and then barked at me. Had someone turned him on? Wound him up? Set him off? He gruffed through his speech so fast, it was over before I realised he was talking to me. I asked for a solicitor.

'A what?' the sergeant said.

'A brief. A solicitor,' I said, loud and clear.

'Sign here,' he said.

I did.

'What is it?' I said after.

'They're your rights,' he said. 'Or were. Now. Follow that officer.'

'To?'

'Fingerprints.'

'And the solicitor?'

'We'll see what we can do.'

He made a telephone call, I assumed to the duty solicitor, but before the door to where I was going was unlocked I heard his conversation begin.

'Jules? . . . No. Sunday . . . Yeah . . . First eleven. Can't do that, I'm afraid. I'm the only fast bowler.'

The door was unlocked and through it I went to . . . another door. She unlocked that one too. The policewoman leading me was silent. Like I was a good catch. I got myself ready for a big bawl in my cell. I was almost looking forward to it. I needed a cell right then, to wail off Roy. The minimalism would do me fine. Just me and him. No disturbances. Just the grimness of it all and the sorrow. I needed the cell.

Off to the photographer. A policeman shooting film coz he couldn't be trusted with a gun. Not next week. Not ever. He'd like to branch out a bit, do weddings and family portraits, maybe. But for now, there was me, holding up my number plate. The procedure holding up my grief. This guy was taking something of a liberty. I can hardly explain. You see, I don't do photographs, or more to the point, I can't do photographs. There are very few of them about. Now there was one more and I got the feeling that PC Bailey wasn't all that interested in my best side or how the light might fall on my bad side. Not a photo for the papers anyway.

Then the man helped me to cover my fingers and hands in black rubber-stamp stuff. He rolled my fingers over ink and looked for all the world like this was his proper job. His attention to detail highlighted his dead-end status. He was too good. I felt kind of sorry for him. To make his job more pleasurable, I co-operated with more *bonhomie* than was necessary. Then, at last, to my cell. In it a bench for a bed, a blue plastic cushion mattress, one inch thick, and a toilet. At last, rest. Alone. I needed to be.

I waited for the policewoman to lock the door but she just stood there, waiting. The silence between us, the gulf between the child and the man taking money at the fair, for the ghost train. Then another woman turned up. The one from the bust all those many moons ago. Just over a week ago. They were both uniformed. Big. Laughing now that they were together. The child is in its seat. The ghost train has engaged with the rail and is now on the move. The women will dangle dish-cloths in the dark to cobweb my face and make me feel the full horror of it. They set up their stand, the big woman with a clipboard and a chair she'd brought in with her. She sat down on it.

'Strip,' she said.

'Sorry?' I said.

'You heard.'

I did as I was told. I handed the garments over one by one. I thought of Imran and the drug squad. His vest holding his body like handlebars, beneath his pink nylon shirt. Maybe even the police could spot the significance of a pink nylon shirt.

I couldn't undo my bra from behind so I dropped it to flop out my breasts and pulled the fastening round to the front. Looking down on myself naked made the tears fall. In rhythmic cascades. Like the fingers of the tide crawling up the beach they crawled down my cheeks and rivered my neck. Between each garment, I had to wait, whilst they searched the seams for concealed drugs. When completely naked, I asked if I could get dressed. I was cold.

'Not yet,' she said, not looking at me.

The other policewoman was staring at me. I covered my pubes with both hands. I stood as if waiting to go to the toilet. My breasts were heavy with the spotlight. My feet were cold on the floor and I moved forward to stand on my shirt which lay across the ground like a dead Indian after battle.

'Move back. Hands by your sides.'

I felt top-heavy. As if I might fall over in a straight stick-like collapse. It was hard to put my shoulders back but I tried. It was the least I could do for Roy, I said to myself. The two women were counting up how many prisoners they had and who was in which cell. Where they'd put any overflow. They might be on a roll.

The woman on the chair wrote everything down. All the names of the garments. Words are just skin, my dad said.

The door to the cell was wide open. There was a clanking of doors and the two women moved quickly to see who it was, as if they were waiting for someone else. I thought of Imran, back at the flat, witnessing the search of my belongings. The emptying of my holiday haversack, all my dirty holiday knickers. A policewoman walked past the cell, dragging a sobbing Elsa. When she saw me, she turned mute. The sobs stopped. Not a peep. I was cold. My shoulders fell down again. Shula wasn't anywhere.

'Now stand on that bench.'

'Sorry?'

'You heard.'

'What for?'

'Stand on the bench.'

'But what for?'

'Do it.'

I stood on the bench. The smaller policewoman stood in front of me with folding arms, examining my body from the side, the side that has the jam splashes down. Enjoying it. Every last inch of it. Enjoying it and not even hiding it.

'Turn round.'

I turned round slowly like a music-box ballet dancer winding down.

'Now open your legs wide.' It went through my mind they might assault me, but the thought drifted off. Of course they wouldn't.

The door to my cell was still open and now that Elsa was banged up, her policewoman came in to join in the party. She looked directly at me, hanging her keys into her pocket but letting the chain hang out, a silver chain. A chain of office. The other two smiled at her. They'd been saving me up for her.

'Has she turned round yet?' she asked.

'Do it again. Turn round.'

'I just did.'

'This officer didn't see.'

I turned round again.

'Legs wide open again and hands in the air.'

'I'm pleading guilty, yer know. There's no need for all this.'

'Now jump off the bench as high as you can with your legs wide open, as wide as you can get them.'

'What?'

'You heard.'

'But what for, though?'

'Jump.'

292

They moved back. The woman on the chair got up and moved back against the wall so I couldn't jump right on her. Spread-eagled, I flew into the air and wished that I could fly.

'Again.'

The second climb up to the bench was harder, showing my bum to the three of them more demeaning than any of it. Them watching me climb up to jump down.

'And keep those legs wide open.'

And I flew, nearly. Nearly.

'And again.'

The third time, I was invisible. The skin a cloth that I couldn't and wouldn't ever take off.

'Right. Let's go and do the other one, shall we? Elsa . . . Groves,' ticking her off the clipboard.

My door locked. The women tittered and giggled down the corridor. Then Elsa's door was unlocked. Elsa sounded like the Marathon Man having his teeth pulled.

Chapter 24

'Elsa's got sod all to do with it. She plaits hair and keeps herself to herself.'

'Let us be the judge of that, shall we?'

They sat on the other side of the table to me. It was five o'clock. Teatime. We'd only just started and I wanted it to stop. I wanted them to stop breathing loudly through their noses. No breath came from their lips, just words to skirt the crime, to measure it up, my involvement, my ability to withstand punishment. The questions started easy enough but I sussed their tactic a mile off. They were getting my tongue loose, getting me to bed myself in with lovely descriptions of my college mates and my tutor and how did I like Brimmington? Wasn't the new shopping arcade a disgrace? I answered as politely as I could whilst inside my mind I tried to fashion up some sort of story. Inside my mind I tried to communicate with Roy for there must be something more after death. More than these two bastards anyway. They prodded me everywhere, home, Mum, Dad, Divine. Country of origin, as usual. A few prods to get the gist of me. To see what I look like when I'm telling the truth. Salesmen do this. Get you at it, so, by the time they're in for the kill, you can't stop your tongue undoing the purse strings, the safe door, telling all. I wanted them to stop. And for a moment they did.

The door opened and a policeman came in with a tray. A tray with a plate of sausage, chips, beans and a cup of tea. Officer McAlpine immediately tucked into the sausage.

'So. Who sent you the smack then?'

He dangled a clear plastic bag in front of me, showing a ripped envelope addressed to Mr Kipling and then another plastic bag with two postcards in it. On one of the postcards there was a picture of a mosque. Taped to the back of it was a bag of white powder.

'I've told you. I don't do smack. I don't buy smack. I don't know where you got that from but it's nothing to do with me. And anyway, I don't know anyone that lives in India.'

'So you knew the letter was from India then?'

'I'm guessing. The picture. The mosque . . .'

They leant forward, to do a visual forensic on me.

'Do you know where we found this envelope? Can you see where it's addressed to?'

'It's nothing to do with me. It's not got my flat number on it, has it?'

'No. But it was in your flat.'

'Was not. Not unless you planted it there.'

'Our friend Mr Imran . . . Reza.'

'Oh Jesus, you've not got him 'ere, have you?'

'He's a hard nut to crack, isn't he?'

'For God's sake . . .'

'He's very upset about all this. Or says he is. Said he found the envelope in your flat. On the mantelpiece. He's trying to say it's nothing to do with him.'

'He's lying.'

'So it is something to do with him?'

'I didn't mean that. I mean it wasn't in my flat. He'll say anything coz he's scared. Jesus, let him go. One look at him must tell you . . .'

'Mr Reza was in the process of opening this envelope. We caught him red-handed. We can hardly let him go, can we?'

'That'd be the stamp,' I said. Quite high-pitched, I was now. 'The stamp. He collects stamps. He's a dealer.'

I picked up the bagged-up envelope and examined it.

'See . . . it's torn at the stamp end. He was trying to get the stamp off.'

I stared into the eyes of the redneck right then. But his eyes were staring into his mate's. I could see them figuring out the circumstances like they were adding up that month's takings.

They both looked back at me and then the redneck said,

'That's exactly what he said. Stamp collecting. Hang an a minute.'

Then he turned to his mate.

'Do you think it's too late to get on to Bradford? Tell 'em to 'ang fire?'

The other officer stood up and did as he was told. I worked it all out then. Simmi's mum in the kitchen with the Bradford police. She'd get a right battering tonight. Of that there was no doubt.

The stamp had a laughing Ganesh on it and I wondered . . . had Simmi's family been Hindu instead of Muslim, whether the envelope might have stayed on the stairs with all the other junk mail. Instead of that thieving little get taking it, for the want of a stamp.

Alone with redneck, a calm descended. I expected him to carry on badgering me but he was breathing through his nose, checking his paperwork. He looked at his watch even though a clock the size of a van wheel tocked right next to his head and then, obviously worried, he got up and left the room. He ignored me completely.

When the door closed on me, leaving me alone, I slouched down for a think and eyed the evidence still on the table, but almost immediately the door opened again and one of those policewomen that had stripped me came in. She stood by the door looking out of the window. I slouched down again. Well, at least Imran was in the clear now. They knew we could never have concocted a stamp-collecting story. At least . . . at least . . . there were very few at leasts. The immediacy of the interview room seemed to ebb away now there was no one in my face. The details of my troubled terrain collected before me at my feet, like debris, damage, death even. For wasn't this the beginning of the end of me? How could I ever be me any more? Perhaps, though, this was the real me. Scared, watchful of decaying possibilities, accepting that the future would for ever be a resurgence of the past, a waste, a pollutant, a foul-smelling reality. When, since my face went, had I ever experienced pure joy? How could I? This was life, this was real. This was the corner I would for ever be sent to sit in, watching. The blame was all mine, the pain all theirs. Vinnie's, Imran's, Simmi's. Simmi's mum. Had they managed to stop the Bradford police, I wondered.

After about twenty minutes, the two officers returned and sat back in my face again.

'And does this Mr Kipling make gingerbread men too, Miss Jackson? We heard, through the grapevine, that you were something of an expert in the cake-making department.'

'Any other bright ideas, Ossifer?'

They were clutching at straws now.

'Well, yes. We've got plenty of bright ideas. Here's one. We were kind of wondering whether there haven't been other envelopes. Maybe there were two or three even. Maybe you already sold your first batch. This appears to be pure heroin, Miss Jackson, though forensic will have to confirm it. Uncut, this stuff can kill. It's not funny. This is not a scene from TV. We've got dead bodies on our hands. On your hands, perhaps!'

He was shouting louder than a small room would demand. I think he wanted his mates outside to hear it all.

'I want my solicitor. And anyway, the scag at Roy's was brown. Not white like that. So it can't be the same stuff, can it?'

They both wriggled uncomfortably in their chairs.

'Who else is dead then?' I said, expecting not to know whoever it happened to be.

One more string to my bow. One more, at least.

'Mikey Granville.'

At that, I coughed. The lapis lazuli coke spoon. Sherlock Holmes. Two and two.

'You know Mikey Granville?'

One more nail in my coffin.

'A little.'

'Have you ever been to his house, on the heath?'

'No.'

'Come on, Miss Jackson. We know you're lying.'

297

'I'm not lying.'

'So you don't recognise DI Mitchell here?'

'No.'

'He gave you a lift from there one morning. You told him all about your rainbows.'

'You were high as a kite, d'you remember? First thing in the morning. I wouldn't mistake a face like yours now, would I, Miss Jackson?'

'Well, funny you should say that, coz I was thinking the very same thing about your face. Right pair, aren't we?'

They were all over me like lice, in my memory, my flat and now all over my fucking face, but my rage, my trying to be snide – it felt on the air like piffling plywood arrows after an elephant. His face was just like everybody else's face. Normal. And that's another one of my handicaps. I don't remember people's faces coz I don't really look at them. Usually, I scan the head area pretending to see. I don't look into eyes, coz no one looks in mine. It's altogether too much work for me constantly to image faces, when all I see are faces that don't like me.

'I wouldn't try the smartarse route, if I were you. You could be in serious trouble, Miss Jackson.'

'What, for an ounce of pot? That's what you call it, isn't it? Pot? You can't lay nothin' else on me.'

This 'Miss Jackson' nonsense is only dished out to demoralise me. 'Misses' don't sell drugs. They type out insurance quotations. They call me 'Miss' to emphasise the gulf.

'And the 3 grams of heroin found in Roy Bold's house. What d'yer know about that?'

He brought out more and more sheets of paper and read them off, not looking at me.

'And what do you know about the 7 grams of identical heroin found in Mikey's headquarters? And what do you know about Mikey OD-ing and dying at three o'clock this afternoon? In his bath. You're in very serious trouble so don't come the smartarse. OK?'

'I was here at three o'clock this afternoon. I want my solictor.'

They could have been lying about Mikey but I didn't think so.

'Just come back from France we hear. D'Envers.'

He pulled out my notebook with my sister's address in and the directions to Hôtel La Rondelle.

'Not a very salubrious area if you don't mind my saying.'

Quiet I was then. Obviously. Death gets the drums rolling. He could hear them too. He got up to take a look out of the window and took a sausage with him. One hand in his pocket, he walked across the room as if to find some smoke signals from the quilt of city buildings all around us, below us, all staring right back at us.

'When arrested, you had over six hundred pounds cash on you. What was that for? Where does someone like you get that sort of money? Grant cheques aren't issued till next week, we checked. So come on, where did you get six hundred quid?'

'I got it off Vinnie. Vincent.'

I wanted it to stop. Now. When I was little and I did something illegal, if it didn't go off right, I just waited until Mum found out. Or worse still, Dad. When they did, they had me bang to rights and punished me accordingly. Interrogations were stopped if I cried hard enough. Not here. They don't buy that stuff in police stations. They are in the business of story production and that can be a long and drawn-out process, long and weary for them, long and scary for me. As in any story, the tension gets progressively more taut until it can't stretch any further. Then it bleeds out all over the place. I hoped it wasn't bleeding all over Bradford but I was too scared to ask.

'We'd like to be able to talk to this Vincent. The doctors are trying to find out what's wrong with him. What drugs has he been taking?'

'He's not well . . .'

'We can see that.'

'I mean, he's just come out of a mental hospital. He's got nothing to do with all this. Just let him go. Elsa, Vincent, Imran. Let them go. They're all completely . . .'

'You need to tell us *exactly* what is going on. Then we'll let them go. Now then. Elsa thinks that *you* sold Roy the smack.'

'Fuck off, will yer. She wouldn't say that. Don't come the

smartarse with me either. I'm not fucking stupid. I haven't even see Roy since I got back.'

'Hit a raw nerve there, have we?'

'Get my solicitor. This is against the law.'

'A drug dealer teaching us the law, eh? Well, what d'yer know?'

'Been waiting all day for me to go turkey, 'ave yer?'

My voice was wavery enough for turkey. I was scaling the decibels. Anger was settling in.

'Well, look at me. Look at my eyes. Crystal fucking clear. Look at my hands. That's fear, that is. They're shaking with fear. I don't do scag. If you were proper detectives you'd have sussed that by now.'

And because I said that, I blew it. I should never have told them I was scared.

'It's surprising what people do and don't do. Lots of dealers don't do scag but they've no qualms about selling it. What about this cannabis then?'

'Guilty. OK? Can I go home now, please?'

'Were you going to sell it?'

'No. I was going to smoke it.'

'So you weren't going to sell it to your pals upstairs? Now, what are their names? . . . Friends of ours, aren't they, Pete? Ah. Here we are. Bev Andrews and Dirk Robertson. Was the cannabis for them? Or was it from them?'

'No.'

'What about this Imran Reza then? Were you going to sell some to him? We're not so sure about this stamp collecting malarkey. Stamps are well known in the drugs trade, as you well know.'

'What are you on about?'

They both smiled at me, one of them tapping his pen on the table.

'Of course. It's not sunk in yet, has it? Two people have died. This is a potential murder inquiry. You have known contacts with Pakistan, Afghanistan and Morocco. Are you beginning to get the picture?'

'Oh fuck off, will yer? You're wasting police time.'

'We've got all the time in the world, Miss Jackson. Though your friend Elsa, is it? She seems in a hurry to get home. Her kid's with the social services right now. Probably in a nice foster home. Not so nice for the mother, mind, is it? The kid'll be fine. She'll probably enjoy it better than home. It often goes that way, doesn't it, Pete?'

'I'm guilty of possessing cannabis. That's it.'

'But what about the five hundred quid?'

'You said six a minute ago.'

'Sorry, six.'

'Ask Vinnie.'

'What was it for?'

'Mind your own fucking business. I want my solicitor.'

'And the coke spoon? Into coke as well, are we?' He shoved the plastic bag with Mikey's spoon in towards me.

'It's not mine.'

'You were holding on to it for someone, is that it?'

'It's Mikey's.'

'It would be. He's dead. All this cannabis is Mikey's too, is it?'

'I've told you. I admit to the cannabis.'

'Well, if you don't cough, we're gonna charge you anyway. Supplying heroin. You won't get bail for that.'

'You can't charge me when there's no proof, no evidence. And which one of you's the nice guy? Whoever it is, you're not coming across.'

'We can extend your stay. And not just yours. All we need is for one of your mates to make a statement. It won't be long before Vincent pops, I have to tell you. Then we can hold you for as long as we like. Let me do you a favour – this is deep shit, Vivian. Climb out of it before it sticks.'

'You'll have to let Vinnie go. He's not well.'

'The doctor thinks he might be putting on a show for us. We can't find anything wrong with him.'

'So are yer saying you won't let us go unless I admit to supplying heroin?'

'Something like that.'

'Even though I didn't?'

'Who supplied it to Mikey? Was it Roy?'

'I don't know, do I? I didn't know Roy did smack. Maybe Roy gave it to Mikey. Or Mikey to Roy. As you pointed out, they're dead, aren't they?'

And I fell forward on the table then. Crying.

'Come on. Come on. What do you take us for? Sit up . . . sit up, I said . . . Now then.'

I wiped the snot and tears with my hands. I peeled strips of Polyfilla foundation from my face, like I was in some horror movie, about to reveal the real me. No handkerchiefs.

'They were using you to stash the smack, weren't they? Roy and Mikey. You were paid for it, weren't you? See. Your face tells such a story – did you know that? It's all beginning to make sense, isn't it? And that's what's bothering you, isn't it? It all making sense. We saw Mikey round your place last night. Your light went off the minute he left.'

I calmed myself. There was no need to be scared. And this was no time to cry. Not in front of them. Not before crying for Roy. He would have to come first. These bastards could wait. This was a time for focusing.

'Listen, Sherlock. You've got it all wrong.'

A joke through tears is pathetic. Truly pathetic. I was ashamed of myself.

All this interest in Roy and Mikey now they were dead seemed ludicrous. Didn't give a toss about them alive. Surely the coppers should be round the junkies' houses warning them about the bad batch of smack? No. They'd do nothing as sensible as that. Instead, they'd spend hours and paper and energy and fuel and all our freedoms, so's to find the person that sold the smack to Mikey who they didn't give a fuck about anyway. And tomorrow the same thing, all over again. Over and over again. Working through the dead bodies as and when they fell in. One after the other. Junkie after junkie. Interview after interview. Macabre. Rolling along.

'How did Mikey know Roy?'

'Roy was Mikey's plumber.'

'Ahhh. So you know something then?'

'What?'

'Mikey's toilet cistern concealed a metal device, watertight. He used it as a stash for the smack. We found the exact same device inside Roy's cistern. We would never have known only Mikey didn't live long enough to put his gear away. Wouldn't that indicate that Roy was involved with selling smack? And selling stashes to store the smack?'

'I thought you said I was supposed to do the stashing. Some detective, you are.'

'Well then, let's look at it another way. Perhaps it really is you who sold the smack. Perhaps you've been selling for some time now.'

I yarled out loud then and thumped the table. He stood up.

'Look, OK. Let's calm down a little. The smack round at Roy's and Mikey's is a different type of smack to that found in your house. So, we get you on possession of smack with intent to supply. Possession of cannabis with intent to supply. Write a statement and get all this over with.'

'You've got it wrong.'

'We found a couple of syringes in your dustbins.'

'So fuckin' what! They're from the man that lived there before me.'

'Do you think the jury will believe you? You – the one clutching a coke spoon when we arrived? With your face, my dear, I'm sorry to say, the jury will believe anything.'

'I want my solicitor.'

'Have you ever sold any controlled drugs to anyone?'

'Never.'

'Not even cannabis?'

'No.'

My stomach was heaving. I really needed the toilet.

'We've lying again, aren't we? If you admitted that, we could at least begin to believe that you were telling the truth about the smack.'

'I want my solicitor.'

The one writing it all down butted in.

'It's one thing selling cannabis, dear. It's quite another selling smack.'

'I know.'

Back to the other one now.

'25 grams of cannabis all together. Well, it's not cannabis till the lab says it's cannabis but for now, it's cannabis. Half of it in your pockets. Half of it on the mantelpiece. Mr Reza swears blind he hardly knows you. Doesn't make sense, though, does it? Him sitting in your flat and opening the mail. What can you tell us about him? I can tell you now, he's not doin' you any favours.'

'He knows nothing about anything.'

'What was he doin' in your flat?'

'Waiting for Simmi.'

'Simmi?'

'His sister.'

'Why didn't he wait in Simmi's flat then?'

'Coz she was getting it ready.'

'What's her address?'

'I don't know. Ruth Street. Something like that.'

'So, you're protecting *her* now, are you? Has she got something to do with the next shipment, perhaps? Imran has a wallet full of flight schedules from Pakistan. What are they for?'

'I don't know, do I? Maybe he's expecting a wife.'

Much snuffling.

'You really aren't helping yourself, are you?'

'No. I want my solicitor.'

The grease on the chips had hardened into lard. I thought about them fucking. The policemen. What would they look like, fucking their wives? What would their wives look like? Him. Baldy. With his collar all loose and relaxed, like he was just knocking off. He would sweat a lot. He was sweating now. Or maybe it was the grease off the sausages. His wife would be small with ribs. Surely a man lying on top would ruin the screw. Wouldn't he have to do press-ups? Wouldn't he have to be fit? Else his heaving mass would squash me, suffocate me. I imagined baldy's thing as a gear stick. I imagined myself holding on to the gear stick of a car with my legs trailing out of the back window. Being taken along for the ride. Open wide. Open wide. He would be a juggernaut, the other one, the one that was supposed to be nice. Thick-set. Moustache. Looked a bit like a football player. Ruddy red neck against white high cardboard collar. Red necks aren't nice. A suggestion of repression in the upper thorax somewhere. He wouldn't bounce up and down on a fuck. Not him. He would lie on me and push in, push in. My head would roll and loll, side to side, catching breath, dripping spit. Water would stream from my eyes. His head would be above mine, to the pillow. His body flab would engulf me and I would lie there, injected with his power, a basin, a receptacle, an open wound. Is that what his wife did? Waited for the injection, the erection? My face felt more ugly than ever right then. I would have liked an injection right then. To swallow me up.

'You can go back to your cell for now.'

They must have felt me undressing them.

'We'll request an extended stay. Maybe you'll come up with a plausible story in the meantime.'

'And a solicitor? Will you come up with a solicitor?'

'We'll see what we can do.'

Elsa echoed all down the cell path. Wailing for her baby. Like someone had killed it. I wanted to shout 'Shula's not dead' but I never. I would have to let her wail.

'Elsa, it'll all be over soon. Don't cry.'

She wouldn't speak with me, ask me anything, talk of Shula, shout at me. Nothing but wail. A scam to wind up the screws, I think. It worked. They were banging on her cell door.

'Crying's not going to help, love. If you could keep it down, else we'll have to get the doctor in.'

I used the toilet in my cell and then sat in the stench.

I wondered about Vinnie. I couldn't get my head round Imran, Bradford, Simmi. So I thought about Vinnie. I couldn't get my head into death. Mikey. Roy. So what was left? Look after them that are still alive. What were they doing to Vinnie? I'd hoped that the cell would surreal me, but it never. It was all too real. Devoid of magic, myth or mystery. I knew what would happen. I knew it'd be over, not when, but it would. Outside, life would go on as usual. But not for me.

I imagined Vinnie writhing, frothing. Lashing his nails down his face, scrawping fork-marked tribal etchings in a frenzy. I imagined him making the same noises as Elsa, holding on to bars, prison bars. There weren't any bars to hold on to, which was great, coz no one could see in, walking past on the way to the coffee machine. I wondered why they made the window so useless. Tiny squares of frosted glass embedded in stone. Twelve squares in all. Each square the size of a sandwich. Squares of frosted glass of sky through which only the shadow of light could be seen. Imran'd find it difficult to get his bearings, to say his prayers. That square glass, that frosted gate to the air was punishment. The heavy dong of the cell door and the clanking keys of the jailer – they were mere theatre. What hurt was to see a curtain across the sky – frosted – to linger in my mind, to remind me that the air is not mine. But there. There for those that are free. Like being in a lavatory. A toilet window. That window, made so thick, so glassy, so marbled in its function – that was the lock, the key, the door, the thing that broke me. It was a temptress, a seducer, a beacon of the fall. An eye glaring down on me. A perspective of imprisonment. A square window, not for looking out of. Not for looking in. There was no 'in'. The 'out' struck out by the iron door that grated on its hinges.

The lid of the door-eye swished back. Someone was out there looking at me. From the outside, you can see in. The cell got smaller and smaller until all there was was frosted window grilling shadows of light over me. As night fell, the street lights blared amber disc patterns on to the wall, headlights sometimes, a moving car over gravel. Not often, though. Elsa had rested but now she resumed. Swearing and wailing. I had to get her out of there.

'So, ready to talk now?'
  'I've talked.'

'What about telling us where the heroin comes from? That'd do.'

'Solicitor?'

'Sorry. Do you have a name for one?'

'No. You have solicitors here. Duty solicitors.'

'Well, he's still very busy, I'm afraid. Do you know where the heroin came from?'

'Doesn't it say on the envelope? Do you have the Yellow Pages? I'll find one for myself.'

'Who sent the heroin over?'

'The only thing I know about heroin is what you've told me.'

'Get back to your cell.'

Mum always wanted me to hang around with decent people. But decent people look down on me. Decent people make aisles for me when I walk past. Decent people are scaredy babbies. Behind the charity they exclude me. They don't want their sons to marry me. Make sure their sons won't want to marry me. But I can see Mum's reasoning. Crystal clear. Whatever decent people do, it's lawful. They don't break the law. They make it. They don't die either, unless they're in an accident. Two deaths already for me. Mum wouldn't buy that and so I would never tell her. She'll never know me now. That's the end of it. Mum who's tried so hard to make me strong has lost me. Another death, almost.

I sat perched on the end of the bench, refusing to partake in the function of the furniture as if to do so was a way of breaking myself down. Then I broke and lay down. My sweaty fingers were ticky tacky against the blue plastic of the mattress and children sucking boiled sweets came to mind. I thought about Elsa's sticky tears rolling off her mattress and on to the floor. I tried to make sure that none of my bare skin touched what could have been cried on, sometime. I felt my face. I scrawped make-up off my face and made tiny balls with it, to throw at the cell door. The aloneness of my face was lost in the loneliness of that cell.

At first, the cell had been all novelty and graffiti. Reading the name of the man from Sheffield who made the iron hinges. Counting window squares. Unstitching the mattress to let the yellow foam centre bleed out of the edges. No fags. No shoes. My body gone over like a set of drawers, a cupboard ransacked. The wailing. The door that reaches from ceiling to floor, as thick a wedge against the outside world as my resolve to keep myself safe, keep me on an even keel. The covered electric light turned low and of a sudden, turned high. A torture device that kept me entertained, counting the minutes of its brightness versus the hours of its darkness. Doors outside clanging open and then closed, slotting iron through sleeves of iron. Voices of women who go home and cook the tea. For a while, I enjoyed all this. The minimalism. But eventually, and then perpetually, my thoughts hovered around the idea of getting out of there. Those lifeboats on the ship from France no longer seemed so ludicrous, considering all the trouble I was in. Anything would have done. I had to think myself up an escape route. A baby rubber ring would do.

Chapter 25

'We unpacked for you,' is how they put it. The totem pole lay down dead.

Simmi came by to drop off some books. Didn't speak. Already she was back in Bradford. Home. In her head, she was. Imran had hired a van to take his sister away from it all. I wouldn't ever see her again. She said I would but I wouldn't. She scowled when I answered the door.

'I'm sorry,' I said. 'I didn't expect . . .'

'Like you said.'

She dropped the pile of books on the hallway floor.

'I won't be needin' books to help my battered wives.'

Vinnie was re-admitted to Seemar. Catatonic, apparently. Wailing Elsa got Shula back but I wasn't up to seeing her for a while. Didn't dare for a while. After Simmi, Irish came round to see me. I cried. I was really good at crying now. He held off from me. I mean, he didn't try any of that arms round the shoulder nonsense, which was great coz it meant I could let rip whilst he made some tea. Then he tidied up a few piles of papers, just a few. As a substitute for physical contact, I think. Each neat little pile stood alien amongst the debris. Soon bored, he rolled some joints. Vinnie wouldn't be able to take his finals. That was final, Irish said.

I didn't mourn a minute for Mikey. I never knew him really. Only the bits that he showed me. Just like no one could ever mourn me. Except our Divine and Mum and Dad. They're the ones who knew me. I suspect others would mourn for bits of me. The Mikey I knew wasn't big enough to get my hanky out for, but still, somewhere beneath all that, he left a void. A still. Unfinished business. Roy. I cried for Roy but, to be honest, even that didn't feel very wholehearted. I was suspicious of myself, for some reason.

I heard the front door open and, as if it was a signal to leave, Irish stood up to go. He wrapped his coat around himself tightly and said, 'Be seeing you,' which probably meant he wouldn't.

'Are you going to see Vinnie tonight?'

'Aye.'

'Give him my love.'

'Aye,' he said.

And I knew he wouldn't. Wouldn't dare.

I let him out of the flat and caught Dirk in the hall.

'Finally home then?' he said, smiling, his head to one side in pretend pity.

'Obviously,' I said. 'Coming in or going out?'

'Just been to drop Bev down the coach station. She's off to Elephant Fayre with Amnesty International.'

'Where's Elephant then?'

'Fuck knows. Somewhere in Cornwall.'

'I'll see yer later,' said Irish, a little frightened of Dirk, I thought, Dirk now wearing a 'big dealer' confidence across his smile.

Dirk. I noticed then his sagging neck. As though all the youthful bits of his face had sunk to the bottom, like sediment. And his hair. If he kept it that long, for that much longer, it'd be more curtain than crown. A man trying to hide the detail of his age.

'See yer, Irish,' I said.

'Can I come in?' said Dirk.

'Course yer can,' I said. 'My turn to make tea, eh?'

'How did yer get on? What brief did you get?'

'Cunningham. He was good. Good in court. Got me bail. They were after sending me over to Pucklechurch.'

'What for? A bit of draw?'

'Scag, Dirk. Scag. They're doin' me for scag, Dirk,' and towards the end of that sentence it was impossible to control my tears.

'Come up to our place,' he said. 'I'll get a fire going.'

Dirk would make me feel looked after, I knew that. I wanted that. In silence we faffed about with keys and the picking up of packets of fags and skins. He held the door open whilst I manoeuvred my way round all the shit piled up against it. We saved what was in our heads for the tea and the spliff. There was a feeling of home. Perhaps even more a feeling of being looked after.

Usually, I eye men the way I would a house. I decide, subconsciously, whether I'd like to live in it, if I had the choice. Some houses don't require much examination. It's obvious, right from the start. I might sit and have a cup of tea in it, but as for living in it, no chance. Men that give off Dad vibrations don't come into the reckoning either. Dirk was like Dad. Practical. Rational. Circumspect.

He went to the loo and I sat in the lounge alone, waiting to tell all about my troubles. I noticed a feeling inside me that I can only describe as a sound. The feeling is the sound of a slowly moving car driving up to a very large mansion house called home. The car reaches round to the front of the house, so that all its windows are in view. The road loses tarmac for gravel. The tyres of the car roll slowly over the gravel, crunching, deep, with a steady certainty, rolling over the stones. Then the car stops. And there is silence. A tangible shudder. That's what it felt like, sat on the couch watching Dirk when he walked back into the room.

'What smack, for Christ's sake?'

'Came in the post for a Mr Kipling. Must've been him that lived here before. On my way out of the court, that DI shithead said I'd be worth more out than in anyway. I think they're gonna watch me from now on.'

'Most definitely,' he said. 'Did you open the letter with the smack in it?'

'No. They did.'

'They haven't got a leg to stand on then. Did you give a statement?'

'Yeah. I put me 'and up for the cannabis. They wouldn't have let us out otherwise.'

'Possession?'

'And supply.'

He caught his breath when I said that. The air in the room changed. It felt like the volume was being turned down. Air volume. Between me and him, though, everything was on full blast. As if we stood out in relief against a backdrop of grey quiet. He walked over towards the fireplace. Self-contained in workman's overalls. First off he stood with his back to me, emptying his pockets. Putting keys and bolts and chains and stringy stuff on the mantelpiece. His pony-tail he lifted and then loosened. His hair fell across his back like a garment spread on the ground before lovemaking. Then raising himself a little, on the balls of his feet, he took the waist of his overalls between pickety fingers and shook. As a woman might delicately shake the cardigan of a beloved child. The ripples of his body, his torso and thighs were clearly visible beneath the thick navy-blue tarpaulin. His movements made waves across the folds of my belly.

Then he turned. I watched him slowly unfasten the press studs down his chest, down to his groin. I watched him yank his shoulders out of their cover. His T-shirted body presented itself like animal meat coming away from its fur. And then the falling to the floor. His feet in a pool of folds and folds of overall. My teeth tingled in my jaw. They were wired and charged with spangles, fizzy and fuzzy. Vibrating on the bubbles. I nearly laughed. The air was charged with the unavoidable. The fact. We were going to do it. As if it were up in lights, the show about to go on. Every moment, action, look and turn of the head was another step on to the stage where the act would begin. Like being called. Your number's up. It was my turn. My turn to feed the hungry cry. The command, the order from destiny to move on, seize my moment, follow my ball of thread right through to its source. To the weaver.

There was a pretend shyness, my body and brain busy with measuring the signals, looking for confirmation, resolution, passion. Understandably my mouth was empty of words. My mind chased for scent, not words or matter or platitudes. We may have seemed shy but in truth, our bodies were too busy to be bantering. That silence could only be filled with goodbye or hello. The hello would be a new-style hello, a hello to cut straight through the matter, down through the root and up to my spark. My fire.

He sat down and took his shoes off, then pulled his overalls over his feet. After, he looked at me. I got up and passed him the spliff.

He searched my face. My scar was gone. Melted away. He looked for me, for my vibration. Never could anyone find me by looking, but he did. He broke through the barrier. Smashed the glass. Then I said I'd make him a cup of tea. He patted the seat next to him, and it was as if each pat patted against my belly, against my unfastening will to keep my clothes on. The feeling came over as thick as a blanket of cloud on a clear sunny day, uninvited, suddenly, unplanned, but now, wanted, wafted and like a draught, it had to be consumed.

I sat down next to him, my hands between my knees, my head facing down to the ground. He took my head, turned it and then sucked it with thirst. I stayed as still as a doll – there was plenty of time for misunderstandings, for him to draw back, forget the whole idea. Only when his hand went into my blouse did I bleed with the fever. The driver of that car shudders with the most powerful thrill of being home.

Afterwards, lying on my stomach, on the couch, looking up and out of the windows to the sky, through the plastic strips of rainbow stuck on to the glass, peeling at the edges, only then did I remember the first time I met Mikey. Here he was. Lying on the very same couch, goofing out. Dirk ran his fingers over the hump of my rump like he was driving toy cars up the ramp of a new Scalectrix. My breasts hung like gourds of future, tickled by the candlewick spread of ridged cotton, like the beach, straight after the tide's gone out.

'You'll still go down, yer know,' his head lying on my arse, his lick and teeth nibbling and soothing, as a sort of keep-me-awake. 'And that draw you had was full of shit. Wax mostly.

That's what me and Bev were fighting about the other day – when you got home from Paris. I didn't wanna sell it. She said we 'ad to. She ripped you off.'

He bit my bum then and I squealed, but not really at the bite. More at the truth.

'They'll still do you for it,' he said.

He might have put a fist in my head to squeeze my brains dry. My head fell to the couch. Gutted. He got up and moved away from me. As though he'd done with me. A chill in the air frightened me. I turned to see where, what, why he was going. His bottom had two red splotches on, where he'd been sitting on his heels. He took the four-seasons mirror off the mantel-piece. From behind the picture of his mum, he took a wrap. He chopped out two lines of cocaine. It worked. I mean it all worked. I can't say how much of the joy was driven by the drug, but *it* was certainly better the second time round. It was certainly better afterwards. It, we, the day, the night – we all worked as one. The memory of my first and natural burst of energy, of the driving pain he gave me, all that was gone. For the rest of the night it was like sucking marshmallow lollipops. In front of the fire. Off our nuts. Awake till the following morning.

And after that, whenever he could, he slipped in to my rooms to see me. Throughout the summer holidays. And sometimes, when Bev was off at one at her festivals, we went to the park and lay by the lake. The lake that she loved so much.

GOING TO JAIL

Chapter 26

The courtroom was of course, my element. Its whole façade presented me with a microcosm of life, that in my well-constructed day to day I was extremely adapted to. The sudden surprise . . . the ambush . . . the random numbers of human bodies who wandered in and then ricocheted out of my life – *they* were my enemies. Unavoidable, challenging and wearing. I needed time. I needed time to get into character. I needed space to feel for my limitations. In short, I would be better cast as a film star. In court, I was one. In court, all my honed skills would have to be taken seriously. I was so practised at spotting other people's dishonesty, insincerity, evasiveness – any ripple on the calm, that I was an expert practitioner of these very arts – arts I deceived myself into believing I despised. I didn't despise artifice. I despised the fact I was never allowed to practise it myself, never allowed to have an inner mind severed from and independent of my outer face. A real life. Well, now I had my chance I'd spend my pearls of wisdom wisely.

The biggest pearl, the corker, was my change of attitude to Ratface. Bodene gave me the idea. I liked the way she was deferential to the judge when he told her off. He seemed disarmed by her good manner. I gave some good manner to Ratface. When he cross-examined me, instead of viewing him as the enemy, I pretended (just to myself) that he was working for me so that each time he built himself up to a climax, each time he did a mini-summing up of my skullduggery, I smiled at him rather kindly.

Then, almost in a whisper, I said, 'No. I'm sorry. It wasn't like that at all.'

I followed up with a smile lent to me by the angels of theatre, a temporary loan in exchange for a story. Then I watched Ratface re-adjust his voice, his feet, his gown. I watched him wipe exasperation from his face and then replace it with a pained expresson of perseverance. An expression he had to dig deep for. He was used to getting his own way, I could tell. He tried every door of my mind for a conflict, some instability, some rippling of the calm. All he got from me was the scarred face of an angel.

Ratface and Bodene. They badgered me all day. Well, I say all day. Half the day in court is spent out of court. Great long rests, adjournments, lunch breaks, lots of conferring over terms and statements, past cases and useless argument. Points of law. Points of law. Plenty of them. I was impressed with Bodene. She seemed to know how to spot 'em. In fact, I'd say she was a master of stretch. Stretching the case out.

The point of law about the wax in the hash turned out to be a very long point. It stretched right through the afternoon. Argument, they called it, which I found quite funny. They weren't arguing with me, no. The barristers and judge had their own private party. The meticulous laboratory technicians of the Home Office did find some evidence of cannabis. The substance yielded almost 15 per cent. The rest was not wax but a combination of semi-toxic tosh, disguised to look like cannabis. The judge in the end decided against me. He decided that, since I thought it was hash, it was hash. There were precedents. There were rules to be followed. The judge followed the rules and Bodene caved in. She had to.

She actually got a bit shirty with the judge at one point. She wrapped her gown around her tight and gave him some lip. Like a small girl clutching her dress against teasing boys. She raised her voice to the judge and begged, yes, begged, he revisit some book she'd picked out for him. And the judge told her that enough was enough. He told her off and afterwards, she thanked him. She thanked him for telling her off. I noticed that on the one hand the judge was irritated by her, but on the other, he quite enjoyed her smiles of deference, the eyes of knowing she kept throwing at him. It was as if they went to the same parties. Ratface didn't have the same sharpness or charisma. He was more like, as my name for him would suggest, vermin chomping at the waste he picked up upon his way.

The competition between the barristers was another game entirely and Bodene, I have to say, had become quite good at it. Perhaps I was being careless, but the idea of the case being a game, tennis for psychos, spiced it up for me. I could only breathe properly when the monotony of hushed learnedness was broken and re-framed into this new warp. Then it all became bearable. The repetition. Tradition. Bowing and scraping. Pantomime. Gesticulation. Salutation. Apologies from the benches. Clarifications from the judge. Directions to the jury. Long silences harnessed up by the flapping of the yapping gowns. Long silences to run away with, up into the clouds of explanation and expectation until *Objection, Your Honour* pops the bubble – pops the truth before it leaves the ether, before it rests as an equation of probability on the cortexes of the jury, their heads like sitting ducks waiting for these bullets all day long.

So at the end of that session, I was free to leave. There'd been so much rain stopping play, the ground was soggy now, soggy with doubt on both sides. Ratface hadn't shouldered one ace serve all day. He hadn't sussed my Divine lie yet. Maybe that was only a matter of time. Bodene had done very well on a number of counts. Her face had stayed perfectly unsurprised when I threw the story of Divine being ill, like she'd heard it a million times before, like she really had prepared a brief. Secondly, her personality had won the jury over and better than that, the judge. And I have to say, she was even getting to me now. Her acting skills were almost on par with mine. It occurred to me that that's what I should have done, law. With my face, I'd have scared the hell out of the witnesses.

When I stepped out of my box at the end of the day, the two grey-haired ladies who sat together in the jury – I swear they smiled at me. Telling me they were going to vote for me. They were on my side. Two down, ten to go.

I had another night of freedom at home. Another walk home, since I'd spent my bus fare in the coffee machine. I would go and see Irish, I thought. Give him a smoke. He might still be cranked up on the whizz, I thought. Whatever, I didn't want to go home straightaway. It felt like prison already there. And besides, story rehearsal was over. My evidence was mostly out. I'd done as much as I could.

Irish's flat was one of those in a big block of flats, one of about five blocks of flats on the east side of an estate of replication. He bought the rent book for a year, off some kid whose mother had died. He'd gone round the world to get her out of his system. Irish had a whole year of low rent in a two-bedroomed centrally heated crate. Jammy bastard. People used to call me that and then laugh.

I stood on the concrete balcony and looked four floors down. Two kids sat on the bonnet of what was once a car. A lady and a man walked along, not together, a few paces between them, both with both hands full of shopping. Their day out. Pension day. The post office was on-site, I noticed. They'd go home and cook that shopping for themselves, alone. Even if they weren't hungry. They'd watch telly and wait for the next pension day. They'd go down to the community bingo if the weather wasn't too sharp. They wouldn't live anywhere else. Ever again. Not so jammy, that.

I rang the door bell. Irish answered the door laughing and when he saw me he laughed even louder.

'For fuck's sake, have I won the pools, or what?'

Vinnie popped his head round the corner. Big grin. Fuck me. It was me who'd won the pools.

'What's this?' he said laughing. 'They've got you in a dress, my God. Give us a twirl then, my lady.'

'Vinnie, how come you're back?'

I smiled wide but I was conscious of my hair, all pulled back, *au naturel*, my face blaring at him. I have to admit, he didn't look at me any harder than usual. His face was soft and alight, his eyes glinting with the excitement of being home.

'I thought you'd been flushed out to sea, Vinnie. What's happening?'

'Well, as you know, I have one of those fathers with a wallet to match his madness. So, due to my illness, inherited, no doubt, I am allowed to take the year again. Though he has given me strict instructions on my place of accommodation and intends to keep in regular contact with my landlady. So. I am under house arrest. You are going through it, I hear?'

'Final day in court tomorrow. Didn't think I'd last this long, to be honest. I should be well banged up by now. Hey, Vinnie, what are you doing tomorrow?'

'Arranging the programme for my year of study. As I am doing now.'

He was laughing at his freedom, whilst I was still trying to organise mine.

'Would you come and be a witness for me, Vinnie? To say you gave me the money, the six hundred quid. It's not lying, is it? Don't suppose you keep copies of your bank statements do you?'

'Hey, hey, hey. Slow down. Calm down. You're supposed to be welcoming me home!'

'Vinnie, I'm in serious shit.'

'Of course I'll help you. Calm down. Bank statements you want, yes?'

'That you could bring to court?'

'Of course.'

'And would you?'

'Of course.'

His little smile was full of power. Heaving it. His eyelids, almost closed, seemed to click like a combination safe, finally teased open.

'What are you doing tonight?' he said, coming close towards me and holding my hand.

'Celebrating,' I said.

'Good.'

'Only I don't have any money. Sorry,' I said, laughing.

'That's fine. No problem.'

'Can I go home and change, Vinnie?' all excited, wafting my dress around like a kid at a party.

'We'll pick you up later. Be with you around seven, all right?'

With Vinnie on the guest list, I knew I was going to get off. I thought such reprieves only happened on telly. The missing star witness running into the judge at the last minute, gasping. Vinnie. A fucking star! A real-life TV reprieve. I ran home like Anne of Green Gables, top of the form. I stripped off and jumped straight into the shower. Overjoyed. Singing at the top of my voice. I even laughed when I looked in the mirror. I'd not done that in a long while. In my towel, I slid on to my bed and rolled some of my torpedoed hash into a joint. I aimed the torpedo at the spliff girl and went as if to throw the blim right at her, but I never. Then I did something which I only do when my life is in the lap of the gods. On a piece of paper, I wrote down, 'I am going to get off.' I wrote in ink. An ink-pen gift from Dad. Black ink, he said, is important. Words written in black ink hold more power than words written in faint. In biro. In pencil. Black ink is permanence, he said. That was one of the only positive images of black I'd ever been able to identify. Words are just skin, he said. Black ink is permanent. I stared at the writing. Then I read it out loud, stared again and visualised myself walking out of the court into the sunshine. I visualised myself swimming in a lake, a warm aquamarine lake surrounded by white sand. The image made me shudder and reminded me that it was time to get dressed.

Then I heard the banging and the shouting. Bev and Dirk were at it again. One of them would have to leave. They couldn't carry on like that. Even though I was downstairs, I was in their flat and no doubt Bev picked up on the vibe that she had company. That she was sharing him. Then one of them did leave. It was Bev, screaming down the stairs. Fucking bastard – stuff like that. Then the front door slammed. I thought I'd go up there, to see Dirk. To tell him about Vinnie. About my good fortune. To give him a way out. He didn't have to stay with Bev. He could be with me now, now I wasn't going to jail.

Still with a towel round me, a come-on if ever there was one, I mounted the stairs. The stair carpet came away from under my feet as if the gods had heard my plan and withdrawn it from me. I was being transported. I was riding a conveyor belt, backwards, going down, right down. I lost my uprightness and fell back-wards, my arm crushed under my tumble, bending backwards on itself. The scream I let out was from a whale calling for its mate, dodging the spears of the hunters. The scream trailed off towards the end, the pain whimpering me. Then I burst into deep breaths of agony. Sick at the wholeness of the pain, of its cutting off from everything, everyone. Of its twanging persistent play on my corded frayed nerves, nerves that up until then had been harmonised with the electrical ingenuity of a Swiss clock. Now they played discordant tunes from the land of hot irons and drilled teeth. I was sick to the stomach with it. Sick that I would for ever feel that relentless pain. As the throbs got worse my sobs got louder and I tried so hard to blanket it. And then Dirk was there, down the stairs, a spliff in his mouth.

'I thought that was her screaming,' he said. 'I thought she'd fallen down the stairs. I was laughing,' he said. 'Oh Jesus, look at the state of you.'

'I lay naked at the bottom of the stairs, my head wedged behind the newel post. He bent down to pull me up and then embraced me. He kissed my face. I wanted to suffocate then. To have done with the pain of it all. He held me, and I waited. I waited for the pain to plateau. To get a handle on its spectrum, for its quiver to be bearable at last, and only then did I consider all else about me. Some time. He kissed my forehead in the whimpering quietness and my eyes at last focused on the circumstance. I sensed we were being observed, as we lay there, as a couple, out in the open, for all our world to see. I sensed the world had taken the very first opportunity it could, to materialise us, to expose us. I looked over Dirk's shoulder towards the front door and saw Bev's eyes staring at me – the letterbox open and her eyes staring in cringe, straight at me.

'Dirk,' I said.

'You fucking bastards. I'll fuckin' do for you, Dirk. You watch me now,' she screamed.

And the letterbox slapped shut.

'I've got to go after her,' he said, getting off me, leaving me, making me hold my arm for myself.

He was in switch mode. He looked back at me, at my arm, and then back towards the door, weighing up which was worse. Broken arm or broken marriage. I noticed his neck rolls. His chin was sharp but underneath it, a concertina of flesh sunken to his throat.

'I've got to go,' he said, almost apologetically, but not quite. 'I've got to stop her.'

My broken bone spoke louder than him and I said nothing. He took an elastic band from his pocket and tied up his hair as he ran to the door. Gone. Full-blown tears from me now.

I sat with one arm out of my dressing gown for some time. Until Vinnie and Irish rang the doorbell. I shouted down the hall for them to hang on. Even that hurt, just the raising of the thorax, the volume of my voice box. All this is connected to the arm in some way? But as I say, I had the measure of it by now. I went to the front door with a face that looked like someone had cooked dinner on it. They both stood back shocked, completely serious, worried.

Irish left us to it. He wanted a drink so he went down to the student union on his own. Me and Vinnie waited for a taxi to take me to casualty. He helped to dress me and saw my nakedness as a nurse would see it. He held me through sobs as a dad and cuddled me as brother. I did it trying to move some of my boxes, I told him.

Down in casualty, he told me how it'd been in Lagos. Rough, it sounded. Bit hard to keep up, all that educated rich-man crap, especially when you don't believe in it. He said he met Fela Kuti in a club but I didn't believe him. He was trying it on. He still believed in his God stuff, though.

'D'yer remember what I said about there being a *big next*?'

'Vinnie, when I listened to your tape, I thought . . . well, to be honest, I thought you'd lost it. Now you're back with us, it might be better to forget all about it. Get on with your work like your dad wants you to.'

'But that's just it. This feels more like work. This wanting to know about life seems to be my only honest desire. I've found out about air and water, fire and wind. They never taught me stuff like that at school. Not even in elementary which, for Christ's sake, is what it's all about. The bloody elements. How can I just cream knowledge off the top without knowing about all the stuff underneath?'

'Vinnie, no one knows about all the stuff underneath.'

'Some people do. They just don't write it down.'

'Like witches, you mean.'

'Yes. If you like.'

'So you're gonna be a witch, are you?'

'No. I'm just saying, there's no point in ignoring it all.'

'So come on then. What's this big *next*?'

'It's the next level of consciousness. The "not" believing what they expect us to believe.'

'They?'

'Them in power.'

'What? The government?'

'Governments. Religions. Educators. Parents even.'

'This is *your* big next, you mean. This is your intellectual way of rebelling against your father.'

'It's not, honestly. It's more than that. I can feel it. Maybe my dad is part of it. Maybe having a dad like mine has made me think more about it. One thing I do know . . . my dad fell for every dummy they sold him. He bought himself manners, a business, good clothes, even a couple of wives. But he's only in this world for himself. That's why he's such a control freak. His world is the only world and he's in charge. I want a bigger world than that. No matter how many flashy suits I have, big houses, wives, the lot, no matter, I will always worry about those with nothing. No money. No power. No idea. If for one minute I thought that the people in charge of this planet were looking after it, us . . . then maybe I'd be more relaxed. You haven't seen what's happening to Africa. What happened to Africa. Africa is supposed to be my country. If I don't like that idea, I can choose England as my country. Neither country fits me. Both countries are so diseased, I fear contamination. I have nowhere to go.

'But when I was mad . . . well . . . when I was mad, I got this message. It was like I was in some kind of meeting of

325

minds, a universal consciousness. The message said that, all conscious people, those who stop and think for a minute, all conscious people will be invited to input their imaginings into the world of universal consciousness. It said that, soon, the real power of humanity will rise to the top and that those in power now, the money people, the violent people, it said that they will be scared. They'll begin to suspect that universal consciousness is no longer the voice of the poet or the artist, something to hype up as entertainment and knock down again as commercial failure. The message said that consciousness is real and that, in the next ten, fifteen years, the conscious human will make connections that stretch as far back as our earliest ancestors. Only when the planet gets respect, as our ancestors gave it respect, will the planet get better. You mark my words. The moment the powers that be fund research into universal consciousness, that is when even *they* believe it. They won't be trying to prove if it is . . . they'll want to know where it is, who it is. Only at the last will they admit . . . that it is. So.'

'So?'

'So what's wrong? Why are you crying? Did something I say connect?'

'So, Vinnie, me arm's fucking killing me. Go and ask them how long they're gonna be?'

Here was a man refusing to mutate. To humour him or yell at him? Or connive with him? Tell him about my weavers. My Polo mint and petri dish. But I'd made it all up. It was nonsense. It was difficult. He was my witness, so I humoured him. For his own good I should have yelled at him. I should have told him that his rantings were no more than that. But how could I not listen to him? Besides Dirk, he was the only true friend I had left. And after all, we're all very very selfish.

'Five minutes,' he said, squeezing my knee. Trying to own me.

'See. That's progress, that is, Vinnie. Now if you were to pass your exams next year, you could help build hospitals like this in Nigeria.'

'Yeah. Sure I could.'

I might have said he could go to the moon, once he's saved up for his rocket. That look on his face.

The doctor was a man any mother would be proud of. Blow dry and clean chin. He was more interested in my scar than my arm. I didn't mind. Took my mind off it a bit.

'How many grafts then?'

'Three,' I said. 'In all.'

'Must have been fairly deep – the damage?'

'Was out for the count for three days and then knock-me-sick painkillers for a week after that. I hardly remember it, to be honest.'

'Third degree then?'

'It is, isn't it?'

'I meant the burn.'

'I know.'

'Jam, you say?'

'Yes.'

'The worst. Like boiling oil.'

I remembered the holes in the walls of the castles – from history. Must have been a lot of ugly people about then.

'It was my sister. She was trying to be grown-up. Helping Mum out. The gas went out on the cooker and she couldn't relight it so she tried to move the pan from one side to the other. I ran into the kitchen and fell over, against her legs. She lost grip of the pan and the jam fell out all over me. Well, actually, most of it fell on the floor but the bit that got me did this. I passed out.'

'That's shock, that is.'

'For three days? Shock?'

'Yep. That's what kids tend to do. System overload, see. You'll need to go down to X-ray with this. It's a definite break. How come?'

'How come what?'

'How did you break your arm?'

'I fell over some boxes. I was trying to stack them.'

'Clumsy, eh?'

'Not as a rule, to be honest.'

327

'Well, clumsy today then.'

'Obviously.'

I went off him then.

'When was your last graft, if you don't mind my asking?'

'Eight years ago.'

'They've come on in leaps and bounds since then. You should try for another. I think they could do a better job than that.'

'Cheers, Doc.'

I hated him then.

We were left behind the curtains for ages, to wait for a taxi driver to X-ray. Vinnie was holding my hand throughout, pretending to be my boyfriend, which was all right. I was quite scared. I'm always scared in hospitals. That shock I was on about – the three days out for the count. I can remember some of it. I was living and breathing, alive and attuned but *still life*. My whole body was out of the equation. I only remember one part of the story. The living-inside-my-head story, I mean. I was another life. I wasn't even human, which is mad, isn't it? I was a crystal. A spinning crystal. The spin went one way, and then the other, but the me in the crystal was a flame. And from my flame I shot out a laser beam, like I saw at the Judy Tzuke concert at Glastonbury. It was a piercing arrow of a light and it stabbed at a mass of black air, making steam rise up. And when the light bounced back and then back again, it hit the steam to make it glitter. Then, like rolling golden spirits, waves of incandescence rolled towards me, so lifelike, I could almost see eyes in there. And tentacles. White gold, white heat, tinged with metallic sheen. Like baby aliens heading for to look after me. But I ran away. In my dream I ran away.

Having a hand to squeeze was a relief. When we went down to X-ray Vinnie helped to push the trolley, like a kid in the supermarket. I had flashbacks of journeys to theatre and I made an idle wish that that was where I was going, and that, when I came out, my face would be back to how it used to be. Like I was an elastic band. A boomerang. An echo. I longed for that true reflection, of who I really was. But nothing came back. Just me and my face. Roy said that the world is enmeshed in elastic bands. Dust-to-dust stuff, I thought he was on about. Population explosions and contractions. Elastic demand. But now, I thought about skin. I remembered what Vinnie said about the face of God being the earth and because of the painkillers and feeling all woozy, I fell back on that. I laid my head soft against the pillow imagining the earth and the universe as one great big elastic band. The tides. The beat. The rhythm. The vibe.

The eventual plaster cast was too large for me to wear my spotty dress to court so yet another problem. Vinnie said he'd stay the night and help me, which was great because it meant my witness was safe. What I didn't want, though, was Bev coming back, giving it loads. Too complicated. When we got home, there weren't any lights on. At night, when Bev and Dirk are home, the fire roaring, the lampshades gold, the light shines through the rainbow stickers on their window. Tonight it was all dark and I was glad. I told Vinnie he had to sleep on the floor and he sighed loudly.

'Yes?' I said.

'Come on. What do you think I'm going to do? With your arm like that?'

'Make spliffs for me, Vinnie. Make spliffs. Vinnie?'

'Yeah.'

'How did you stop being mad? Just tablets?'

'No. They didn't help. They just smothered me. Actually, it was my dad that helped in a funny sort of way. He told me that, in old African culture, people who were in fact suffering from temporary insanity were revered. For their insight. It was believed they were in contact with the gods. Nowadays nobody takes any notice of them, or their insight, since no one can see what they're looking at. He said my insanity might have meant something if I'd been studying properly. Behaving myself. He told me not to get distracted by fads and phases but to look straight ahead – look where I was going. That way, he said, my insights would all be pointing in the same direction.

Of course, he was talking about wealth and growth and the road to Allah but I understood it in my own way. So now, I'm steady as I go. Forward.'

Even with my arm like that, after fifteen minutes in bed he couldn't keep his hands to himself. At first I protested, an elbow in the ribs, but through the quiet of the night I got lonely. My painkillers wore off and the spliffs wore in. The pain of severed bone hummed and hovered in the background like some awakened god from the abyss, demanding respect, attention, obedience. And all the rest of me, every inch of me not broken, was glad and alive with the freedom of health. Awake. In excellent working order. So I twiddled my toes and compared that to the hum of the broken bone. Like playing a penny whistle. I fluttered my eyelashes and compared that to the hum of the bone, the breath of an angel's harp. And Vinnie stroked my breast. I played that back to the numbing hum of my groaning bone pain and that was jazz and blues and rain. Tenor sax to water the brain and run over the groans of the pain, making it still, background, beaten, the shade for all that's light. Yes, I let him. I let the dark silhouette of his black head move up and down to soothe me. He was shiny, purring, silent and black. Like a cat. In the black of the night, we were both outcasts from what is and what isn't. We were a secret. Off the record. Just a quiver. We meshed with just the silken threads of our humanity – for to keep the basket sturdy which would hold on to life until the morning came. Out of my mind, I was.

He was my Polka. Polka was my cat, when I was a kid. After the jam, after the hospital, after the house turned into a living tomb, Polka sat with me, day in and out, in the garden. She lapped me, snuzzled under my arm and slept in my bed. She was the only one that didn't know about my face. Sure, she must have seen it, but it didn't matter to her. She was my friend. I never spoke to Divine because I had Polka. I only nodded at Mum and Dad, to say I was in pain, hungry or not. I didn't like to get out of bed. It took a long time to get me out of the house, to the parks, to the zoo. Dad bought a car.

Funny thing was, I don't think we ever would have got a car, but for my face, the jam. And funnier still, I knew that the car wasn't for me. It was for Mum. Coz Mum was about as quiet as me, on this face of mine. Keeping mum, as they say. Dad told Mum it wasn't her fault – my face, that is – and Mum told Divine it wasn't her fault either and when Mum cried in the evenings, when the news came on the telly and they turned the telly off and I could hear from my bedroom, I heard Dad and Divine comforting Mum, saying it wasn't her fault. But it was. She was the one cooking jam. And it was Divine's fault for pretending to be grown-up. And it was Dad's fault for not carrying me off to the hospital in his arms like he did Divine. No. He didn't do that for me. Dad waited for an ambulance. And just then, just as Vinnie made horrible slurping noises in my ear, I wondered if Dad got the car so's such a thing might not ever happen again. He bought his own little ambulance.

In the car I felt safe. I sat in the car whilst they went to look at the animals. With Polka. Then Polka got run over by a car. I never spoke at all after that. I never went out in the car after that. Divine couldn't cope at all then. She took all the guilt on singlehanded. Mum wouldn't come near me. Dad got confused. Like me, Divine hardly left the house. Divine brought school home with her, the books, the writing, the disciplined study. She plaited my hair, read to me, made cakes for me. And I repaid her with silence. She owed it to me. She owed her life to me. I gave her a vacuum in which to act out her guilt and she worked it to the bone. Never was I left alone. When she was not at school, she created a fantasy world around me, not letting a breath of wind disturb me. Just with my eyes, not with lungs or voice box or even arms held out for hugs, just with my eyes, I watched her every step with jealousy and sometimes evil. I would have liked to kill her. In my head I spun about the possible ways to do this. I got locked in.

And then one day, I realised I couldn't speak. Not wouldn't. Couldn't. One minute I was locked in. Then I was locked out. There was no place left for me to be, because I'd wiped out all the footpaths to my heart. They took me to see a woman who made me play with bricks. And water. Lots of decisions were made about me. Special schools and tests. Instead of being coaxed, I was dragged. Instead of being encouraged, I was forced. The patience of the carers had reached its brim. Instead of being asked, I was told. Luckily my brain grew and with the growth came space. The gift and memory of choice blossomed inside me. The reality of it. The link to it, to having it, was my voice. The link to my past was my voice. The future held only two choices. To kill myself. Or to kill Divine. The only other option was to speak my mind. That was my only thread with the world. So I at last spoke.

'Please don't send me to a special school,' I said.

Letting Vinnie feed off me was just plain old weakness, choosing the not altogether unpleasant feeling of being caressed. We woke early. He helped to dress me in a white T-shirt with the arm cut off. A black shirt and black skirt. With the cricked neck of an artist, he dabbed make-up on to the lumps of my scar and stood back and said fine. He called a cab to take us to Irish's flat, where Vinnie's belongings were stored, for to root out the bank statement. The one thing I knew that morning – I mean, I really knew it – not just hope, not just wishful thinking, not just blindness – I knew I wasn't going to prison. Wasn't a broken arm punishment enough?

No. It was not. As the taxi chugged over the cobbles outside the court and the door was flung open for me, as I lowered my head to alight, as I adjusted my hearing to daylight surround sound, the brumming of engines called me. I looked over towards the court and saw bikes, lots of bikes and spider jackets glinting in the sun. The Taras had come. The way they were arranged there, spoking out from their leader in the centre, they looked as a huge metallic tarantula might look, shiny and furry, menacing but playful. Unlike a tarantula, they were noisy. One of them must be in court today, I surmised. Come along to give him some moral, no doubt. I watched Vinnie, shuffling for change in his pockets, already the metal engines of the bikes searing through me. I was trying to be calm. My head needed peace.

The taxi drove off and Vinnie came over to support me. We

walked away from the bikes but then turned because I heard my name called. It was Dirk. In clean white T-shirt, washed and ironed by Bev, no doubt. Navy-blue jeans, new, fitting well round his knees, the pipe of the leg hugging his boots in tune, comfortable. His hair was out and flowing, newly washed but he hadn't shaved. There was growth. His hair was feeding from the sun. He walked towards us. His mouth smiled prayers of white teeth from the shadow of his growth. He was so happy to see me.

As he got near to us, the Taras blew their horns. Some had those musical horns that play a tune. Maddening. The noise, along with the engines, was fantastic. He was upon me and almost bent over to kiss me but I used my plaster cast as a defence.

'Sorted, then,' he said, holding my fingers that were stuck out of the end of the cast, like I was still so very far away, like he was helping me over some troublesome puddle.

'Dirk, what are you doing here? Where's Bev?'

I pulled my hand back and moved closer to Vinnie.

'We've come to see you.'

'See me what?'

'We've come to see you in court.'

He pointed with his thumb back to the bikes.

'To give you a vibe. Help get you off.'

'Vinnie'll get me off. He's come to give evidence for me.'

'Well done, Vinnie. See what I mean? It's working already.'

I wasn't angry with him. I just didn't need him on my case right then. I felt Vinnie's hand tense around my shoulder as Dirk inspected the plaster. Then Dirk did the worst thing he could possibly do.

He took out his blue pencil that he keeps behind his ear and bent down to write on my virgin armour-cased arm. Since I had Vinnie just where I wanted him, I really couldn't gamble on Dirk's copywriting skills right then.

'Dirk!' I said with my angry head on.

'What's wrong with yer? I want to be the first,' he said with a horrible smirk in his eye, pulling my fingers towards him.

Before writing, he looked up at Vinnie and gave him a smirk too. Vinnie's hand went even tighter round my shoulder.

'What d'yer wanna write, Dirk?'

I turned to face him head-on then, so that Vinnie couldn't see me and I glared. I glared intensely, so he'd think about the consequences, the complications, the loss, the future. The unknown. My eyes said all of that. All of that in that one long glare. It was easy.

'I was only gonna put "See you at HQ",' he said, popping his pencil back behind his ear. 'I'm off to live there. There's a room free. Overlooking the river. I wondered if you . . .'

'Listen, Dirk. I've got to go. I've got to get Vinnie to my brief.'

I let my tongue lick my top lip. To say yes. Yes, I would come and live with him in HQ. Yes, I would like to see that rainbow again. That's all I could see. The river and the rainbow. Blue-bottles and Pot-Noodle cartons didn't come into it.

'So this is Vinnie, is it?' Dirk looked him up and down as if examining the threat.

'Dirk, Vinnie. Vinnie, Dirk.'

Some fucking time to be doing the introductions. Politeness creeps in everywhere still. Holds things up. Obscures light. Pushes down him that would rise up. Deflects attention. Creates patterns for comparison. A virtual and meaningless reality. A bastardisation of electricity. As the duel progresses and the two men take fifty paces back, the need to kill is no longer an issue of intelligence. It is wrapped in the sheath of a sword, the barrel of the gun, the death clothed in etiquette and the inherited male reflex of target practice. But right then, I needed politeness. I didn't want truth rushing out of every eye, seeping from the twitches of our mouths, creating a new situation when in court, in ten minutes, I'd be facing the more important situation of my freedom.

'How you feeling, Vinnie?' said Dirk. 'I heard you weren't too well. Lost the thread a bit, eh?'

'I'm fine, thank you.'

'Eat this, Viv, before you go in? It's a bit of Manali. Then you'll feel all right, whichever way it goes.'

334

And there was the snout of it, the snout of the truth, trying it's damnedest to break forth out of Dirk's big mouth, out of his arm patting Vinnie's shoulder, his eyes laughing at him as he passed me the blim. I chewed the blim into bits, small bits for the stomach to get a hold of. I was trapped now. The only place I could go to was inside my head. Away from the truth on the pavement and the lies in court. Dirk was dragging the truth towards my witness. Vinnie wasn't Vinnie. He was my witness. I had to stop this meshing of the energies. At times like this I know for a fact that our energy is not just a hunch, an idea, a poet's chisel. Not just some appendage that sails around on the boat of our words. That energy, that prediction power, that wave of fear or revulsion or expectation – that is matter at its most keen, most powerful. Yet, just as the crest of that energy hits the beach, like froth, like bubbles, we let it slip through the atmosphere and pretend to ourselves that it was never there. Out of fear, probably. Or our inability to fit the truth into the grovelling hands of the mathematical hag for her to mark and score and equate and root in squares of one-dimensional nonsensical matter. The lid of the paranormal is still, in any case, left only slightly ajar. When the lid is wide open, coincidences will be extinguished and our energies will fall into each other's arms, lovingly. By talking – I think I mentioned my packing cases needing to be strapped over to stop the contents falling out during transit – by talking I interrupted their energy flows, diverted their curiosities and calmed the atmospheric storm about to build up.

When less interesting matter, like burning jam, has seeped deep inside the rods and cones of the brain's inner eye, as it did to my eye, then the more interesting matter of earth's energy circulates the iris as the wind blows waves in a cornfield. I am seen but I'm invisible. I am touched, but by who? My energy plays bumper cars all day long, in the moonshine and sunshine and human-eye knowledge shine.

Chapter 27

When I introduced Vinnie to Bodene and showed her the bank statement, she grabbed hold of my face (scar side) and pinched it hard, chubby with congratulations. Grinning, she was. I could see her teeth.

Off she trotted to inform the prosecution of the good news. When she came back I wanted to grab hold of her cheeks. I wanted to kiss her. The heroin charge would be dropped. They'd lost their nerve, she said. Would I now plead guilty to a lesser charge of intention to supply cannabis? she asked me, a glint in her eye, her nose already smelling the kill. No, I said. Not bloody likely. Good, she said, and went away again. When she came back, she wasn't grinning. The judge had accepted the prosecution's application to drop the heroin charge.

'So we don't need Vinnie now,' I offered.

'Yes, we do,' she said.

'What for?'

'You need someone on your side.'

'What for?'

'To say what?'

'He can say a lot,' she said.

I didn't understand.

The problem, she said, was that the judge, not known for his lenience, would like to see some justice done in this particular case. Some result.

'Well, they've got me on possession,' I said. 'There'll be a fine for that, won't there?'

'When there are Class A drugs involved and unfortunately for you, two circumstantial deaths, then it's a little bit more serious than that. The judge will want to set an example. You could well be that example. For just the cannabis, you're looking at six months, twelve if you're found guilty of supply.'

No way. Not a chance. I was going to walk.

I let Bodene talk to Vinnie and set off for the cells through the back door. I walked through as a wizard from some other world, taking special interest in the chairs and the table. The bulb without a shade. The uniformed messengers of the monarch manacled by their very own misunderstanding. These thoughts made the grey walls seem false, of papier mâché even, as if any minute they'd come tumbling down like a child's last castle in the sand. The man with batman tattooed across his forehead would have to believe in the walls, I thought. To take them away would be to plunge him into the abyss. To take them down slowly might be, in the end, more enlightening and I imagined him sat on the floor, stacking the bricks and counting the many ways that bricks could be re-stacked, re-shaped, to make some other sort of building – a building that might shelter him from the storm, perhaps. I imagined all this sitting on my plastic chair, holding my arm in its sling as if it were a nuisance.

At last my name was called. I came up from the cells, as the actress. The final day. All could have their final say. The shiny wood against my footfall was slippery, like the fickleness of the jury. It had to be trodden on with care, with respect, its thudding sound, a sound of applause for progress made to the dock. Yet it wasn't a dock. It was a bridge. I was standing on the bridge of a ship. The crew were all there, seated. Their beards and metal collars, their denim and leather, their tattoos and boots up on the bench like they were at the bus stop, some of them. Their constant murmur and chortling was like guitar music in the desert, folky and fresh, fuzzy and friendly.

And so to the jury now. They have come in and are not sat tight and tuckered in their benches, but leaning over one another to grab a last word, a smile, a note or two about the day ahead. I couldn't hear the gowns flapping or the judge thudding. The bows of the ushers were drowned out by the clomping boots of the bikers, their helmets clacking together, like planets clashing in the skies.

Bang, bang!

The judge has arrived. Settle down now, please. Make yourselves comfortable. The show is about to begin.

All rise! *Get up. Stand up.*

You should have seen the jury sit back when the judge told them that the heroin charge had been dropped. And then the clatter of applause and general hoo-hah! from the public gallery. The jury were definitely on my side now. What a waste of time all that was, they were thinking. Here was a girl stitched up, they were thinking. And as if he'd read my mind, the judge put a stop to all that.

'Now you must decide,' he said, 'on the one charge of supplying cannabis, is the defendant innocent or guilty. This is still a grave charge. You are being asked to make an important decision. You will need all your concentration to ensure you make a correct decision.'

I felt as if I was on some ride. As if I was being taken somewhere, over obstacles, through gates, up through levels of consciousness. This last stretch of the journey would be the hardest. It was the closest to the top of whatever mountain I'd been climbing. If I kept my head, I would soon be free. Just one last day, one last act, one last task to complete.

Because of the dress rehearsal, day one, because of the jury getting used to my face, day two, used to seeing past it (surely by now), day three (I have calculated, that on average, people begin to see past my face after an approximate accumulated period of visual contact lasting a mean time of one hour and seventeen minutes) and because Bodene pointed out my absent solicitor during interrogation and because the heroin charge was dropped . . . and because every other associated detainee held in the cells was black and no charges were laid against them, I felt my train about to move out of the station. There was Dirk. He was on it. On the train. Waving. Now he was pressing his nose with his finger. A cocaine treat for later, he was saying. I prepared myself for a long and winding ride through the wide open spaces of the countryside.

But Ratface might still pick up on the fact that Divine was

nowhere near Vietnam when Vinnie lent me the money. She was in Paris the day I was arrested. He must have sussed this by now, surely? Surely? Bodene hadn't. Maybe I was in with a chance. I had to be. I could feel it. Lights were coming on inside my head. I was out of my mind.

Most of the evidence from the plod hadn't held sway. It should have been watertight. But it wasn't. The lies had fallen out of their mouths like gravel from the beaks of feeding birds. Unwholesome lies had dropped on to the truth of the court like boulders on to bare toes. And the pain of the assault still lingered on, in the memory of the judge and the even bigger memory of the jury. My lies were altogether more believable. I had given the command performance I promised I would. My lies were from the film of reality, the tragedy that was played out over and over again on the telly, in the papers, in the subconscious sea. All reflected in the pond of their brains. The jury was on my side. Well, it was until it registered that the Taras weren't going to shut up. They were behaving like the game was over. Be quiet. For God's sake, be quiet. The jury was on my side right up until the moment the judge looked over his glasses at the noise and then, with such an irritated expression, he nodded to the flappy flappy gowns of the ushers. He shook his head in resignation. The jury saw him do this and they too began shaking their heads. The Taras seemed unaware of the plot I was starring in. They were destroying my finale. Then one of them giggled out loud and shouted, drawing more and more attention to . . .

'Silence in court, please,' gavelled the judge, now beside himself.

The crows squawked in indignation. The usher took the gavel as an instruction, as permission to go up to the men in their spidered jackets. His gown took on the mantle of the unarmed priest, his demeanour the same, as if he were the only one brave enough to confront the heathens poisoning the atmosphere. Dirk didn't have much control over them. I could see him, at the end of the pew, sitting back, staying out of it. The jury looked back and forth, from me to the bikers, trying to measure up my relationship to them. The twelve good men looked hurt now. As if I'd been conning them all along. They began a very new case against me, all on their own. I felt the swell of the jury's support drift away from me. It was back to square one, almost. Except now, I had the Taras as the backdrop to my crime. I was back in the dock.

Bodene up.

'I would like to call to the stand Vincent Abala.'

Vinnie's little body in the witness stand was all I had to defend myself with. We were two creatures of the same ilk. Here was Vinnie, small, black. More me than the louts on the bench. Here was someone that the jury could have mercy on, for precious knows, up until then, they had wanted to be merciful. Someone had to lose. Someone had to be the underdog. To balance it all out. There had to be a victim in all this. If it wasn't me, then it was Roy and Mikey. And I would pay dearly for their lives, even though I wasn't to blame. Someone had to pay. I stared hard at the back of Vinnie's head when he took the stand. All my energy was directed at Vinnie as he swore to tell the truth. All I had to work with was my head. One broken arm and one cuffed arm, it was as if I had finally been cut down to size. To just a head.

I remembered the Tarzan movies of my childhood. When, walking through the jungle, the great white man falls into quicksand and is soon up to his neck in it. He looks all around for something to cling on to, something he can use to drag himself out of the monstrous mush. That was me. They were after my head. My only chance of survival was to find my spirit, my concentration, my imagination. With wide eyes and massive concentration, I imagined a thread between Vinnie and me, a common silk that joined us but in turn separated us from the louts, from their rustling and stamping of feet, from their sniggers. When he spoke I leant forward and weaved a vein of truth between us, an air of family and belonging. When he mentioned my name, I closed my eyes and imagined us as lovers, unable to reach out to each other, separated and isolated by a web of lies construed to destroy us. I really went for it. This, as I said, was my Broadway. The jury would see me and Vinnie as one. The louts as another. The plod as another. Themselves as merciful.

'So the bank was just closing, Mr Abala?'

'It was.'

'And you say that the money you withdrew consisted of predominantly twenty-pound notes and not ones and fives as given in evidence for the prosecution?

'I do,' said Vinnie indignantly.

'That's OK, Mr Abala. I've checked the charge sheet. What you say is correct.'

She passed the charge sheet round for everyone to have a look at. Everyone that mattered. Benky and Ratface. Then she held up the bank statement, the trophy, the certificate of truth. Flappy usher wasn't so flappy now, I noticed. Not so keen to pass the trophy round. His gown had gone all limp. All this anti-climax threw Ratface off the scent completely. Took the wind out of him. At last we'd managed to wipe that smirk off his face. Divine really was sick now. She was real. She was in Vietnam. In the light of all this new evidence, my Divine lie was in the dark, invisible, insubstantial.

'And you say that whilst in custody you were required to remain in your cell naked for quite some time?'

'Objection, Your Honour.'

'Your Honour, I merely seek to establish that the treatment in the cells as described by the accused was not just an isolated incident or indeed exagerrated. Rather, the rule as opposed to the exception.'

'The police are not on trial, Miss Bodene. Please question the witness regarding matters pertinent to the case in question.'

'And, Mr Abala, you can confirm that Miss Jackson required this sum of money in order to secure a passage to her ailing sister in Vietnam.'

'I can.'

'No more questions, Your Honour.'

Bodene down.

Ratface up.

'Mr Abala. Can you tell the jury where you were taken to, once you were released from custody?'

'Seemar Psychiatric Centre.'

'No more questions, Your Honour.'

Ratface down.

Bodene up.

'Your Honour, I have just one more point I'd like to clarify . . . Mr Abala, why were you sent to the Seemar Psychiatric Centre on release from custody?'

'I was there the day before. I'd been diagnosed as suffering from stress. I didn't have my medication with me, when they arrested me. I asked for a doctor to prescribe something for me, but they refused.'

'They refused? The medication? Or the doctor?'

'Both.'

'And what effect did this have?'

The court was in complete silence. No squeaking, not even from the louts.

'I became anxious. Eventually I tried to . . . I tried to . . .'

Vinnie couldn't talk any more, he was crying. It was all going swimmingly well again. I wondered exactly what Vinnie had tried to do but then remembered myself again. My concentration. To bolster the tragedy some more, I thought of my dad and how he would rip his shirt and have done with me. The pain in my broken arm came back right at that moment, as if on cue, to lend a helping hand. My tears, so easy now, fell like rain on thirsty plants. I asked my screw for a tissue and then motioned that I hadn't an arm to dry my own tears. She uncuffed me and I dabbed my face fine-style.

'Thank you, Mr Abala. You may step down now.'

Vinnie turned round and gave me an I-did-it-for-you look, slightly predatory, I thought. Like I owed him something. Worse than that. Like he had no doubts I'd pay him back. I looked over to Dirk. He sat slouched, his arms folded, his smile on me. A full smile. Expectant. Time for the summing up.

'Ladies and gentlemen of the jury. We have 25 grams of low-grade cannabis, weighed out into four separate packets. We have six hundred pounds in cash found on the defendant's person. We have a pair of scales, found at the house, the dishes showing traces of cannabis resin. We have a written statement, in the defendant's own handwriting, stating explicitly that she supplied cannabis. Ladies and gentlemen of the jury. It is inconceivable, is it not, to imagine that this young woman was not engaged in drug trafficking, albeit of a minor nature. Yet, now she says it was all a mistake. The police, she says, were mistaken. Indeed there were mistakes. Her mistakes. Two in all. Her first mistake was to have engaged in criminal activities contrary to the Drug Trafficking Act. Her second, that of getting caught. Do not be seduced into believing that this defendant is a mere pawn in a much larger and more dangerous organisation and could therefore not have known the nature of the crime in which she was involved. And do not be misled into thinking that the defendant can only speak the truth when there is a solicitor present in the room. This defendant is an undergraduate at our local college. She is studying business and economics. She understands the concepts of profit and loss. Demand and supply. This extra-curricular activity of hers is a corruption of the education supplied to her at the expense of the tax payer. I ask that you find the defendant guilty of that which she has confessed to in her handwritten statement. I would also . . .'

Then he stopped, struck his breast and asked if he could sit down. He drank some water and puffed and panted a bit and then waved at the judge, like he was saying 'Not playing any more'. He might have been shot by some secret hunter's arrow, from the public gallery. An arrow must have shot straight through to his solar plexus which he held now, with both hands.

'Is there a problem, Mr Greaves?'

'Yes. Uhhr. Your Honour. I'm unable to continue. A terrible pain in my chest.'

An usher flapped over and led him out of the court. This threw me. And the jury. I wasn't sure whether Ratface doing that was a good move. Who were the jury going to feel sorry for now, I wondered. On balance, I finally decided he'd done me a favour. Not on purpose, obviously. Maybe he really didn't have the stomach for it. Nah! It was just too much hard work. All that prosecuting. It's not surprising that his heart rebelled. Cut off in his prime – this could only help me, I decided. His argument was away on the air to nowhere. So too him. Out of the court, out of my mind and hopefully out of the jury's mind too.

I soon came to my senses. Of course, this last falling down of the case against me smacked too violently of an uncalled-for divine intervention. There was no need. I was doing all right without Ratface having a heart attack or whatever it was. This wasn't turning out like a proper story. My obstacles were being blown out of the water, one by one, not by luck or coincidence, but by some force I couldn't quite identify. The forces of justice, maybe. As if God himself were angry at the waste of time, at the dressing up, at the lies and contrived so-called attendance to the common good. It was God who put the heroin on the charge sheet and God who dropped it off again, after the damage was done, after the lies that created the charge were, to all the world, laid bare of care, integrity, truth. Now, God was getting impatient. He wanted to have done with it. He'd had about as much as he could stomach of Ratface. God's intervening in this way stole my glory. I was running this court case, not him. How could I claim to be responsible for a heart attack? I couldn't.

Vinnie sat next to the louts in the public gallery. Suit and tie. Shiny forehead. Straight face. His serious head on. I couldn't look at him.

Bodene got into the swing of things then. So did I. I began to play with my scarface. I stroked it and pretended it was irritating me, that it was sore. I didn't have much make-up on so it looked vicious. I pretended to be embarrassed about it. I drew attention to it. I pretended nerves and swung my head from judge to jury. I looked down to my knees. I thought of Dad and *his* face. If he could see me now. I got ready to chuck out some more crying. Now was the time for tears. Let them flow and flow and flow. Have pity, dear jury, on this miserable monster before you. I looked over to Dirk and he put his thumbs up to me. Through the tears and the wiping of my face I saw his thumb for me. He pouted a kiss. For me. He was the one. Mine. Soon I would be free. Soon I would be on my way to HQ to live in sin. Bodene was finished. She sat down. There was quiet. Now it was the judge's turn.

'Ladies and gentlemen of the jury, I now charge you to come to a decision that will reflect the quality of the evidence laid before you. You must decide: Did the defendant supply cannabis or not? The weight of guilt or innocence must be measured against the evidence put before you in this court.'

(He nodded his head in the direction of the scales, the money, the hash, the syringes, the coke spoon, the statement that said I, Vivian Jackson, sold wacky backy to some kid on some estate of replication, some time ago.)

'If you should find the defendant guilty, you must ensure that her guilt is beyond all reasonable doubt. I must also remind you, before you retire to consider your verdict, that appearances, pathetic or otherwise, can be deceptive. Oh, and one last point, which I'm sure our learned friend would have put forward, had he not been taken ill so suddenly. Please remember that the defence does not deny that the defendant wrote the statement, in her own words, with her own pen. That is perhaps something on which the jury would like to ponder. I trust you will return with the correct verdict.'

His head was surrounded by mist. Or was it steam? I turned my face to him, full on. This was the end. But it felt like a beginning. There was no wood, no ground at all, beneath my feet. Just my head, and Benky's head. The way he looked at me, I got the feeling there was mist around my head too.

'The jury will rise and leave the court to consider its verdict.'

Bang, bang, bang!

All rise!

The whole room stood.

And then the nod.

A NOTE ON THE AUTHOR

Joanna Traynor was born in London and grew up in the north of England. Formerly a nurse and a sales person, she now works in the computer industry. In 1996 she won the Saga Prize for her first novel, *Sister Josephine*. She lives in Devon.